ARE WE THERE YET

A SWEET ROAD TRIP ROMCOM

SAVANNAH SCOTT

CONNECT WITH SAVANNAH SCOTT

You can connect with Savannah at her website
https://SavannahScott.website/

You can also follow Savannah on Amazon.

For free books and first notice of new releases, sign up for Savannah's Romcom Readers email at https://savannahscott.website/romcom-reader-email/

For Jon
Thank you for the road trips ...
for weekends at the coast, cruises, and nights sitting around campfires.
Thank you for letting me ride shotgun.
Here's to the journey, and to taking it together.

For the road-trippers, and all who live with wanderlust in our hearts.
May your journeys bring you sweet surprises,
and may each new day be an adventure.

Maybe we'll meet along the way.

~

Take the risk and go where the road leads you.

~

1

RILEY

If you don't know where you're going,
You might wind up someplace else.
~ Yogi Berra

The world is full of people who know what they want to be when they grow up. I am not one of those people. The closest I've come to feeling like I found my life's purpose has been my summer job at the local coffee shop in my hometown of Bordeaux, Ohio.

I swipe at a splash on the counter and tuck my rag into my half-apron. Two more weeks of working as a barista at Bean There Done That. In fourteen days, my best friend, Madeline, and I will pack up to head back for our senior year at UCLA.

The shop door swings open. Madeline's brother, Cameron, and his best friend, Ben, walk in. I smooth my apron. Why? It's not like the apron police are coming through town. I just need something to do with my hands. And my mouth. I know that sounds beyond weird, but I'm a blurter when I get nervous, it's like someone shoots me with a double shot of truth serum and I just start blabbing the first crazy thing that comes to mind. And then I keep going like a runaway car in need of a brake pedal, spilling all my inner thoughts without a filter.

And, believe me, when it comes to being around Cameron, I need a filter and a brake pedal, among other things. Cameron Reeves is as gorgeous as his name makes him sound. He's about six feet tall, which is the height I always wrote in my *ideal man list* in my journal. Yes. I have a list of qualities I want in a man. And the one approaching the counter ticks all those boxes —except two.

He's my best friend's older brother.

He barely knows I exist.

That is, unless you count the fact that I'm a fixture in his life. Cameron probably gives me as much thought as he gives his sofa. It's there. It's always been there. Comfortable, reliable, old sofa.

"Hey, Riley Bo Biley, Fee Fie Fo Filey!" That was not Cameron.

You know how every hot movie star has their supporting man? The dorky sidekick, or the life-of-the-party guy who provides a contrast to the hot, overwhelmingly perfect, leading man. Well, Cameron's wingman is the charming, goofy, effervescent, Ben.

"Hey, Ben. What can I get you today?"

So far so good. Not a blurt or babble. Maybe if I just focus on Ben, I'll avoid humiliating myself in front of Cameron.

"I'm feeling the need for one of your iced mochas, Rye." Ben lowers his voice to a conspiratorial whisper even though he and Cameron are the only customers in the shop right now. "But make sure you make it. You're the best barista here. Don't tell the others I said that."

Ben winks. It's not a flirty wink. Well, it is, but you have to know Ben. He flirts with life. Winking is part of his regular arsenal of interactions. Hugs, smiles, compliments, all just flow from Ben. He scatters kindness like a confetti cannon.

I take Ben's payment. Cameron steps up to the counter, completely oblivious to the fact that my pulse just kicked up about ten notches. It's like a stampede of happy little horses start galloping through my veins. Giddy-up! There's Cameron!

"Hey, Riley."

"Hi. Hey. That color shirt looks great on you. The rust brings out the flecks in your hazel eyes. It even makes the green stand out. All the colors. How does one shirt make someone's eyes look that amazing?"

Whaaaaa?

Cameron doesn't even dignify my blurting with any reaction. He's calm and focused, as usual. Ben smiles a goofy, playful smile at me. He's obviously thoroughly entertained by my word vomit.

"And that apron looks lovely with your eyes, Rye Rye," Ben says, super unhelpfully.

My apron is around my waist. And it's black, sporting a few stains from the workday. It might compliment something, but my brown eyes aren't it. Ben's just being his typical goofball self.

"I'll take a medium oat milk latte with one packet of stevia," Cameron says.

"Walking on the wild side, are we?" I say, in an attempt at a joke.

Cameron smiles. At me. But not really at me. I mean, yes. He's smiling in my direction. But it's more of a smile you'd give your puppy, or a toddler who managed not to tip their trike over when they rounded the corner at the end of the block. It's not a *Hey, Riley, I think you're adorable and I can't live without you* smile.

Sofa. I'm the sofa.

"Oat milk latte with stevia for the man in the rust colored shirt."

Dork-alert! Gah.

I promise I form cohesive, not-weird sentences ninety percent of the time. Okay. Seventy-five. Fifty. Alright. Fifty.

I glance up toward the ceiling, take a breath, and then I gather my wits enough to start working on the two coffee orders. Once Cameron and I are in the same room for a little while, my nerves always settle. It's just whenever he makes an entrance, and I have to reel in my feelings and reactions, that I act like a complete bumbling idiot. Or when he gives me certain looks. Or when he wears a backwards ball cap. Or when we go swimming and I see him shirtless. Or ... well, let's just say, Cameron can draw out my flabbergasted, uncoordinated side more than anyone else on earth.

"What are you two doing this afternoon?" I ask over my shoulder.

"We're heading to Satterson's Garage," Cameron says without any other explanation.

Cameron isn't always a man of few words, but he's also not one to elaborate unless he's in a certain mood. That relaxed, chatty mood is one of my faves. Oh, who am I kidding? All Cameron's moods are my faves.

After his uninformative answer, Cameron stands off to the side of the register, looking like a dream in his rust colored shirt and jeans. His sandy blond hair has streaks of lighter blond from the summer sun. He's got that young Liam Hemsworth look to him—simultaneously scruffy and clean-cut.

"Duke says he has a surprise for us," Ben adds.

Duke's the local history teacher. His family owns the garage in town. He also coaches little league and usually stays connected with his players, even after they leave town to go off to college. Both Cameron and Ben played ball for years on our local team, the Mighty Fireflies. Yeah. I know. We come up with some doozies for naming things around here, trust me.

"A surprise from Duke? I wonder what that could be," I say as I set Ben's iced mocha on the counter.

"I dunno. Duke seems pretty excited," Ben says. "What time do you and Madeline get off work? You could come with us."

"We've got another hour. Then Sarah comes in to cover the rest of the afternoon until closing."

Hardly anyone comes in here after the lunch rush these days. It's too hot out, and most people are hanging at the Res or trying to stay cool in their homes.

Madeline must hear her name because she comes out from the back.

"Oh, hey guys."

"Hey, Mads," Ben says. "I was just asking Riley if you two wanted to come with your brother and me to Satterson's after work."

"Why would I want to go to Satterson's?"

"Duke has some surprise," I explain.

"Oooh. I love surprises. Count me in."

Cameron walks away and takes a seat in one of the booths along the wall. Ben wags his eyebrows at both me and Madeline and turns to join his best friend.

"That guy is like a junior Duke," Madeline says.

I laugh. "I never thought of it that way, but you're so right. Such a shameless flirt, but harmless too."

"He should give my brother some lessons. Apparently, Cameron was dating a girl at San Diego State for a few years. Ever since they broke up, he's been as winsome as a piece of paper."

That's some piece of paper, if you ask me. Of course, I'm not telling Madeline that. She'd freak. Do you know how hard it is to have an insufferable, incurable crush on a guy and not be able to dish about it with your bestie? It's excruciating, let me tell you. Madeline and I share everything—right down to our favorite outfits. Usually, if either of us faces a dilemma, we hash it out over popcorn and diet soda, or one of my fab coffee creations. But when it comes to Cameron, I'm on my own.

I knew about Cameron's breakup. I saw it on his social media. He didn't post the breakup, but that girl stopped appearing in every photo, so I put two and two together. And yes, I stalk Cameron's socials. I prefer the term, scan, or peruse. Stalking sounds so ... stalkerish.

Our shift wraps up. The guys hang out in their booth until Madeline and I finish cleaning up and Sarah arrives to take over. Then the four of us head over to Satterson's in Cameron's car. Ben's in charge of tunes since he's riding shotgun. His taste in music is decent. I love matching music to the occasion. But it's not like we're actually on a long trip. Everything in Bordeaux is within five or ten minutes of everything else. We pull into Satterson's and Duke strolls out toward Cameron's car.

"Hey, guys," he says, leaning his arm over the passenger door and tilting his head so he can peek through the window.

"Oh, hey, Madeline and Riley. I didn't expect you two. Wait out here for a minute. Okay?"

"Uh. Okay," Cameron says.

I'm as confused as he sounds.

Cameron leaves the A/C running in the car so we don't melt. A few minutes later, Duke comes back out.

"Okay. Coast is clear. I just had to make sure it was cool for all four of you to see what I've got to show you."

Now I'm dying to see whatever this is.

We follow Duke in through the main door that leads into the small office off the service bays. Then we walk into the garage where two cars are up on lifts, and a blue vintage VW van sits in the far bay. Duke walks past the two cars in for service, nodding to the mechanics at work as he goes. Then he stops in front of the van.

"What do ya think?" Duke asks.

He's beaming, waving his hand at the van like he built it from scratch. Knowing him, he just might have.

"She's a beauty," Cameron says.

Cameron's eyes are glistening, and he's got this killer smile which is on full display right now.

"Right?" Duke answers. "This family who lives on the outskirts of town was getting rid of her. She'd already had so much work done, including a complete engine rebuild, so I only had to do a little more. "

Ben lets out a low whistle. "This would be the perfect surf mobile. Right, Cam? Couldn't you see a couple of boards on top while we pulled into the parking lot at Sunset Beach to catch some waves?"

Cameron nods. His eyes haven't left the van. He gently reaches out and runs a hand along the hood.

"She sure would." Cameron looks over at Duke. "What are you going to do with her? Keep her for your family vehicle?"

"I considered it. But Shannon wants something more updated. She's all about the bells and whistles for Bridgette. I made this safe enough so I would feel good about toting my family around in it, but Shannon's happy with our Honda."

"So?" Ben asks. "Are you selling it?"

As if he's in the market to buy it. Maybe he is. I don't know Ben's financial situation, but I'm guessing it involves student loans. He's about to start his first job out of college at a resort off the coast of California. Until then, he's been living it up on his parents' dime all summer. He's calling it his gap summer. He's definitely mastered the gap aspect of things.

"It's already sold," Duke says with this smirky grin.

Cameron's face falls a little. No one else seems aware. But I notice everything about Cameron. He wanted this van. Badly. I resist the urge to walk over and put my hand on his back to reassure him. It's a sweet van. I'd love something like this one day. Ben's right. It's the perfect ride for a beachy life. This may be my last year in California, though, so I should not be entertaining ideas about beach-worthy vehicles.

"Who'd you sell it to?" Cameron asks Duke.

"Well, that's the surprise. And it's also why I had you four wait in the car. This van ... well, the proud owner of this van is standing right here."

Duke points to me, and I reflexively look over my shoulder. Nope. He's definitely pointing at me.

"Me?" I ask when I look back at him.

"Yep! Isn't that awesome? Your dad came in the other day and saw me working on it. I was doing some finish work on the interior. He and I got to talking. He had actually stopped in to ask me to help him find something as a gift for his daughter."

"For me?"

I'm still in shock.

"He figured you four were driving to California. What better way to go than in a 1979 VW bus?"

"So, this is mine?" I ask again.

Cameron shakes his head and chuckles. "It's yours, Riley. Your dad bought you a vintage VW."

"Well, you're driving it," I say.

"What?" Cameron asks.

"When we drive back to UCLA, you're driving. I call shotgun."

I look Cameron in the eyes. He's smiling that same smile he had when he first saw the van, only now, that smile is definitely directed at me.

2

CAMERON

There's more to life than VWs ... but not much.
~ Anonymous

Riley stands there, nearly bouncing in place, staring up at me.

"Okay. Twist my arm. I'll drive your van to California."

"You will? Okay. Alright. Good." She nods with each word. Then she says, "Wait. You will? Really?"

I nod.

"Yes! Oh my gosh! Yes!"

Riley jumps into the air. She turns to Madeline and gives her a hug. "This is going to be epic!"

Then she turns to Duke, hugs him, and says, "Thank you! ... Thank you. Thank you. Thank you. You're the best!"

Duke beams and holds Riley in a hug. She bounces away from him and makes this little squealing noise.

Then she turns to me. "Thank you, Cam."

Her face is soft and so happy. She's almost always happy, but this is like usual Riley joy times ten. She throws herself into my arms and gives me a huge hug, rocking us side to side a little and giving me an extra squeeze for good measure.

"I didn't do anything, Rye. I'm just agreeing to drive your van for you," I mutter into her hair.

She smells like a coffee shop. Chocolate, espresso, warmth, and something that reminds me of home. Riley leans back and smiles up at me, her arms still wrapped loosely around me.

"It's not nothing, Cam. I'd freak out if I had to drive the whole trip. I trust you." Her face shifts from serious to giddy in a nanosecond. "And we are gonna have so much fun!"

Ben pipes up. "What about me? Everyone gets hugs but me?"

Riley bounces away from me and gives Ben a big hug. "Can you believe it, Ben? This is my van."

"It's sweet. Your dad's amazing."

"Oh my gosh! I have to call him! Duke, thank you. Thank you. Thank you. Thank you."

"You already thanked me plenty, Riley," The look on Duke's face says he's not tired of hearing her gush—at all. Her joy is contagious.

"Let me show you a few things, and then you can call your dad," Duke says.

"Yes! Show me everything, Duke. I want to memorize this van. I want to sleep in her. I want to drive her so slowly through town just so everyone can admire her true beauty."

Duke shakes his head at Riley. She's ridiculous, but we're all so used to her. Besides, Duke's just about as crazy as Riley. If you put Duke, Riley, and Ben in a room together ... well, let's just say they shouldn't be left unattended.

"Technically, it's a bus. But you call it what you want. Just please don't call her a car," Duke says.

"I never would. Never. As if she's a car. She's an icon. Like Diana Ross or Bette Davis. Only more surfer-y. Maybe she's like Gidget."

"You gonna name her?"

"Of coouurrrse." Riley puts her hands on her hips and draws out the phrase.

Like, duh, who wouldn't name their van?

Me. That's who. But leave it to Riley. I'm pretty sure she named her backpacks every year through high school. I know she named her bicycles. Mrs. Spokes, Limoncello, The Blue Beast …

I look back at the van. My smile breaks free again. This is such a sweet ride. And to think, Riley's dad bought this for her. It's not even her graduation year.

Duke slides the side door open and starts touring us through the features, recounting what the previous owners did and what improvements he made. The more he talks, the thicker the feeling of anticipation grows between the four of us.

Ben and I were already slated to drive with Riley and Madeline back to California in two weeks. Our parents are best friends, so despite us all being over twenty-one, they conspired to plan this road trip once they found out Ben and I landed jobs at a high-end resort on Marbella Island off the coast of California. Instead of Riley and Madeline waiting another month to leave for their last year at UCLA, they're coming out with us. They each applied and were accepted for temp jobs during high season at the resort.

I can't complain too much about our parents meddling. They're footing the bill for the hotels, gas, and meals on this trip. If I didn't know better, I'd say they were vicariously reliving their youth through us. More than that, they want me and Ben to look out for Riley and Mads.

Originally, I was going to be driving Riley's old car from Ohio to California. It's a four-seater that's seen better days. This van is a massive improvement.

Driving a VW bus down Route 66? It doesn't get more iconic than that. Who knows the next time I'd ever have a chance to take a trip like this. In one month, I'll be working full time. No more whole summers off to hang out and fritter time away like it's an endless commodity. From here on out, my life will be filled with my career and only short spurts of designated time off.

Ben and I were lucky enough to find jobs together. But you never know how long our lives will run on parallel tracks. Taking this trip with my best friend and my two baby sisters is the chance of a lifetime.

I look over at Riley. She's intently listening to Duke explain how he moved the battery placement to be more optimal. Her big brown eyes practically gleam with excitement.

Sure, I know Riley's not exactly my sister, but she may as well be. We grew up together. She and Madeline are as inseparable as Ben and me. Obviously, she's not the girl she was when Ben and I took off for undergrad four years ago. I'd have to be blind not to notice she's grown up. But for all intents and purposes, the beautiful young woman coming unglued with excitement in front of me may as well be my sister.

Duke finishes touring us through the finer points of the van, including the special storage spaces, the added convenience of a camp stove, overhead compartments, and the improved seating arrangement with a smoother mechanism for turning the rear bench into a bed. He replaced the front chairs with captain's chairs, but they match the interior and feel like they were original to the bus. I take a seat in one and Riley sits next to me, looking over with an ear-to-ear grin.

"What's the sound system like?" she asks Duke. "Do I need to rely on my bluetooth speaker for our road trip soundtrack?"

"Are you kidding me?" Duke asks. "This thing is fully upgraded. I kept the vintage look, but you've got an AM/FM stereo, a CD player, and bluetooth capacity. This is a fully loaded sound system. And I embedded speakers in the front door panels and the rear roof."

Riley rapidly taps her feet on the floorboards like she's running in place. Her knees alternate bobbing up and down while she squeals at a decibel that might just break the windshield.

"You. Are. The. Best! It's official. I'm naming my first child Duke."

"As you should," he says without skipping a beat.

"Wouldn't your husband need to have a vote in what you name your child?" I ask.

Riley gives me this smile like she's the girl who just got given a VW bus on a day that's not a holiday or a special occasion. "My husband will be so smitten with me he will leave that minor detail up to me. And when I tell him how Duke was the one who refurbished the van that took me across the U.S. for one of the greatest road trips ever, and then that same van became my favorite car ... vehicle ... sorry, Duke ... ever. Welp, my husband will say, name our kids anything. Name them Cheeto and Frito for all I care."

"Wow," I say.

"Wow is right," Riley answers. "I mean, think about it. The woman carries the child. She should be able to name it. What does the guy do?" She pauses, turning a telling shade of pink. "You know what? Don't answer that. The point is, I will be bearing our children. I get to name them."

Then she turns to Duke. "If my baby's a girl, I'll name her Duchess."

Duke cracks up. We all do. No one is as ridiculous and somehow simultaneously adorable as Riley.

My phone rings. It's Mom.

"I should take this," I tell Duke and my friends.

I step off to the other corner of the garage.

"Hey, Mom. What's up?"

"Hi, sweetie. I wanted to let you know we are having the Stewarts over for dinner. Can you pick up a loaf of garlic bread at Kroger?"

The Stewarts. That's Riley's family.

I ask my mom if Ben can come too. Of course, she says it's fine. He's as good as family. When I hang up, everyone's saying goodbye to Duke. Riley's going to leave the van at the garage for a few days so Duke can finish a few minor things he's working on. To me, it's already beyond perfect. But Duke says there's finishing touches he's dying to add. Maybe Riley *should* name a baby after him. You could do way worse than Duke.

Dinner consists of our parents nearly talking over one another as they plot the details of a trip they aren't even taking. Riley can't stop smiling.

Right now she's looking over at me, making crossed-eyes and sticking her tongue out. She's trying to make me laugh so I'll become the center of attention. I'm returning the favor by flaring my nostrils back at her. Are we being juvenile? Sure. When you grow up with someone, it's easy to revert to antics you pulled when you both were much younger.

"What do you think, Cameron?" my mom asks.

"Um ... about what?"

Riley giggles quietly. She may not have made me laugh, but she did her job. Now I look like an idiot who wasn't paying attention. Because I wasn't.

"Stopping at some museums to add a touch of culture and education to the trip."

"Isn't the point of this trip to get to California?" I ask, regretting the words as soon as they're out of my mouth.

Dad chuckles good naturedly, which usually means we're in for a lecture.

"Son. The point of this trip is so much more than merely driving from point A to point B. You'll be driving a highway that's chock full of historical significance. There's so much to be done and seen along the way. Of course, as you get further west, there may be more cacti than points of interest, but the desert has its own beauty. And of course, there's the Grand Canyon, the Petrified Forest, Four Corners ..."

My dad prattles on about all the things you can see between long stretches of wasteland once you pass through Missouri. Fabulous.

The adults resume their excited chatter, planning where to stop, and even reminiscing about road trips they've taken. Madeline nudges Riley. They have some sort of silent conversation between themselves. It's like they can read one another's minds. Not a word is spoken, just a series of facial expressions followed by shrugs or nods. Then Madeline says, "Riley wants to look up the best museums along the route. May we be excused to go do research?"

"Oh! That's an excellent idea, darling," my mom says.

"Want some help?" Ben asks, barely cloaking his desperation to escape.

"I'm great at internet searches," I volunteer.

Riley beams. Madeline shoots me a glare full of daggers.

I don't see why. If she can weasel her way out of parental suffocation, why shouldn't Ben and I be able to join in?

"Yes, Cameron. Go help the girls," Riley's dad suggests, as if it was his idea in the first place.

Ben hops up so fast his chair nearly tips over.

He quickly recovers with a charming, "Thanks for dinner, Mrs. Reeves. It was delicious."

He grabs his plate and takes it through to the kitchen. The three of us trail after him.

Once we're in the kitchen, Madeline says in a hushed voice, "If any of you make us stop at a museum to add culture and education to this trip, I'm hitching a ride with a complete stranger."

"Right?" I add, thinking we're all on the same page.

Yes. Route 66 will be cool to ride along. But we are on a mission to get to Marbella Island. We don't need to drag out the trip more than necessary.

"We can focus on making good time and getting to each designated stop daily. No need to make this trip longer than it already is," I say.

All three of them look at me like I've lost it.

"What?"

"Seriously, Cam? You want to rush this trip?" Ben looks nearly hurt.

"We're definitely not rushing this," Riley adds.

My sister jumps in, saying, "I just don't want to get all stodgy and focus on the historical relevance as if we're studying for a history final. I do enough of that from September through May. This trip should be fun with plenty of stops at places we may never see again in our lifetime. But fun ones. Ones we choose, not the list foisted on us by our parents."

"Agreed," Riley says. Then she looks at me with this pleading look. "Is that going to be okay with you?"

I don't know what to say. I like exploring and adventure as much as the next guy. But we're talking a two thousand two hundred fifty mile trip. That's thirty-three hours of straight travel time, if the weather and traffic are good. Not to mention stops for restroom breaks, meals, and sleep.

We're not going to know where the best hotels are or where to eat if we don't make a plan and stick to it. We could get stuck in the middle of nowhere. I don't tell my three closest people in the world about my hesitation.

Instead, when Riley looks up at me with those doe eyes and her eyebrows raised, I just say, "Yeah. Sure."

RILEY'S JOURNAL
(AKA "GLADYS")

July 10th

Hey Gladys,

So much happened today!

First of all, I have to tell you about the VW. Yes. *My* VW bus. It's a 1979. I never knew I was into vintage cars, or vehicles, as Duke would say, but man, oh man, when I saw her, it was love at first sight. Daddy decided he wanted me to have a more sturdy, reliable ride since we're traveling across the country to go back to LA. And this sweet girl happened to be sitting in Satterson's Garage when Daddy went to talk to Duke. She's blue with white trim and a dark gray interior. So, my dad bought her—for me.

Can you believe it, Gladys? I know you can. I have the best dad in the world.

So, of course, when Duke told me it was mine, I squealed and jumped. I hugged everyone in sight—well, I stopped short of hugging the two mechanics I barely know.

But I hugged Cameron. Oh, yes I did.

Best. Moment. Of. My. Life.

Gladys, I wish you were really here. We'd put on one of your old records and dance like we used to when I was little. Do you remember teaching me the Jitterbug? I do. I always will. I'd tell you about hugging Cameron and you'd pop on a record and we'd dance like no one's watching in your living room.

Anyway, back to the hug with Cameron. That hug was better than finding out Dad bought me the van. Hands down. I'd give that van up for another hug like that. I'm crazy, I know. But it is what it is.

If you were here, you would ask me why I'd make such a sacrifice. And I'll tell you.

Cameron hugged me back.

He didn't give me that little one-two pat on the back. He didn't pull back. No. He held on while I bounced with joy in his arms. He even bent down and said, "I didn't do anything, Rye." I freaking love when he calls me Rye. His voice in my hair felt like a secret only we shared. I could have sworn he inhaled, like he was soaking me up. But I know better. If anything, he got some of my hair stuck in his nose or something. When it comes to Cameron, I'm in a place worse than the friend zone. I'm in the sister zone!

Ohhh. I almost forgot. When Cameron came into Bean There Done That, before we even went to Satterson's, he looked so good. He was wearing this rust colored T-shirt. It's just a T-shirt, I know. But rust is a color you don't see every day. Who am I kidding? He could wear puce or beige and I'd be swooning. But he wasn't wearing puce or beige. He wore the heck out of that rust T-shirt. And it made his eyes pop. So, yes. I blabbered on about his eyes. He acted like he didn't notice my verbal version of Niagara Falls. And you know what? I'm pretty sure he didn't.

Cameron never notices me. He's not mean or arrogant. He's just oblivious. To him, I'm just another family member. I'm like a housecat he's had for too many years. Now when he looks at me, all he thinks of is cleaning the litter box or sprinkling some kibble in my dish. Otherwise, he hopes I find a sunny spot to go lick myself and fall asleep out of his way. Not literally me … cat me. You understand.

Gladys, something has to give. I can't be pining away for Cameron like this year after year. But you know me. I can't help myself.

You know more than anyone since I tell you EVERYTHING. All the guys I've tried to date are held up to the impossible measuring stick that is Cameron Reeves. And they don't even make the half-way mark. Maybe one day someone will, and I'll be put out of this misery of unrequited crushing. It's the WORST.

So, besides the usual Cameron obsession, and the gift of a totally refurbished van for the trip, we also had dinner at the Reeves' house. All the parents were in full-blown planning mode, as if they'll be taking this trip instead of us. It's pretty cute, if you ask me. They're so excited and brimming with ideas. Which reminds me. I'm going to make a bucket list for this trip. What's a road trip without a bucket list?

Right? Right.

There are only thirteen more days as of tomorrow until we shut that van door and hit the road. Also, I want to put together a killer road trip soundtrack. You taught me that, Gladys. Life needs a soundtrack. It makes things so much more magical. Well-written songs help us to say things we never could find the words to say. Music gives us a place to feel all our emotions, and lyrics help us know we aren't the only one who ever felt this way.

Of course, this playlist is going to have to be massive.

Cameron, the keeper of all facts and details, said something about the drive time being over thirty hours of just driving. That doesn't count stopping at attractions, and eating, and all the other possible delays.

I'm practically giddy thinking of it all. What a grand adventure, as you'd say.

Did I mention that I asked Cameron to drive and then called shotgun? Yep. I did that. But I'll let Ben or Mads ride up front sometimes too. It's only fair. And maybe I'll even drive on a straightaway to give Cam a break every so often. There are miles and miles of Texas, or so the song says.

There's so much goodness ahead, I can barely sleep thinking of it all.

Thanks for being the best secret keeper ever, Gladys.

3

RILEY

The sweetest part of leaving home is
knowing, beyond the shadow of a doubt,
that you'll always carry it with you."
~ Unknown

"Come here, you little goofball," I say to Poppy.

Of course, she runs in the opposite direction.

Madeline and I are babysitting for the MacIntyre's tonight out at their home which sits on a property everyone in town calls The Old Finch Place. Well, Madeline's actually the official babysitter, but since I'm doing a whole lotta nothing until the trip, she invited me to tag along. The evening isn't cool, but it's not boiling, so we're outside trying to wear the kids down before bedtime.

Poppy squeals and runs past me just out of arm's reach. She's nearly six and cuter than should be legal. Owen, her baby brother, is two and a half and full of enough energy to light up a small city. He chases after Poppy, screaming her name. We're playing some mutated version of tag that has elements of hide-and-go-seek, and possibly some musical chairs thrown in for good measure. There aren't clear rules and Poppy tells people they're "out" whenever she's about to be caught.

"You're it," I shout to Madeline.

She gives me a look and laughs, knowing I'm being as random as Poppy.

"No! You it!" Owen shouts at me and then bursts into a fit of giggles.

"No. You're it!" I say, grabbing for him, pulling him to myself and then swinging him in a circle in the air.

"Put me down, Wiley! I tant be it up hee-uhw."

He's still smiling big. I set him down and he smacks his little hand on my thigh as soon as his feet hit the ground.

"Now you it!"

"You better run, then!" I say, taking off after him, but modifying my speed so he doesn't trip trying to get away from me.

I veer to the left toward Poppy. "I see you, Poppy."

She's hiding behind a bush.

"No you don't!" she whispers, almost to herself.

I look over at Madeline, and decide to cut Poppy some slack. Without any warning, I chase my best friend down, darting this way and that around the yard until I catch up with her and tag her.

"You're it!"

Madeline's doubled over, her breath coming in and out as rapidly as mine, and she's laughing between gulps of air.

"Okay! Ready or not, here I come!" she says.

Owen lets out a shriek even though he's far from Madeline. Poppy stays quiet behind her bush. I hustle away from Madeline toward Owen. He's a good shield.

We keep playing our made up game for another twenty minutes or so, then the sky grows dusky and the fireflies come out. We grab the mason jars off the porch and run after the glowing beetles, capturing them until our jars look like magical lanterns, flickering with bioluminescent bursts of yellowish light.

We leave the jars on the porch and take the kids upstairs. Madeline holds Poppy's hand and I carry Owen on my hip. He's a chunky little guy, and his weight feels double when he collapses into me, resting his head on my shoulder.

After teeth are brushed and jammies are on, we tuck the kids into their beds and read each of them a story. I sing a soft song my mom used to sing to me, called *I Love You Up to the Moon,* first to Poppy, and then to Owen. Madeline and I pull the bedroom doors shut behind us and tiptoe downstairs to hang out in the living room.

Lexi's the best to babysit for. She leaves out a little basket in the kitchen full of microwave popcorn, soda, cookies, and a note that says help yourself to whatever you want in the fridge or pantry. Madeline and I pop popcorn, and then we take our snack and soda into the living room and plop onto the couch.

"I told Ben and Cam they could come over once the kids were asleep so we could talk about the trip." Madeline tells me.

Why does just the mention of his name make me wonder what my hair looks like after a rousing game of whatever that was we were playing? I hadn't even thought once about my looks all night.

Madeline's got her phone out—obviously texting the guys.

She looks up and says, "They'll be here in about fifteen or twenty minutes."

I take a deep breath, trying not to let my nerves show to Madeline.

She doesn't seem to notice I'm coming slightly unhinged at the mention of her brother.

"I still can't believe your parents gave you that van!"

"I know. It's crazy, right?"

"For average parents, yes. For yours, not so much."

"What's that supposed to mean?"

I pop a piece of popcorn into my mouth and let it melt on my tongue.

"You know."

She just looks at me like I do know. I'm not sure I do.

"Your parents give you everything."

"Oh. Yeah. I mean, they are very generous."

"True. But they're extra generous with you. Think about your older brothers. Did either of them get a car during college, or even for graduation?"

I squirm a little.

Why should I feel badly about getting a van as a gift? I didn't ask for it. I rarely ask for anything. But Madeline's right. I don't really have to. My parents pay for my school, still send me a weekly allowance, and Mom takes me shopping as soon as I'm back in town. They furnished my dorm. Now that Madeline and I share an apartment, they pay my rent. And they helped us fill our place with all the things we needed to get set up when we moved in.

"I guess they look at me as their baby girl."

"Which you are. It's not a bad thing. I'd love to be in your shoes."

Madeline's family is more of a you-earn-it type. They also don't have quite as much money as our family, not that it ever mattered to me. Our parents grew up here in Bordeaux and have been best friends since childhood. My dad travels to Dayton to do architectural work. Madeline's dad works as an electrician, running the family business that was handed down to him.

After hours, the two men set aside their professional lives and function on a level playing field, as far as I could always tell. My mom has always been a homemaker. Madeline's mom sells Mary Kay. Not at the pink Cadillac level. Her side-business always made her enough to pay for summer camp or some extra frills for the family, as far as I know.

But Madeline's right, even if they had the money, her parents aren't the type to give their grown children automobiles. Madeline has scholarships and student loans, and she works part-time in the library on campus to pay for books. Her parents paid for part of her education, but they only supplemented the overall cost.

"Are you ..." my voice trails off.

"Am I what?" Madeline asks from over the rim of her soda.

"Jealous?"

I don't know if I'd be jealous if the shoe were on the other foot. I might be, though jealousy isn't something I usually experience. I wouldn't blame Madeline for being envious of my situation. If she only knew the pitfalls of being raised the way I have been, she might not covet the spoils.

"I'm not jealous. At least not too jealous. Would I like my own sweet vintage van to drive around campus and take to the beach? Sure. Who wouldn't? But mostly, I'm just happy for you. Besides, I know you. You'll share."

"I totally will. You can drive it whenever you want. You know that."

"I do."

I take a swallow of my soda and lean back into the sofa cushions.

Madeline might wish she had a van, but she has something

I want way more than cool transportation. Lately, I find myself desperately wishing someone would steer me into my future with greater clarity. One thing Madeline has that I lack is a sense of where she's headed in life. She's wanted to be an elementary school teacher since we were in high school, maybe even longer.

I just want to be with Madeline as long as possible, so I applied to UCLA when she did—to get a bachelor's with a major in education. Later, I found out Madeline picked that school for two reasons. They focus on teaching in the inner cities, and it's close to the beach.

Is Madeline hoping to stay in LA after we graduate? We haven't dared talk about life after college. It's like neither one of us feels prepared to face the fact that twelve months from now, we'll be out on our own, trying to do all the adulting things. She's far more ready than I am. Even in my internships at local schools, I find myself feeling a lot like many of the kids in class: recess is still my favorite part of the school day.

A knock at the door breaks through my thoughts.

"That's prolly the guys," Madeline says, getting off the couch and walking into the hallway.

I stay rooted in my spot. Who knows what I'd do or say if I joined the welcoming committee.

"Hey, hey, hey!" Ben's voice carries too loudly through the foyer.

"Shhhh," Madeline shushes him. "The kids are asleep."

"Oh. Yeah. Right. Right," Ben answers her in a hoarse stage whisper.

"You are going to officially drive your wife nuts," she says, shaking her head as she reappears in the living room doorway.

"First, he'll have to find a girlfriend. These things go in order," Cameron says.

His voice carries in from the hallway, and my stupid body

gets chills. I remember the summer his voice changed. It was never super-high, but when it was transforming into the voice he has now, there were some very squeaky moments.

"Anyway, back to my wife," Ben says, completely unfazed by Cameron's reality shot. "I'll drive her nuts in the best of ways. I'm going to make an awesome husband and father. Plus, we brought pizza, so stop complaining about me and dig in."

Cameron rounds the corner, wearing a gray T-shirt that says *SDSU Alumni* and some black basketball shorts. Why? Just why does this man look so good? I look down at my popcorn, shaking the bowl a little and then look back up. Cameron's setting the pizza box on the coffee table.

"Soda's in the kitchen. Please be quiet and help yourselves," Madeline says.

The guys come back from the kitchen carrying sodas. Ben has cookies and a bag of chips too.

"Dude," he says to Cameron. "We really should look into a babysitting gig. It's a sweet deal. Look at the way they get to eat!"

Madeline rolls her eyes at me. I just laugh. Ben's hilarious. And, being around him makes me feel better. If someone as outrageous and silly as Ben can land an actual job his first summer out of college, there's a chance for me. At least, I'm hoping there is.

Madeline grabs plates and we all dig into the pizza while Cameron takes the floor like he's the CEO at a board meeting.

"Okay, guys. I figure we should split up the responsibilities of preparing for this trip between the four of us. The better prepared we are, the less likely we'll run into a situation that puts us off schedule."

"We don't start work for a month, Cam," Ben says. "We leave in less than two weeks. We've got wiggle room. Chillax, my man."

Cameron crosses his arms across his chest. He's in bossy mode, which should make him seem obnoxious or unattractive. I'm sorry that it doesn't. He's got this calm, take-charge air about him that makes me feel like I can relax and everything will be alright.

These days, I rarely feel like everything will be alright. My whole life I've been a kept woman—okay, a kept child. But still. I've relied on my parents for everything. With Cam in his organized, serious mode, I know we'll get to California just fine. All I have to worry about are the snacks and the soundtrack.

I figure I'll help the planning along by volunteering to take on those two tasks.

"I've got music and snacks covered," I say, beaming at Cam.

He gives me a serious look. His arms are still folded across his chest. Can I help if I picture him somewhere down the road in the distant future, telling our kids it's time for bed? He's just so authoritative right now.

"I was talking more along the lines of figuring out how long each leg of the trip will take, what gas stations, restaurants, and most importantly, hotels are along the way. We'll need a first aid kit and provisions, and we need to know all the basics about your van, like where the spare tire is, what kind of gas mileage it gets, where the windshield wiper controls are. You know, the basics."

"Oh," I say.

"What are we doing, going on a trek in the Amazon rainforest through ancient lands occupied by a cannibalistic tribe?" Ben asks just before popping his pizza slice in his mouth and taking a huge bite.

Cam gives Ben a wry grin.

"Provisions," Ben continues, chewing and swallowing while he talks. "First aid? All these plans? Dude. We're a group of twenty-something, Gen Z nomads out for the adventure of our lifetime. Stop throwing your thermal wet blanket on our trip."

"You'll be happy for my thermal wet blanket when we need it. I mean thermal blankets. Whatever. You'll be glad I forced us to make some concrete plans."

"I say we live by our wits and take each day as it comes. We've got the rest of our lives to live by some calendar app and a list of reminders. This is our last hurrah!"

Ben looks at me and Madeline as if he's running for office and wants to secure our votes. I'm all for a fun trip. So what if we don't make it to a hotel one night. We could sleep in the van. We'll have snacks, and we'll make sure to always get gas before we run low.

But things being as they are, I'm team Cameron, ride-or-die.

"I think Cam has a point," I say.

"Thank you, Riley," Cam says, smiling at me.

Our eyes connect. I try to hold his stare, but he breaks it and gets right down to business.

By the time Lexi and Trevor are home, we've devoured the pizza, and we've decided Cameron can determine the length of drive time each day and key stopping points. Each of us can do our own research and add in landmarks or events we want to stop for, but we'll only allow a certain amount of time each day for sightseeing. Cam would love to do this trip in four days, five max. My parents already told us to stretch it out a little so we can make the most of the experience.

At one point during our planning session, Ben told us about a friend who drove to his girlfriend's graduation in Boston last year right after he graduated from SDSU. The two graduations were only four days apart. Ben's friend drove the whole forty-five hours in three days, only stopping at rest stops for naps. And then, after her cap and gown ceremony, he proposed.

Madeline and I swooned like most girls would at this story.

Cam just said, "That guy should have splurged on a plane ticket."

On the surface, Cam's definitely not a romantic, but under that layer of responsibility and drive, I know he's got a side that is itching to let loose and throw caution to the wind. Maybe this trip will help him relax and take some risks.

4

CAMERON

Anyone can be a father,
but it takes someone special to be a dad.
~ Wade Boggs

When I come down the stairs Saturday morning, still in my pj bottoms, Dad's in the kitchen looking like he's ready for a day of work.

"I told Mabel we'd come by and change her air filter and the batteries in her smoke detectors today."

"We?"

"Yes, son. I told her *we'd* be coming."

"What if I have plans?" I chuckle, loving the new feeling of teasing my dad.

"I'm pretty sure you don't, since you've been giving me your Saturdays all summer."

"You'd be right about that. Give me a minute to hop in the

shower and grab something quick for breakfast, and I'll be ready."

"Don't keep me waiting, the cool of the morning won't last long enough for you to get pretty."

I take the stairs two at a time, shouting down, "I was born pretty!" Then I add, "Good genes, I'd guess."

My dad's voice trails up after me as I grab an outfit and cross the hall to take a shower.

"Darn straight it's good genes. You look just like me."

I laugh as I turn on the water, inspecting my reflection in the vanity mirror. I do look a lot like my dad. I'll never tell him I think so. I don't usually think about my looks all that much. I know I'm not ugly. Any girl I've dated always called me cute, or even gorgeous, but that's what girlfriends do—until they don't. People put too much stock in looks. Effort is what will get a man where he wants to go—focus and effort.

Mabel's house is only a few blocks away from my childhood home. She's one of the seniors in town. Some tasks are more than she can handle—especially the ones involving climbing a ladder. So, people around town pitch in to help keep Mabel's home maintained. I've grown up with Mabel being like a second grandma to me. She's a little quirky, but that's kind of par for the course around here. We're salt-of-the-earth people here in Bordeaux, but we've also got our eccentricities, and some of us more than others. Don't even get me started on Cooter Shartz. That man gives new meaning to the word strange.

Mabel's standing on her porch wearing a hot pink velour tracksuit when we pull up in front of her house. She waves an animated hand and walks toward the car.

"Oh, look at you, Cameron. My my. Have you grown since the last time I saw you?"

"I think that was last week at Kroger. So, no ma'am, I'd have to say I probably haven't grown since then."

"Well, you look older, and just so handsome. He reminds me of you at this age, Doug," she says to my dad.

"Only, I was way cuter. Right, Mabel?"

"You know me and my memory. I can't rightly say."

She gives me an exaggerated wink—one I'm pretty sure my dad sees too.

"Well, we'll just get to it," Dad says. "The air filter and your smoke detector batteries, right?"

"Thank you so much. I made you a casserole to thank you. Don't forget to stop in the kitchen to take it with you when you go."

"Aww. You didn't need to go and do that, Mabel."

She really, really didn't.

"I most certainly did. I got the recipe from Midwest Living."

"That's an actual publication?" Dad looks part confused and part concerned.

"Well, yes it is. It's even online. Just about anyone can enter a recipe to the editor and they'll publish it in the coming month or so. I even had a few published here and there. This one's pretty basic. Just ground beef, canned cream soup, tater tots, canned beans, and cheese. They called it Sunday Scramble. I thought that name made it sound like it's got eggs in it, so I renamed it."

"What do you call it?" Dad asks, taking the bait.

"Tots and Creamy Beefarini."

Dad and I look at one another. I have to look up at the tree branches overhead and breathe through my nose while biting the inside of my lip. If I look at Dad or Mabel, I'll lose it.

"Okay, welp. Thanks for that, Mabel. I'm sure Jenny will be grateful not to have to cook tonight."

How my dad is keeping a straight face right now, I'll never know.

I take one last inconspicuous gulp of air, and then smile over at Mabel and nod politely. Dad and I spend the next hour doing minor upkeep on her home. Dad even brought a can of WD-40 to grease the locks and hinges. He always goes the extra mile. That's how I was raised. Good enough isn't good enough. Add something extra and you'll get somewhere. Mabel's smile as we're leaving says it all.

I carry the casserole to the car and set it in the back seat.

"One can only hope we get rear-ended on the way home," Dad says with a half-smile. "That casserole flying off the back seat would ruin the interior of the car, but it just might be worth it."

"Your car would smell like Beefarini forever."

Dad glances over at me and we both laugh.

"Our whole house is going to smell like Beefarini tonight."

"I think I'm meeting Ben at Mad River Burgers tonight," I say hopefully.

"Invite him to supper instead," Dad says in that *don't even try to wiggle out of this* tone.

Great. Now, not only do I have to eat Tots and Creamy Beefarini, but Ben's going to have to endure Mabel's cooking with me. I'll owe him one, big time.

"Do you have plans right now?" Dad asks.

"Not right now. Later, Ben and I are meeting a group of friends at the Res to swim."

Our reservoir is a man-made lake that feels as real as if God put it there himself. It's a hangout for families and all us younger adults during the summer. High school kids cluster together in one area of the beach. Couples try to find a secluded spot to themselves, and fail. There's no hiding a budding relationship from the prying eyes of Bordeaux. Kids run in and out of the shallow water that hits the shoreline, while moms sit on blankets and in lawn chairs watching them from a short distance away.

The Res has been a backdrop for my life. It's where I learned how to swim, and later to water ski. It's where I had my first kiss, and where I asked my prom date to the dance. The guys and I used to hang at the Res, and when the first one of our friend group, Steven, got his driver's license, we all rode out there like we owned this town and nothing could hold us back from our futures. I've taken dares to run into that water when it was just above freezing, and I've had some of my best heart-to-heart talks with Ben out there, sitting in the back of one of our trucks, or laying on top of adjacent picnic tables, staring up at the stars while one of us pours our heart out to the other.

I may not have been given a brother by birth, but I got the next best thing. Ben's my ride-or-die. And I'm his.

"I thought we'd grab a cup of coffee at Bean There Done That," Dad suggests.

Dad never grabs a cup of coffee for the sake of simply caffeinating. To him, a trip to a coffee shop is a mission to impart wisdom or correction. With our trip across the country coming up so soon, I'm pretty sure this will be some sort of send-off speech.

"I've got time," I say. "Let me treat you this time."

Dad looks over at me and nods once. He's not smiling, but his eyes are warm.

It feels good to step up and be more of a man with my dad. Things are changing so quickly. I'm no longer a kid coming home from college, even though nothing about this summer feels much different than any of the past four. Under the surface, I have a constant daily awareness that I'm at a turning point. From here on I'll be a grown up, not merely in age, but in every other way. I'm on my own dime. I've got to support myself and make my way in the world.

My mom's already talking about turning my room into her "she shed." A she shed? She's got plans for lavender on the walls and floral curtains. There's talk of a "little daybed with an eyelet comforter," and storage for her Mary Kay business. I'm being replaced—edged out by a midlife frilly pastel takeover of what was my haven for eighteen years, and my soft place to land the last four. Mom says not to worry. I can always stay in my old room when I'm in town—on the daybed covered in lace and surrounded by flowers. I may not make it through one night with my manhood intact.

But on the other hand, Mom's earned that room. She's devoted herself to me and Mads for twenty-three years. Come to think of it, she ought to be allowed to paint the whole house lavender and hang garlands and lace from every corner if that's what she wants to do.

"... Does that sound good?" my dad asks as we pull into a diagonal spot in front of the coffee shop.

"What?"

"I lost you there for a few minutes, huh?"

"Yeah. I was thinking about the future of my bedroom."

Dad chuckles. "You saw what your grandma did to my old room."

"Yeah," I laugh. "I don't think the Mattel warehouse has as many Barbies as Grams had."

Dad shakes his head, a wistful smile on his face. Grams passed away nearly eight years ago. I was just fifteen and Mads was thirteen. Grams had a personality a lot like Ben's. Colorful. That's a word I'd use to describe my grams. Gramps left us six months later. Everyone in town said he died of a broken heart. I'd have to agree. The two of them had a love affair that was almost embarrassing to witness. Where

Gramps was this quiet, steady man, Grams was a ball of sunshine and energy.

They should have clashed, but Grams told me whatever could be a cause for conflict in a relationship was often a blessing in disguise. In her words, *when you learn to live with someone, you eventually take the good with the bad. And what you thought were defects might turn out to be their best qualities—attributes that benefit you more than you expected they would. I used to fight your Gramps, trying to make him come out of his shell, be more spontaneous, take initiative without always having to weigh out the pros and cons. But if he'd have lived life my way, we'd have nothing to fall back on, no stability. He's the ballast, and I'm the wind. He keeps us from keeling over, and I make sure we move along.*

I'll never forget that talk. I was fifteen. I had been dating my high school girlfriend for six months and we were in the middle of our first real fight. Instead of talking to Ben, I went straight to Grams after the last bell. She opened the cookie jar, poured me a glass of milk, and sat at the dining table listening to me pour out my heart. I explained how right I was and how wrong Maryann was. Grams never corrected my foolishness directly. She never sided with Maryann, but she shed a bright light on how relationships worked. Knowing how much she and Gramps loved one another, and having grown up in the shadow of that love, made me take note of every single word she said.

Maryann and I broke up that summer. Sometimes what you think is bad, just is. Or, at least it's not a fit for you. We were not a fit. Maryann constantly complained about me and tried to change me. High school was supposed to be fun, not a series of disagreements with a girl who obviously should have been dating someone far different than me.

Grams died that year, leaving me with memories, imparted wisdom, and a hole in my life no one has ever filled.

Dad and I walk into Bean There Done That.

"What'll it be, Sport?" Dad asks as he walks toward the counter.

"I'm treating you," I remind him.

He shakes his head. Then he turns to Riley who's manning the register. "I'll have a black coffee."

"That's all?" she asks. "Can't I get you a muffin or scone? Or maybe you'd like to try an espresso drink?"

"Just black coffee."

Dad's face isn't stern, but it's set.

"Is this because I'm treating?" I ask. "I can afford a muffin, Dad."

Riley looks at my dad with this sweet smile on her face.

"Sarah just made some lemon-blueberry muffins with a swirl of icing on top that are seriously delicious enough to make you reconsider all your life choices. How about I throw one in as a thank you for fixing my grandma's sink last week."

I look over at dad. I didn't know he'd done that.

He just shrugs.

"A black coffee, and a muffin on the house," Riley announces.

"What's your pleasure, Cameron?" she asks, and then immediately blushes.

Her next words come out like a rushing stream. "Um. I mean ... to drink. What do you enjoy drinking? Today. What would you like to drink?"

She lets out a long breath, and instead of looking directly at me, she glances at my dad with her eyebrows raised, her eyes wide, and her lips pinched to the side.

He just smiles an amused, but warm smile at her.

"I'll take whatever you suggest, Rye." I say.

She literally blows a breath out that sounds like "whhhh-hfff," and then seems to give herself an inner pep talk or something, because she straightens her back and says, "I suggest the caramel frappe, but it's not made with oat milk or stevia. I guess I could modify it that way if you wanted. But there will still be sugar involved."

My dad glances between the two of us.

"I eat sugar. I just don't overindulge. But if you suggest the caramel frappe, then give it to me the way you think I'd like it best. And throw in another muffin."

"Okay, Cam." She smiles at me, takes my money, and then turns to make our order.

"She's sure grown up over this past year," Dad mentions, as if he hasn't seen her almost daily over the summer whenever she's hanging out with Madeline.

I look across the counter at my sister's best friend. Her back is turned toward us, and if I didn't know who she was, I'd be tempted to check her out— from her long brown ponytail to the curve of her hips. And, yes, she's no longer even a teenager. She'll be turning twenty-one while we're on the road. I guess we ought to do something to celebrate her. That's a big birthday. I'll bring it up to Madeline tonight.

"Yeah," is all I say to my dad. But he looks at me like one man to another, knowing full well I had some not-so-brotherly thoughts about Riley just then.

"Does she have a boyfriend?" he asks.

"How should I know?" My tone comes out a bit more clipped than I expected, so I change the subject. "Let's find a table."

Once we're seated, Riley shows up with our two drinks and muffins on little plates. "Enjoy," she says, turning away as quickly as she came.

"So," Dad starts in. "I wanted to take you out to talk before the time gets away from us and you four hit the road."

I take a long pull through the straw of my frappe. It's

sweeter than my usual drink, but refreshing and delicious. My eyes drift to behind the counter where Riley's rinsing out the blender and wiping down the area around the espresso machine. I'll have to thank her before we leave.

"You're about to start your life. Really start it. Going to college is a big step, but there's still a sense of external structure and safety on campus. Once a man graduates and has a job, he's really moving into adulthood."

I nod. I'm well aware of my stage in life. It's practically all I think about.

"Now's the time to set your sails, think about your goals, decide what matters most and go for it. If you want a wife or a family, it's time to date with more intention. Dating becomes more purposeful when you know you're looking for the woman who will spend the rest of her life with you."

Says the man who married his high school sweetheart.

He doesn't need to worry about me and my "future wife." I'm not in the market for a relationship, serious or otherwise.

"And you'll want to think about upward mobility. You've got opportunities I never had, Cam. I don't want to see you waste them. This resort's a dream job, and going in at an assistant manager level at your age, straight out of college, welp. That's not something everyone gets a shot at. You still need to think ahead. Don't rest on your accomplishments. Ask yourself what's next. Where are you headed? Who are the people who will help you get there?"

"I think about all that," I assure my dad.

I roll thoughts like that through my mind practically non-stop. I don't tell him that.

"You've raised me to focus and go after what I want."

"I sure have. I just want you to remember what you've been taught."

"I know. You always said, there's no second chance when

working with electricity. Act like your first action is life or death. Treat all opportunities as if they were your one shot."

"Exactly," my dad says, leaning back in his chair and finally taking a bite of his muffin. He smiles and says, "She was right. These are delicious."

He doesn't take long savoring his food. He's got a lecture on the brain—nuggets of truth and wisdom he wants to hammer home before I set off to start my own life for good.

"I appreciate the lessons my work has taught me," Dad says. "Electricity is a cruel teacher. Get it right or feel the shock of her repercussions. And I've had to sustain the business my father built. I've done my best to fill his shoes and earn the trust of this town. You're only as good as the job you do."

"I know all that, Dad. I'll make you proud, I promise."

I wish he'd say I already do make him proud, but that's just not my dad. He loves me. I know that. But he shows his love by pushing me to be my best, to avoid errors, and to do better than he has because I have advantages he never had. He helped provide that leg up, so I owe him my best efforts as a thank you.

"You'll do great out there," Dad says.

It's the closest thing to an atta boy as I've gotten in a long time, so I'll take it. "Thanks, Dad. I won't let you down."

5

RILEY

The nice thing about living in a small town
is that when you don't know what you're doing,
someone else does.
~ Immanuel Kant

My mind feels twitchy and scattered as I flit from my dresser to my closet, to my bed, pulling things off hangers and out of drawers and piling them on the mattress. Two suitcases sit open and empty amidst the piles of clothing.

We each get to bring a limited amount of luggage to go on the roof rack Duke installed on top of my van. He attached the cutest little ladder too. I picture using that roof as a hangout long after we've made it to California. We can drive out to the beach and sit up there looking out at the ocean. That is, if we make it to California. At this rate, I'll never be packed in time to leave.

Mom pushes my door open past the smidge I already had it cracked, and pops her head in.

"How's it going?"

"Gah!"

"That good, huh?"

"How am I supposed to only pack two suitcases?"

"I already told you Dad and I would box up whatever else you need and ship it to your apartment in LA once you're back from the island. Don't worry."

"I know. It's just we've got a week on the road, and then the six weeks we'll be working at the resort. I need way more than I can fit in these two bags."

"Island living is simple, sweetie. Shorts, T-Shirts, a few sundresses, flip flops. One pair of knock-em-dead shoes, and a dress to match. You're golden."

"Easy for you to say." I flop onto the only open spot on my bed.

Mom moves further into my room. "Let me help, will you?"

"You don't have to ask twice. I need all the help I can get."

I wouldn't be so wound up, but I keep picturing Cameron's face when he arrives to pack up the van at our house later tonight. He'll have his arms crossed across his chest, and his face will be all serious like a dad when you're home past curfew. Then he'll make some snarky remark about whether I need so much stuff. I have to get a jump on this and figure out how to pack all my necessities into two suitcases. I usually pack that much for a long weekend!

With Mom's help, we finish selecting things that match, and then we pare my choices down to fit into two bags. Granted, I have to sit on one to get it to close, but it's done. We load everything into the back of my parents' car, along with my barista box and my guitar. Those are non-negotiables. You never know when you'll be stuck in the middle of some desert, with only tumbleweeds and dirt as far as the eye can see. At that moment, you'll crave an espresso drink like you never have before.

Enter the barista box.

I'm going to fill the mini-fridge with essentials like flavored creamers, milk, two bottles of cold brew, chocolate shavings, and whipped cream. I'll make sure the ice trays are filled too. In the box I have a few syrups, some cocoa powder, coffee grounds, my battery operated frother, and a hot plate and pan for boiling water to use in the french press. I've also got a selection of biscotti and small butter cookies since those will travel better than muffins. Thankfully my bus, which has yet to be named, has an outlet. I could just smooch Duke for his ingenious upgrades.

My friends can thank me later.

Tomorrow we take off early in the morning, but tonight we're loading the van, and then we're going to the send-off party Ella Mae put together for us. The MacIntyres are hosting it at their farm with a bonfire. Ella Mae is a social media influencer who lives here in town. She's thirty, but she's as cool as anyone my age. She's always been someone I look up to. Just a few weeks ago, I took her place in the annual Red, White, and Blue, and Corn Too parade as Miss Corn Husk.

Oh, girls. Be careful what you wish for! I have wanted to be Miss Corn Husk since I was in junior high. Maybe even in elementary school, now that I think about it. When Ella Mae passed her crown on to me, I was so honored. But that parade ride was the itchiest experience of my life. The whole dress is made of corn husks. It's slightly stiff and incredibly scratchy. If I think about it too much, I start itching even today. All that said, I wouldn't have traded that experience for anything. Growing up in this ridiculously small town, Miss Corn Husk was kind of a big deal. And I got to be her. I won't do it again, but I'm glad I had my moment of corn-laden glory.

Aiden bought the MacIntyre farm when I was in high school. Of course, it wasn't called MacIntyre farm until he bought it. One summer, I came home from college, and Aiden had a wife, two adopted children, and a baby on the way.

Things change like that when you go away. The place that seemed like nothing ever happened while you lived there year after year, ends up experiencing radical milestones in your absence. People die. Babies are born. Someone new moves in. Someone else moves away. And all that change makes it feel like it's not quite the same place you left—like that place of your childhood memories is somewhere that can never be reached again.

Loading up the van takes a little over an hour. Cameron doesn't comment on my suitcases, even the overly fat one. But when it comes to my guitar, he definitely gives it the side-eye.

"What?" I ask in a challenging tone.

I've gotten past my initial nerves from when we first drove up, and now I'm in my second phase of my usual reactions to Cameron—a lot less awkward, and a little more sassy.

"That's a big item to take on a cramped road trip."

"Music is life," is all I say before turning to hand the case up to my dad so it can be strapped onto the roof with our suitcases.

I step inside the van and unload the contents of our family cooler into the fridge next to little packs of baby carrots, some energy drinks, bottled protein shakes, and a container of hummus. Mom fills the ice trays with water and hands them over to me. I set my box on the floor next to the back seat.

"What's that?" Cameron asks.

"Have you considered a job with the TSA? Maybe immigration?"

He just stares at me, waiting for my real answer.

"It's my barista box. You know, all the essentials for making coffee drinks."

"I brought instant," he says.

I clutch my heart. "Say it isn't so."

"What?"

"Instant coffee?"

"Yeah. Why? What's wrong with that?"

"Cameron. Cameron. Cameron." I tease.

But I'm not really teasing. No human on earth should drink instant coffee, not when the world is filled with glorious beans from tropical climates around the earth, just begging us to roast and grind them to perfection and then make all sorts of delicious drinks from the resulting elixir.

"Whatever. Bring your barista box. Just know you're keeping it near your seat if it crowds anyone."

"Fine. But you may just change your tune when you're stuck somewhere in Timbuktu with no cell service and all you want is a frothy frappuccino to soothe your travel-weary soul."

Cameron looks nearly horrified at my suggestion that we may be stuck somewhere remote.

Despite his screening every item that goes into the van, we end up finishing packing, and then we hop into our separate cars to drive to the MacIntyre farm.

My dad drives out of Cam's neighborhood down a few other streets lined with houses until we reach the country road lined with a low wooden fence that edges up along pastures as far as the eye can see. Cornfields alternate with low grass and the occasional barn and farmhouse until we reach the tree with the dent in it and the gravel driveway just beyond.

We pull up the driveway and find parking along the edge. As soon as I step out of the car, I notice Madeline and Cam standing near the barn with their parents. My oldest brother, Brian, is talking to Madeline's dad. Brian lives in Vandalia. He must have come out here for my send off. My other brother, Pete, lives in North Carolina now with his new wife. Both my brothers seemed to slip straight from adolescence into adulthood without a hitch. Maybe I don't know the particulars, but they're each married and holding down good jobs now.

Brian's head turns toward us when Madeline squeals and runs in my direction.

"It's tomorrow! Can you believe it?!"

Madeline's voice sounds like a string of excited emojis. Seeing her snaps me out of whatever inner spiral I was swirling down about my brothers' neat and tidy adult lives.

I jump up and down a little with Madeline. "We're going on an epic road trip!" I scream.

"It's going to be so, so ... EPIC!" She pulls me into a hug. "And then we're going to live on an island for six weeks! What is our life?"

"I know!"

I needed this—needed Madeline. I'm still twenty, turning twenty-one in five days. I'm not graduating for another ten months. I've got nearly a year to figure out what I want to be when I grow up. Right now, I need to throw myself into this trip and not miss a drop of it.

My eyes lift to see Cameron studying us from his spot near the barn. Ben is talking to him, but his gaze is fixed on me and Madeline and our display of excitement. I raise my hand and wave at him. He tips his chin in response. His arms are folded across his chest. He looks commanding and serious. I feel my cheeks heat. Hopefully, Madeline doesn't notice.

I remember us at younger ages. Cameron was always more of a rule follower, but not always so serious. At least, not that I remember. He used to let loose more often, regularly teasing Madeline and me. He'd act annoyed by us, but he'd look out for us too. I guess that's what growing up does to a guy—they get more stiff and less playful.

Just then, Duke shouts out, "Let's get this party started!"

Scratch that last thought. Not every grown man loses his inner childlikeness. Duke is a riot. He's always joking around and making any event more fun.

Madeline hooks her arm through mine.

"Look, Riley."

She points to a banner tied between two poles in front of the goat enclosure. It says, *Happy Trails to Riley, Madeline, Ben, and Cameron!* Underneath those bold words it says, *Don't forget the town that loves you.*

"Awww," I say, leaning into Madeline. "That almost makes me want to cry."

"I know. Right? So sweet." She pauses, looking around at all the people gathered on Aiden's property. Then she leans into me and says, "But between you and me, I'm so ready to ditch this place. I miss the beach and all the things we can do in LA."

I don't answer her. I love the beach. I love living in LA—for now. But a part of me doesn't love the crowds, the traffic, and the constant sense that nothing ever shuts down. Maybe I'm just a small-town girl at heart. I'm pretty happy in Bordeaux. But if Madeline weren't here, I wouldn't want to be here either.

Aiden rings the black, cast iron dinner bell that's right outside his back door. The hum of conversation dies down, and he stands on the back steps preparing to say what he has to say.

"We want to thank everyone for coming out tonight to see these four off on their road trip across the country. For Ben and Cameron, especially, we want to say we'll miss you two. Don't forget the good things you've had here. And you know you will always be welcome back. No matter where you go, Bordeaux is still home, you hear me?"

Ben and Cameron both nod. Ben shouts out, "Bordeaux forever! Go Corncobs!" like a dork.

Cam shakes his head, but there's a little grin tugging at the corner of his mouth.

"You'll find out soon enough," Aiden continues. "You can travel anywhere you want, but you won't find another place like this one."

He's biased, of course. He's got an amazing property, a great job working for himself, and a wife and kids he loves. Not everyone's as fortunate. But I have to agree, Bordeaux is special.

"Now, without further ado, I'm going to hand things over to Ella Mae, who pulled this gathering together, and practically turned my farm upside down in the process."

Ella Mae steps up to the stair below Aiden and waves at everyone. "Hey, everybody! I just want to give you a quick rundown of what we're doing tonight. We'll start with some food. And I want to thank everyone who brought a dish. Mabel, that ambrosia salad is looking extra special."

Mabel waves to everyone like we don't know who she is. Madeline and I exchange a glance and giggle softly into one another's shoulders. My arm is still linked with hers for some reason, and I'm not even trying to let go of her right now.

"Everyone can help themselves to food. I understand Jim brought his guitar so he can play a little for us. Then, we plan to do some square dancing and roasting of marshmallows. But, most importantly, don't forget to head into the barn where I've got a money tree sitting on a table. Let's send these kids off properly. There's also a pile of hay bales set up in there. Be sure to take a pic with these four hometown kids with the polaroid I've got sitting out. We want to capture the memories for them."

Ella Mae looks up at Aiden.

He nods and she reaches over for the bell. "Okay, people! Let's eat!" Ella Mae pulls the bell cord and it clangs. The crowd meanders toward the folding tables set up at the end of the driveway in a grassy patch under some trees. We load up plates and find seats in lawn chairs or on blankets, some of the younger guys hop up on the fences and balance their plates while perched there like the iconic country boys they are.

I turn to Madeline who's sitting in a chair next to mine facing the fire pit. It's still too light out for the fire we'll be burning later.

"I saw this bumper sticker in town the other day."

"Yeah?"

"It said, *Why look for your white knight on a handsome steed when you can have a redneck in a Chevy truck*?"

Madeline laughs hard, which gets Ben's attention from across the way. "Hey, you two. No fair telling jokes without sharing with the rest of the class."

I turn to Madeline and whisper, "The funniest part was it was on the bumper of a Ford."

We both giggle some more. Ben stands and walks over to us. "Spill it. What's so funny?"

"You," Madeline says. "You've got a little something ..." she points to her chin.

Ben's chin is clean as a whistle, but he takes the bait and starts wiping. Madeline shakes her head like he missed the spot and she points to her chin again. They go through this exchange a few times before Ben thinks to pull out his phone to check it like a mirror.

"Madeline!" he shouts, obviously not at all upset. "Oh, you did not want to do that before a week-long road trip."

"I so did."

"Sleep with one eye open. That's all I've got to say."

"I will if you will," she says in a flirty tone.

It's not at all fair of her to take that tone with Ben. I don't think he's got a thing for her, but I know Madeline has a crush on a guy in our program at UCLA. She needs to keep things with Ben obviously platonic.

Ben rolls his eyes and then makes that *I'm watching you*

signal with his two fingers flying from his eyes toward Madeline's face.

All of a sudden, there's a commotion from near the goat enclosure. A child squeals and other children are shouting things like, "Get them! Get them!" and "Come back here!"

When I look up, chickens are running pell-mell all over the back area of Aiden's property in front of the animal enclosures.

"I didn't even know he had chickens," I tell Madeline.

"He just got them this summer."

The chickens run toward the crowd of people, and one of them finds the bags of marshmallows Em set out for roasting later over the bonfire. Maybe it's the rooster. He's got a beautiful plume of feathers on his head. He starts pecking like he's on a mission, and the bag tears. Then he goes for the gold, plucking out a marshmallow and pecking at it until his beak is white and sticky. Meanwhile, other chickens are darting here and there, mostly trying to reach the rooster and the other bags of marshmallows.

People get busy chasing chickens, which is a sight in itself. One person will lunge for a hen, but miss as the hen darts away, and then another person dives to catch the runaway bird, but she's too fast for them. People are shouting, running everywhere, zigging and zagging, arms flailing and grasping for the runaway hens. Bags of marshmallows are scattered and a group of birds is devouring random marshmallows.

Aiden rings the dinner bell.

"We need to catch the rooster!" he shouts into the crowd of people. Some of us stopped moving as soon as the clang of the bell rang out over all the shouting, but some people continue chasing the loose chickens. Children are running all over screaming, even after Aiden tried to get everyone's attention.

Aiden holds up a bag. "I've got corn to lure him with. I need someone to scatter it while someone else grabs those bags of marshmallows away as soon as he's distracted. The hens will follow him once I have him in the coop."

Cam steps up. "I'll scatter the corn."

My hero.

I can't help it. He's not mine. And, he's hardly a hero. He's just scattering corn, but tell my heart that. Aiden hands Cam the bag of corn and Cam takes it, looking all serious and focused.

Within minutes, Cam's got the rooster eating nearly out of his hand while Ben grabs up the marshmallows, and Aiden sneaks behind the rooster and grabs him. Aiden knows how to hold the bird, but it's obvious this guy is not happy about his snack being interrupted. Hens keep sneaking marshmallows that have fallen on the ground, but the mayhem has mostly subsided. Aiden deposits the rooster in the coop, and sure enough, hens start moving in that direction. It's sort of magical to watch them all make their way over to where the rooster is penned up in one of the roosts.

"Typical," Madeline mutters to me.

"What?"

"All the girls flock to the hot guy. Even if he's a menace."

I laugh, but wonder if there's a story I'm missing in her analogy. Madeline and I share everything with one another. At least, I think we do. I obviously don't talk to her about Cam. Is there something she isn't talking to me about either?

Once it's dusky out, Aiden lights the fire, and Jim pulls out his guitar and starts playing *This Land Is Your Land*. It's an interesting choice, but no one seems to bat an eyelash. They don't even flinch when he hits the end of the song and starts playing it again. And again. Apparently, Jim took up guitar later in life, and now he's mastered his song. He's a regular patriotic, one-hit wonder.

Ben walks over to me and Madeline. "I'll be singing this

song in my sleep. Or dreaming of a maniac chasing me down Main Street with a guitar, crooning this song on an endless loop."

"Be nice," Madeline chides Ben.

"Says the girl who made me wipe my very clean face until I nearly gave myself an exfoliation."

Madeline just giggles and shrugs her shoulders.

Ella Mae eventually cuts Jim off. "Thanks, Jim. We've appreciated your contribution to the celebration. We're going to start the square dance now."

A few other local men, mostly farmers from the outskirts of town settle into chairs around the fire. Ella Mae sets up a miniature speaker with a mic and announces, "Ladies and Gentlemen, grab your partners. We're about to be entertained by none other than Hey Diddle Diddle, Fiddle in the Middle."

People pair up around the fire and in the gravel and dirt areas between the house and the barn, facing one another in the usual starting formation of four couples standing in a circle.

Ben walks up to Madeline and asks her to dance. "I'm not dancing with Cam or Esther, so maybe you'd do me the honors?"

Madeline rolls her eyes and softly shakes her head, but she extends her arm to Ben, giving me a look before walking away with him. I'm left standing alone, but I barely have time to think about it because the caller starts to shout out dance steps as soon as the music begins. I watch Ben and Madeline. We've grown up dancing square dance and two-step to the point of being able to do it in our sleep. They move together like it's second nature. No sparks, just two friends enjoying an old-fashioned summer night under the stars around the bonfire. These are the things I miss when I'm away at school.

I'm so caught up in watching two of my best friends dance

that I startle when Mabel walks up to me. Cam's trailing behind her like a scolded puppy.

"Now, see here, Cam," Mabel says, even though her eyes are locked on mine. "A pretty girl like Riley shouldn't be standing off to the side watching the festivities. Do what's proper and ask her to dance. Your grams would be fit to be tied if she saw you standing off like you were holding up the barn with your backside instead of asking a young woman to dance."

Even with only the glow of the firelight, I can see Cam blush.

I turn my eyes away from him back to Mabel. "It's okay, Mabel. I'm fine."

I can't look at Cam, but I feel him standing there. My gaze drifts to the couples do-si-doing around the farm.

In a low voice, Cam asks, "Riley, do you want to dance?"

Mabel nods her head like her work here is done and she backs away, probably off to meddle somewhere else, or maybe to dance with her boyfriend, Walt, who is Duke's dad.

"Why, I'd love to dance, Cameron," I say, my playful exaggeration hopefully disguising the slight quaver in my voice.

Of course, the inner me is doing some sort of cheerleader formation where the squad throws me in the air and I do a back tuck from their basket toss before landing. All the air whooshes out of my lungs at the thought of dancing with Cam. On the outside, I'm just barely holding myself together.

Cameron extends his hand and I manage to take it. His palm is big and warm, easily engulfing mine. He clasps my hand gently, but firmly enough that he can tug me forward until I'm in step with him. We wait for the first song to stop so we can join in on the next. Cam keeps my hand in his, his eyes roving across the dancers, his head lightly bobbing to the downbeat. I don't think he even realizes he's still holding my hand, but I sure do. Every nerve ending in my body seems to be linked to my fingers, palm, and knuckles right now. Little zips of energy burst through my chest and down my legs.

The song ends, and Cam leads me to a spot where three couples had been dancing, easily compensating for the absence of a fourth. We take our spot and dance together. It's not a slow dance, but every time the caller says, "Swing your girl, promenade," Cam has to hold my hand and place his other hand on my back. It's the closest we've been besides hugging. And Cam's a great dancer, fully in charge of the both of us, moving with the beat and pulling or pushing me just right.

I'm nearly floating on a cloud a half hour later when we break for a drink. My nerves have somewhat subsided the more we danced. Cam's quiet, so I fill in the gap by rambling on about our trip.

" ... and, I've got a bucket list." I say, wrapping up a long stream of words about my plans and everything I've done to prepare.

"I know," is all Cameron says at first. But then he adds, "I've been instructed to look it over and try to be accommodating."

I can't help but laugh a little. "Oh? And just who instructed you in this road trip etiquette?"

"My mom."

"Well, God bless her. Someone needed to help you get that pole out of ... to just calm down a bit and relax."

Cam looks over at me and rolls his eyes. "There's no pole involved. I'm thinking of our safety. And it would be nice to get to the island before our jobs start to get familiar with everything. I only went there once for my final interview."

I hadn't considered how Cam would feel about starting a new job. I kick myself a little for being so self-focused.

"Sorry, Cameron. I wasn't thinking about pre-job nerves. Even if we do stop here and there along the way, we'll have plenty of leeway to make it to the island with a few days to spare before we all start work."

"It's not nerves," he says with a little too much emphasis.

"Oh. Okay. Whatever you say."

The music starts again. "Do you want to dance some more?"

I look up into his eyes. Do I want to dance with him? Um. Yes, please.

"Do you?"

"I could dance," he says with a small smile.

"Okay, then. Lead the way, partner."

We dance another round of dances, and then Ella Mae thanks the band. The four of us are ushered into the barn where townspeople line up and take photos with us at the makeshift photo booth made of hay bales. Ella Mae put together props on little sticks for us to play with in the photos, like paper mustaches, glasses, corn cobs, and bandanas. After that, Ella Mae presents us with the money tree. The town put in over a thousand dollars.

Cam takes the microphone to thank everyone on behalf of the four of us, and when he's done, Ben grabs the money tree and holds it over his head, shouting, "I'm rich! I'm rich!"

Various people take turns stepping up to the mic to say something funny or encouraging as they wish us safe travels, or they bestow some heartfelt wisdom like, "Don't chew any gum you find under a table at a diner." Then Ella Mae surprises us by giving each of us a T-shirt that says *Go, Corncobs* with a hashtag of *#BordeauxOhioForever.*

It's already ten by the time people start saying goodbye. It's a process with us. You don't just say goodbye and walk to your car or truck. Nope. You linger. And then you walk a little closer to your vehicle and chat a little more. It's a ritual, and we're all so used to it, we don't question how it works. I only notice since

I've been in LA where most people don't take the time to wave or greet one another at all, even old friends.

Eventually, we make it to Dad's car, and he drives us home so we can get to bed. We plan to leave at six in the morning. I don't know why it has to be that early, but I'm carefully picking the hills I'll die on this trip, and departure time's not one of them. I can sleep in the van once we're on the road.

Oh, who am I kidding? I won't sleep. I'll be way too excited to even shut my eyes.

RILEY'S JOURNAL

July 23rd

Well, Gladys, we're leaving tomorrow.

Tonight was our official send-off. And it was a farewell done as only Bordeaux can do it. Ella Mae threw a bash at the MacIntyre farm. I won't bore you with all the details, but I will say this: I danced with Cameron.

He asked me.

Don't get all excited, Gladys. Mabel forced him. She gave him a doozy of a guilt trip. And you know Cam, he won't turn down a chance to do what's right.

Oh, Gladys. Despite my nerves, it was as close to heaven as I've been on earth. I'm sure of it. I'm also sure Cameron might as well have been dancing with Memaw as far as he was concerned. I'm as invisible as the Saran wrap over Esther's Watergate salad.

Do you think there will come a day I won't blush and babble at the sight of him? Or am I going to spend the next week turning various shades of pink and red?

I'll get over him eventually, Gladys. Don't we all get over the hum and rush of our first crush? If anything, six or seven days cooped up in a van together should kill any infatuation I have, and kill it good. They say absence makes the heart grow fonder, so maybe forced proximity works the opposite way. A girl can hope.

I'm resolving to start this last year at UCLA crush-free. You'd tell me to give my young heart the chance to fall for someone who notices me. I know you would, Gladys. As much as you love Cam, you wouldn't want me pining away for a guy who can't see me. Besides, even if he noticed me and then by some miracle, fell for me, Madeline would die if something romantic ever developed between her brother and me. And I don't know what I'd do if I lost her. I should always put my best doe before a bro, right?

I'm lying here in my bed, now that the night's events are over, the van is packed, and my family's all in their rooms. We leave in seven hours. This is the last time this room will really be mine. Of course, Mom won't do a thing to it quite yet, since I'm coming home for Christmas and probably for spring break, but after this year, I'll be out of college. Ben and Cam are moving on this year. Madeline and I are next.

I can hardly sleep between the excitement of our trip and all the feels of saying goodbye to Bordeaux, and to my room, and to everything familiar. In just over a week, I'll be a part-time barista on an island I've never even seen in person, and then it's back to LA where life is flashy, and I'm one among many. I'm glad I went to LA. But it won't ever be home. I need a slower pace in a smaller setting. At least I learned that about myself. That's something.

But I'm getting ahead of myself. I've got my road trip bucket list tucked away in the front of my backpack. I decided to copy it out of my journal so I don't have to pop this notebook open every time I go to check something off. I like to keep what I've written here between just the two of us, as you know. The more I open this journal in front of Cam and Mads and Ben, the more they'll want to know what I've written in these pages.

As usual, talking to you helped.
Thanks for always being in my corner, Gladys.
I miss your hugs and the way your eyes crinkled when you laughed.
Do you think anyone will ever miss me the way I miss you? I sure hope so.

Goodnight, Gladys.

6

CAMERON

It takes courage to grow up
and become who you really are.
~ E.E. Cummings

"Is the tank filled?" Mom asks.

She sets a plate of pancakes and sausage in front of me with fresh squeezed orange juice. She's not usually up making us breakfast these days, but since we leave in a half-hour, she's going overboard.

"We're all gassed and Duke checked the oil and tire pressure. We've got a new battery. Nothing to worry about, Mom."

Mom nods and smiles a thin smile. "Can I get you anything else, Madeline?"

"Mom, sit down and join us." Madeline says. "You're making me nervous."

"Sorry, sweetie. It's just my way of keeping the tears tucked away until I'm looking at the rear bumper of the van."

"Awww, Mom."

Madeline stands from the bar stool and wraps Mom in a hug.

"You aren't helping the tear-stopping situation here, Mads," Mom says, her face buried in Madeline's hair.

She sniffles, grabs a napkin off the counter and wipes her eyes, and then she busies herself cleaning up the bowl of pancake batter and all the other pans from breakfast.

"Why did you two have to grow up so fast?" she asks with a forced note of cheer in her voice.

There's no hiding the sadness. Everything in me wants to fix this for her. But to do that, Madeline and I would both have to move back to Bordeaux. No offense to the town where I've grown up, but I'm ready to spread my wings. I've wanted to get into the hotel management business for years—to travel, to see places outside this town. I want to be a part of providing people a place to get away from life as they know it, to give them adventures and memories that are bigger than what I've had.

I try to say something consoling. "Mom, we're only one FaceTime call away, and we'll be home for the holidays."

"I know," she says, smiling over at me. "I'm so proud of both of you. Don't worry about me. I'll get some hobbies. Or something."

"You'll have the she shed," Madeline says, giving me a devious look.

"About that," I say. "Why my room? I mean Mads' room is way more girly already. You wouldn't have to do as much to convert it."

"She's not officially moving out yet."

"Mmmm," I hum over a bite of pancake and sausage. The combination of the two is the best way to eat breakfast—dripping with syrup.

I swallow and start to say, "Well, she's not ..."

I let my words trail off. I was going to say she's not coming back after this year either. But I think my mom has enough loss on the brain for one day.

"She's still your baby," I say with a smile.

"I am," Madeline adds, obviously catching my gist.

"You both are," Mom says, looking between us. "Be safe and call us at least every few days. A text to let us know you're okay and that you made it to the next destination on your trip would be nice."

"Mom, we'll be fine," Mads says, at the same time as I say, "We'll text. We'll even send videos."

"Okay," Mom says, shoring herself up with a deep breath. "Okay."

She nods once. And then Dad comes in from wherever he was. He loops his hands around Mom's waist.

"You okay?" he asks quietly.

"Mm hmm," she says. "I will be."

"Yes you will." Dad looks at both our plates. "Eat up, you two. It's going to be time to go. Ben and Riley will be here any minute."

He doesn't have to tell me twice. Who knows what kind of food we'll eat along this trip. I've done some planning for stops, but I'm not the only one voting on our meals. I exhale a long breath. Ben, Madeline, and Riley. I love them, but usually I'm the only voice of reason when the four of us are together. Here's to a week of being the unpopular opinion. If I left it up to them, we'd probably end up in California by the end of September, not mid-August.

Ben's the first to arrive. Madeline and I are rinsing breakfast dishes and loading the dishwasher. Mom's still milling around the house, tidying things that are already tidy. Dad's in the living room, probably reading something.

I hear Ben's voice from the family room. "Mrs. Reeves, you

are looking exceptionally beautiful this morning."

"Give me a break," I mutter to Madeline.

She giggles.

"He's just Ben. He can't help himself," she says, rolling her eyes.

"Why, thank you, Benjamin," Mom says.

You can hear the near blush in her voice.

"We ought to be able to bottle that charm," I tell Madeline.

"You could get a prescription. It might do you some good," she teases.

I whip at her with the dish towel I'm holding. She dodges me and makes a face.

Ben shows up in the kitchen. "Any breakfast left?"

"We just finished cleaning up. There are a few sausages left-over in the fridge. Didn't you eat?"

"Yeah. I ate. My mom fixed a feast. But I'm hungry again. Sue me."

"Help yourself," Madeline tells Ben, waving her hand toward the fridge.

"Anyone want to bet Riley will be late?" Ben asks, opening the refrigerator door and perusing the contents like he lives here.

"That's just mean," Madeline says.

"Or accurate," I say.

Just then I hear the front door open and shut.

"I'm heeeere," Riley shouts. "Let's get this road trip on the road!" That's followed by, "Oh hi, Mrs. Reeves. How are you today? I hope you're doing better than my mom. She was a mess." There's a pause and then, "Don't tell her I said that. I feel so bad for her. She and Dad are right outside waiting to send us off."

"Your secret's safe with me, Riley. And yes, I'm a bit of a mess too. But I'll be fine. It's just hard letting you kids go. It's so fulfilling, watching you grow up and find your own lives. I guess the best word for it is bittersweet. There's a pain that's nearly as gripping as labor. But we made it through birthing you into the world. I guess we'll make it through this one too."

Their voices die off, replaced by a stretch of silence, and then I hear Mom say, "Thank you, dear."

Riley shows up in the kitchen doorway. She's wearing cutoff jean shorts and a graphic T-shirt that has a sketch of Taylor Swift's face on it and the words *It's Me, I'm the Problem, It's Me.*

"Nice shirt," I say with a small chuckle.

She looks down at herself like she forgot what she was wearing and giggles nervously. Then she says, "Consider yourself warned."

She fidgets a little with the hem of the shirt.

A memory slams me from out of nowhere. Ben and I had gotten back from a baseball game our senior year in high school. We walked into the kitchen. Riley and Madeline were baking cookies. The whole house smelled like chocolate and sugar. We rounded the corner into the kitchen. Riley had a dusting of flour across her face and she was laughing at something Madeline had said.

Something felt different. I saw her everyday. That day stood out. I remember being uncomfortable, and not sure why. Maybe it's the way she's standing in the kitchen now, but it feels like I'm seeing her for the first time. Like she's not Riley, my other sister. She's a young woman ready for an adventure. Her eyes meet mine, snapping me out of my thoughts.

"Everyone ready?" I ask.

"Let's do this!" Ben says.

He's holding a breakfast sausage link in one hand and an apple in the other.

Our parents line the lawn like six parade goers, hugging each of us repeatedly and saying things like, "Watch your gauges," and, "Call us for anything," and "Don't pick up hitchhikers."

Even after we're buckled up and pulling away from our home, they stand at the edge of the yard, watching us and waving frantically.

I glance in the rearview mirror at Ben, "Next stop, adulthood."

"Not so fast," Ben says. "We've got a few detours first … like Indianapolis for lunch. And Springfield for our dinner … and the Grand Canyon, and …"

I shake my head and focus on taking in the shops on Main Street and all the familiar sights of Bordeaux, while Ben carries on listing stops we'll make on our trip toward our future.

Riley cues up her playlist. We're not even on the outskirts of town when the Ramones' *I Don't Wanna Grow Up* blasts through the speakers.

"That's what I'm saying," Ben shouts from the back.

"It's barely light out, could we listen to something less …" I look over at Riley.

True to her request when she first asked me to drive her van, she's riding shotgun, her legs bent and her feet tucked under her.

"Less?" she asks, looking at me, but then looking away.

If I didn't know better, I'd say Riley's nervous. She's got no reason to be. This trip is all she's been talking about. I'm a good driver. I won't let anything happen to us if I can help it.

"Less loud and thumpy?"

She smiles an amused grin.

Then she says, "Okay, grandpa."

She thumbs through her phone and switches to an old sixties ballad about children getting older.

"I sense a theme, Peter Pan," I joke, glancing over at her.

"Just the first few songs," she says quietly, looking out the window at the properties lining the two-lane highway.

"Are you okay?" I ask.

"What? Yeah. Of course. Yes. I mean I didn't sleep all that great. But I'm good. You?"

Her answer's the usual flurry of words that seems to be her default ever since we all went away to school. I don't remember her being like this before, but maybe I wasn't paying attention. I was a high school boy. We aren't notorious for being tuned into anything at that age but girls and ... well, girls. And Riley never fell into the category of "girls," at least not in that way. She's just Riley.

Anyway, I learned my lesson in that department. College taught me more than how to run a hospitality business.

I glance at Riley. She's waiting for my answer.

"I'm good. Why don't you sleep now? I promise you won't miss anything. Just a whole lot more of this before we hit another big city."

I gesture with one hand at the flat grassland with occasional houses, the small highway, and the scattered semis riding alongside us.

"Okay," she says, looking back over her seat toward my sister. "If I manage to sleep, wake me before we hit the state line. Okay?"

I give Riley a questioning look.

"I need to take a photo at each of the state welcome signs. It's on my bucket list."

She says it like I'm actually pulling over at every single state line along this trip. I quickly do the calculation. Indiana, Illinois, Missouri, Oklahoma, Texas, New Mexico, Arizona, California. That would be eight additional stops. Yeah, no.

"I'll slow down," I assure her. "So your photo doesn't blur."

Her nervousness seems to evaporate at my comment.

"What? No. We're getting out. We have to. We need a group

shot at each one."

"Have to?"

"When is the next time the four of us will take this trip?"

"She's got a point," my ex-best friend says from the bench seat in the back.

"I think it sounds fun," my traitor of a sister adds.

Riley smiles over at me.

"Fine," I concede. "We'll pull over. Now get some sleep. You only have about forty-five minutes til we're in Indiana."

I'll pull over for this one state line. I happen to know they put a really nice arch over the highway with a decent sign there. That should satisfy Riley. We'll see about the rest.

Riley curls up in her seat, her head against the window. I glance over at her while she fidgets, trying to get comfortable.

"Hey, Ben?" I say.

"Yeah?"

"Throw me my hoodie, would ya?"

"Sure."

I glance into the rearview mirror. Ben stands and fishes around in the storage behind the front seats. Then he hands me my hoodie. I pass it to Riley.

"Here. Roll this up. It's a better pillow than your window."

She looks at me, her doe eyes wide, and takes the sweatshirt from me.

"Thanks."

"No problem. Just don't drool on it." I wink at her.

She shakes her head, rolls up the sweatshirt, and snuggles into a position she must find comfortable, because within five minutes, she's breathing softly. Madeline and Ben are having a quiet conversation in the back. I occupy the next forty minutes by thinking about my new job at the resort while wide open fields stretch out to either side of the highway and Riley sleeps peacefully in the chair next to mine.

7

RILEY

When you go on a road trip,
the trip itself becomes part of the story.
~ Steve Rushin

"Riley," someone says.

"I think she's down for the count." Ben's voice. That's Ben.

I try to crack my eyes open, but I'm so very cozy, and I feel like snuggling in my bed a few minutes longer. Wait. Why would Ben be in my bedroom?

"Riley," Madeline says.

I feel a light nudge to my shoulder, so I crack my eye open. Just one eye.

Cameron's neutral expression greets me from across the way. His arms are crossed across his chest, making him look stern, but still so attractive.

Cameron? Why is Cam ...? Oh, yeah. We're already driving to California.

I sit up and stretch, Cam's sweatshirt falls down along the door when my head lifts. That sweatshirt. It smelled like him. I wanted to bury myself in the smell of a soap made of white flowers and cream and something musky. I know it's weird to say a man smells like flowers, but Cam does. Manly flowers, subtle and heady—like something that grows wild in the woods. Which is funny, because Cam is anything but wild. He should smell like a stapler and a ruler, or a filing cabinet—something orderly.

I chuckle.

"What's so funny?" Cam asks.

"Just something. Nothing, really."

I stifle a yawn with the back of my hand, and look around. We're parked off to the side of the road. Madeline and Ben are up off the bench seat and crouched behind me and Cam. Cam's sitting sideways in the driver's seat, studying me.

"Ready to take this epic photo at the state line, sleepyhead?" Cam asks.

"Definitely ready!"

I open my backpack, grab my phone and my selfie stick, and then I hop out onto the shoulder of the road. Ben and Mads slide the back door open and join me. Cam rounds the front of the van and we all stand in the grass off the side of the highway, looking up at the sign that hangs on a substantial metal arch spanning the whole four lanes of I-70. On a royal blue background with an outline of our state, it says, *Ohio. Come Back Soon*.

"Where's the welcome to Indiana sign?" I ask, looking at Cam, as if he'd know.

"There's not one."

"What?"

"This is what you get, Riley." Cam barely hides the note of irritation in his voice.

It's a pretty cool sign, but it's telling us goodbye, not ushering us into what's next. I square my shoulders. Okay. So, we didn't get a welcome to Indiana. We got this instead. And Cam pulled over to take pictures, which is super sweet of him, and totally puts him outside his tidy, organized, scheduled comfort zone. I'll make the most of this.

"Okay. It's okay. Let's pose here and I'll take a selfie of all of us."

We huddle up, Cam and Ben on the inside and me and Mads flanking them. I pop my phone into the selfie stick and hold it out at arm's length. Cam drapes his arm around my shoulder as naturally as if he does this every day. I nearly drop the camera like a grade-A clutz as soon as the weight of his arm lands across my back. I feel his nearness, and I smell that delicious, manly smell—the same one that lulled me to sleep in the van. Cam squeezes me in toward himself. My heart hammers in my chest.

I attempt to regroup, giving myself the world's quickest pep talk to get it together. *It's okay, you big goof. He's just putting his arm around you for a photo. Settle down.*

"Okay, everyone," I yell. "Say, Ohio!"

We all say, "Ohio!" and I snap the picture which ends up with all of us pursing our lips in the shape of the letter O.

"Um, maybe try again," Madeline says, laughing. "We look like we're blowing bubbles."

"Or like we're about to kiss this state goodbye," Ben offers.

"One more," Cam says. "One."

I shoot him a little look, which involves me having to turn my head to meet his eyes. Cam drops his gaze to mine. Our faces end up six inches apart from one another. His long lashes and the stubble on his face from not shaving this morning are right there, begging me to reach out and touch him. I feel my cheeks heat.

I shake my head slightly, and say, "One more like this, and then a jumping one. Okay?"

I look to Cam for his approval. He gives it with a light nod.

"Say, ABC!" Ben says.

I don't have time to question his logic, because my friends all say, "A, B, C!" I join them on the C. When I check the photo, it's perfect.

"How did you make that happen?" I look at Ben in wonder of his jedi photography skills.

"Easy. Saying C makes you end with a smile. Not like cheese, which ends with –eese, and makes you look like you're biting down to get fitted for a retainer."

Cam taps his watch. "Are we taking this jump shot, or not?"

"Abso-freakin-lutely!" I tell him.

I walk about twenty feet away, adjust my selfie stick to turn it into a tripod, and jog back to where everyone's standing. On the way to my friends, I say, "On three, we jump!" I turn to join the picture and count, "One ... two ... three!"

We all jump. The camera on my phone makes the automated shutter sound. I run over to it and check the shot. It's great. We're all at some stage of jumping or coming back down, and the Ohio sign is perfectly captured behind us.

"Happy?" Cam asks, pausing to look at me, but then walking toward the driver's side of the van without another word.

"Yeah," I say, even though he can't hear me anymore.

Once we're buckled in and back on the road, I turn to Cameron.

"Thank you."

"No problem. That only cost us twenty minutes. I'll make up the time somewhere."

"I have no doubt you will," I tell him.

I don't laugh. And, believe me, I want to. There's no way we need to keep track of this trip by the minutes. Adventures are measured in moments and memories, not minutes. I almost say that to Cam, but I restrain myself like the nearly twenty-one year old I am.

I'm grateful the photo shoot seems to have eliminated my shyness around Cam. At least for the time being. I should feel one hundred times as nervous when I think of his arm draped over my shoulder and the way he pulled me close, but I don't. I just smile a private smile thinking of him, and then I remember I'm trying to squash my Cameron obsession, so I focus on the small clusters of trees along the road.

We drive along the highway further into Indiana. There's not much to see in this part of the state besides a lot of open land, regular overpasses, the occasional nondescript building, and distant copses of trees scattered here and there.

I pull out my phone and quickly look over the photos we took. Then I send Ella Mae the shot of us jumping along with a thank you text for the multi-purpose selfie stick she bought me as a going away present. This thing is going to come in so handy at every state line.

I queue up the next set of songs for our trip. I've got today's tunes set up in eras. Yes, Tay Tay, you're not the only one with eras. We're starting in the 1960s and moving through to modern releases, all with themes of America and the thrill of a new adventure. I've got the whole list written in the back of my journal in case we lose Wi-Fi and I have to improvise.

Born to Run by Bruce Springsteen starts up, I open my back-pack and pull out the piece of paper I've been working on for the last two weeks.

I need to bring this idea up quickly or we'll pass the first spot where I want to stop.

"So, I have a bucket list for this trip."

Cameron groans. He literally groans. Madeline chuckles at her brother's reaction, or maybe she's laughing at me and my bucket list.

Ben says, "I love the idea of a bucket list! Let's hear it, Rye."

"I'm not going to share the whole list with you now. I'll drip it out over the trip. But I do have a few things that fit into today's possibilities—you know, besides the welcome signs at Indiana, Illinois, and Missouri."

Cameron shoots me a look like I just asked him to get out and push the van the rest of the drive to Springfield. I think that's where we're planning to stop tonight. I'm counting on it. There are things I want to do in that city. It's the official birthplace of Route 66. Yes, the road unofficially begins in Illinois at the original historical starting point in Chicago. But Springfield was the town that named the route. It's the city that has the plaque saying it's the birthplace of The Mother Road.

"The first thing on the list is coming right up."

Cameron's "No," comes so quickly, my head nearly spins.

"You don't even know what it is," I say.

"We just stopped, Riley. This is a drive to get us to California. We need to actually move to get there."

"Cam, we're taking an iconic drive down historic Route 66. Do you even realize how many cool things are along this road?"

"I do. And that's why we're nipping this in the bud right here and now before we get much further. Can you imagine if we stopped at every little kitschy place, roadside diner, and Mom-and-Pop stand that claims to have a stake in the history of this highway?"

"Ohhhmygosh! That would be amazing!"

Cameron shakes his head. "It would take us a year. Ben and I would lose our jobs. You and Mads would never graduate. But that's beside the point. We're on a timeline. We're not stopping at everything on your list. You'll get ... one thing a day."

"It would not take a year. And one thing a day?" I pause. "Let's put a pin in that thought. Anyway, before we pass it, the world's largest candle is in Centerville. We're only five minutes away and it's only a two minute detour off the highway. And, bonus! There's a candle outlet right there."

"Wow." Cameron deadpans.

Madeline chimes in. "It sounds kind of cool. World's largest candle."

"Is it actually a candle?" Ben asks.

"Well, no. I don't think so. The website photo makes it look like it's made of concrete. But it's still cool. It's a landmark. And it's fun."

"I say we stop," Ben says.

"No," Cam says, a note of finality to his tone.

"I think we should," Madeline adds.

I sit quietly. It's three to one, if we're being democratic, but I have a feeling those stats won't impress Cameron. He's like the driver of a bullet train in Japan, needing to be within seconds of his predetermined arrival time. I'm hoping Madeline and Ben will fight this particular battle for me—that way I can save my challenges to Cam's assumed authority for the next few things on my list.

I study the set of Cameron's jaw, the way his gorgeous eyes stare dead ahead, focused on the road, and unwavering. As irritating as he's being, I still find his steadfast temperament hot. I'm so whimsical and uncertain most of the time. There's something comforting about Cam's steadiness and determination. He's not mean. He's just clear on what he thinks should happen.

He glances over at me. I can feel my eyebrows sitting higher on my forehead and my head tipping the slightest. I don't dare speak. My nerves are revving up like a Formula-One engine. Gah. I thought those were gone for good now that we've settled into the trip.

"Okay," he says softly. "We'll stop for this ridiculous candle."

"Yay!" I shout, shimmying in my seat.

"That was too easy," Ben says.

I shoot him a look. He doesn't need to poke the bear when we just had a win.

We pull off and drive to the Warm Glow Candle Company Outlet Store. The candle is sitting right in front of this tudor style shop. It's probably fifteen or twenty feet tall. I make everyone pose in front of the candle.

Cam says, "Everyone use the restroom as long as we're here."

"Okay, Dad," Ben jokes back.

The whole stop takes about fifteen minutes. Cam stands around with his arms folded while Madeline and I peruse the candle shop, smelling various candles and goofing off.

We load back up and hit the road.

Once we've been back to driving for about ten minutes, I say, "You know, if I were in charge of welcome signs at state lines, I'd make a giant head of Abraham Lincoln and put it on the side of the road right after you drive into Indiana. They could have holes for us to put our heads through next to Abe. One could be, like, maybe ... Mary Todd Lincoln's body and then your face would show through like it's her head ... another could be ... Ulysses S. Grant. Who is in charge of these state welcome signs anyway?"

"Your mind is so random," Ben says.

I turn around and look at him. "And that's a good thing, right?"

"Let's go with a good thing. Sure," he says, chuckling.

"You love my randomness."

"Who wouldn't?" Ben says.

I glance over at Cam. He looks typically unimpressed.

"Abraham Lincoln was born in Kentucky."

"But he moved to Indiana when he was seven," I answer.

The look Cam gives me makes me wonder if he thought I never paid attention to history in school. I ignore his look and decide to goad him on instead. "Admit it, Cameron, you'd love being Ulysses S. Grant."

"Um. Nope. Can't say I would. I'd love staying on the road and making time."

"Just think how much cooler that sign would be—especially better than having nothing there to greet people. What were they thinking? This is the midwest. We greet people. Here we just entered Indiana, and no one officially welcomed us."

I raise my hand and make a flourish with it across the air in front of me like I'm framing a marquis. "Welcome to Indiana. Birthplace of Abraham Lincoln."

"A sign like that would just cause a traffic jam," Cam says. "People would be constantly stopping there to take photos. Someone would probably end up hurt. It's the side of a highway, not an amusement park."

"It would cause a traffic jam because it would be awesome. Right, Mads?"

"I think it would be cool," she says. "They should have a Frederick Douglass peephole too."

"Done!" I say, as if I'm the new ambassador of state signage.

My playlist continues as the soundtrack to our trip. *Go Your Own Way* by Journey fades into *American Pie* by Don McLean. I start singing along. Cam quietly drives beside me, glancing over with a possibly amused expression from time to time.

Every time the lyrics talk about driving a Chevy, Ben shouts "Drove my VW!" It doesn't rhyme, but we're all laughing, and even Cam starts singing along.

I fight dropping my jaw when his voice joins ours in the chorus. I turn in my chair and look at Madeline. Then I subtly point to her brother while I mouth, "He's singing along!" She giggles, but we all keep singing straight through to the end of the song.

We make it all the way to Indianapolis after two hours of driving, plus our thirty minutes of stops for my bucket list items. Cam blows straight through Indianapolis without even asking if anyone wants to stop, and I don't complain.

I do mention, "We're only twenty minutes from Collinsville where there's the biggest bottle of ketchup. It was even featured in the Twilight movie."

Cam looks over at me. I'm not sure if that's a smirk or the start of a smile.

"We're not detouring to see a giant bottle of ketchup."

"I'm not asking you to go two hours north to the largest covered wagon in the US."

He lets out a breathy chuckle. "Well, isn't that a relief?"

8

CAMERON

A journey is best measured in friends,
rather than miles.
~ Tim Cahill

"I think I need a donut burger!" Riley exclaims, looking up from her phone. "No. I know I do. I need this in my life. Donuts and burgers, it's like bacon and pancakes. This I *have* to try."

It's totally not like bacon and pancakes. Also, we are not stopping for a donut burger.

Riley's been scrolling quietly for the past half hour. Apparently, all that effort went into her searching out unusual food combinations to suggest as a pitstop.

"Is that on your bucket list?" I ask, dreading the response.

"Nope. I just found it. In Terre Haute we can get a donut burger at Fifi's. And the donuts are even square. I wonder if that makes them taste different."

"I'm pretty sure putting a burger between them makes them taste different."

Ben chimes in from the back. The bench seat is where a second row would be in most vans—about six feet behind where Riley and I are sitting. The way Duke fixed this bus up, there's storage behind the front seats, and then a whole lot of open space. There's a built-in table and a fold-down chair for when we park if we all want to hang out in the back of the van.

"Sorry, Rye. Looks like Fifi's closed," Ben says.

"What?! No! What are we going to do?"

"I'll buy you a burger and a donut and you can improvise," I say. "When we stop for lunch. In St. Louis. That's only two and a half hours from here, if we don't stop to see any more landmarks."

Riley gazes over at me with those big brown eyes. I wish she wouldn't look at me like that. It makes me want to cave. I've been holding out. No giant bottle of ketchup. No Hoosier Hill—the highest point in Indiana, at a whopping one-thousand-two-hundred feet. I think that's not even the elevation of the Hollywood sign. But yes, Riley mentioned it. And yes, I shot her down. I also narrowly avoided the Teeny Statue of Liberty Museum. In Indiana. Apparently, that's an actual thing. Correct me if I'm wrong, but the Statue of Liberty is in New York. Riley didn't pout for too long over my rejection of a stop at the miniature version of the Liberty Island landmark.

"We're passing through Terre Haute," she says.

"We are."

I see it coming. Another item. I keep my eyes on the road so I don't have to look at Riley's imploring expression. *Stay strong, Reeves.*

"Forty minutes south of here is a ginormous statue of a giraffe on someone's private property. It's on the highway by Shakamak. Isn't that a fun name for a place?"

It's like Riley has these magical powers. She sits silently until I finally give in and glance at her. Her eyebrows are raised expectantly.

"Shakamak," she pauses. "Say it three times fast. Shakamak. Shakamak. Shakamak."

She turns to the back and looks over her seat. "Say it three times, guys."

I'm now surrounded by three grown young adults who are chanting *Shakamak*. And not just three times.

Riley looks back at her phone. "Also! Oh my gosh! There's a private farm with an actual zebra who lives with the other animals."

"We have zebras in California. There's a whole herd at Hearst Castle. And, of course, the LA Zoo."

Riley rolls her eyes. "So, no stopping until St. Louis?"

"Not if I can help it."

"What about the Indiana-Illinois state line?"

I consider this. "If we stop there, will you table all requests until after St. Louis?"

"Yes!" She does a fist pump.

Then she looks back at Mads and Ben. "I didn't have any other requests before St. Louis, so don't worry guys. You aren't missing anything big."

"Whew," Ben jokes. "I thought we'd miss seeing the world's largest toothbrush."

"Nope. That actually tours around to different cities," Riley says without missing a beat.

"I was kidding, Rye Rye."

"Oh. Well, anyway, everyone get ready! We're only ten minutes from the state border with Illinois!"

Riley nearly buzzes with anticipation, her eyes as fixed on the road for the next ten minutes as mine are. I hear Madeline and Ben talking about something in the backseat, but the details of their conversation are drowned out by the songs coming through the speakers.

We approach the state line.

Riley sees the sign before I do.

"Seriously?" she says. "That's the sign?"

I look out and see it. There's a small green road sign—the kind you see everywhere for on and off ramps, only smaller. My guess is, it's two feet by three feet, if even that. In neat lettering, it says, "Illinois State Line."

"Do we need to stop?" I ask.

Riley doesn't say anything. Her crestfallen expression says it all for her.

I pull over.

This is officially the lamest sign in the world. There are probably bigger signs welcoming people to our town of twenty-five hundred. I know there are. But Riley wants pictures at every state line and that look on her face is killing me right now.

"You're pulling over?"

"Yeah. I don't want us to go through this trip with you lamenting that you missed getting a photo of this border. So, let's make it snappy."

"I could kiss you, Cameron Reeves! Thank you! Thank you. Thank you. Thank you."

I chuckle at the idea of Riley kissing me. She's so animated and bubbly when she's happy. It makes me want to do more dumb things just to put that smile on her face. Only, not really. We do have a schedule to keep. But now my mind is having the weirdest thoughts of Riley kissing someone. Not kissing me, of course, but kissing someone. I haven't ever seen her as a person who kisses anyone. She's just Riley. But I guess she might kiss someone if she were into them or they were dating.

I shake my head to dislodge that weird train of thought, and make my way over to the sign which barely comes up to my shoulder.

Riley has us all gather around the sign. She's down on the ground beneath it, pointing upward. The rest of us frame the sides, and we all point at it too. Riley pushes the remote to the selfie stick and the camera clicks. Then she says, "Make a face that says, *What the heck*?" We all scrunch up our faces like we can't believe this sign is even here. The camera clicks again.

We hustle back to the van, and we're on the road to St. Louis in less than five minutes after we unloaded.

"I love these pictures!" Riley says after we're all buckled in and rolling again.

Then she declares, "I'm writing my congressman about that sign."

"These aren't your congressmen. We're in Illinois. This isn't your state."

She ignores my logic. "This is so unpatriotic! Whatever happened to a sense of welcoming people into your state? Could they get more boring than, *Illinois State Line*?"

Riley looks back at her phone. "Still, I love these photos. Thanks, Cam."

"No problem."

Madeline and Ben fall asleep sometime shortly after we cross into Illinois. They slump toward one another, and after a while Ben ends up with his head on my sister's shoulder.

I whisper to Riley, "Get a shot of that."

She turns around and captures the moment on her cell. "Total blackmail pic."

"Right? That's what I was thinking."

We're quiet for a while. Riley pulls a notebook out of her backpack along with some Red Vines and Beef Jerky. She offers me some and I take a few of each. She tucks her feet up under her and writes in the notebook for a while. Then she looks up at me.

"Did you always know you wanted to be in the resort business?"

"Always? Probably not always. When I was little, I wanted to be a major league baseball player and play for the Cincinnati Reds. That was after I wanted to be ... nevermind."

"What?"

I look over at her. "You can never bring this up again."

She rubs her hands in anticipation. "I'll do my best. Depends on how juicy it is."

"I wanted to be the Tooth Fairy."

Riley barks out a laugh. She tries to straighten her face. Then she laughs again.

My sister stirs, but settles back to sleep.

"Shhh."

"Okay. But, Cam. That's so cute!"

"I was young. Anyway, major leagues was my real life's ambition."

"Really? You gave up the whole tooth fairy thing so easily?"

"Yeah." I chuckle. I can't believe I told her that. I never told anyone I wanted to be the Tooth Fairy. I seriously had my heart set on it for a while.

"I was barely good enough to play ball through high school. It was one of those dreams you have as a kid before you figure out that life isn't magic and you have to be more practical."

"Working at a resort seems pretty magical, if you ask me."

"I imagine it will have its moments. But it's work. And work is work."

"What do you mean by that?"

Riley adjusts herself so she's tilted more in my direction, her shoulder rests against the back of the passenger seat.

"Work has ups and downs. You're lucky if you get to do

what you love. But they call it work for a reason. There are always personalities to endure, problems to solve. There'll be days where you want to throw in the towel no matter what you do."

"Huh."

She stares out the front windshield.

"What about you?" I ask. "Did you always want to be a teacher?"

She snort-laughs. Then she brings the back of her hand up to her face and giggles.

"No. Not at all."

"Is that a funny question? I mean, you are in your Bachelors of Education."

"I am."

"When did you decide on that major?"

Riley looks over at me. Then she glances over her shoulder at my sister and Ben who are still sound asleep and slumped together.

"Can you keep a secret?"

"Sure. Of course."

I have the urge to cross my heart or do a pinky swear like we used to when we were so much younger. I look over at her. She's not that kid anymore. That's for sure. Riley's objectively beautiful in a girl-next-door kind of way. Her long, chestnut brown hair is pulled up into a messy bun right now, but sometimes she wears it down in waves. She's got the brown eyes to match her hair, besides those big eyes, her petite features fit her face. She has this childlike quality that makes you forget her age. Riley's probably one of those people who will seem young forever because of her zest for life. But when I look at her right now, with that pensive expression on her face, she seems less carefree and more like a woman than I ever realized. Huh.

"I picked my major because Mads chose education."

I'm quiet. She seems hesitant and I don't want to say anything to make her clam up.

"I honestly don't know what I really want to do. I love working at the schools for our internships, but mostly because I get to know the kids and play with them during recess." She pauses. "That sounds so dumb, huh?"

"Not at all. I always liked recess best."

She smiles, but it's not her usual unabashed smile. Then she says, "You were a straight-A student."

"I was, but that doesn't mean I loved studying. I just worked hard to get good grades. I mostly did that so I wouldn't lose my chance to play ball."

"I never knew that."

"So, you don't want to be a teacher?"

"Not really. Is that horrible? I'm here, letting my parents pay tuition for a degree I probably won't ever put to use."

"It's not horrible. A lot of people never use their specific degrees. Having a degree still gives you a leg up in a lot of ways."

She smiles a little more warmly.

"So, if not a teacher? What?"

"That's the billion dollar question." She looks out her window and then back in my direction. "I have no idea."

"Well, you don't have to know yet."

"Right. I have ten months."

"You have the rest of your life."

"If only."

"You do. Think about it. My mom started taking piano after Mads went to college. People start new things all the time. You can try something on and switch if it's not a fit."

"Not if I want to be a doctor."

"Do you?"

"No way! Just the thought of blood makes me queasy."

"Well then, you're set."

"Maybe I am." She doesn't sound convinced.

We ride along in silence until we see a sign that tells us we're three miles away from St. Louis. Riley sits up and starts paying attention. I'm focused on trying to make sense of the maze of freeways interchanging and layering with one another.

A few miles later she shouts, "I see the arch! Guys, wake up!"

My sister rouses first, sits up, and Ben's head abruptly drops to her lap. He wakes from the impact and looks around, an expression of supreme grogginess across his face.

Riley looks back at them while she points out the windshield. "It's the arch! I wonder where the welcome to Missouri sign will be."

Just then I see it in the distance, sitting on a thick signpost attached to the side of the bridge that crosses from East St. Louis over the Mississippi river.

"Um. We're not getting out for it. There's no way. Get your camera ready, and I'll slow as much as I can."

Riley looks out the windshield and lets out a huff. But she grabs her phone and captures a picture just before we drive under the sign.

"Welcome to Missouri!" she says. "Let's go up in the arch!"

9

RILEY

As soon as I saw you,
I knew a grand adventure was about to happen.
~ Winnie the Pooh

I'm gearing up for a fight. I desperately want to go up the arch. The whole arch experience would add an hour or so to the schedule. So far, Cam has had a mini conniption fit for each detour or added landmark I even suggested, let alone the ones we actually stopped to see. But this is the arch. I'm going to have to insist. I won't do an actual old-fashioned protest where I sit on the riverbank and refuse to get up until Cam relents. At least, I don't think I'll have to resort to that kind of tactic.

I repeat myself, "Come on, guys! Let's go up in the arch!"

"I heard you the first time," Cam says.

His voice is slightly firm, but his expression looks ... mischievous. His eyebrow lifts momentarily, and he's got this little glint to his eye and a smirk to his lips. I've rarely seen this look on him, but I'm here for it. Let's face facts. I'm here for all of Cam's facial expressions, tones of voice, and moods. It's darn near pathetic.

"I've got plans for St. Louis, Sunshine."

"Sunshine?"

Is that a nickname? Or does he just call people Sunshine when he's feeling snarky? I reel in my inner cheerleading squad, sending them straight to the bench. There will be no pom-poms rustling over the nickname, Sunshine. No one's doing the splits or even jumping Herkie over this.

Sunshine. I stifle the smile trying to bust out to match the nickname.

"You're missing the point," Cam says. "I'm telling you I've got plans. Don't ruin them, please."

"Hmmm."

I consider his words, but also take into account his suddenly revived energy. Should I just capitulate and let Cam determine what we do here? Or should I insist?

"Who nominated you the leader of this expedition?" Ben says from the back seat.

"Yeah. Just because you're behind the wheel doesn't make you into some dictator." Madeline adds in her typical younger sister tone. "I'm going to start calling you Stalin."

"Have a little faith, would you?" Cam says to me, completely ignoring the back seat comments.

"Okay," I say. "I'll entrust our entire time in St. Louis into your hands, Cameron Reeves. And I'm hoping you know what it means for me to do that. I've had dreams of going up the arch for most of this summer."

"Faith," he says, nodding once like he's got this.

It's kind of hot the way he takes charge. I know. I'm trying to turn the heat down, or at least resist it. But can I help it if

Cameron's so naturally alluring? It would be like setting a hot fudge sundae in front of me, warm brownie, homemade ice cream, the perfect sauce-to-dessert ratio, and then telling me not to drool or take a bite.

Who am I, Mother Teresa? I am not.

At least I'm not actually drooling over Cameron—usually. And I'm definitely not biting.

I'll keep trying to resist him, though. I have to.

Cam navigates through the city streets near the waterfront like he lives here.

"Have you been to St. Louis before?" I ask.

"I've been a few times."

Huh. The mysteries of this man.

"When?"

"On break. To visit a friend I met at UCSD."

His face grows a little serious.

"Girl friend or guy friend?"

"Yep."

He doesn't say anything else. I'm nearly itching to ask more. I assume from his answer it was a girl—a girl he liked enough to take his break to come visit. The arch no longer appeals to me. I want to get the heck out of this city and whatever memories it holds for Cam, especially the ones putting that look on his face.

But like a cloud that drifts in during an otherwise sunny day, Cam's expression shifts, his ease and happiness returning. He announces, "We're here," before turning into a parking structure.

None of us say anything. For a man who poo-pooed the state line stops and the awesome tour of the candle factory outlet store, he sure is excited about a parking structure in the middle of a part of the city mostly filled with nondescript skyscrapers.

Cam takes the ticket from the dispenser, finds a space, and locks the van behind us. He gives one last glance to the roof rack, looks around the garage, and seems satisfied, because he pockets my car keys and wordlessly leads us to the elevators. Once we're at street level, Cameron starts walking away from the waterfront—away from the arch. I'm dying to remind him where the arch is, but I actually feel more compelled to give him the benefit of the doubt.

We walk to the Hilton. It's a towering building among other concrete and glass structures.

"Are we staying at the Hilton?" Madeline's voice is incredulous.

"Yeah. No." Cam says over his shoulder. "We're sleeping in Springfield tonight."

He walks confidently to the bank of elevators and pushes the button to go up. Like a bunch of lemmings, we follow him onto the car and watch as he depresses the button to the top floor.

"We're getting lunch."

"At the Hilton?" Ben asks. Then he lets out a low whistle.

"It's not that pricey. Their lunch menu has salads and side dishes that will be just right. Besides, Memaw slipped me a hundred at the bonfire and told me to spend it all in one place."

"Gotta love Memaw," Ben says.

We exit the elevator into a rooftop bar called Three-Sixty. The indoor area is sleek with gray and metal bar stools and exposed steel and ductwork on the ceiling. The only color accenting all the clean industrial chic vibe is a vibrant yellow. There's a balcony outside with a view of the ballpark and skyline. Out the other windows you can see the river and a pretty full view of the arch.

I nearly squeal as I take it all in. I'm just about twenty-one, the youngest of the four of us since Madeline turned twenty-one a month ago. Cam must read my thoughts.

"They don't card up here before seven in the evening."

I nod, following Cam out toward the patio. We're sitting outside!

The waitress brings us our menus. Cam tells us all to order what we want. He's treating—well, he and Memaw are treating.

Madeline looks over at him after we've placed our order and says, "I'll follow you anywhere, my dictator!"

Ben says, "I'm not committing to following you quite yet, but you did good, bro."

I don't say anything for fear of blurting. I'm feeling suddenly shy and out of place again. I focus on Madeline instead, waiting for my nerves to settle. I look over at Cam, he's got his aviators on and he's leaned back casually in his seat like he belongs here. He's glancing out at the view. The sun hits his hair just right, showing off the highlights. I want to reach out and run my fingers through it like some crazed hair-obsessed stalker.

"Come look at this view," Madeline says to me, saving me from myself.

I stand and follow her to the edge of the balcony. Trendy steel beams and crossbars run the entire length of the edge of the outdoor patio, but a plexiglass barrier keeps us from being able to lean on the railing. The feeling that you could just swan dive off the edge takes my breath away. The city sprawls out around us.

"This is amazing," Madeline says.

"Better than the Indiana State Line," I joke.

"Um. Yeah." She chuckles. "But I think we made the most of those stops. A great trip includes some silly things and some breathtaking. I've got a feeling we'll get our fair share of both."

I smile over at her. "Are you nervous to start our jobs on the island?"

"Nah. What's the worst that could happen? We get fired and have to leave the island and go back to our apartment on campus early? Oh well."

"Maybe keeping the jobs will be harder than losing them. I'm a good barista, but I've never served people who cared this much about the quality of their drinks. The guests at this resort are world travelers. They've had cappuccino in Italy, espresso in Turkey, Blue Mountain coffee in Hawaii."

"You're a great barista. You'll do fine. And I don't even know what my job entails. But whatever it is, we only work until two and then we have the whole afternoon and evening to lounge around on an island, checking out guys and working on our tans."

I giggle. Madeline can be a tad boy crazy. She definitely has her sights set on this guy in our program, but she's also a harmless flirt at times.

"Maybe we'll finally find you a boyfriend."

"I'm not looking," I tell her.

"You never are. That's where you've got to call a friend. I'm here for you, Riley. You're adorable and fun. You're a catch. I don't know what holds you back, but my challenge to you during our six weeks on Marbella is to have a little fun with someone of the opposite sex. It wouldn't kill you to stop acting like a seventy-year-old widow who lost the love of her life."

"We'll see," I say, staring out at the view.

I may not be seventy, but I basically did lose the love of my life. Not that I ever had him, but it's all the same when it comes to matters of the heart. Maybe he's not even the love of my life. But, he's something—and I feel the loss of what we could have had too much when I'm around him for too long.

"Are you dealing with my brother?"

"Huh?"

"You know, riding shotgun this whole day. Is he getting to you?"

"He's fine. Not getting to me."

Not in the way she means, at least.

"We can switch out. Maybe Ben should ride up there for a while. We could ride together in the back."

"Sure. That's fine."

Cam approaches us. "Food's here. Let's dig in. I've still got one more surprise before we get back on the road."

I'm dying to ask him if it's the arch, but I know he'd rather me just let the day unfold, so I keep my inquisition to myself. The food is amazing. We split a gourmet pizza. Madeline and I share a salad. The guys get a couple of appetizers as meals. After we eat, we ride the elevator to street level. It's eighty-five out and humid. Being in the city only magnifies the heat. Still, Cam insists we walk the few blocks to the riverfront.

When he turns to take the ramp that leads under the arch, I can't help myself. I bounce on my feet, throw my arms around him and say, "You're taking us up in the arch!"

His arms wrap around me, probably in an attempt to keep us both from going down to the ground from my sudden outburst. When I pull back, I feel my cheeks heat. My eyes dart to Ben and Madeline. They're both obviously amused by me. I look back at Cam. He's smiling.

"I told you, have a little faith."

"You planned this all along?"

"I did," he says, holding the door so I can pass through.

To prove his point, Cam whips out his phone and presents the gal scanning tickets our pre-paid admission. We spend a little time in the museum under the arch. None of us seem to be in too much of a mood for historical enlightenment or the movie about how they made the arch. The doors to a tram car slide open like an elevator, and we climb in, taking four of the five seats facing the center. The glass door slides closed and then a metal door behind it shuts us in. This is not an experience for the claustrophobic. The only windows in the whole capsule are on the door and we don't see anything for a few minutes. Then, we just see the wall of the interior of the arch, a few pipes—nothing much.

Cam's knee and elbow graze mine. I feel every teeny brush or bump of our skin. My mouth goes dry. I try to remind myself to stop feeling so much for this man. Maybe by the end of the trip he will annoy me so much I'll be better equipped to shun these surges of excitement zinging through me. Right now, I feel like I could power the tram with my nerves and giddiness alone.

We exit the car and walk up this ramp to a wide platform with little rectangular windows on each side. We lean against the wall to stick our faces right up to the windows. The Missouri side includes views of the old courthouse, Gateway Park, the stadiums, and a panorama stretching miles off into the distance. On the other side, we see the mighty, and muddy, Mississippi. Riverboats hug the bank. There's a casino across the way, and bridges with cars crossing over in both directions.

After we've had our fill, we take the tram back down and walk to the parking structure.

"I call shotgun!" Ben shouts as we near the van.

"Rock, paper, scissors!" Madeline shouts, winking at me. Under her breath, she whispers, "You can never make it easy on a guy. Always make them work for it—no matter what it is."

I shake my head at her, but go ahead with the rock, paper, scissors competition next to the van.

Madeline mouths paper to me and she throws down scissors. She throws down scissors again when it's her against Ben. Ben picks rock.

Once we're settled in the back seat, Madeline says, "Ben always picks rock."

"How do you remember that?"

"I've known him my whole life."

"Me too, but I never paid attention to that."

She just shrugs.

"Do you guys mind if we take a road that will add seventeen minutes to the trip?" Cam asks.

"You want to add seventeen minutes?" Madeline's tone is taunting. She adds a gasp for dramatic effect.

"I actually want to probably add about a half hour. There's a renowned stop I want to make before we hit the road for Springfield. You'll thank me."

"Lead on," I say.

"What's gotten into my brother today?" Madeline asks. "I thought he was all about keeping things on schedule."

"Who knows? I'm not complaining, though."

"Yeah, me neither."

In no time we're at Ted Drewes, and Cam's explaining it's a shop for frozen treats that has been serving frozen custard since 1930. We each get a cupful and eat it on the drive from St. Louis into the rest of Missouri.

I wait until everyone's at least halfway finished with their dessert before I bring up my next bucket list item.

"So, I have a request," I say, aiming my words toward Cam.

"Let me guess," he says. "Another bucket item?"

There's no bite to his tone.

"Yes, actually. It's another bucket item. It's the Fanning 66 Outpost. With ... wait for it ..." I pause for dramatic effect. "The world's largest rocking chair!"

"Wow. Now that's something we *have* to see," Cam says, sarcasm dripping from his voice.

I ignore his tone.

"We do!"

I decide to sweeten the deal. "Besides, they have restrooms and classic pop."

"Take me to your rocking chair," Cam says, mechanically, like he's an alien.

"Man, you're a bigger dork than I am," Ben says.

"I second that," Madeline says.

I guess I have a thing for hot dorks.

10

CAMERON

I would like to travel the world with you twice.
Once to see the world.
Twice to see the way you see the world.
~ Anonymous

"It's a forty-one foot rocking chair!" Riley shouts as she hops out of the back of the van.

She runs over to the place where this red chair that could seat twenty or more people stretches toward the sky. She does a twirl like she's in *High School Musical*. Other tourists look at her and smile. The smallest—well, actually the biggest—things make Riley exceedingly happy. I picture her face when we walked into Three-Sixty. Sheer awe. Then there was that hug under the arch. Totally unnecessary. It wasn't like I was going to pass through St. Louis without going up in the arch.

The chair is emblazoned with the words, *Route 66 Red Rocker* at the top, and *World Famous* at the bottom. World

Famous. There's the Eiffel Tower. The pyramids at Giza. The Great Wall of China. Now, we have this roadside monument, which I only learned about over an hour ago. Apparently, whoever painted it suffered enough delusion to use the words *World Famous*. Gotta appreciate the hubris of whoever made that claim.

"I'm pretty sure the guy who painted that is off his rocker," I mutter to Ben.

"Good one!" Ben says, laughing. "Off his rocker. Yeah. Maybe he's the *chair*man of the Fanning Outpost. Get it? *Chair*man?"

"I get it," I say in a purposely deadpan tone.

"Let's take a picture!" Riley shouts from underneath the rocking chair.

She darts back to the van and grabs that tripod/selfie thing of hers. Before she even has it set up, an older couple walks over to her and the husband offers to take our photo.

We gather up under the chair and pose, throwing our arms over one another's shoulders, then we take one with the girls down in front of us and me and Ben standing behind them.

Then Riley says, "Let's all pretend we're sitting down."

We squat like we're in invisible chairs. Just before the camera clicks, Ben loses his balance, wobbling and trying to stabilize himself by leaning on my leg. His impact pushes me to the side. I tilt into Riley. She squeals, grabs onto my shoulder and flails, trying to grasp onto Madeline. We're now like those pinging balls businessmen keep on their desktops—ricocheting off one another in a chain reaction. The four of us end up in a heap under the statue, laughing and scrabbling to disentangle ourselves. I'm splayed across Riley, Ben's elbow is jabbing my ribs. Riley's legs are crossed over Madeline's.

I look down at Riley's face. She's cracking up so hard, she curls into the fetal position, cradling her abs while a tear leaks out of her eyes. Then she snorts, which makes her laugh even harder. I'm doing a pushup away from her slumped, hysterical form. She looks up at me and tries to say something, but then she gasps and collapses into more laughter.

Ben's up and off me. Madeline has extracted herself from the dogpile. Now I'm the only one down here with Riley, perched over her in an awkward pose that looks like something it totally isn't. I do a burpee move to jump up and away from her. She wipes at a tear, shakes her head and stands up, walking over to the couple holding her phone.

"I got a whole buncha them photos," the stranger with Riley's cell says. "I hope you don't mind a few with you all in a tangle on the ground there. I thought you might like the memory. Sometimes the worst of times in the moment make for the best of times in the rearview."

"Aren't you the sweetest," she says. "What was your name?"

"I'm Jeremiah and this here's my bride, Cindy. We're heading to the Grand Canyon. It's been about thirty years since we've been."

"Wow! We're going to California. Madeline and I go to UCLA. Cameron and Ben just got jobs at a resort on Marbella Island."

"Ooooowee. Them's nice jobs. Workin' on an island at your ages. That'll be somethin' alrighty."

"We've got two weeks til we need to be there," Riley says. "And I plan to stop at every cool landmark and state line along the way!"

"Well now, that'll be a lot of stoppin'," Jeremiah says. "But you know, I can't say I blame ya. You never know when you'll be back this way. We always thought we'd take the boys. Now they're grown and have their own families. I retired in the spring, so we finally got the gumption to make the trip. You're right. You make the most of this experience. Yessir. That's a good call."

Jeremiah pauses and then he taps his chin with his finger. "You know, if you like seein' the state lines, you ought to stop at the spot they call Stand on Three States."

"What? Where is that?" Riley nearly bounces on her toes.

I do a mental scan of the trip route, trying to imagine how far out of our way this suggestion would possibly take us.

"Oh, it's right on your way. You can stand on Kansas, Oklahoma, and Missouri all in one step. Just look 'er up. You won't have to go too far off the Mother Road to find it."

"Thank you so much! And thanks for taking our pictures."

"Wasn't a thing," Jeremiah says.

Riley leans in and hugs both Jeremiah and Cindy before joining us to check out the inside of the store. She pauses to capture a photo of the long mural down one side of the building with old-fashioned automobiles and motorcycles and a gas station painted to look like you pulled up to this spot seventy or eighty years ago.

This girl. It's like every moment is one she hopes to capture and commemorate. I've known Riley my whole life, but we've basically been separated for four years while I was away at college. Sure, we saw each other every summer at family functions or around town. In some ways, though, it feels like I'm just getting to know her.

The Fanning 66 Outpost looks like an old west general store —all wood, with a porch that has normal-sized rocking chairs. Inside the store looks like a log cabin, complete with a stone fireplace in one corner. A few freestanding wooden shelves hold travel snacks and enough Route 66 souvenirs to outfit every traveler that passes through here for a year. The beverage refrigerators have the widest array of sodas, from vintage brands to the unusual.

Ben opens one of the doors and holds up a bottle.

"You guys! There's no way! They have sodas for each dictator! And, what do you know, they have Stalinade: The Real Red Soda."

"Oh my gosh! We have to get that for you!" Madeline squeals to me. "Unless you'd rather have Fidel Castro's Havana Banana."

"I'm good," I say, meandering away from the sodas. This place is unreal.

Riley pauses in front of another fridge of sodas. "Look at this! Bacon soda. They even have bacon with chocolate."

"That stuff will give you cancer," I say from over her shoulder.

She jumps a little. Obviously she didn't know I was standing right behind her. Those doe eyes widen and she looks up at me. She gets this taunting look on her face and she wags her eyebrows in an almost flirtatious way.

"I dare you to drink some."

"Are we in junior high?"

"Come on, Cam, live a little."

"I just lived a little—a lot, actually. I ate lunch overlooking the entire city of St. Louis. I went up in the arch. I ate frozen custard. I'm good."

"You need this in your life," Riley says.

I watch her grab the soda, walk toward the front, hold up a few *Fanning's Outpost Route 66* shirts and select one, before she meanders over to the cash register.

"Let's wrap things up," I shout over to Mads and Ben who are still giggling like two little kids in front of the soda fridge. "Use the restrooms if you have to and meet me at the van in five."

They look at one another, then turn to me and in synchronized unison say, "Okay, Dad."

They can mock me all they want.

With our stops at candle shops and rocking chairs, and ridiculous state line photo shoots, we've added nearly two hours to this day's drive already. We have two more hours til we reach Springfield. It's already three thirty. We'll just get there in time to check in, find a place for dinner, and get a good night's sleep if we head out now.

Somehow, Riley's next to me again. The three of them play rock, paper, scissors for this coveted spot in the van. Ben offered to drive twice, but I'm good. I don't exactly relax well as a passenger.

As soon as we're buckled up and heading back for the highway, Riley says, "Too bad we won't be here at night. They light up the rocking chair and you can see it from a pretty good distance down the road."

"It's a shame to miss that," I say.

She reaches over and playfully swats my arm.

"You know what you need?"

"I'm sure you're about to tell me."

"You need some bacon-y, chocolatey goodness!"

She follows that statement with a flick of a bottle opener. She turns the bottle opener toward me. It's shaped like a highway sign and it says Route 66 on it.

"I even got a cool bottle opener. It's a practical souvenir, just like my T-shirt." She turns toward the backseat. "Anyone else need a bottle opener?"

Madeline takes the opener from Riley, while Ben announces that he put my commemorative dictator soda in the mini-fridge for a later date.

"Do the honors," Riley says, handing me the glass bottle of dark carbonated liquid.

"I don't really drink soda."

"It won't kill you. Not one bottle, or one sip. Just try it."

"Maybe you should be in marketing instead of education," I say without thinking.

Riley's face falls momentarily, but then she twists her lips and her eyes drift up toward the roof. She lets out a soft hum.

"Try the soda, Cam."

I reach out, taking the bottle like I'm accepting the elixir of death.

I put my lips to the mouth and take a miniscule sip.

"Drink it like you mean it!" Riley says, giggling.

I move the bottle back to my mouth and take a good chug. The flavors come in layers. Something caramel, like a usual soda, but a little more syrupy. Then there's the smoky hint of bacon and the deep bittersweet of chocolate. It's not bad. I definitely wouldn't choose it, but it's not as bad as I thought it would be.

"What do you think?"

"Not bad. Not great. But not bad."

Riley grabs the bottle. She takes a chug. The muscles in her throat bob as she swallows and I watch as she licks her lips, closes her eyes and then lets out a little hum of appreciation.

"Where has this been all my life? It tastes like the county fair!"

"Like livestock and a sweaty crowd?" I tease.

She shoots me a glare. "No. Like that bacon dipped in chocolate. You know, the stuff they serve next to deep fried Twinkies, which are also the bomb."

"I avoid all that mess," I confess.

"How are you even in your twenties?"

"I plan to live way past my twenties—because I don't pollute my body with that kind of junk."

"It's a sweet indulgence, not your daily meal. You need to break out of that shell, Cameron."

The complaint hits a little close to home. Stephanie said the same thing.

She passes the bottle back to me and I have the sudden urge to down the whole thing just to prove I'm not as buttoned-up as everyone thinks I am. Instead, I take a decent sip and pass it back to Riley.

She smiles a satisfied grin and says, "That wasn't so hard, was it?"

"I know how to let loose, Sunshine."

There's that nickname again. I don't know what got me to start calling her that. It fits her like a glove. She's like this bright light, always illuminating situations and drawing people to herself. I don't usually give people nicknames. I glance over at Riley to see if I can gauge her reaction.

She smiles a shy smile at me, and then shifts so she's glancing out the window on the passenger door.

We're making good time between the Outpost and Springfield. Riley's got her playlist queued up. She's quiet for a while, aside from singing along with some of the songs she chose. Eventually, she grabs a few pages of paper from her backpack and hands one to Ben and one to Madeline. Then she announces we're playing Road Trip Bingo. She must sense that I'm on the way to protesting.

"You're playing. I'll track your sheet for you. Don't be a stick in the mud, Cameron. I promise you'll have fun. At the very least, it will help you pass this last hour of the drive."

She looks over at me for the first time since I called her Sunshine. She's glanced at me here and there, but hasn't held my gaze. I don't know if she likes the nickname or if it bugged her, and I'm not about to ask such a private question. Why does it even matter?

"Okay. Okay. We'll play. Tell me what we're doing here."

"Yay!" Riley says, bouncing a little in her seat and doing a shimmy with her shoulders. Easy to please. That's her. It's kind of endearing.

"Okay, so. Each of our Bingo cards have different signs and things we might pass on the road. When we see one, we check it off. The first person to get a straight line of checked boxes wins."

"And what do we win?"

"First shower when we get to the hotel room, and pick of the sleeping arrangements."

"Winner gets to pick tomorrow's stops," I say before I think better of it.

"Oh! You're on, cap-i-ton! Like a prawn. You're going dawwwn."

"Ladies and gentlemen, she raps."

Ben chimes in from the back. "There are four of us. I may just win. And Rye Rye, if I win, I can be bribed. Like, I'll take a little of that gourmet popcorn you bought at the Outpost if you really want to sway me into stopping somewhere."

"What about me?" Madeline says. "I could win. And, I can be bought too. But not with sugar. And I have no desire to sit next to my brother. But I'm sure I can name a price."

"And if I win," I say, with a glint in my eye as I spear Riley with a look. "We are making time tomorrow. No largest this or smallest that. No detours to stand at a state line."

She nearly pouts.

"Okay, maybe a state line. But we're not veering off Route 66 to find the place that three states intersect."

"If you win," she says. "That's a big if, mister."

Riley reads me all the items on my sheet. I try to memorize them. Deer, stop sign, caution, exit, crosswalk, truck, lane ends ...

"I feel like I'm at a disadvantage. The rest of you get to look at your sheets and I have to remember mine by heart."

"Too bad, so sad," Riley says.

She giggles and it reminds me of times we all played board games or hide-and-seek when we were kids. I look over at her. Riley's not a kid. Not even close. Even at the end of a long day, after the wind blowing her hair around in St. Louis, and the walk we took downtown, and even after falling over in the grass under that rocking chair, her wavy brown hair falls around her shoulders, framing her face and drawing attention to her brown eyes. She looks like she's had a day, but the look suits her.

I wonder if Riley's dated much in college. She seems like such a free spirit. I can barely imagine the type of man who could be good enough or interesting enough to make her want to settle down. Not that she'd settle down. But when she gives her heart, he's going to be one lucky guy. Whatever she does, she does it one hundred and ten percent.

We're each shouting out things like "RV Park!" or "Speed Limit!" when Riley shouts, "Uranus!"

Ben cracks up. "What did you just shout, Rye? I know you didn't just spot Cam's ..."

"She didn't!" I cut him off before he says it.

"No!" Riley says, giggling. "It's Uranus."

"Sorry to disappoint, but I'm fully clothed back here."

"Thank everything holy," Madeline says.

"Ha ha," Riley says. "Uranus, Missouri. It's a place. For real. They even have a fudge factory."

"Say it isn't so," I murmur.

"It's so true," she says. "We just have to stop here, Cam. They even have a standee where we can poke our heads through for a photo."

I don't even want to ask what that standee entails.

I'm about to put my foot down when Ben says, "This, I have to see."

Echoes of Riley telling me I'm a stick-in-the-mud and need to lighten up ping against memories of Stephanie complaining that I never let loose.

"Okay!" I shout. "Take me to Uranus!"

My three passengers crack up and I hand my phone to Riley so she can enter the details into the maps app. Turns out we're only five minutes from Uranus. I mouth that sentence to Ben in my rearview mirror and he busts out laughing all over again.

We pull off the highway onto a service road that's actually labeled Route 66. The large neon sign has a rocket ship with a UFO over it and the words *Uranus Fudge Factory*. A small metal sign along the road says, *No ifs, ands, or butts*. They're really rolling with the whole town name. Along the front of the parking lot are all sorts of oddities: a dinosaur statue, a Phillips 66 fuel tanker. The buildings, with an old-west facade, form a semicircle at the back of the parking lot.

While I find parking, Ben says, "Wait! I have to tell you what we're in for here."

"Okayyy," I say, feeling a bit wary, considering I'm parked under a sign that says *Welcome to Uranus.*

"This place isn't actually a town. This guy wanted to name this place Uranus and declared himself the mayor in 2015. Ever since then, it's grown as a tourist spot. Also, they're only open for another forty-five minutes, so let's go get some fudge!"

We make our way through the general store, sampling fudge, and buying a few flavors to take with us, and then Ben buys his first souvenir of the trip—a T-shirt that says, *I (heart) Uranus*.

"I will not be seen with you when you wear that. Be forewarned."

"Ten bucks says you're wearing this in public before the trip is out."

"Oh, you're on. I'm for sure not ever wearing that."

"Famous last words, my friend. Famous last words."

Before we leave the fake town of Uranus, we ask a young couple to take our picture while we pose in the standee. Yes. It's a view of a zebra, elephant, giraffe, and hippo all facing forward. In other words, we're featuring their backsides in our photos. And yes, we put our faces through the holes that are ... well, you figure out the rest.

If that's not me loosening up, I don't know what is.

11

RILEY

The world is a book,
and those who do not travel only read one page.
~ St Augustine

"BINGO!" I shout when I spot a yield sign on an on-ramp merging onto the highway.

"Noooo!" Cam moans beside me. "We'll never make it to California."

He pauses, looks over at me, and then says, "I did mention that the privilege of calling stops only lasts one day for the winner, didn't I?"

"Stalin," Madeline coughs into her fist.

"Dictatorship," Ben coughs after Madeline.

"Since when is being concerned and responsible akin to ruthless, tyrannical fascism?" Cam asks.

"I'll take that day—tomorrow," I tell Cam. "And we can play again when we're driving. I've got other games too."

"I'd expect nothing less," he says, seeming not exactly disappointed.

Huh. Maybe I am getting to Cam a little bit. Not in the way I want, of course. I really need to plant my feet in reality. It's not like Cam and I are taking this trip across the country together, only to end up finding true love in one another's arms like we're the co-stars in a road-trip romcom. He's Madeline's older brother. And I may be less invisible than I was before we left this morning, but I'll never be a real woman in Cam's eyes—the kind of woman he wants the way a man longs for a woman.

He's staring at me.

"What?" I ask.

"Promise me you'll get us to Amarillo by bedtime tomorrow."

"Define bedtime," I retort, with a wag of my eyebrows.

"Take a road trip, they said. It will be fun, they said."

"You're having fun. Admit it."

Cam holds up his fingers like they're pinching something, only he leaves a little space.

Yeah. He's having fun.

And for some reason, that makes me ridiculously happy.

We roll into Springfield at around seven. We've eaten fudge and gourmet popcorn, and I finished that amazing bacon soda, but for some reason my stomach is screaming for me to eat—after I shower. What is it about traveling that makes you feel so scummy? We sat still all day. Well, except for the stops I suggested, and our trip up the arch, and lunch on top of the hotel. I guess all that added up.

We check into the hotel I basically begged Cameron to book for tonight: the Best Western Route 66 Rail Haven. I had looked it up online and thought the surrounding area was going to be more iconic. Instead, we've got a few auto repair places and some other free-standing businesses across the street. It's very ... *we're staying overnight on our way through town.*

The property is clean and cute. The rooms are themed and the whole vibe retains a classic roadside motel feel while being updated. I really wanted to stay in the Elvis room with a pink Cadillac bed frame. Elvis himself stayed there. But it only has one king bed, and we're sharing a room between the four of us every night to save money.

We end up in a suite with one king bed and a double-single bunk.

"I call the king bed for me and Mads!" I shout as soon as we pop the door open with our keycard.

"Rock, Paper, Scissors for the bunk!" Ben shouts right after me.

Cam rolls his eyes, but sets his suitcase down and starts the game with Ben right away. Ben throws rock. Cam throws paper. I catch him winking at Madeline right after he wins.

"Looks like I get the bottom double, bro. Enjoy that top single."

"Just you wait. When I get Bingo, I'm calling the king bed, and you can sleep on the floor."

Cam just shakes his head like that's never happening.

"Can I shower before we get something to eat?" I ask the group.

It turns out everyone feels as grungy as I do, so we take turns each toting a change of clothes into the bathroom and showering. By the time we're all clean, it's just about eight.

"So ..." I start in cautiously.

It's been a long day. I'm pretty sure Cam would like to lie down on his little double bed on the bottom bunk and have someone hand-feed him pizza that we order in. And, while I'd love to be the tribute for that experience (call me a giver, I know), I'm not going to settle for pizza in this hotel room when we can add yet another memorable experience to this day.

"No," Cam says, before I even finish my thought.

"What? You don't even know what I was about to say."

"Whatever it is, it inevitably involves driving, stopping, taking some photos, and a lot of energy I just don't have after this day."

I reconsider my suggestion.

"Welp. Okay. If you insist. I was going to suggest a sixteen minute drive to Lambert's in Ozark. They literally throw your rolls at you. It's actually called The Home of the Throwed Rolls. You can get all the great southern comfort food. You know, chicken and dumplings, chicken fried steak, St. Louis style barbecued pork steak ... and there's the hubcap cinnamon roll. But you know, we don't have to do that."

"You had me at southern comfort food," Ben says.

"We have to have our rolls thrown at us," Madeline adds. "Now that I know this is a thing, I have to experience it."

"I'll throw something at you if it makes you happy," Cam says to his sister.

He looks at each of us, then he turns and grabs my keys off the hotel desk, and says "Come on, then."

I squeal and jump a little.

"How do you still have the stamina of the Energizer Bunny after the day we've had?" Cam asks.

"It's a gift."

He chuckles. I try not to stare. His eyes crinkle at the corners, and his mouth turns up in this subtle and sexy way. His hair is still damp from the shower. He's got on a white polo shirt that reveals his arm muscles and fits across his chest just right. He's wearing plaid shorts and black flip flops. He looks a little tired from our full day, but also casually comfortable.

I wave my arm toward the front seat, giving it up to Ben,

while I climb into the back with Madeline. As much as I love riding next to Cam, I'm missing my bestie.

I settle into the back seat bench and turn toward Madeline. "So, tell me your high and low for today?"

"High: definitely eating overlooking St. Louis. That was so amazing. Low: when Ben fell asleep on me."

We giggle. "Was it that bad?"

"Probably not. I'm just not used to sleeping with someone."

"I should hope not," I joke.

"Yeah. And sleeping sitting up is not ideal. But really, this day had no lows. What about you?"

I don't tell her my high was my conversation with Cam when she was experiencing her low of a sleeping Ben leaning onto her.

"High: all of us falling over at the Outpost under the rocking chair. Low: that state sign that was too lame for words."

"You are so silly."

"Why?"

"Your high on a day when you saw the entire city of St. Louis and the Mississippi River, and then went up in the arch, is all of us falling on top of one another?"

"I measure my highs by how memorable they are. I loved those other things—of course, I did. I would have hated to miss them, but the four of us falling when we were posing for that picture is bound to be something we'll never forget. We can go back to the arch or Three-Sixty. We can't go back to that moment, so it's my high."

"Hmmm." Madeline pauses, looking at me with a warmth that always makes me remember why she's my best friend. "There's more to you than most people know, Riley."

I can't help that my eyes drift toward the driver's seat where the back of Cam's head is all I see of him.

"Don't let him get to you," Madeline says, following my line of vision.

"I don't. I'm rubber. He's glue."

"You're going to make such a good elementary school teacher. You always remember those things we said when we were their age. Your students are going to love that about you."

I haven't ever confessed to Madeline that I'm struggling to find my purpose, and I've for sure never mentioned that I'm ninety-nine percent sure I'll never be a teacher. She'd be so disappointed. By the time she graduates and has a classroom of her own, she won't care so much if I find another path. If only I could find that path, or at least a road sign pointing me in the general direction of that path.

When we pull into Lambert's parking lot, we have a hard time finding a spot. This place is popular, even with less than an hour til closing and the dinner hour for most people having ended a few hours ago. I tell Cam, Mads, and Ben to go on in and get us a table. Then I run around to the side of the building to capture a photo of the mural that shows Lambert's years ago. The caption on the mural says, *Home of Throwed Rolls - Four Generations and Throwing.*

Inside the restaurant is all wood with long wooden benches that almost look like church pews flanking each side of wooden tables on both sides of the restaurant and down the middle. The walls are covered in vintage signs, and the decor includes all sorts of knickknacks.

We're seated. Cam's more quiet than usual. I'm sitting next to Mads, across from him.

"You okay?" I ask quietly while Ben and Madeline debate whether we should get what they call Pass-Arounds or just order salads and pig out on rolls.

Cam's hazel eyes soften as he looks across the table at me.

I'm not going to read into the expression on his face. I am definitely not.

"Just tired. Driving takes it out of you, ya know?"

"I don't, really. You did the heavy lifting there. I really appreciate it. I think I could drive this trip, but I would have been a ball of nerves trying to make sure we stayed on course."

"Yeah."

He huffs out a laugh. It's not mean, just truthful.

Why does he have to be so attractive? This sleepy, sedate version of Cam makes me want to offer him a backrub—which, I'm totally not doing, even if I'm known at school for giving the best shoulder rubs during finals.

I feel my nerves creep up while I'm staring at him.

Gah. I was doing so well.

I pick up my menu and turn to Madeline.

"What's the consensus?" I ask Ben and Madeline.

"It depends. How hungry are you?"

"I was really hungry earlier, but now I'm so-so."

We all decide to share Pass-Arounds—macaroni with tomatoes, fresh fried okra, fried potatoes, and black eyed peas. Madeline and I split a salad. Ben and Cam share fried chicken. The Pass-Arounds are really the best thing I've eaten in a long time. Worth the eight-hour drive if you ask me.

Then the rolls come flying! It's the most fun thing, and could almost be my new high for the day. Servers in red suspenders and bow ties stand at the ends of the aisles and shout, "Rolls! Hot Rolls!" or diners raise their hands in the sign that they are ready to catch to get a waitstaff's attention. The waitstaff chucks hot rolls at customers. We're not talking short distances either. These guys are hurling rolls over the heads of other customers, five, six, seven, even ten tables away.

We raise our hands and catch the rolls ... or not. That's even funnier. One roll bounces off my hands over toward Ben and

Cameron. They both grab for it and miss because of the interference of one another. The roll plops onto the middle of our table, and we all fall into hysterics. The next one is even funnier. Madeline raises her hands, catches the eye of a server. He hurls the roll her way. For some reason, she drops her hands and squeals. The roll hits her right in the face. We all laugh harder than we were already laughing.

"The goal is to keep your hands up. Like this," Ben says. "It's so much easier to catch when you keep your hands up."

"Ha ha," Madeline says, breaking her roll in half and biting into it. A hum of appreciation follows that bite. "Why are these so good? I could eat these forever."

We don't have time for dessert since we arrived forty-five minutes before closing, but we're really too full to indulge in sweets anyway.

"I feel like I'm the Pillsbury Dough Girl," Madeline whines as we step into the evening heat and walk toward the van.

"I still say we should have gotten rolls and sorghum to go," Ben says.

I step back so he can ride shotgun again. For some reason, ever since my nerves kicked up at dinner, I've had a hard time looking Cameron in the eyes without butterflies exploding in my stomach and my palms getting slightly sweaty.

Back at the hotel, we all brush our teeth and change into our pajamas, and then it's lights out. I don't think any of us could have stayed up another minute after the day we've had. When the lights are out, I hear Ben and Cam saying something indecipherable to one another in the other room.

I shout out, "Thanks for driving, Cam!"

"You're welcome, Riley. Sweet dreams."

"And me," Ben says. "You want to thank me for agreeing to all your pit stops. Right, Rye Rye?"

"Yeah. Of course I do, Benny. Thanks!"

I grab my journal and turn on the flashlight on my phone to jot a quick entry.

Before long, the room fills with the kind of quiet you only experience in a hotel. Traffic out front creates a white noise. The hum of the A/C or the clunk of the thermostat occasionally fills the room. I drift off to thoughts of Cameron and the day ahead.

12

CAMERON

The greatest part of a road trip
isn't arriving at your destination.
It's all the wild stuff that happens along the way.
~ Emma Chase

"Good morning, sleepyhead," I say to Riley.

A little squeaking noise accompanies her yawn, and then she lets out a drowsy hum. With her head still on the pillow, Riley glances around the hotel room as if to attempt to orient herself.

She glances back at me. "Where are Madeline and Ben?"

"They went to the lobby to get coffee and to ask where we can get a good breakfast. I needed a little quiet, so I stayed back reading. You can get ready, and we'll go meet them."

It seemed harmless, sending them out and staying behind.

Riley stretches her arms overhead, and then gives me a

drowsy look. She turns onto her side and snuggles back into the mattress.

Her voice is raspy and sleep-drenched. "I could sleep forever. How are you up and dressed already? What time is it?"

"Eight."

"Oooooh. I just remembered. I get to call the stops today!"

She snaps up into a sitting position and throws off her covers. She's in a matching pajama top and bottom. Pink with little ... what are those? Cinnamon rolls? Yes. Her pajamas have tiny cinnamon rolls all over them. Of course they do.

I've grown up seeing Riley in pajamas. There's no telling how many times Riley and Madeline had sleepovers. Not to mention our family camping trips, or the times our family joined hers at their cabin on Lake Michigan. It shouldn't matter that Riley's sitting on the edge of her bed with sleep-tousled hair and a pink hue to her cheeks. She's just Riley.

"Huh?" I ask. She's staring at me like I missed something.

"I said, are you going to sit there while I get ready?"

"Um. No. Nah. Nope. No. I'll just ..."

I hook a thumb over my shoulder at the door. Then I stand, setting my book on the desk.

"You know where to find us?"

"Yep."

I walk across the parking lot. Ben and Madeline are in a conversation with the clerk at the front desk.

"Riley's awake. What's the plan?"

"College Street Diner, Steak-n-Shake, or the world's largest Bass Pro Shop?" Ben says.

"For breakfast?"

"They've apparently got something like a resort there. But the snack shop is really just coffee and baked goods in the morning."

"Well, you know what Riley's gonna want. If it's the world's largest anything, she's going there."

"She might surprise you."

"She always does," I mutter.

We walk back to the room. Riley's dressed, and her hair is pulled back into a ponytail.

"We've got choices," I tell her. "But since you're the Road Trip Bingo winner, you get the final vote."

"I already checked the travel blogs," she says, stuffing her pajamas into her suitcase and zipping it up. "The best two breakfasts are a little place called College Street Cafe, and the classic, Steak-N-Shake."

"There's also a coffee shop inside the Bass Pro Shops," Ben adds.

"I saw that, but it's not really breakfast-y enough for me," Riley says. "Plus, if we go there, we'll end up getting lured into the shop, and it will take us hours to hit the road. I've got big plans for today. And, even though they have live alligators on the property, I'm going to have to pass on the Bass."

"Good one," Ben says, laughing.

"What?" Riley asks.

"Lured into the Bass Pro Shop? That's classic."

"Oh my gosh! I didn't even mean to do that!" Riley answers, beaming at Ben.

Seeing the two of them together is like staring straight into the sun.

I shake my head. Riley's definitely anything but predictable. I would have bet my breakfast she'd want to see the Bass Pro Shop.

After we strap the luggage on top of the bus and check out, Riley ends up picking the Steak-N-Shake. Mads and Ben order biscuits and gravy. Riley orders eggs, bacon, and a hashbrown covered in cheese sauce. I order two egg whites scrambled, wheat toast, and a coffee, black. Riley teases me relentlessly about needing a senior menu. I don't tell her I prefer eating off that when a restaurant has one. She calls me Grandpa for the whole meal.

After breakfast, Riley announces, "We've got three quick stops here in town before we get back on the road!"

"Three?" I ask.

"Quick."

"Hmmmm."

"First, we're going to see the world's largest noodle outside the Kraft factory. Then we'll see the world's largest fork. And then, we'll see the world's largest statue of a foot. You'll be happy to know I'm completely skipping the giant golf club."

"Remind me why we're destined to see all these larger-than-life items on this trip."

"What do you mean, why? Don't be a fuddy-duddy, Gramps. It's fun—pure whimsical, frivolous fun. You should try it sometime."

She winks at me. It's playful—like her. Something in me pauses. She's Riley, the same girl I grew up with. She's the girl who got gum stuck in her hair when she challenged Madeline to see who could chew the most pieces and then blow the biggest bubble in sixth grade. I remember her sitting in our kitchen while Mom rubbed peanut butter all over her pigtail and froze it out with ice. She's always been a bit goofy, sometimes awkward. Just Riley.

I keep my eyes on the road and follow the voice navigation Riley pulls up on her phone. Of course, at each landmark she's picked in Springfield we have to get out. At the fork, we all pantomime bringing a fork to our mouths. Then we fake feed one another. Ben and I grab one another in a headlock and act like we're force feeding one another. At the noodle, we all make our arms into curves over our heads. At the foot, we each kick one foot toward the camera. The shot looks awesome with the perspective making the soles of our shoes nearly look bigger than our heads.

Finally, we're on Highway 44 with Springfield behind us. I passed up the option of stopping at the car museum, even though it sounded cool. Knowing Riley, we've got a long day with more stopping than rolling ahead of us. The sooner we hit the road, the better.

"So, we've got one hour and fifteen minutes before our first stop," Riley tells me.

She's back in the passenger seat, her feet on the dash, and her phone out with the maps app open.

"We're going to stand in three states at the same time."

"I'm sure it will be life-altering," I say with an expression that matches my level of enthusiasm.

"Cameron Reeves, I refuse to let you poop in my Cheerios. I am excited about this moment in my life. Here I am, a girl from a town barely anyone knows exists, and I'm going to stand on three states. If you don't want to stand in three states, you can sit in the driver's seat and pout about having to stop, or whatever it is you're going to do while we make memories."

She smiles over at me with a spitfire look still lingering in her eyes.

I smile back. "I'll get out."

"Don't do it just for me," she teases.

"Wouldn't dream of it," I tell her. "I might as well get that same bucket list item checked off."

"Wait! What? You have a bucket list?"

Ben chimes in from the back seat. "Yeah. He wants to be regular, stay fit, make it to California with the least amount of fun possible, and get straight to work. It's a simple but worthy list."

"Be regular?" Riley asks. Then she looks at me and says, "Ohhh ... gross, Ben!"

"Why do you think he never eats anything that could contaminate his god-like bod? He's a conscientious guy."

"TMI!" Madeline shouts, but she's already in a fit of giggles. "It's so you, though, Cam."

"I have fun. I'm going to work at a resort for Pete's sake. How much more fun can a guy be than that?"

"I'm pretty sure the guests are the ones having fun in that scenario," Ben says.

Riley sits quietly beside me, apparently lapsing into another bout of shyness that seems to overcome her now and then. I can't blame her. Who wants to hear about whether I'm regular? Leave it to Ben.

"So, give me the rundown of the day," I tell Riley, hoping to draw her out again.

She lightly shakes her head. "No way, Cam. I'm a vault. You'll just have to wait and see. I'm dripping the details out over the day. I have it all planned out."

Then she looks at her phone and shouts, "Oh my gosh! I never called Mom and Dad!"

"It's okay. I called them last night after everyone was asleep."

"You did?"

"I figured they needed to know we made it. I called all three sets of parents."

"I'm FaceTiming Mom now. Dad will be at work, but she should be home."

Riley pulls up the FaceTime app. Her mom's face fills the screen after a few rings.

"Hey, baby girl! How's the road trip? Tell me everything!"

"It's awesome, Mom. So much to tell you. We went to this place in Springfield where they actually throw rolls at you from across the room."

"Lambert's?" Mom asks.

"Yeah! How did you know?"

"Your dad and I went there years ago when Brian was little and I was pregnant with Pete. We took a vacation to the Ozarks. How fun that you went there."

Riley rattles on about our trip yesterday. Hearing it from her vantage point sounds so much more exciting. Then she turns the camera so we all can say hi. The hour or so between Springfield and the state border flies by pretty quickly. Before I know it, we're veering off the highway onto a state route with grass and trees on either side.

"See that sign?" Riley shouts, pointing to a sign smaller than my grandma's old TV.

I don't answer and keep driving.

"It said, *Kansas*!"

"Riley, please. We're going to the three states marker. Can we just get there instead?"

She momentarily pauses, but then concedes.

We pull off onto what almost seems like a private paved road, a fenced ranch runs along one side and trees with wild grass lining the other.

"Are you sure this is the way?"

"Google says so."

Just then the end of the road we've been going down comes into view. Trees encircle a cul-de-sac, and off to the back side of the turn-around sits a stone monument that might be six feet tall. It's basically a random pillar out here in the middle of nowhere.

"It's so ..." Riley starts to say.

I say, "... lame" at the same time as she says, "... awesome!"

Riley completely ignores me and hops out of the van. Madeline leans forward and whispers in my ear, "Let her have this day, would you?"

I pause. "Yeah. I will."

Ben's already out with Riley walking toward the statue that looks like it could be a stack of stones someone cemented together and put at the front of their property.

A square concrete slab is on the ground with an engraving of the three states: Missouri, Kansas, and Oklahoma. There's a large dot representing the spot where we're standing at the junction of all three. Riley starts hopping from state to state on the map. She steps off Kansas and onto Missouri, and says, "Dorothy, you're not in Kansas anymore!" Then she hops onto Oklahoma and starts to sing the show tune with that name, but stops before she even finishes the first word because she hops back onto Kansas and chants, "There's no place like home! There's no place like home! There's no place like home!" while clicking her heels.

I shake my head, but I can't help the smile breaking free across my face.

"Come on, guys. Let's get pics!"

We pose in front of the mini-monument. Then Riley has us all stand around the plaque on the ground with our toes pointing inward while she takes an aerial view photo of our feet.

"Okay, loooooad 'em up, cowboy! We've got a state sign to be at in one minute."

"One minute?"

Madeline shoots me a look. I smile a forced grin. I'm sure I look half-crazed. My sister's right, though. I don't want to be the cloud in front of Riley's sunshine. I need to let go of my agenda today and show my friends I can roll with it like the most flexible of people.

"I'm so flexible I should be in Cirque du' Soleil," I mutter to Ben.

"TMI, dude," he says with a chuckle.

"Says the man who brought up my bathroom habits in mixed company."

"You earned that."

"Yeah. Maybe I did."

Riley's right. One minute later we're at the sign that says *Welcome to Oklahoma*. It's a larger white sign with a star surrounded by various colors. And it's bigger than some of the signs we saw yesterday.

We pull over, hop out, take some shots, and are back in the van in no time.

"We're getting to be pros at this," Riley says, her smile beaming over at me.

How can I say no to a smile like that?

We may end up sleeping in the desert in ninety degree heat, the voice of reason in my head reminds me. *Let her have her fun,* this other voice says. I decide to listen to voice number two until after lunch. We can always make time if we have to later in the day.

"Okay," Riley says, turning to face me. "We've got a little detour here that won't even mean stopping unless you count hitting the brakes at a stop sign. We're just going to zip through Miami, Oklahoma to see their darling historic downtown area. There's a gateway to Route 66 sign which I will snap a video of without even asking you to slow down."

"We could stop if you wanted to," I offer.

"Why Cameron," Riley says, batting her lashes exaggeratedly. "Aren't you just the sweetest."

I shake my head, follow her directions, and in just over

twenty minutes we're driving through a town that looks like it never aged past the 1930s. Old brick and stone buildings line the street. A classic marquee tops the theater. Riley reads us the history of the town after she films the Gateway to Route 66 scrolled arch that spans overhead. According to her sources, this is the longest Main Street on the whole stretch of the historic Mother Road.

We're back on the freeway in no time and I'm feeling calm as can be when Riley announces, "We get to drive for an hour and seven minutes now. Then we're going to see a whale."

"A whale? In an aquarium?"

"You'll see." She wags her eyebrows and winks at me.

I barely see a blush rise up her cheeks before she turns away. She's such a puzzle.

I glance over at Riley. The sun is glinting through the van window onto her brown hair, showing off the varied hues of chestnut, blond, and even a little auburn. She's intently studying her phone, posting photos of our trip to social media, it looks like. If I didn't know her so well, I'd be taken aback by her natural beauty. She's so effortlessly attractive. I could be a guy on a road trip with a beautiful, fun-loving woman riding shotgun. But I'm not. I'm the voice of reason among a group of free-spirited friends. One who is my sister, and one who may as well be.

Riley turns on the radio. Her playlist starts with *Oklahoma.* Riley breaks into the song, belting out, "OOOhhhh-klahoma …" Annnnd … thus starts the show tunes section of our trip. For some reason, Riley knows every song, and she sings like she's auditioning for the leading role in each play.

Over the next hour, we rotate through songs about Route 66. When Riley queues up Bing Crosby and the Anderson Sisters, she pauses the song before it gets going. Then she magically whips out printed lyrics and hands two sheets over the back of her chair to Madeline and Ben. I sing as much as I know of Bing's part and Ben joins me. The girls sing the female lines. And we make our way toward this mysterious whale, singing about getting our kicks on Route 66.

Despite the redundant landscape, I guess we're actually doing just that.

13

RILEY

It's a big world out there.
It would be a shame not to experience it.
~ J.D. Andrews

"This is the whale?" Cam asks.

His arms are folded across his chest and he's staring at the eighty-foot structure that sits partially submerged in what once was a private swimming hole.

I link my arm through Madeline's and stroll toward the whale.

"It's hot enough to fry bacon on the sidewalk," I say.

"My phone said ninety."

"All I know is I wish they still allowed swimming in this pond. I'd jump into that water in a hot minute."

"And catch some algae-born disease," she jokes.

We walk toward the giant attraction together, the guys a little way behind us.

"This is the Blue Whale of Catoosa," I explain to Madeline. "It was made by this guy for his wife as a gift because she loved collecting whale figurines."

"Awww. That's the sweetest. I hope I find a man who will build me a whale someday."

"You do you, boo. I'd rather have a man build me a house, or take me on adventures."

"Well, I don't want a whale, of course. But a man who would do all this for his wife. That's love."

"It is."

We both sigh. Cam and Ben catch up to us, and the four of us enter through the mouth of the whale. When we're barely inside the head, Ben says, "Geppetto! Someday I'm going to be a real boy!"

"Don't count on it," Madeline teases Ben.

"Oh, I'm not. I'm all man, Mads. All man," Ben jokes back with a wink.

He runs toward the rear of the whale where a ladder is attached inside the tail and clambers up to the top in no time. Then he stands on the fins and flexes his biceps.

"See this, Mads? All man right here."

She shakes her head. "He's ridiculous."

I snap a picture of him and he hams it up for the camera.

"He's cute, but he knows it," I say.

"Doesn't he, though?"

Cam walks up behind me and Madeline. I feel his presence without even turning to see him. And when I do spin to face him, I have to check myself. Cam's a little travel-worn. There's a light wind coming across the pond and through the cut out holes in the side and top of the whale. It lifts his hair so that a lock falls across his forehead. His hands had gone from being tucked into his crossed arms to being stuffed into his pockets.

He takes one hand out and combs it through his hair, and then our eyes meet. For some reason, he makes me want to mess with him today. I'm feeling a temporary boldness.

"You know, we're a half hour southwest of the world's largest totem pole, just thought you'd want to be aware."

"You don't say."

"I do. Of course, we'd be backtracking to go see it. It's actually a totem pole park. This guy carved a bunch of them as an art exhibit."

"Mm hmm."

Cam's face is priceless. He's trying so hard not to react. Madeline knows just what I'm up to.

She joins in. "Awwww. Totem poles? I think we should go!"

Cam gives her a look. His reaction's not as disguised as it was when I started ribbing him.

"Have you ever just blown a half hour on nothing? You know, like taking thirty minutes of your life to do something that won't achieve a goal and might even be a complete and utter waste?" I ask him earnestly.

"Sure."

"Like, when?"

Madeline seems to bore when Cam's obviously finished taking her bait, so she walks toward the ladder to join Ben up on top of the tail.

"I can't think of a specific situation on the spur of the moment. That's like when people ask you to share your most embarrassing experience. No one can think of those things on the spot."

"I can."

"I bet you can."

"Let's see ... there was the time I wore a white shirt that didn't seem see through when I was dressing in the early hours before my morning class. That was until I was walking around campus and people kept looking at me funny. They'd glance at my face, glance down at my shirt and then look anywhere else. The guys were the worst, some of them did double takes. When I think of it now, I still get a crazy flipping sensation in my stomach. Gah! I was such a spectacle and I didn't even know it. Let's just say I wasn't ... well, anyway ... I kept thinking I had something spilled down the front of myself from breakfast. Thankfully, Madeline and I had our first class together and she told me. I rushed back to the dorms and changed as soon as our prof said, 'See you Wednesday.'"

Cam's face looks—well, it's not quite judgmental. It seems like he's trying to steel his features.

"Then there was the time I sat in ketchup at the student union. A huge red blob was smeared on the back of my pants and I never knew until I got home and changed. Guys were checking out my backside all day, and I just assumed it was all the squats Madeline had made me do in the gym that week."

Cam shakes his head. A bare whisper of a smile forms on his beautiful lips.

I'm blurting now, and I can't help myself. Cam's close enough for me to smell his scent. The sun is making the flecks in his eyes more pronounced. I wish he didn't have this impact on me, but I can't seem to get a grip on my tongue right now.

"Of course, not all my embarrassment comes from wardrobe malfunctions. Though, I've had plenty of those, to be sure. There was the time I got into the car with Mads after we had been studying at the library. I had to stop to check out a book before I left. She went ahead of me to the car, and told me to meet her in the lot. I walked right out of the library, pulled open Madeline's passenger door, and sat down. When I looked over, some guy was sitting in the driver's seat. I screamed so loudly. It was blood curdling. The guy just stared at me like I was nuts. Here he's in Madeline's car and I'm the one who gets looked at like I'm a crazy person. As if that weren't bad enough, someone knocked on the window of the passenger door right after I encountered this axe murderer sitting next to me, and I screamed even louder. I turned to see whoever was knocking. Madeline was standing outside the car. I hopped out of that guy's passenger seat without even saying a word. It wasn't Madeline's car, obviously."

This time Cam chuckles and his eyes crinkle with his laughter. "Riley, you are a piece of work."

"I know, right? My point is, if you do enough embarrassing things, you've got an arsenal to pull from whenever anyone asks that question. I'm guessing you don't do many things that embarrass you."

He's serious for a moment. Then he surprises me by saying, "I guess I usually don't take enough risks to have things go sideways."

"Risks like retracing your steps on a cross-country trip to visit a totem pole park?"

"Nah. Not that kind."

I laugh lightly. "I wasn't serious. I don't want to see the totem poles."

"You don't?"

"Nope. I've got other stops planned. I thought we'd grab lunch here. Then we won't have to stop for an hour and a half —heading west, not backtracking and going east."

Cam smiles down at me. "I could do lunch. And this day isn't as crazy as I thought you'd make it when you won the rights to make us stop whenever you want."

"I can be reasonable with the right motivation." My words come out in far too flirty of a tone, but Cam doesn't seem to notice.

"And what's motivating you today, Sunshine?"

I feel myself starting to blush at that nickname, so I turn and feign interest in the concrete whale.

"Lunch, Reeves. Lunch is motivating me!" I say over my shoulder. "Let's get some pictures on this whale so we can gorge ourselves on diner food."

Cam and I stand side by side at the bottom of the ladder. He slings his arm around my shoulder and I indulge myself by leaning into him. He bends a little so his head is in the frame. I can feel his breath across my cheek. I think my eyes flutter shut for the briefest moment.

Get it together, Riley.

Mads and Ben stick their heads down from up on their perch on the tail. I snap a selfie. We take about ten more photos on the whale, and then we head back to the van.

The Boomerang diner has old-school red booths with formica tables rimmed in silver edging. It's all very retro. The menu has all my faves. Mads and I decide to split mini-potato skins and pickle o's. Cam gets a plain burger. I shoot him a look that says I'm about to call him Gramps throughout the whole lunch.

He turns to the waitress and says, "On second thought, make it a bacon cheeseburger."

All three of us stare at him like he's been abducted and returned with a surrogate being inside his host of a body—one who obviously has way better taste than the real Cameron.

"What? A guy can order a cheeseburger when he wants."

Ben orders next. He flirts shamelessly with the waitress, who looks old enough to be his mom. Then he asks for the Frito boat which comes with chili, onions, and cheese.

As soon as Ben hands Shirley his menu, Cam says, "He is not eating that Frito thing. Bring him a cheeseburger and fries."

"What? Why not? Everyone else ordered what they wanted."

Cam looks at Ben. "I'm not riding the next few hours with you in a van after you eat a plate full of chili cheese Fritos." Cam looks at me and Madeline. "Should we put this to a vote?"

"Fine, fine," Ben concedes. "Give me the same thing he's having."

The food is delicious. We're full and happy when we leave.

"I'll drive the next leg," Ben offers.

"Okay," Cam says, easily, tossing the keys over to Ben who catches them effortlessly.

The move brings to mind the days I'd hang out to watch the baseball team practice after school, or attend their games—all to watch Cam in action in those white pants. Whoever designed baseball uniforms would get a thank you note from me if I could find her. Trust me, it's a woman.

"You're going to let Ben drive?" I ask.

"Did you not want him to?"

"No. I'm fine with him driving. It's just ..."

"I was pretty controlling yesterday?"

"Well ... yeah."

"Someone told me I needed to take more risks. So, here I am tossing the keys to Ben. I'm going to nap in the back seat with Madeline."

"What if I want to ride shotgun?" she jokes.

"What if I want to sit with Mads for a while?" I ask.

We really are relentless. Poor Cam. Then again, he's an easy target, and it's so fun to get a rise out of him.

"I want you riding shotgun, bro," Ben says. "Even if you're going to fall asleep on the job."

I sit next to Madeline, Cam takes shotgun, and Ben is at the wheel. We stop quickly for gas and then we're on the road.

"Try not to get a speeding ticket," I say to Ben before we reach the highway.

"I'm like a Formula One driver, Riley. No need to worry. I've got mad driving skillz. That's skillzzz with a Z."

"Okay, Mario. Just don't get us into trouble."

He winks at me through the rearview mirror, and sets his phone so the GPS directs our route.

The last thing I say before we're on the highway is "We're headed to Pops 66. We've got about an hour and a half before we get there."

~

"I WANT TO KISS YOU, RILEY." Cam says.

His voice is low and secretive, and I feel it everywhere.

"You what?"

"I want to kiss you. I know it's a surprise. And I shouldn't just spring this on you. But please, may I kiss you?"

"Cam, we can't kiss here. Mads and Ben will see us. You have to wait til we're alone."

"I've waited too long, Riley. I need to kiss you now."

"Now?"

"Yes. Now. You've been driving me crazy. I need you. You told me to take risks. This is me taking a risk."

I told him to take risks. Actually, I didn't tell him. He just mentioned that he doesn't. Then he ordered a bacon cheeseburger. And now, this? How does one go from a bacon cheeseburger to a kiss? Especially the kiss I've waited a lifetime to experience.

"You really want to kiss me?"

"More than I've ever wanted anything."

"Riley?"

"Riley?"

"Riley?"

Cam's hand grips my shoulder. But, he's not caressing me. He's actually shaking me a little.

Huh? What's going on?

How is Cam calling my name and kissing me at the same time?

"Riley, wake up."

"What? ... Where am I? ... Cam?"

I look up into his eyes, trying to reconcile how we went from nearly kissing, to him hovering over me and lightly shaking me. I glance around. We're on the highway in the van. Cars and trucks surround us on both sides, and stretch out as far as I can see through the front and back windows. Madeline is sitting next to me on the bench seat, the same way she did when we took off from the diner.

It was a dream. *Please, please, please let me not have been talking in my sleep.*

I look at Cam again. His face is a mask of neutrality. He obviously wouldn't be looking at me like that if I had been calling out his name or puckering up in my sleep.

Would he? No. He most definitely would not.

"There's a situation. Traffic started to slow and now we're all being held here until they handle everything."

"What kind of situation?" I ask, stretching my arms overhead and sitting fully upright.

I can't look Cam in the eyes. That dream felt so real. He was basically begging me to kiss him. No. Correction. He was begging to kiss me. His face had been right in front of mine, our eyes locked. The longing look that overtook him made him sexier than ever—which is beyond what I can explain because his effortless hotness is pretty much staggering. But, Cam when he wants me—whew.

That's not the real Cam. He doesn't want me. He wants to let me know we're having a situation, not to kiss me senseless.

"Apparently, there's an obstruction on the highway. At least that's what Google Maps shows," he calmly says, as if he didn't just tell me a kiss from me was the thing he wanted most in the world.

Because it isn't. And he didn't.

14

CAMERON

Map out your future – but do it in pencil.
The road ahead is as long as you make it.
Make it worth the trip.
~ Jon Bon Jovi

"I was hoping to make it to Amarillo tonight for a steak dinner at the Big Texan," I say. "I don't think we'll make that whole distance at this rate. Who knows when we'll start moving again. And from here it's four more hours of drive time alone. We'd have to skip all stops, and we'd still pull in around bedtime."

I look straight at Riley. Today's stops are up to her and she knows it.

She still seems a little out of it from her mid-afternoon nap. Sometimes naps will do that to you. She won't look at me. She's back in her shy, evasive mode for the time being, apparently.

She slowly turns those doe eyes on me. "I really wanted to stop at Pops 66."

"Is Pops as impressive as that whale?" I ask, teasing her lightly.

"More amazing." Her voice is quiet.

"What is Pops?"

"It's a soda ranch."

I can tell Riley senses me relenting before I even say a word. I see the glint in her eyes when she looks up at me. She's going to Pops and she knows it. Our conversation is only a formality now. I have to make her work for it, though.

"A what? A soda ranch? I'm sorry. A ranch, by definition, is a large plot of land where the homesteader raises domesticated animals. Did they tame some wild soda out here on the open range of Oklahoma?"

Riley ignores my faux objection.

"There's a sixty-six foot tall neon soda bottle out front, and they sell over seven hundred types of soda." Riley pauses, and looks at me with a plea on her face. "They even have salad at the restaurant."

I chuckle. She's appealing to the health-driven side of me.

"Low blow, Sunshine."

Madeline looks at me funny. I shrug. I like the nickname. It suits Riley.

I already know we're stopping, and I'm trading my steak dinner for whatever Riley's about to ask.

Ben abandoned the driver's seat about fifteen minutes ago, killing the engine and joining us in the back of the van. It's obvious we're going nowhere for a while. It's over ninety degrees outside and the van is only slightly cooler after running the A/C while we were driving. With the engine off, it's getting stuffy in here quickly.

Ben suggests we use this time while we're stuck to look up

options as to where we'll spend the night if we don't go as far as Amarillo. I agree, since I'm relatively sure we're not making it to the Big Texan tonight. I'm considering whether I'd eat steak for breakfast. Hands down, I would.

Madeline and Ben whip out their phones. Riley looks out the windows and then picks hers up too.

"If we make it to Pops, we'll be less than a half-hour away from the Tiger Safari where you can sleep in a yurt like you're in Africa with the wild animals only yards away." Riley says. "If we weren't in such a hurry, we could sleep there."

"Sleeping with tigers?" I ask.

"Not right with them. Just near them."

"I'd sleep with one eye open for sure. Nope. I'd sleep with both eyes open."

"Dude, that's not called sleeping," Ben says.

"Exactly."

Ben says, "Hey, Elk City is halfway between here and Amarillo. It's an actual town. We could stay there."

He's scrolling options and then he smiles. He pulls up a video on his phone.

"Guys! We have to do this. We have to!"

Madeline says, "What?" Ben hands her the phone, and she says, "Yes! We have to!"

I remind Ben. "It's Riley's day to call the stops. If she agrees to this, we'll have to do it. But if she says no, in all fairness, it's a no."

Riley takes Ben's phone from him, watches the video, looks up at Ben and says, "Oh, yeah we do. We totally have to do that."

Meanwhile, helicopters circle overhead with news station channel numbers on their side panels. They're obviously filming something we can't see.

"See if you can pull up a news feed so we can see what the hold up is here," I suggest.

Madeline finds a livestream.

"A cow? All this is for a cow?" Madeline says. Then she adds, "Lulabelle would be proud."

Lulabelle's one of the cows in Bordeaux that continually breaks free from the ranch where she lives and meanders through town. She's never caused a freeway shutdown, though. This is pretty epic, even for Lulabelle's standards.

This cow or bull is running along, darting on and off the freeway and honest-to-goodness cowboys with lassos are chasing it. A few guys in tractors are on the chase too. They're dressed like you'd expect ranch hands to be, and they are closing in on the fugitive bovine. The cow darts left and runs until it's almost cornered, but then zig-zags to the right. We're all huddled around Madeline so we can watch over her shoulder as the scene unfolds on her cell.

"Hey!" she exclaims. "There we are! That's the roof of our van. She's only a little bit behind us."

Riley stands to look out the window of the van door toward the access road which runs alongside this section of the highway. On screen, the cow is running from the access road to the strip of grass that edges along the freeway, then toward the highway, and back again. The newscaster is giving a play-by-play from the helicopter. "She's going toward the highway. Oh. Nope. She ran back toward the side road. Come on, guys! Get ahead of her."

He sounds more like a sportscaster for the NFL than a news man reporting a cow on the loose.

Then he says, "Okay. Okay! It looks like they've got her cornered. He's going for it. Get 'er! Get 'er."

On screen, just to the side of our van and one lane over, we watch as one of the cowboys lassoes the cow. They try to get her to lie down, but she's bucking, obviously resisting the abrupt end to her impromptu outing. One cowboy hops out of his saddle. Then a man who had been riding on one of the tractors joins him to help attempt to subdue the cow.

"They need to hogtie her," I say to no one in particular.

Before I have much time to think, I swing the van door open. We've been sitting stock still for over forty minutes. We won't be moving until this is resolved. I make eye contact with the driver of the SUV in the slow lane next to us, cross in front of her and walk through the grass toward the access road. I can hear my friends shouting from behind me, especially Ben.

Ben's saying, "Dude. Where are you going? Cam! Come back here."

When I approach the scene where the men have the cow lassoed, I nod to the cowboy still on his horse. He's holding his steed and has control of the other man's horse as well.

There are some benefits to growing up in the sticks. This is one of them. I know cows.

"Need a hand?" I ask.

I hear Ben jogging up behind me. "Cam? What gives?"

"We just need to lay her down. Then we can tie her until the trailer gets here," the man on the horse says.

"We can help," Ben offers. I nod in agreement.

The two cowboys circle the cow whose eyes are wild from her adventure. Probably the awareness of all she's been through has suddenly hit her. She's definitely jacked up on adrenaline. I figure these men know cattle infinitely better than I do, but I've spent some summers working local dairies and ranches over the years, so if they need me I could pitch in.

"Let's get her to the grass," one of the men suggests.

The man holding the lasso starts to lead her over. The cow

probably has slowed down enough to recognize a food source. She surprisingly gives up her previous fight relatively easily.

Once we're in the grass, I suggest, "I'm no expert, but maybe we do what they do after birthing? We could run the rope under her front quarters and coax her into a lying position."

"Good call," the man not holding the lasso says.

The cow is now grazing like she's got all the time in the world to hang out while the freeway sits full of travelers unable to move because of her escapades.

Ben and I stand out of the way while the cowboys run the rope under her belly and then give it a tug once it's up near her shoulder blades. I hold her eyes as she surrenders and lies down. One of the men on a tractor walks over to the cow and hogties her four legs together.

"Thanks a bunch. We appreciate you being here to give us some back up, " one of the men says to me.

"Not a problem," I say, turning to Ben and walking with him back to the van.

"Man, that was awesome! You think we got to be on TV?"

I laugh. Of course he wants to be on TV.

I hop into the passenger seat. Ben gets into the driver's seat. Mads and Riley start peppering us with questions and excited comments about us going out there.

"You were on the news!" Mads says. "That guy in the helicopter said, *What's this? We've got a civilian walking over to the scene. Wait, there's another one. I hope they know what they're doing. Seems like one of them's saying something to the cowboys.* Then he just went on about the cow going to the grass and the man tying her legs so she wouldn't get away again."

"It pays to have worked on a farm," I say. "Obviously, they knew what they were doing. I just figured they might need an extra hand."

"We're micro-famous!" Ben says.

"What even is that?" I ask. "How can fame be micro? If you're famous, it means people know about you."

"Welp. Around here, they do now."

"Yeah. You better get yourself a shirt that says, *I'm the guy who stood by while they hogtied old runaway Bessie.*"

"We weren't just standing around. We were on standby—their second line of defense. We showed that cow she was outnumbered."

"You tell yourself that," I joke.

Ben starts the ignition. We're still in a virtual parking lot, but apparently there's a little movement ahead.

I look over my shoulder at Riley. For some reason, her reaction matters. She's beaming at me. She doesn't say anything, but her smile makes me feel like a hero. It's every big brother's dream to have his little sister look up to him. This feels like that, but oddly different.

"Let's check out Pops," I say.

"I bet you can get another bacon soda," Ben teases.

"Maybe just a diet coke."

Madeline says, "No way! We're not going to a place with seven hundred sodas and you walk out with a diet coke."

"Let's play Road Trip Bingo!" Riley suggests, saving me from being prescribed another weird soda.

Though, I'm sure once we're there I'll be subjected to the whims of these three.

Riley whips out the printed cards from her backpack as the traffic starts to slowly roll forward. This time, I'm not distracted by driving, so I can focus. I fully intend to win the right to choose our stops tomorrow, and I'm counting on a game that's at least fifty percent determined by chance to make it happen.

Pops 66 is a fun stop. It's surrounded by open land on all sides. The large soda bottle isn't lit yet since we still have some time before the sun sets. We're all ready for a bathroom break, and it's as good a place as any to top off the gas. Of course, the main attraction is the soda—that and the wall with shelves full of old-fashioned candy. We decide to wait to eat.

Riley stocks up on some sodas at the cash register. There's an entire section of the fridge called the Sodasgusting section. They've got buffalo wing soda and beef jerky soda. Then there are more sweet flavors like peanut butter & jelly, maple bacon and sweet corn. Sweet corn. I picture guzzling a can of creamed corn and nearly throw up a little in my mouth. Why? Just why would anyone in their right mind make that soda? Still, if there were a way to ship it, I'd send Duke a can to make him laugh.

They've got coffee soda, which seems redundant to me. Peanut butter and jelly? No. I love a good PBJ, but when I picture dunking that sandwich in soda, I have to pass. There are also a few flavors that don't sound so bad, like butterscotch and lemon meringue pie.

We're back on the road after about a half hour at Pops—which included taking photos inside along the wall of sodas, and more photos outside by the giant pop bottle.

Ben still wants to drive, and Madeline begs for a turn riding shotgun, so I'm in the back seat with Riley. I only need to check off two more squares before I win at today's Bingo. I'm hoping everyone's distracted with their sweets and drinks for long enough that I can win this and secure my spot as tomorrow's guide.

Riley puts four sodas in the mini fridge and passes me one that's pear flavored.

"It'll almost be like drinking a pear juice, only bubbly."

"What? No dreadlocks surprise? No buffalo wings?"

"Oh, we got buffalo wings. We're all splitting that one. It's a rite of passage. You must drink the buffalo wing soda or we'll let you out here and you walk a mile."

Welcome back, sassy Riley. It's not that her shy side isn't

intriguing. It is. I'm just baffled as to why she'd be shy around me. We're practically family. Still she can be so hot and cold—not cold, exactly. Just aloof or tongue-tied. And then, with barely a moments' notice, this playful side shows up. It keeps things interesting, if nothing else.

"You might want to hold out on that pear soda and save it as a chaser for this one. Who knows what a soda named after a chicken appetizer will taste like."

"I could go to my grave happily never knowing the answer to that."

"And yet, you won't. Will you?"

She glances over at me with this mischievous look in her eyes. Her lips pucker slightly and she bats her lashes slowly.

"Huh? No. No, I won't."

I don't know if it's the way time seems to morph when you travel. Hours either blow by or drag. A day feels like a week. A morning passes like a minute. Lines blur. People feel like they've suddenly become your world. I glance up at Ben and Madeline sitting in the front seats. They don't seem different to me. Ben's still my crazy, loyal, goofball of a best friend. My sister's still my sister. I look back at Riley. She seems different. I can't put my finger on why or what changed. It's like she's just another girl, not my surrogate sister. And if she were just another girl, she's definitely not average. She's ...

I shake my head.

"Give me the soda and let's get this over with," I say.

"That's what I thought," she says.

And then she licks her lips. Not intentionally, she just does it. Riley has lips. She's always had lips, obviously. Why am I studying them like I'm about to do something I shouldn't? Her lips are soft and full, naturally a rosy pink except a little sheen from where she just wet them. *She's Riley*, my inner voice of reason reminds me.

Riley hands the soda over to me and our fingers brush when I take it from her. Our eyes lock. She pulls her hand back and wipes the condensation onto her shorts. I track the movement, and then look in her eyes again.

"Stop stalling, and drink," she says, oblivious to the situation she's put me in.

What am I thinking?

I crack off the lid with the bottle opener Riley hands me and take a swig.

Gah! I should have taken a sip, not a full gulp. Man. This tastes like watered down, bubbly barbecue sauce. Trust me, if that sounds at all good, I'm not doing the disgusting taste in my mouth justice.

"Gross!" I exclaim. "So gross! Who makes this? And why? Ugh! This is so nasty. I'm going to be tasting bubbly chicken wing aftertaste when I burp!"

Madeline, Ben, and Riley all laugh.

"You're laughing now. It's your turn next."

I hand the bottle to Riley. She looks me in the eye and puts it to her lips. Then she takes a chug. Her throat bobs. She pulls the bottle away and licks her lips.

"Ewwww. Yeah. Not my favorite. This is just ... wrong."

She unbuckles, walks up to the front seats and hands the bottle to Madeline and Ben. They both take turns drinking and shouting about how disgusting the soda is. Meanwhile, I spot one of my last two Bingo items outside the van.

I shout out. "Fifty-five miles per hour!"

"I'm only going sixty. Chillax, Gramps," Ben answers.

"No," I say with a chuckle. "I got another square on my Bingo card."

"Bingo!" Madeline calls out.

"What? Noooo!" I cry out.

"Oh yeah, Baby! I got Bingo. All I needed was the speed limit!"

"I'll drink to that," Riley says, lifting her lemon cream pie soda into the air.

I lift my bottle of pear soda and we clink the necks of our bottles together.

15

RILEY

In life, it's not where you go—
it's who you travel with.
~ Charles Schulz

It's after seven when we pull off the highway to make our way into Elk City. Because it's summer, the heat is hanging on, and the sun will stay out for at least another hour or so. We're all hungry and ready to see something besides the inside of my van—regardless of how awesome this van is. I still can barely believe it's mine.

"Let's go to Mountain Man's. We can get food there too. We'll find a room for the night afterward," Ben suggests.

"Sounds good," Cam agrees.

The road takes us past a few scattered older farms and some rural businesses which seem to be closed or relocated. Mostly, it's more wide open space with trees here and there. Another small American town. Stop lights hang from overhead lines at the intersection. On the corner across the street sits a gray building that looks like an old Seed-N-Feed, with a matching barn style roof. The parking lot is mostly empty. It is a weekday, so that makes some sense. The front of the building has an image of a bearded man wearing a pelt hat with the animal head still attached. The caption says, *Bury the Hatchet at Mountain Man's.*

I already love this place. This. This is what we're supposed to do on our trip—drive into unknown towns we didn't plan to visit, find a place where the locals hang out, and have a night of unexpected fun. The inside of Mountain Man's has a few long wood tables, and a waist-high wrought iron fence separating the eating/viewing area from the axe throwing section.

Yes. Axe Throwing!

We are doing this!

We order a Hatchet Jack pizza and garlic knots to split, and Cam, bless his heart, gets a salad with grilled chicken. We all decided we couldn't stomach any chicken wings after that pop this afternoon. I'm trying not to stand too close to him, or look at him, or catch his eye, or smell his very manly, very Cameron scent right now. After sitting with him in the back seat, I don't know what to think or feel. He seemed to be ... I don't know. I'm sure he wasn't doing what I wished he were. It's probably all because of that crazy dream—which also is playing on an uninvited infinite loop in my brain. *You've been driving me crazy. I want to kiss you. I need you, Riley. I need to kiss you now.*

After we've signed waivers and had our professional coaching session on how to throw an axe, we take our spots in two of the "caves" in the main room. We are taking turns in Bear Cave One. Madeline and I sit on stools behind the little wrought iron fence while the guys stand side by side facing their two targets. Cam throws first. I'm not the least bit surprised when he gets a bullseye. Is there nothing he does poorly? He's perfection. I cheer and whoop and shout, "Way to stick it!" Madeline looks at me with a curious look. I dial it way back and tell myself to go just as crazy when Ben lands his throw.

Ben throws and the axe hits the target, but a few inches off to the side of center. I jump off my stool and throw my hands in the air, screaming, "Go, Ben! Woot woot!"

Madeline looks over at me. "What is wrong with you?"

She's smiling, but her look tells me she thinks I drank a pop laced with something mood altering back at Pops. Not that they sell mood-altering sodas there. I'm pretty sure they don't.

"I'm just encouraging them," I say.

She laughs and shakes her head.

Cam throws again. He hits the mark on the target, of course. I clap like I'm at the opera, soft and dignified. "Well done, Cameron," I say softly.

"Oh for Pete's sakes. Seriously?" Madeline says.

"What? Too tame?"

"Yes, Goldilocks. Find your happy middle ground, you loon."

Ben throws. He gets closer to the bullseye this time.

I let out a simple, "Go, Ben!"

Madeline turns to me and nods. "I knew you could do it."

"I feel like a dog on a leash," I tell her.

"I'll give you a treat when the food gets here."

The guys throw one more time and then swap out so Madeline and I can try our hands at this. Madeline's so focused, her tongue peeks out. It's super cute, and I tell her as much. She does about as well as Ben. He whoops for her, and Cam says, "Good going, Mads."

I throw and my axe hits the wall above the target and then it bounces back. I duck and cover my head, curling into a standing ball—as if that's going to protect me from a boomeranging blade.

My axe lands with a thud in the middle of the plywood cave. I walk over and pick it up.

Ben is cracking up. Mads too. Cam quietly asks if I'm okay.

I totally am. And I'm going to make this axe my minion. It will do my bidding before we leave this place.

Madeline throws again. She's not as close to the bullseye, but she still hits the target.

I say, "Way to go, Mads!"

She says, "That's all you're going to cheer for me?"

"You said dial it back," I say with a wink. "Besides, I have to focus and get my axe game on. This is serious business."

"Just don't end up in the hospital tonight."

"Har har. Now be quiet so I can get in the zone."

The guys are chanting my name from their place behind the fence. I pause to take in the sound of Cameron saying, "Ri-ley! Ri-ley! Ri-ley."

I focus, holding the axe the way they taught us, using a two-handed grip, not too tight, not too loose. I close one eye and line the axe up with that magical dot at the other side of this cave. I silently repeat what the coach said: *Lean back, raise over-head, release in front of you.* When I let go, I close my eyes, afraid of the returning axe. Of course, my eyes should be open, but shutting them is a reflex—as if not seeing the axe sailing back to me will be better than watching my impending doom sail at me from midair. I hear a solid thunk, and then the shouts of my friends. Even some employees and another couple who walked in a minute ago start cheering. I pop one eye open to glance at the outcome of my throw and then I start jumping around like a Bruins' cheerleader, throwing my arms overhead and bending my knees in a tuck and then a double hook.

Yes. I hit the very outer edge of the target. No. I did not make a bullseye. I'm about as far from a bullseye as you can be without falling right off the circle, but I'm on there.

The coach comments, "That's about the most excited I've ever seen someone over a near miss."

"Thank your lucky stars she didn't get a bullseye," Cam tells him. "She'd be running around kissing everyone in the place in celebration."

He looks at me and winks. I almost pray for a bullseye—if it's a ticket to kiss Cam, I'd kiss that old man and his wife at the corner table to have my one chance with him. Not exactly the scenario I've dreamed up over the years for our first kiss, but I'd take it.

Needless to say, I never throw a bullseye. Madeline gets close. We eat our pizza. It's beyond delicious. And the bread knots? Well, you just have to be a complete buffoon in the kitchen to mess up something made with bread, butter, herbs and garlic. And they did not mess these up. No they did not.

Cam happily eats his salad while we indulge in carbs and fat. We finally taunt him into eating a bread knot, and when he does, he actually closes his eyes in bliss. I'm so dumbfounded by the expression on his face, I can't even find the words to tease him. I'd like to see that look on his face after a night spent kissing under the stars. And I need to lasso that thought and hogtie it, for sure. There will be no kissing Cameron Reeves, so there's no use letting thoughts like that run loose like a cow on the access road. Back to your pen, wayward thoughts!

We leave Mountain Man's, bellies full and smiles on our faces. I'm hooked on axe throwing. It's like bowling, but way more dangerous and hilarious. Though, as you'd suspect, I can be a lethal weapon with a bowling ball. Sports aren't really my thing—except swimming. I do love to swim. And cycling. Those are more my speed. And now, axe throwing. I smile at the thought.

We stop at the first hotel we saw on the way into town. Cam gets out and asks about a reservation for the night. The clerk tells him they're unusually full because of some Ranch, Farm & Livestock Expo going on this week. She also tells him, "Good luck finding a room," as he turns to leave the lobby.

He reports all this to us when he pulls open the passenger door to hop back into the van.

We drive to two more hotels while Mads and I search travel reservation websites for availability. They are both full.

"Should we drive on to Amarillo and make a late night of it?" Ben suggests. "I've got energy to spare after that axe throwing and pizza pitstop."

"You say that now, but this day is bound to catch up with you."

"We could trade off driving."

"I'll drive," I offer.

"You sure?" Cam asks, looking back at me.

"Yeah. I'm good to drive for two hours. If I get drowsy, I'll tell you."

"I'll ride shotgun to keep you awake," Cam says.

We all agree, so I hop out of the back and swap spots with Ben. He may have said he's ready to drive, but it's nearing nine and he drove a lot today. As soon as he's settled in the back seat, he grabs a pillow and puffs it next to the window so he can lean on it.

"Look at Mister Wide-awake," I whisper to Cam.

He looks back fondly at Ben and shakes his head. "He would have muscled through, but there's no need for heroics. We've got this."

"Yeah, we do," I say, loving the sound of the word *we* coming out of Cam's mouth.

I'm too tired and happy to try to fight my attraction right now. I'll resist more tomorrow when I'm rested and have coffee running through my veins.

We're barely fifteen minutes into the drive to Amarillo when Mads and Ben fall fast asleep in the backseat.

I don't know what possesses me. Maybe it's the darkness surrounding us, or the residual high from axe throwing, but I ask Cam a question that's been nagging at me since lunch yesterday. Was that only yesterday? Sheesh.

"So," I try to keep my tone easy-breezy, casual as can be. "This friend you have in St. Louis must be pretty special for you to have taken your break to visit."

Cam's entire demeanor changes. He had been relaxed—his face calm, eyes softly focused on the road ahead. He's never completely at ease, but he was pretty chill. When I mentioned his friend, his shoulders went stiff. I think I even see a tick in his jaw, which is definitely clenched a little.

He's quiet for a beat and then he says, "Hey, we should call our parents. We didn't think of that earlier. It's an hour later there, too."

I look over at Cam. I'm not nervous—either that, or my curiosity is overriding my nerves.

"So, I hit a nerve? Your friend is a pretty uncomfortable subject? I can drop it."

I have a hunch who this *friend* is, and his reaction only serves to confirm my suspicions.

Cam's head turns toward the passenger door so I only see the back of him.

"Let's call our parents," I suggest.

I shouldn't have pushed. I didn't realize how much this would bother him.

"Stephanie," he says, turning back toward me. "Her name was Stephanie. Is. I guess. I mean, it's still her name."

"I take it she was a special friend."

"Girlfriend, yeah."

"Sorry."

"Yeah."

Cam's quiet. I focus on the road, giving him space for whatever he's feeling. He's a vault when it comes to private matters. I'm surprised he even gave me what he did. And, I can't say I feel too great having nearly forced him to talk about it.

After about fifteen minutes of deafening silence, Cam turns to me. "She was my girlfriend for two years. Came to San Diego from St. Louis. We met through friends at the beginning of our sophomore year. After a while, I asked her out. She said yes. We became inseparable."

Now I really regret asking. As much as I want Cam to spill his heart to me, spilling about another woman isn't really what I had in mind. But I opened Pandora's Box, so I get to deal with the contents.

"I wasn't the only one interested in her at the time we started dating. As a matter of fact, four friends including me all professed our intentions to ask her out to one another one night over a friendly game of poker."

He chuckles at the memory, but it's not a full laugh, more one filled with bitter irony.

"We didn't know how bro code applied when none of us were dating her and we all had feelings at the same time, so we played cards to see who won the rights to ask her out."

"No way! That's so ..."

"I know. But we didn't know what to do. And luck was a lady that night—at least for me she was. I won. The other three said they'd back off until I struck out. They were that confident I would."

He shakes his head.

I try to imagine what it would be like to be the woman four guys played cards over. The thought disturbs me and thrills me in equal measure. More than that, I can't fathom what a woman would have to be like to incite this kind of competitiveness and desire in four friends. I suddenly feel self-conscious. I'm riding next to Cam wearing only jean shorts and an old T-shirt with my favorite pair of Converse. I'm not ugly. I'm more—forgettable. Obviously.

"So, I asked Stephanie out the next week. I was going to ask her out that Monday, but I chickened out. Tuesday, I realized it wasn't going to get less intimidating. I approached her at the Student Union while she was eating lunch. She offered me a seat. I joined her and her friends. After lunch, I offered to carry her tray to the trash. While she followed me, I casually asked what she was doing that weekend. She said she was just planning on studying and hanging out with her friends. I invited her to an open mic night at a campus hangout. She said yes."

He's staring ahead like a bigger piece of him is back in that moment than here in the van with me.

"I didn't act excited or show her how I felt right then. I just said, *Cool. I'll see you Saturday. I'll pick you up at seven*. But inside I was freaking out. I texted Ben as soon as I walked out of the Union. He called me back and flipped out enough for both of us. Thankfully, he wasn't one of the four guys with a crush on her. That would have killed me. Ben and I, as close as we are, have never fallen for the same woman. I don't know what I'd do if that ever happened."

"You're so totally different. He's so ... Ben. And you're so ... you probably have different tastes."

It's the first thing I've said since I first pushed this subject into the light. My voice feels foreign and sounds like a pin popping a balloon. Cam doesn't seem to notice.

"Anyway, that was the beginning of two years of dating Stephanie. She never came to Bordeaux. I wanted her to meet my family, but she's really tight with her sister and brother, so she wanted to be home every break. I went to St. Louis twice one summer and three times the next. That was the summer before our senior year."

"What happened?" I ask.

Give me a T-shirt that says *Glutton. Glutton for Punishment.* I can't help myself. I don't only have romantic feelings for Cam. I truly care about him, regardless of the way he makes me feel and the things I wish I could have with him. I'm feeling this whole undercurrent as he relays the story of his relationship with Stephanie. If he wants to tell me, I want to listen—to be here for him. Maybe it will help him to talk about it.

"Ha," he laughs out a sort of barking laugh. It's the most caustic sound I've ever heard him make.

He's quiet again. I'm about to tell him he doesn't have to tell me if he doesn't want to when he says, "She found someone more interesting."

I glance over. Cam is running a hand down his face and then raking his fingers through his hair.

"She broke up with you?"

I can't help the note of incredulity in my voice. Who on earth would have him and let him go? I could seriously give this woman a talking to. Not that I want her to have Cam—I mean, her loss, for sure—but I can't imagine being the fool who walked away from him willingly.

Cam glances at me briefly and then turns toward the passenger window. "I broke up with her."

I don't ask. We ride along for a while. I don't know how much time passes. I keep thinking of things to say, and not one of them feels right. I could prod with more questions. It's obvious this story has layers. It's equally evident that he'd tell me if he wanted me to know.

A sign along the road says *Amarillo - 30 miles*.

I turn to Cam. In a soft and careful voice, I say, "She's an idiot."

16

CAMERON

If you make the mistake of looking back too much,
you aren't focused enough on the road in front of you.
~ Brad Paisley

"She's an idiot," Riley says.

I stare into the darkness. "Maybe I am."

She doesn't answer me, and I appreciate that more than she could know. I've listened to Ben telling me it's not my fault for over a year now. I don't need platitudes, though I know Ben means well. What I need is more like what Riley's given me over the past hour or so—silence, and a listening ear.

I look over at Riley. There's barely enough light to make out her features. Still, I'd know it was her. Certain people are so much a part of your life you feel their presence without even having to see them. Riley's like that.

"Tell me five great things about your ex," she says out of the blue.

"What?"

"Tell me five great things about your ex."

"Why?"

"Humor me, hot shot. I just want to know."

"Okaayyy. Um. She was—is—really smart. Book smart more than street smart. She's driven. You know? Straight A's. Pre-med."

"Is that one thing, or three? Or four?"

"It's kind of one thing."

"Okay, four to go."

"Even though she's smart, she knows how to let loose and have fun."

"You say that like it's a bad thing, not a positive trait."

"It was ..."

I think back to Stephanie's words. *You're always on, Cameron. You need to learn to lighten up and have some fun once in a while. It's like I'm dating someone from the House of Lords—so serious. Let loose for once.*

"She didn't think you could let loose?" Riley asks as if she can read my mind.

"Something like that."

"Welp."

"What do you mean, welp? You think I can't let loose?"

"I'm just sayin', you need to work that muscle a little—your fun muscle. But you make up for a lack of spontaneity in other ways."

"What ways?" I'm basically begging for a compliment here. It's pathetic.

"You're a gifted leader. You always consider the big picture. You're goal-oriented. You look out for others. You're loyal. You have fun when you know it's good and safe to do it. But if you think things are going to go sideways, you make sure you and everyone you care about avoids the worst."

She glances over at me. "Sorry, I'm rambling."

"It's okay."

Riley continues. "Think about this trip. We'd probably be broken down somewhere without gas, having forgotten to inform our parents of our progress, and sweating out the night on some wild prairie if it weren't for you. There's a time for fun and a time to be responsible."

She sneaks a glance at me and then looks back at the road. "Besides, who can have fun when someone they care about is making the ability to let loose seem like something you have to prove as if you're earning a Boy Scout merit badge? Fun should be uninhibited. It's like fruit on a well-tended tree."

Riley's voice has gotten faster and faster the more compliments she spewed at me. It's like sharing her view of me made her nervous. It's actually cute when she gets all rattled.

"Thanks. For all of that."

"It's just the truth." Riley pauses and then resumes her odd mission of getting me to talk about Stephanie. "Okay, so she's smart, and she can let loose. Is she beautiful?"

I wish I could see Riley's face right now.

"She's pretty. I mean, yeah. She's attractive."

"Okay. Three down. You're doing this. Two more and you progress to level two."

"Level two?"

"Yeah. Like in a video game. You master level one, you go to level two. So, two more things."

I think. *What was great about Stephanie?* I should be able to come up with two more things. I spent two years of my life with her. I thought I was going to propose to her our senior year before everything blew up. I picture that night. Nothing could have prepared me for what happened. I showed up to surprise her, and there she was, looking at another guy the way she looked at me in the early days of our relationship. When she leaned in to place a kiss on his cheek …

"Cam?"

"Huh?"

"I lost you there. Two more things. She's gotta have two more awesome qualities. Does she floss? Good hygiene? Is she nice to old ladies? Does she do charity work?"

"I already told you she's family-oriented. She loves her siblings." My voice is clipped.

I take a breath. Riley's not the one at fault here. She's just unearthing all this stuff I've conveniently buried.

"Home stretch, Reeves. One more."

"She …" I can't believe how hard this is. And why do I need to even do this? Something about the way Riley's asking for this ridiculous list makes me want to give it to her.

"I've got it. She tutors Freshmen in biology."

"Ding. Ding. Ding!" Riley says quietly, but with animation to her voice. Then, as if she's a WWE announcer, she says, "Ladies and gentlemen, we have a winner. Cameron Reeves finished round one and is progressing to level two."

As serious and uncomfortable as this topic is, somehow Riley makes me laugh.

She continues to use her announcer voice. "Okay. Level two may seem easier on the onset, but it's actually harder in some ways. Are you up to the challenge, Mr. Reeves?"

"I'm up for it. Bring it, Sunshine."

"Okay. Tell us five horrible things about your ex."

"Really?"

"Yep."

"What's the purpose of this?"

"Trust me. I've got my methods, as crazy as they may be. You're already feeling better. Am I right?"

"A little, actually. Yeah."

"So, five things that make her awful."

I skip the obvious. Not sure I'm ready to go there with Riley.

"She can't see the value of a good man when he's committed to her."

My throat feels dry and my eyes almost burn.

"You know, maybe that's enough," I say.

"You need this, Cam. Tell me you've done this with Ben and I'll stop."

"Ben?"

"Yeah. Tell me Ben has gotten you to really share your thoughts about Stephanie."

Stephanie's name sounds wrong coming from Riley's mouth. It's like Stephanie's invading this space—taking over one more thing and ruining it.

"No. Ben and I haven't done this."

"Four more, Cam. You've got this."

"She's self-centered." Understatement.

"She's not really all that fun. And she's definitely not funny."

"Burn!" Riley says. And then she adds, "Mwahahaha. You're doing great. Two more. Make them good—or horrible, as the case may be."

"She belittled my choice of career."

Riley's suddenly quiet. All her playfulness seems to have evaporated in an instant.

When she speaks her voice is soft, like the tone you use with a child who needs comfort.

"Cam."

That's all she says. My name. Not even my whole name. It's the shortened version that only my family and closest friends use.

"Yeah. That did suck."

"I will cut the woman. Are you serious? Your career?"

"You'll do what?" I can't help but chuckle.

"She doesn't deserve you."

"You don't even know her. You're making me paint her in a bad light right now."

"Fair enough, but that last one was a doozie. Sorry. I lost my neutrality for a minute there. I'm back. One more. One more horrible, awful, very bad thing about this ex."

"Ummm … Oh! Yeah. She's not into holidays."

"Sacrilege!" Riley shouts it so loudly that Madeline and Ben stir in the back seat. She sees them rustle around and starts whispering. "Who doesn't like holidays? That's just inhuman. What kind of doctor is she going to be? Don't say pediatrician. It can't be."

"Pediatrician."

"Gah. A pediatrician who hates holidays. Cam. What on earth?"

"I know."

I have to laugh, even though the pain in my heart still feels raw. It's not really Stephanie that I miss anymore. I see that more than ever right now. It's just the fact of what I went through with her—for her.

"I wasted two years," I say quietly.

"Education comes in all forms," Riley says almost to herself.

"What?"

"School of hard knocks, Cameron. You had to endure this breakup. But I bet you learned some valuable lessons."

"I might have. I don't really know what I learned." I look out the window. Then I say, "It wasn't all bad with her."

I don't know why I feel the need to defend Stephanie to Riley right now.

"I'm sure it wasn't. You're hot, smart, funny, thoughtful. You'd be a catch. I'm sure she wasn't the only girl interested in you at school. You stayed with her for a reason. And it wasn't only because you won her in a game of poker."

"I didn't win *her*. Sheesh, Sunshine. You make me sound like some land baron from the eighteen hundreds. I won the chance to ask her out."

"Potato, Po-tah-toe."

"You're ridiculous. You know that, right?"

"I actually do."

And she said I'm hot? Obviously, she's talking objectively. Still, it's been a while since a woman said anything remotely close to that to me.

"You feel better, right?" she asks.

"Actually, yes. I do. Why did that even work?"

"I have no idea."

"You don't?"

"No. I just figured you keep things so bottled up. Letting it out had to help. And I knew asking you directly about her and the breakup would just cause you to throw up walls, so I made up a game."

"Huh."

"Pull up the address. We're exiting into Amarillo in a mile."

I plug the address for the Big Texan into our maps app. Then I turn around and call out to Madeline and Ben. "Time to wake up. We're in Amarillo."

Ben stretches and looks around. Then he answers in a groggy voice. "Already?"

I look over at Riley when she parks the van and mouth, "Thank you."

She smiles an easy smile back at me.

17

CAMERON

One's destination is never a place,
but rather a new way of seeing things.
~ Henry Miller

"We're in Texas!" Riley shouts in her scratchy morning voice.

I love the sound of it for some reason.

She's still in bed. My sister's asleep next to her—soundly snoozing right through the boisterous announcement of our location.

"Yep. We're in Texas, little lady," Ben says in an exaggerated East-Texas accent. "Care for some vittles?"

"No! You don't get it!"

Riley rubs her eyes and surveys the room. We barely took in our surroundings last night when we finally checked in around eleven. The walls and ceiling are wood-paneled in a rustic, knotty pine. The bed frames match, and there are ranching artifacts on the wall. and Navajo woven patterns on the chairs. Even if Riley hadn't shouted, *We're in Texas!,* one look around would give that fact away.

"What's wrong?" Ben asks Riley.

"We missed it! We missed the *Welcome to Texas* sign! We zipped right past it in the dark last night and I didn't even think of it. And now we're an hour and a half past it."

Her shoulders slump. She lets out a huge yawn. I can barely stand the look on her face. She's clearly crestfallen.

"We couldn't have taken a picture at the sign in the dark anyway," I say in an attempt to console her with logic.

"Hello. Flash? Yes we could have. I'll get over it. I just wanted a picture of each one. It's not the same without that one. I mean, it's Texas."

"Have you seen the Welcome to Texas sign?" I ask her. "It's not very big. It's green with the Texas flag on it."

Riley looks at me funny. "How do you know?"

"I might have looked it up."

"Awww. Cam, you looked up welcome signs?"

"I had to know what we're up against—for the sake of planning."

She smiles over at me. But her smile's short-lived. She's really upset about this. I get it. I collected quarters as a kid. Missing one meant the collection would remain incomplete until I had every single state in my tri-fold album where I displayed them all.

I don't know what motivates my next actions or words. Maybe I'm sleep deprived. It could be the look on Riley's face right now.

I walk over and sit on the edge of her bed. She collapses back onto her pillow.

"I'll bring you back here sometime." I promise. "We'll stop at that sign and get a picture."

She looks at me like what I said is actually as crazy as it sounded.

"Or not," I add.

"You'd do that? When?"

"I don't know. Maybe it's far-fetched. I mean, when are the four of us taking this trip again?"

She nods. "It's okay. I'll really get over it. I know it's silly. It was just one of my things on this trip."

"And you've made it our thing. I wish we could have gotten that photo."

"I'm just going to have to realize I'm chronicling reality. And, reality was that we missed that sign."

"It was still a good drive," I say.

She nods up at me, the memory of our conversation obviously on both our minds.

"We could green screen it," Ben suggests.

"What?" Riley asks.

"You know. We'll get a green screen, take our photo, then we can pop a shot of that welcome sign in the background. Bam! You've got your Texas state line photo."

Riley laughs enough that her eyes crinkle up. "I'll think about it, okay?"

She yawns again.

"You need more sleep," I tell her.

Her hair is mussed and I have the oddest urge to brush it off her cheek. I'm not sure if this is some sort of therapeutic transference where I now feel something for Riley because she helped me yesterday, or what's going on right now.

Why would I suddenly be drawn to Riley?

She's obviously beautiful, so it's no wonder I have a primal reaction to her. I'm a guy. We notice beauty. As attractive as Riley is, that's not what's got my attention right now.

I take a breath, reminding myself this is Riley. She's my baby sister's best friend. She's as good as family to me. And I'm a mess—as evidenced by all the facts she pulled out of me on the drive last night. I'm in no place to entertain thoughts about a woman, especially not Riley.

Riley turns her big brown eyes on me and gives me this soft smile. The urge to kiss her takes me by such surprise I practically shoot off the bed like a bottle rocket just to avoid acting on it.

"Are you okay?" she asks.

She has no idea. I'm not okay. Not at all. I'm having thoughts and feelings I definitely shouldn't have about her. I have to sort this out. I can't be looking at Riley like she's some other girl. She's so much more than that.

"I'm okay. Just need to ... I'll be back." I move toward the restroom even though I only used it fifteen minutes ago. Before I step inside, I say, "Ben and I are getting breakfast. Do you want to sleep some more or come with us?"

"I think I could sleep. Will you bring food back?"

"Sure. I'll get something full of carbs and grease to go."

"Mmmmm," she says in a happily drowsy voice that is not helping my situation in the least.

I shut the door of the bathroom and lean back on it. *Get a grip, Cam.* My breathing comes more quickly than usual. *What is happening to me? One night of her helping me face my breakup and now I feel like this?*

I turn on the faucet and flush.

Should I have flushed first? I think usually the sound of the flush comes first. Maybe they won't notice. I dry my unwashed hands and walk out of the bathroom. Riley and Mads are asleep in their bed. Or at least Riley's fast on her way to sleeping again. Her face looks peaceful—breathtaking. She is breathtaking. It's okay if I know that about her. Last night she said I was hot. It's an observation. I don't have to do anything about it.

Ben's looking at me with a completely amused look on his face.

"What?" I ask.

"Nothing. Let's get breakfast."

"Yes. Food. Sounds good."

About seven minutes down the road from the Big Texan is a restaurant called Youngblood's Cafe. The outside of the building is tan and nondescript, but the parking lot is full—always a good sign when it comes to picking a spot to eat.

The interior is wood—wood walls, wooden tables, wooden cashier counter. A buffalo head stares down over the tables from one wall, rifles hang on another, there's a brick fireplace with a hearth, and various Texas memorabilia covers spaces all around. Long tables and smaller ones fill the room and booths line either side of the walls.

The hostess approaches us. "Welcome to Youngblood's. Two fer breakfast?"

"Yes, ma'am," Ben chimes in. "Um. Lacey, ma'am."

She smiles over at him. "You aren't local. Passin' through Amarilluh?"

"Yes, ma'am. We're staying at the Big Texan on our way to California."

"Shame," she says with a wink at Ben.

Never one to know a stranger, Ben continues the conversation. "Shame we're passing through, or shame we're going to California?"

"I'd imagine both. I've never been to California. I don't have any desire to neither."

She doesn't take Ben up on his obvious attempt at fishing for a compliment.

"Okay, handsome. Here's yer menu. Coffee's on me this mornin'."

She hands me my menu with a smile.

"Why thank you, Lacey. That's awfully sweet," Ben says.

He's using that voice. It's one-hundred percent different from the voice he uses with me.

"Oh, I can be real sweet, handsome. Don't you know it."

She gives Ben a wink and sashays off. I stare at Ben, shaking my head.

"What?" Ben says, looking at me. "It's harmless fun. You should try it sometime. She knows I'm passing through. I know she's flirting. We both feel good about ourselves. No harm, no foul."

"Are you sure?"

"Sure about what?"

"No harm, no foul."

"We both are playing. It's fun. No one's hurt. What's with you this morning? Like, why'd you duck into the bathroom and fake going a second time after sitting on Riley's bed? And why did your face look like you saw a ghost? You're acting weird—even for you."

"What's that supposed to mean?"

"It's like your usual uptightness, but magnified times fifty. Did something happen between you and Riley while Madeline and I were innocently sleeping in the back of the van?"

Ben wags his eyebrows like I have some salacious story to tell.

"Riley? She's Riley, Ben. And what could even have happened? We were driving."

He smirks at me. "I don't know, but something sure did."

"She got me talking about Steph, that's all."

"Wheweeee. How'd she do that?"

"I talk."

"Yeah. You're a regular blabbermouth. You broke up a year ago and all I got was the bullet point version of what happened the night you thought you were going to take things to the next level. And then a little more dripped out over time, but it's been like pulling teeth. I'm not complaining. I know you. I get it. It's not like we're going to sit braiding one another's hair while we talk about our feeeeelings." He cups his hands under his chin and bats his lashes. "But seriously, I know the breakup has continued to eat at you. Maybe it's what's keeping you from a little harmless flirtation with a waitress here and there."

"Nope."

"Yeah. Nope, is right. Face it. Even on your best day, you'll never be as charming as me."

"You who are also single."

"Right. By choice, for now. I might have fun making women feel good about themselves. Innocent flirting. Nothing else for now. I'll know when someone warrants more. And I'll bring it then. You can count on it. None of this ducking into bathrooms to pretend to relieve myself when I've got feelings for a woman."

"Who says I've got feelings?"

He just stares at me. Then he makes a show of lifting his menu and rattling off options he's considering ordering.

I look at the menu even though I know what I'm going to order. A loud burst of laughter fills the room as a group of older men gathered around a large center table crack up over whatever one of them said. It's a scene that's all too familiar. We may be in Texas, but I can tell these men probably grew up together. They might have raised their families together, or worked for one another. Now, they meet at Youngbloods for coffee or breakfast—maybe daily, could be a few times a week. Seeing them almost makes me homesick. But then I think of Marbella Island and my future in resort management. I'll have something different—something I chose and pursued for myself. And Ben will be with me—pain in the rear that he is.

"It's not feelings," I say again.

"I'm getting Huevos Rancheros."

He completely ignores me.

"And you're getting egg whites scrambled, with a side of whatever vegetable or fruit they have." He pauses. "Oh! And I need biscuits and gravy. I'm pretty sure a place like this knows how to make some biscuits that'll be worth eating."

He's all nonchalant and casual. I know he's trying to get a rise out of me.

"So, how 'bout them Astros?" I ask.

"Shut up!" Ben cracks up. "You have feelings. Just bend. Give me something here. I slept through the good stuff. I'm dying, Cam. You and Riley. This is so classic."

"First of all, there's no *me and Riley*. Second of all, it's not classic, whatever that means. And third. No. You're acting like a seventh grader discussing who likes who. We're grown men—about to go into our first job to launch our careers. There's no *me and Riley*."

Ben stares at me like he's calling my bluff.

"You're so extreme," I say. "You always jump into the deep end. Feelings. We left Ohio two days ago. How would I have feelings that I didn't have then?"

"Call it what you will," Ben says. "But it's not nothing."

The waitress, bless her heart, shows up at this moment with two cups of black coffee.

"Hey, sugar," she says to Ben.

What's with this guy? On one hand, I'm used to it. But then again, can you ever really get used to people reacting to your best friend like he's a movie star?

"Well, hey there, uh … Felicia. What a beautiful name."

She titters. What on earth? It's an actual titter, like she can't control herself in Ben's presence. Meanwhile, I sit here like yesterday's mashed potatoes at the back of the fridge. It's crazy. I'm hot. Riley even said so.

Riley.

RILEY'S JOURNAL

July 26th

Hey Gladys,

Two more days until I turn twenty-one. No one has mentioned my birthday, so I won't either. I can just quietly slip into official adulthood. Maybe no one will notice. I'll celebrate with you, Gladys. I wish I could really celebrate with you.

Remember those cakes Mom used to make before Dad or someone finally convinced her my fave was from Oh, Sugar!? Some women are bakers. Others, not so much. She made up for it in enthusiasm—Okay. She totally didn't make up for it, but she *was* enthusiastic. They were horrible though, weren't they? I mean. How do you mess up cake? But she did.

And Dad would choke down a piece every year, always saying, "Mmmmm," afterward. I bet he'd have said more if he weren't battling choking on dry crumbs. They sort of reminded me of kitchen sponges that had been left out too long. Maybe that's why they call some cakes sponge cake. I sure hope not.

Besides the ever-looming reminder that I'm one year closer to official adulthood without being any closer to having a clue about what I want to be when I grow up, I did drive the van last night. Everyone seemed to need a break. And I felt like getting to know her. She needs a name, but I haven't found one that fits her quite yet.

Names are so important. Like Cameron. Yes, Gladys. I'm still fighting my attraction, but when it's late and you're alone together driving, it's a little hard to put up a fight.

Did you know Cameron's name means *crooked nose*? I'm relatively certain his parents had no clue. It's a Scottish name. And I'm figuring in Scotland having a crooked nose means you held your own in a fight. Who knows? Cameron's nose is perfect, not crooked at all. That word crooked doesn't apply to one thing about him.

Just tell me, Gladys. Where's the off switch for my feelings? If you know, send me a sign.

Last night, I got him talking about his ex. Her name was Stephanie. I will forever have a hard time smiling at women with that name after what Cam told me. I'm sure some Stephanie out there is wonderful. Maybe many are. They'll have to prove it. Her name has been ruined for me. She belittled his career, after all. Who does that? Stephanie. That's who.

I can tell she broke his heart. They were together for two years. All that time, and I was just two hours north of him, willing to be something she couldn't. He said she was attractive. I'm sure she was more than that if four guys fought to have a chance at dating her. The photos of her on Cam's social media are pretty.

Am I jealous? You know I am. But, you'd be so proud. I never let Cam know how envious I was. I actually care about him—it's not just attraction for me.

So, I set all these confusing, unrelenting feelings aside and focused on helping him. He said I did help. That meant the world to me.

Maybe Madeline's right. I just need to date someone. I've been keeping myself on hold for Cameron, as crazy as that sounds. I knew there'd never be any hope for us. Even if he somehow, one day, saw me as more than a second little sister, there's still the reality that Mads would lose it if we started dating. Which we aren't. Maybe she'd get over it. But, knowing Madeline, she would feel betrayed. The last thing I want to do to her is betray her.

I will say it felt great to help him bleed the wound about his ex, though. Maybe friendship is all Cam and I will ever have. I'll have to take what I can get with him.

I'll tell you this, Gladys. For your ears only. Sitting in that front seat while he rode alongside me, laughing and sharing his thoughts and feelings—it's probably the highlight of the trip for me. I've got a bucket list of places and things I want to see and experience, but not one of them measures up to having Cam drop his walls for a few hours with me.

Madeline's waking. We're going to hit the road again soon, I think. We've got planning to do—the four of us—and then another day of adventures.

I'll always love you, Gladys, and miss you more the longer you're gone. I bet you'd love all these old main streets. If you look at any of them just right, you can imagine them in their heyday. I bet you'd like that.

Written in Amarillo ... in a room you'd love very much ... sitting up next to a sleeping girl whom you love with your whole heart.

18

RILEY

Most of us are always in haste
to reach somewhere else,
forgetting that the zest is in the journey
and not in the destination.
~ Ralph D Paine

"What time is it?" Madeline asks, rolling over and looking at me.

I've got two pillows stuffed behind my back. I'm still in my pjs, and I've been journaling while I let her sleep. The guys are still at breakfast, but Ben just texted that they are on their way back with food.

I close my journal and turn to look at the clock.

"It's nine fifteen."

"What? I slept in so late."

"You needed it."

"I don't see why. All I've done is sit in the back of the van and get out to eat, pee, or buy something."

"Travel. It takes it out of you in its own special way."

"Well, I'd better get ready."

She says that, but makes no effort to move.

We chat for a bit, and it feels so right. I haven't had enough one-on-one time with my bestie on this trip. I pull up maps on my phone and we look at our options for the day. We consider possible places we'd like to visit. Madeline has the power today. She gets to call the stops. I don't want to direct her. I just want her to know her options. When we feel like we've got some ideas in mind, she looks over at the side table where I set my journal.

"What were you writing?"

"Just a journal entry. I write stuff. You know: what we did each day, things I'm thinking about. Stuff like that."

My fingers itch to move the journal somewhere safer, as if it's going to fly open of its own volition, spilling my innermost thoughts and feelings all over the bed for Madeline's shock and disbelief. I take a deep breath instead. I'll pack it into my backpack as soon as no one's paying attention.

"I didn't know you still journaled. Remember your diary?"

"Yes." Do I ever.

Cameron and Ben got a hold of my diary on one of our multifamily camping trips, and they teased me relentlessly about an entry I had written about a TV show I used to watch. I had a celebrity crush on the teen son in the sitcom family and I had written something about him. Ben and Cam ran around the campsite tossing my diary between them while I chased after them, shouting for them to give it back. They were making swoony faces and air kissing while they said things like, "Oh, Clark, I love you." And, "Clark, you are in my dreams. I wish I could meet you."

It's a wonder I still have a crush on Cameron after some of the stunts he pulled, but I was in sixth grade and he was in seventh. It's not like he was at the apex of maturity back then.

I didn't journal for a while after that traumatic and embarrassing moment. But, when Gladys passed, I missed her more than I imagined possible. One day, I randomly started writing a letter to her. It opened me up—especially since I couldn't tell Madeline all the things that were stirring around in my head about Cam, or about my lack of direction in life. Journaling helps me feel like I've got someone who's in my corner—someone who doesn't judge me and who has no investment in the outcome. Gladys would only want me to be happy—that's all she ever wanted for me when she was here.

"Cam and Ben can be such juvenile jerks."

"They were thirteen."

"Still."

"I think they've matured a bit since then."

Madeline laughs and the door pops open.

Ben walks in holding two paper coffee cups, and asks, "Who matured? Since when?"

"Not you, ever," Madeline answers, smiling at him with a warm smile.

"You got that right," Ben says with a wink. "Maturity is for boring people."

Then he starts singing a song from *Peter Pan* about not wanting to grow up. He and Madeline both played Darling children in the musical in high school. That song could be my theme song right now.

"We brought pancakes with sausage and bacon," Cam announces, holding up a bag of to-go containers.

"My hero!" I shout, bounding off the bed to grab them from him.

Not to be outdone, Ben holds up the coffee cups, "And coffee!"

"My hero!" Mads shouts. "Give me that caffeine!"

Cam's eyes meet mine and he smiles an almost shy smile. It feels like a private thank you for last night. Normally, this kind of smile from him would send me into a spiral of blurting and nerves. Today, I feel less overwhelmed by him—but also more. If only he knew.

"Thanks," I say, still looking him in those gorgeous hazel eyes.

His voice is soft, and possibly even affectionate, when he says, "You're welcome, Sunshine."

Maybe it's just my overactive imagination ascribing meaning where I want to see it. Cam's definitely lighter than I've seen him in a while.

I turn and bring the bag to the bed where Mads and I dig in. The guys sit—Ben on their bed, Cam in the desk chair—and we start planning the day.

With a mouthful of a bite of pancake, Madeline declares, "No offense to your awesome van, Rye, but I need to stretch my legs today. Can we plan to stop early?"

Cam looks sheepish when he says, "Please no mocking me. I have an actual bucket list item for Amarillo."

"Steak," Ben says.

"Yeah. Steak. I don't want to pass through Texas without eating a steak."

It's odd how this is the moment I realize Cam never directly asks for anything for himself. He might dominate a group with his strong leadership, but he's usually aiming for whatever he thinks is best for everyone, not his own whims. Also, he eats like a teen girl preparing for prom, or a yoga instructor who believes food is strictly an energy source. Cam asking us to stay here for food is pretty much the ninth wonder of the world.

"Of course you get steak," I say without consulting anyone.

Madeline gives me a not-so-subtle side-eye.

"That is, if your sister agrees, obviously, since she's in charge of calling stops today."

"Thank you," Madeline says to me with a satisfied nod. "What did you have in mind, Cam?"

"I want to eat a steak here. They open at ten, but we all just ate. Maybe we can find something to do around Amarillo for a few hours and then we can grab lunch at the restaurant. They also have the famous seventy-two ounce challenge."

"What's that?" Ben asks.

"If one person can eat a seventy-two ounce steak on their own, they get it free. And they get a T-shirt, I think."

"Are you going to eat that steak?" I ask.

"No way. I'll barely finish ten ounces. I would like to watch whoever's trying to eat that massive steak, though."

"Deal," Madeline says.

We figure out our plans for the morning, Mads and I take turns showering, and then the four of us load our suitcases onto the top of the van and head to Cadillac Ranch. It's about fifteen minutes from the hotel.

"Shouldn't we stop to buy paint?" Ben asks.

He's sitting next to Cam, riding shotgun while Cam drives. Madeline and I are cozied up in the back seat. I feel like hanging with her today. Our hour together in the hotel wasn't nearly enough.

"I already have paint," Cam says.

"You do?" all three of us say simultaneously.

"Guys. Seriously? Way to boost a man's confidence. Yes. I have paint. I knew we'd want to stop and experience this place. I didn't want to mess with finding paint on the trip, so I packed some. It's in the cabinet behind our seats."

I'm in awe, and I can't help the smile that breaks across my face thinking about Cam purchasing spray paint just so we can stop here. He's full of surprises. And it's at this moment, I know. I will never be able to be completely happy being just friends with him. I may be forced to keep that spot in his life, but my heart will never join me there. I will always ache, knowing how I feel and what I wish we could have.

I try to imagine life ten years from now—Cam's married to some gorgeous woman. She's probably tame, interesting, goal-oriented, and never blurts under pressure. Her hair never flies all over the place, even on a windy day. She lets Cam call the shots, and he dotes on her. They have two darling children and the most obedient dog in the world. And they live on an island where Cam manages a resort while she sunbathes and never gets burnt.

In my version of our future, I'm still single, trying to figure out what to do when I grow up—at age thirty-one. Mads is married too, to someone who deserves her awesomeness. We're all home over a summer vacation or Christmas to see our families, and I have to sit in the corner pining away as I watch Cam place an adoring kiss on his wife's temple while she hands off one of their sleepy children to him.

"What is that face? Oh my gosh. You look like someone died," Madeline whispers over to me.

"They did," I say without thinking.

Her face contorts.

"I mean. No one died. We're good. We get to paint! Woo hoo!"

I pump my fist in the air for emphasis, and my eyes drift to Cameron who looks back at me in the rearview with a concerned look on his face. The same look he'll give his wife one day. Gah. I shift so I can focus on the scenery outside the van. Whoever said a rich imagination is a gift never had to sit six feet behind their lifelong crush while picturing his future in technicolor detail.

We drive through town and then veer onto a frontage road out in the middle of wide open space. Far off in the field are what used to be ten Cadillacs buried into the ground, so about two-thirds of each car remains visible. Originally, they were an art piece commissioned by a billionaire. Now they've been stripped to their frames.

After we park, Cam grabs a bag out from the cabinet and hands each of us a can of spray paint.

"So you know the history of this place?" he asks me when he catches up with me.

"Yeah. Pretty much."

"Stanley Marsh III asked some hippies from San Francisco to create a tribute to the evolution of the tail fin on the Caddy. They buried these cars in 1974. People started coming onto the property, taking pieces off the cars, or vandalizing them with spray paint. Marsh tolerated the participation from the locals, even though it ruined his original intent. Something much bigger rose up over time. This attraction became something people travel from all over the world to experience."

His bicep bumps my shoulder as he emphasizes his point with physical contact. I feel instantly charged as if someone plugged me into an outlet. I think I might be blushing. I hope Cam thinks it's the heat, even though it's still only in the low eighties.

"What's the takeaway?" he asks, wagging his eyebrows and smiling down at me.

I'm loving this carefree side to Cam. It reminds me of how he was before he left for college.

"If you put art in public, hire security?"

Cam chuckles. I'm hoping this ease of his is a byproduct of

having gotten some of his thoughts and feelings about Stephanie out of his system last night.

"No. Well, maybe. But I was thinking more along the lines of being flexible and trusting when things don't go as we thought they should. We might remember these cars and learn to anticipate better things in whatever's going to come next."

"That's awfully optimistic of you."

"I'm not really a pessimist."

"No. I guess you aren't. I'd say you're more of a realist."

"To my core."

He nods. Then he turns and shouts, "Catch up, you two slowpokes. We've got some cars to vandalize."

A small crowd of people gather around the cars. It's still early in the day. Probably, the later it gets, the more people will come. The distinct smell of paint fills the air. The cars are coated in so much spray paint they look like the cover of a psychedelic Beatles' album. We shake our cans as we walk around to find the spot that calls out to us.

Mads stops and announces, "I'm painting daisies."

Ben stops at the car next to hers and says, "I'm painting, *Ben was here.*"

"So original," Mads teases him.

Ben holds his arms out to his sides and says, "I'm as original as they come, sweetheart."

I thought I knew what I wanted to spray. Nothing here will last. Within hours, whatever we paint will be painted over by some other tourist, eager to make their mark on this historic piece of collective art.

Suddenly, it hits me.

I walk toward the last car, wanting some space from my friends to do what I'm going to do. I pass a couple speaking German and teaming up to spray the image of a butterfly on the side of a car. When I reach my spot, I open my royal blue can and start spraying.

G. R. This one's for you.

I stand back and watch as the paint drips down a little from some of the letters. I stare at the words, hoping someone remembers me the way I remember her. Maybe she can see me right now and she appreciates this temporary tribute to the impact she made in my life.

I whisper, "I miss you, Gladys," and then I cap my paint can.

I'm lost in thought when Cam comes up behind me, his breath a tickle across my neck.

"G.R. Is that your boyfriend?"

His voice sounds restrained, tight and earnest.

"I don't have one—a boyfriend, that is."

"Who is G.R.?"

"A friend."

"Huh. Want to see what I did?"

I nod and follow Cam around to the other side of the car the German couple was painting.

When I see what he painted, I can't help but smile. Somehow, Cam painted the outline of a light blue VW Bus. Under it he sprayed, *Best Trip Ever*, in bubble letters.

"You're an artist," I say.

"Nah. I just like trying my hand at things. And, I'm a perfectionist, so I may have looked up a tutorial or two before the trip."

"Seriously? That's so unfair. I want a do-over."

He hands his can to me and says, "Have at it. We're in no hurry."

"No hurry, huh?"

"Nope. Not today."

19

CAMERON

I have found out there ain't no surer way
to find out whether you like people or hate them
than to travel with them.
~ Mark Twain (Tom Sawyer)

"That steak was ..." Madeline's voice trails off. "I'd give up a lot of things to have that steak again."

"Like what?" Ben asks.

Riley's driving, Madeline's in the shotgun seat. Ben and I are in the back. I've got the maps app open. It's Mads' day to call the stops, but I plan to keep her informed of our ultimate goal —making it to the Grand Canyon for sunset tomorrow.

"Let's see ..." my sister trails off.

"Guys? Would you give up guys?" Ben asks.

"Don't be dumb."

"It's a legit question, because I loved that steak. It's probably the most memorable steak I've eaten in a while, but I wouldn't give up dating to have more of it."

"Of course you wouldn't," Madeline teases.

"I would," Riley says.

Madeline turns to her. "Easy for you to say. You don't date."

Huh. She doesn't?

"I've dated."

"Reeeeallly?" Madeline pushes. "And when was the last time you went on a date?"

"Not this summer. We've been home."

"No. Obviously not this summer. But when?"

"Last year, okay."

"With?"

I shouldn't be listening so intently. Why should I care when Riley last went on a date? At least I know she hasn't been dating much, or my sister would be telling a whole other story right now.

"A guy at school." Her voice lowers so I can't hear the name she says to Madeline. "We went out. Okay?"

Madeline nods, obviously picking up on the same note of irritation in Riley's voice as I am.

"I would for sure not give up dating for that steak," Madeline says. "But, I'd give up ... sugar for a week. Or watching *The Bachelor*. Or ... I'd give up romance novels for a week."

"That's some steak, then," I tease.

"What are you saying, Cam?" Madeline asks, looking back at me.

"Just that your romance novels are pretty up there on your priority list. And, for the record, I'd give up your romance novels for that steak too."

"I knew it!" Ben shouts.

"What?"

"I knew you read those things."

"I don't," I say with a laugh.

Riley's eyes meet mine in the rearview mirror. We've been doing a lot of that since one of us has been in the back and the other in the front more during this leg of the trip. She wags her eyebrows like I'm busted.

"I don't," I say to Riley only.

I don't really care what Ben or Mads think. But for some reason, I do care if Riley thinks I'm curled up on a Friday night reading about how the man of someone's dreams wins over the woman in some story.

"I think it's great if you do," Riley says. "More men should read romance. They might learn a thing or two."

"Here, here!" Ben says. "Pass me your Kindle, Mads."

"You've got plenty of ammo, Ben. You don't need my Kindle."

"Oh, I know that, sweetheart. I'm planning to school your brick wall of a brother on the finer points of romance."

Madeline chuckles, pulls open her bag, and hands Ben her Kindle.

He fires it up and starts reading from the page Madeline's already on in her current book.

Ben starts in a masculine voice, but then shifts up an octave when he realizes it's a female point of view. "Jameson loops his hand behind my neck and leans toward me. Our eyes meet, and in a soft, careful voice he asks, *Is this alright?*"

Ben pauses, clearing his throat. "Man, Mads. This is heavy duty. Do we want this Jameson guy kissing our girl here?"

Madeline laughs nervously. "On second thought, hand me the Kindle."

"Oh no. Not on your life. We need to see what's going on here," Ben teases.

Riley's eyes find mine. She's smiling with an amused look on her face.

Ben changes his voice to sound more effeminate again. "I can't find words, everything in me feels pliant. My nerves zing like I've been plugged into an electrical socket." He chuckles. "Sounds dangerous." Then he keeps reading in this exaggeratedly girly voice. "I simply nod, giving Jameson all the permission he needs."

Ben dramatically looks around at each one of us. "She gave him the nod, people. This is it. He's moving in for the kill!"

Madeline has covered her face with her hands. Riley is lightly laughing and shaking her head, glancing back at me every so often like we're sharing a secret.

Ben continues. "Jameson moves in, brushing the hair away from my cheek."

Ben looks up from the Kindle. "Bro's got moves. That's definitely an A plus on the romance-o-meter—sweeping her hair off her cheek. Classic." He turns toward me. "Do it like this, though, Cam. Look in her eyes the whole time."

Ben leans toward me and feigns brushing my hair back with the back of his hand while he stares in my eyes.

I shake my head while swatting his hand away.

I glance at Riley again. She nods like Ben's not wrong. For some reason, I make note of the fact that Riley likes her hair swept away from her face. I can't help picturing the two of us, facing one another, me looking down at her, her giving me a silent nod, my hand lightly grazing her cheek as I gently sweep her hair back over her shoulder. I can't look in the mirror at her right now. It feels like she'd see all my thoughts as if they were written on my face.

"Jameson moves toward me, claiming my mouth," Ben reads. "Oh yeah, bro! Claim that mouth! Don't just kiss her. Claim. That. Mouth!"

It's like he's rooting for a tied home game in the final quarter with two minutes left on the clock.

"You're such a dork!" Madeline gasps out between laughs.

I look at Riley, she's laughing as hard as Madeline. When our eyes lock, though, I feel something—a tug. It's the same feeling that had me shooting off her bed and toward the bathroom a few hours ago.

"Our clothes are wet from the rain," Ben reads. "Man. This guy. Kissing in the rain. Are you hearing this Cam? Under a waterfall, in a pool. In a box, with a fox. Sam I am. This guy knows how to kiss. Take notes, my man."

"I don't need to take notes," I tell Ben.

"Obviously," he says with such insincerity I shove his shoulder.

I can't control where my eyes go—straight back to the rearview mirror. This time, Riley is the one to look away, a slight flush to her cheeks. Is this embarrassing her? Or is she just amused by Ben?

"Jameson moves his hand to my back, holding me to himself while he continues to kiss me like I'm his last breath, his only concern, the one thing he can't live without." Ben looks over at me.

"Dude. I think I might be doing this all wrong."

He's dead serious.

I lose it. I can't help myself. The look on Ben's face. He looks like he just failed a final exam.

He doesn't stop there, though. "I mean, think about it. Have you ever kissed a girl like she was your world?"

His voice is pensive, his face serious, and the three of us are roaring with laughter. He's too funny. He chuckles then. "Nah. Who cares? No one ever complained about my kissing. This is just a book. You know when you'll kiss a girl like she's your everything?"

"When is that?" I ask, my laughter subsiding.

"When she *is* your world. That's when."

Ben powers down the Kindle. "Enough of today's romance lesson. I think that's given you something to think about, young padawan."

"Thinking about you kissing?"

"Sure. Why not?"

"Um. Probably for one hundred reasons. That's why not."

"Suit yourself."

"Madeline, I'm concerned for you," Ben says as he hands the Kindle back to her.

"Why?"

"All that fluff is setting the bar way, way too high. What if you meet an awesome guy and you hit it off, but he kisses you like you only matter a lot."

"What's wrong with that?"

"Exactly," Ben says. "But in your mind, Jameson is kissing this woman with everything he has. She's his world. You're kissing a guy who really likes you, but you're thinking, *Hmmm. Why isn't he kissing me like Jameson kisses that woman?*"

"Sochie."

"Sochie?"

"Yeah. Characters in romance novels sometimes have weird names."

"Again. My point is made. All this living in fantasy could ruin reality for you."

"Not a chance," she assures him. "I might set the bar high, but I know the difference between romance on page and real life. Trust me."

"If you say so. I'm just trying to help you out."

"Okay. Doctor Phil," I joke.

"You know, if that guy ever retires, I'd make a great host of a show like that."

Riley looks back at the two of us. Then she smiles at Ben. "You actually would."

Madeline announces, "Texas, New Mexico border, one mile!"

"Oh my gosh! Look at that!" Riley exclaims.

We all stare out through the front window. A good distance down the road, the dividing point between Texas and New Mexico is prominently set off. As we get closer, the details become clear. Two angular stone pillars with the native sun symbol carved into them support a rectangular yellow sign that spans the two lanes and the shoulder of westbound I-40. On the overhead sign it says, "Welcome to New Mexico—Land of Enchantment."

"Now that's a welcome sign," Riley says, as she pulls over just past the sign and we all hop out.

We run back to the side of the road so that the welcome sign is behind us, and take a bunch of selfies. I whisper something to Madeline and she smiles.

When we get back in the van, Madeline tells Riley, "Turn around the first chance you get."

"Why?"

"Because I call the shots today."

"And we're backtracking?"

"Trust your bestie, girlfriend."

I'm smiling from the back seat, keeping my eyes trained out the side window so I don't give anything away. Riley does as she's told and finds a turnaround about a mile down the road. We head in the opposite direction, going east. She looks back at me. I train my features to be still.

"What is going on, guys? You're up to something, Cameron James Reeves."

"Ooooh. All three names," Ben says. "She's serious."

"Don't worry. It's a good thing," Madeline assures Riley.

A few moments later, Mads says, "Okay. Get ready to stop in less than a minute."

When our goal is in sight, Madeline says, "Okay! Stop!"

Riley looks around. We're in the middle of basically nowhere. Yellowed summer grass spreads out in all directions. Riley searches the landscape out the front of the van, and then she sees it.

"You guys! Really?"

"You couldn't get one on the way out here," I explain. "So this will have to do."

"Oh my gosh! You guys are the best!"

Riley grabs her phone and hops out. Ben looks confused, but he follows along. When we're on the side of the road, he catches on. About thirty feet from the front of the van is the *Welcome to Texas* sign. Yes. It's the one between New Mexico and Texas, not the one we missed when we crossed over from Oklahoma, but it's better than nothing.

Riley sidles up to me as we walk toward the sign. In a voice meant only for me, she asks, "Was this your idea?"

"Madeline's calling the shots today."

"Under your influence, I think."

"Hmmm."

"You're the best, Cam."

She beams up at me and I'd be lying if I said I didn't want to drive her back to Oklahoma so she could get the actual shot she wanted right now. I don't really know what's happening to me. She's Riley. A relationship of anything more than friendship wouldn't work between us for so many reasons. But try to tell my brain that right now—or whatever part of me seems to be waking up to her for the first time in all these years of knowing her.

20

RILEY

She wasn't where she had been.
She wasn't where she was going.
But she was on her way.
~ Jodi Hills

It's mid-afternoon when we pass a royal blue road sign that says Tucumcari on the top line. Well, it actually says ucumcari. The T is torn off. A list of amenities for travelers is indicated in a sort of twelve-days-of-Christmas style underneath the city name.

"Thirty Modern Stations, twenty-four restaurants, fourteen hotels ..." Ben reads aloud as we pass. "What are modern stations?"

"I don't know. But we need to find out," Cam answers from the back.

"Are we stopping here?" Ben asks.

"I need to go," Madeline says. "It's time for a pit stop."

Every time she says, "pit stop," she uses the accent of this character from the Cars movie who was Italian, so it comes out "peeeet stope."

"Tucumcari!" I shout.

"We've established that, Rye," Ben answers.

"No! You guys. I thought we'd be here at night one night. I wanted to stay here. There are some of the best neon signs on all of Route 66 in this town."

"Here? Are you sure?"

"Yes! I wanted to stay at the Roadrunner Lodge Motel!"

"What's special about the Roadrunner Motel?" Ben asks.

"They have everything restored like it's back in the sixties. And ... wait for it ..." I pause for dramatic effect. "They have Magic Fingers beds!"

"What?" Madeline asks.

"Oh my gosh! Tell me you know what Magic Fingers beds are. Don't let me down, Mads."

"Um. No. Are they shaped like a hand, like those cool chairs from back then?"

"No, silly. They're beds that vibrate. You put a coin in this box at the side of the bed, and the whole mattress shakes. It's so cool."

"Does it shake all night?"

"No. I think like a minute or something."

I look back at Cam. He's smiling at me, again. He's been so much more smiley ever since our talk. On one hand, I'm grateful to see the weight lifting. On the other hand, it's making my goal of resisting him so much harder. He's attractive no matter what, but Cam giving me private glances in the rearview mirror and smiling like that? Well. He could cause a ten-car pile up.

"I'm a little bummed we aren't going to get to stay there," I admit.

Madeline starts rattling off directions to me. I'm at her mercy today. It's been good so far. She hasn't really had a lot of great options as to where to stop. There's a lot of highway surrounded by open land with chaparral and scrub plants for miles and miles through this stretch of Route 66. There haven't even been distant cliffs along the horizon for the most part. Though, there's a mesa off in the distance now. Just one.

We drive through Tucumcari on Old Route 66, which takes us past vintage motels and gas stations. Some are closed for good, left where time abandoned them, a neglected memory of what they were. Others are revitalized, but maintain the 1960s feel. We come up to the Roadrunner Inn.

"Stop here," Madeline says.

"Why?" I ask.

I pull into the parking lot anyway.

"We may as well see if we can use their lobby restroom if they have one. At least you'll get to see the property."

Cam gets out from the back and approaches the main office. The three of us follow behind him.

The man at the desk greets us. "Welcome to the Roadrunner. Do you have a reservation?"

"No sir, we don't," Cam says.

"Well then, what can I do for you today?"

"We're passing through on the way to Albuquerque. We need to use a restroom if you have one. And my friend here is about to turn twenty-one on this trip. She's heard of your motel and she wanted to stay here, but the timing didn't line up. She really wanted to experience the beds."

Cam remembered my birthday.

"Ah. The Magic Fingers," the clerk says.

"Yes. That's what made your establishment stand out to her."

"It's definitely a selling point," he says. "I remember traveling with my parents as a boy. Those Magic Fingers beds were —well, magical. I used to beg my parents for a quarter back then. A quarter could buy you five candy bars. Five. So, asking for a quarter was a big deal. And my dad would put up a fuss. But somehow, he'd pull a quarter out every time. I think the fuss was for show so I never took it for granted. I'd climb up on the bed and pop the quarter into the metal box. That bed would start vibrating, and it wasn't gentle or relaxing in the least. More like it was trying to shake the rest of your change right outta your pockets. But I loved it. So, when we had a chance to revamp the rooms here, I knew we had to put that feature in."

I look around the lobby. Then I look back at the man behind the desk.

"You want to see one of the rooms?" he offers out of the blue.

"Could we?" I ask.

"I'm not one to say no to a birthday girl."

"It's not my birthday yet."

He ignores me, grabbing a key ring and telling us to follow him. When we get to a room on the lower level, he opens it and waves us in. The room is clean, and it definitely feels like we've stepped back in time. We stand there looking around, even though there's not much to see after the first few seconds.

I'm about to thank him for letting us see inside a room when he turns to me and says, "If you needed a quarter, I happen to have one right here. Go on. Sit on the bed."

He pops the quarter in my hand and I walk over to the bed. I put the quarter in the slot, and sure enough, the bed starts shaking like a cheap carnival ride. I can't help myself. I start laughing. Ben plops down on the end of the bed, and in no time he starts laughing too. I fall backward onto the mattress, Ben collapses, his head next to mine, legs going in the opposite direction. The hotel manager tips his chin to Madeline and Cam. They take his hint and join us. It doesn't take more than a few seconds before Cam and Madeline are laughing along with Ben and me while the manager looks on with an amused grin on his face.

After we've been jiggled for about a minute, the machine turns off. The manager offers us another quarter. We gladly take it. This time, all four of us lay across the bed like a bunch of sardines. The laughter starts up as soon as the vibrations kick in. My eyes glance over Madeline's head to find Cam watching me. His eyes are crinkled and his mouth is open in a full laugh.

When our time runs out, we all stand and file out onto the walkway outside the room. The manager locks the door behind us, and then he directs us to a gas station up the road that he says has "relatively clean" restrooms.

"Don't forget to stop at TeePee Curios," he adds. "You're bound to find a few things you'd like there."

"Will do," Ben says.

The four of us walk toward the van, but Cam lingers behind, pulling some money out of his wallet. He shakes the man's hand, gives him the money, and then he walks over to us and gestures for me to toss him the keys.

"I'll drive the next leg. You and Mads can hang out in the back."

We pull out of the parking lot onto Route 66 and I say, "Thanks, you guys! That was totally worth the stop."

"I need one of those Magic Fingers things for my mattress!" Ben says.

He's already scrolling on his phone. "You guys! There's a vintage Magic Fingers massager system on Ebay! It's less than fifty bucks. Check this out. It says, and I quote, it quickly carries you into the land of tingling relaxation and ease."

"Is that what that was?" Cam deadpans.

"I got carried there soooo quickly," Madeline says.

"To the land of tingling relaxation or the ease?" I ask.

"Both, I'd say. Yep. Both."

We're all laughing as we roll into the gas station. We top off the tank, use the restroom, and then we stop at TeePee Curios where I get a few kitschy things to add to my growing Route 66 collection. I pick up an arrowhead for Cam. I don't know why, or how I'll give it to him. It dangles on a leather lace—in case someone would want to wear it as a necklace. We take a bunch of photos under the neon sign and in front of the teepee entrance to the shop. Then we're on the road again with a little under three hours of driving left until we reach Albuquerque.

Madeline and I entertain ourselves playing cards in the back of the van. The guys are talking about Marbella Island up front.

"So, you're turning twenty-one. Are you excited?" Madeline asks me.

"I should be, right?"

"I was so excited for my twenty-first. Well, you know that. It just felt like a rite of passage. Like I'm officially a grown up now."

Madeline's only two months older than me. We celebrated her birthday at the beginning of summer.

"I'm looking forward to seeing what life on the island will be like," she says.

Thankfully, she's not pressing me more about my feelings surrounding my birthday. I'd tell her. I just don't want that conversation to veer into the whole *becoming a teacher* territory.

"I wonder if there are any cute boys our age working at the resort," Madeline says.

"I thought you liked Max."

"I do, but we've never really officially dated yet. I can't get a read on him. He's so friendly. I think we have chemistry. But whenever I've been sure he was going to make a move or ask me out, he hasn't. One time I was so sure. He even asked me the classic question."

"The classic question?"

"Yeah. Are you busy Saturday?"

"Oh. Yeah. That's pretty much a date-precursor."

"Right? That's what I thought! Then, when I said I didn't have anything going on, he asked me to get together to work on our homework for Human Development."

"Noooo."

"Yes. So, we studied. He did order pizza. But we just studied. Every so often, I'd look up and see him staring at me. I'm starting to wonder if there's something wrong with me."

"Believe me. There's nothing wrong with you."

Ben's voice carries back to us. "Nothing wrong with you Mads. If a guy just asks you to study he's either completely in the friend zone, or he's overwhelmed by your awesomeness and he's nervous. If he doesn't get it together and ask you out, you've got two choices."

"Oh, tell me, wise one," Madeline jokes, but I can tell she wants to hear whatever Ben's got to say.

"Either you ask him out, or you wait. Well, technically you have three choices. You can move on."

"Ask him out?" She doesn't sound averse. More curious than anything.

"Yeah, the thing about that option is you'll end up wondering if this guy will ever take the initiative, or is he going to leave that up to you? And do you care?"

"Oh. I care. I'm all about being pursued. I'm not afraid to reciprocate, but I need a man who isn't sitting around waiting for me to make all the decisions and take all the action."

"A guy like me," Ben waggles his eyebrows.

"Like you, only not," Madeline clarifies.

"Dude. You aren't dating my sister," Cam says.

"Obviously. I'm just saying I'm the type of guy who takes initiative and action. I don't wait for a woman to ask me out."

"You take initiative with anything that moves and shows a sign of life," Cam jokes.

"Ha! As if."

We're all laughing at Cam's comment and Ben even joins in. It's one of his best qualities—the way he can laugh at himself.

Once the guys resume their conversation, Madeline and I take up where we left off, only I notice her voice is much quieter. The back seat feels private, but obviously Ben easily overheard everything we were saying. How he managed to track his conversation with Cameron and still follow what we were saying is beyond me.

"So. What are you going to do?" I ask.

"Not sure," she says. "I guess I'll see where things stand when we get back to school. Unless I meet the man of my dreams on the island."

I smile at her. "Gin!"

"What? No fair. You distracted me by talking about boys."

"That's not in the rules. I can use any means to gain an edge."

"That's just cruel."

I lay out my cards and we count my points. I tally everything on the sheet and then re-deal the cards for our next hand.

"What about you?" Madeline asks.

"What about me?"

"You haven't even told me who you have a crush on all year. Every time I've set you up, you've made some excuse."

"I've been busy."

"All year?"

"I don't know. I'm just not in the mood to be set up."

"I think you've got a crush on someone. Why don't you tell me who?"

My eyes betray me, flashing toward the front of the van.

"No one you really ... it's complicated."

"Ooooh. Complicated is the best. Is he a teacher?"

"Gross. No!"

"He could be a TA," Ben unhelpfully adds.

"Nope."

"I've got a friend you'd really like," Ben says. "Maybe I should give him your number."

Cam looks back at me. I can't tell what he's thinking from the look he's giving me.

Oh, Cameron. If you only knew.

21

CAMERON

If you can't get someone out of your head,
maybe they are supposed to be there.
~ Anonymous

We're heading east again—on our trip out west.

I think about how only three days ago, I would have thrown down over this decision. How can something so intrinsic as a need to stay on schedule become upended in me over such a short span of days?

Madeline may be calling the shots today, but Riley's definitely giving her strong input. It's kind of like when Mom would say, *I don't know. Ask your dad*, and then proceed to rush to get to Dad before we did. Then she'd tell him what he thought and coach him in what to tell us when we asked whatever we had gone to her about in the first place. Madeline may be in charge, but Riley's pulling the strings. And, I'm doing exactly nothing about it.

According to Riley, we just *have* to experience the quarter-mile rumble strip called, The Musical Highway.

"Shhhhhh!" Riley announces. "It should be right around here."

Sure enough, a sign at the edge of the road tells us we're approaching the section of highway we want. I slow to exactly forty-five miles an hour, and an instrumental version of a line from *America the Beautiful* plays loudly enough for us to hear it through the car. Apparently they installed metal plates under the asphalt in this section of the road to create this experience as a social experiment to help people choose to drive the speed limit.

"That was so cool!" Madeline shouts.

"I loved it so much!" Riley agrees.

I drive to the next possible turn-around and get us going westbound again. It was a pretty unique experience. Worth turning around and adding ten minutes to the trip? Yeah. Probably.

"Thanks, Cam!" Riley says from the back seat.

Making her happy—definitely worth it.

"Just doing what today's designated guide tells me," I say with a wink.

Riley twists her lips into an adorable pursed expression. Her eyes crinkle at the edges. I waggle my eyebrows once. What am I doing? Heck if I know. It's like someone walked me into a room and took off a blindfold I didn't even know I had been wearing. Now, I see her. I can't unsee what I see.

"Speaking of which," Ben says. "I think we are due for another round of Road Trip Bingo. We need to determine who gets to call tomorrow's stops."

"What about another game instead?" Riley suggests.

"Like what?" Ben asks.

"Well, there's Hot Seat, Never Have I Ever, Cows on My Side, Name That Tune, The Movie Game ..."

"What are you?" I ask teasingly. "The road trip cruise director?"

"I did my research."

Riley gives me a quick, definitive nod. I smile back at her.

"Hot Seat!" Madeline says.

"How's it played?" Ben asks, walking right into it.

"Each person takes a turn in the hot seat," Madeline says. "Everyone else gets a turn asking the person in the hot seat a question. The person in the hot seat has to answer—kind of like Truth or Dare. Only, in our version, we made it like two truths and a lie. The person in the hot seat gets one lie each round. The other passengers guess which answer was a lie. Whoever guesses the fib gets a point. If no one guesses, the fibber in the hot seat gets all the points. At the end of everyone taking a turn in the hot seat, points are tallied. If there's a tie, we go into a final, to-the-death match between the people who tied."

"I say Cows on My Side sounds pretty good," I suggest.

"What'cha hiding?" Ben asks.

"Nothing. You know me. I'm a boring, open book."

"You're definitely boring," Ben says too easily. "But you're no open book."

He's not wrong.

"And it's scout's honor as to whether you're lying," Madeline reminds us. "You could lie, but we will find out the truth one day. And when we do ... welp, I wouldn't want to be you, you yellow-bellied-liar."

"Oh. My. Gosh!" Riley says, laughing hard at Madeline. "You're so intense. What are you going to do to the person who lies and doesn't fess up?"

"I have so many pranks I have yet to pull. An entire arsenal. Don't make me put them to the test."

Riley's still chuckling. "Okay. Okay. And, Ben, I think we missed the Reeves gene."

"What one?" I ask.

"The one that turns you into Stalin and this one into some scary version of a female tyrant."

"Say what you will," Madeline teases back. "But I will not be crossed."

"Cows on My Side it is!" Riley shouts.

"Here! Here!" I shout.

I don't know what Riley has to hide, but Hot Seat is looking scary from where I'm sitting.

"I'll start," Madeline says.

She makes her hands into some fake gangsta sign and says, "Brang it, people."

"You asked for it," I say.

"Oh yeah? What goes around comes around, bro. Think well on that little tidbit."

"Riley's right. You're scary."

Madeline beams like the scary woman she is.

"Okay," Ben says. "Hmmmm ... What's something you're glad your mom doesn't know about you."

"Going for the jugular right out of the gate!" I say to Ben, raising my fist for a bump.

He bumps and makes the fanned out finger gesture as his hand pulls back. Always extra, that's Ben.

Madeline pauses, taps her chin with her finger and says, "That I snuck out to go to senior night at the reservoir."

"I think Mom knows," I say, glancing at my sister in the rearview.

Riley giggles. It's pretty cute. I'm kicking myself two ways: first, for never noticing how truly cute she is, and secondly, for noticing now. Nothing good can come of this. Let's say we date. As if I'd take these feelings and thoughts as far as acting on them. She'd have to reciprocate or give me some kind of green light for me to do that. She's not, and she won't. But if she did ... well, let's say we dated. Then what? She's going back to school. I'm going to work on the island. It would technically be a long-distance relationship, even though we'd only be two and a half hours away from one another.

Then there's the whole thing about our families. Unless we were getting married, our parents would not smile on me dating Riley. They'd be right, too. There's no guarantee we'd last. And if we broke up, the entire fabric of a lifetime of friendships, shared vacations, and basically being found family to one another would crumble based on the fact that I couldn't get Riley out of my system and had to act on this attraction. Those stakes are so high I can barely take my next breath when I think of them. Do I want to be the one putting our family bonds on the line? I don't. Not at all.

The biggest reason acting on my attraction would be foolish is sitting smugly next to Riley, glaring at me right now. Madeline. She would freak to the point of needing restraints and a sedative if I so much as thought about dating her bestie. Madeline's highly possessive. Plus, she thinks of Riley as the sister she never had. She'd see my interest as crossing a line. I see it too. So basically, I'm screwed.

"Cam?" Madeline says.

"What?"

"I said, it's your turn to ask me a question."

"Oh, yeah. I'm just thinking."

Madeline rolls her eyes at me.

"What's your biggest fear?" I ask.

"Easy. Bats."

"Bats? How did I not know this?"

"You should. Those things are creepy."

"Do you have a hidden talent?" Riley asks.

"So many," Madeline says with the most serious look on her face. "I can do a perfect Scooby Doo impersonation."

"Let's hear it," Riley says.

"Not until everyone votes," Madeline says. "Okay! Time to vote."

We all chime in, guessing which of Madeline's answers is a lie. I pick bats. Ben says she can't do Scooby Doo. Riley picks the Res because she thinks our mom knew.

"It was bats!" Madeline shouts. "I think they are adorable. Have you seen them up close? They have cute little faces. Plus, they're blind. How can someone be afraid of them? They're harmless."

"What's your real fear?" I ask.

"Ask that another day," she says. "Who's next?" She throws in, "Ruh-roh, Raggy" in a perfect Scooby Doo voice. We all laugh.

"We're almost to Albuquerque!" Riley shouts. "We'll have to put a pin in the game."

"We're actually in Albuquerque," I say. "There's no Welcome to Albuquerque sign."

"That's just wrong," Riley laments.

Ben pulls up the address of the AirBnB we reserved and starts reading off the directions to me from his phone instead of putting it in maps.

"Just put it in the map app."

"Nah. I'm your map app today. I'll get you there."

"Whatever floats your boat. Just don't get us lost."

"I have a suggestion," Riley says.

"Shoot," I tell her, sneaking a glance in the rearview and catching her eyes again.

"Madeline really didn't get a fair shot at calling stops since there wasn't much to see today. Can she have a do-over tomorrow?"

"Team Madeline?" I tease.

"Whatever," Riley says with a knowing smirk on her beautiful face.

"I'm good with that. You, Ben?"

"I'm good with it. Madeline, what's your favorite road trip treat?"

"Bribery? Really, Ben?" I ask.

"Oh yeah. You know it. I am not beneath stooping to paying off the guide to make sure I have a say in the stops. Riley has automatic sway with Madeline. I'll buy my way in."

"I make my own decisions," Madeline says. "And, Red Vines."

A few miles into town, we pull off the highway and follow the directions to a residential neighborhood where we've reserved a three-bedroom, two-bath house with a pool, hot tub, and firepit. We're barely in the door when Ben walks straight into one of the queen bedrooms and says, "I claim this one!"

"No Rock, Paper, Scissors?" I ask, wagging my eyebrows at Madeline and Riley. We're all onto Ben, aka Rock Man. I nearly teased him, calling him, Ben The Rock Johnson, but that would give away our secret knowledge.

"Nah, man," Ben says from the bedroom. "That game hasn't been kind to me this trip. I'm not feeling the luck."

From the sound of his voice, he's already lying in bed.

I look at Riley and Madeline, "Well, I guess that means I'm in the other queen. You two okay sharing the king?"

"Yes! A king!" Riley says, pumping her fist in the air.

I rouse Ben off the bed and we grab the suitcases from the roof of the van and wheel them into the house. Then we order pizza and all retreat into our rooms to change into our swimsuits.

Ben and I are already in the pool when Madeline and Riley walk out through the sliding doors onto the covered porch where the firepit sits surrounded by an outdoor sectional. The whole style of the home feels like a nod to the pueblo Native American architecture. It's light terra cotta colored stucco with wide wood beams integrated throughout the house and porch. The broad back deck is really a low wood platform made for entertaining. There's plenty of room for a large group to sit around the firepit comfortably.

The girls take one step down off the porch, and they're standing on the concrete surrounding the pool and jacuzzi. Riley's wearing a royal blue suit that's not a two-piece, but it may as well be. It's a one-piece which has wide open sides and two rings holding the top and bottom pieces together. It's cut low in the front and high on the hips. Her hair is down from the ponytail she's had it in all day.

I've seen Riley in swimsuits for as many years as I can remember. I probably saw her in swim diapers at some point. Yeah. Yeah. It's not the sexiest image to picture right now. But maybe I should be thinking about that—Riley in swim diapers. Nope. Not working. Not when she's standing fifteen feet away from me looking like she stepped out of a swimsuit magazine.

Madeline says something and Riley tilts her head back in a laugh. Riley grabs her hair and tosses it over her shoulder. Then she looks over at me and Ben and dives into the water. A line of bubbles trails behind her before she emerges halfway across the pool.

"Didn't your mom teach you it's rude to stare?" Ben says quietly to me with a chuckle.

"Shut it," I tell him.

"Mm hmm. Good thing you feel nothing but brotherly affection for her."

I send a spray of water in Ben's direction—as if it's his fault I can't do anything about the way Riley's affecting me.

"You know who doesn't feel brotherly affection for Riley?" he continues.

"Who?"

I'm watching Riley as she surfaces again, tilting her head to the sky so the water runs down her face and neck and her hair falls in one brown sheet behind her. She's a vision.

"Me," Ben continues. "Riley's not my sister. She's not my pretend sister. She's just a really attractive young woman with a killer swimsuit and a great sense of humor. I'm definitely not her brother."

I turn to Ben so quickly I surprise myself. "You will leave her alone," I growl quietly.

"Because you feel like a brother to her? Is this your brotherly overprotectiveness coming out?"

He's pushing me. I know it in my right mind.

"This is me setting a clear and healthy boundary. Because no one in this group of four people is doing anything but being the best of friends on this trip."

"If you say so," Ben says.

"I do," I say.

Madeline shouts, "Pizza's here!" just as a faint sound of the doorbell rings through from inside the house.

Riley hops out of the water, grabs a towel, wraps it around herself, and walks through the house with Madeline. Ben and I hop out and follow them.

The pizza guy is around our age, maybe a year or two younger.

"Thanks for bringing us dinner," Riley tells him. "Oh my goodness, this smells so good. Is it as good as it smells?"

He smiles warmly at her. "I like it. And I'd say that even if I didn't work there."

"Did we get the right kind? What's your best seller?"

"Yeah. Pepperoni, as common as it is, is our best seller. Ours is good. They put garlic butter on the crust. I doubt I'm supposed to tell you that."

He smiles a conspiratorial smile at Riley. I think it's smarmy. She seems to think it's cute.

"I hope you like it," pizza guy says. "Are you here in town long?"

Pizza's getting cold, bro. Time to deliver and move on.

"Nope," Riley says, obviously not at all interested in eating hot food. "We're just here for the night. We're headed to California. Did you grow up here?"

"I did. If you want some great donuts in the morning, I know just the place."

Is this guy going to ask her out to donuts?

"We'd love to know the inside scoop on good donuts," Riley says, smiling warmly at the pizza guy.

He's good looking, I guess, in an *I skateboard whenever I'm not at work* sort of way. He's wearing loose fitting jeans, a white T-shirt and a knit cap in eighty-five degree weather. His mid-length shaggy hair pokes out the bottom edge of his beanie.

I resist the urge to wrap my arm around Riley's shoulders.

"You've gotta try Bristol Donuts," he tells her. "It's a double-decker bus turned donut shop. You order downstairs and then eat upstairs."

"That sounds great!" Riley says with her usual enthusiasm.

Ben steps up, thanks the pizza guy, grabs the pizza, and turns to take it out to the back patio.

Madeline follows Ben, leaving me, pizza boy, and Riley together on the front porch.

"Here," pizza guy says. "Gimme your hand."

Riley sticks her hand out, not knowing if this guy murders

people on his off hours. For all we know, this pizza delivery gig is just a cover for his involvement in organized crime.

But Riley smiles up at him, her big doe eyes all wide and sweet.

He gently grasps her hand and tips it over so the palm is facing up. Then he writes something right on her hand with a pen he just dug out of his pocket.

"I'm Deuce, by the way."

"Riley. Nice to meet you, Deuce." She pauses for longer than she should, and then as if she just remembered I'm here, she says, "Oh. This is my friend, Cameron."

"Hey," Deuce says to me.

Deuce. Who names their kid Deuce? Someone in the mafia. That's who.

"Pizza's getting cold, Rye," I say.

She looks over at me like I'm her dad and I just told her it's curfew.

I stare at her. She stares at me. Deuce looks between us.

"Enjoy the donuts, Riley."

He gives her a two-finger salute and a wink and walks two steps backward before spinning on his heel to head back to his car. The car with the pizza slice on top of it.

"What was that?" I ask once he's out of earshot.

"What was what?"

"All that." I gesture toward Deuce's car and then back at the spot where he was standing and then at Riley. I basically look like I'm conducting a symphony or directing traffic after drinking too many cups of coffee.

Why do I care? She flirted with the pizza guy. So what? It's probably Ben's teasing that's got me all in knots. I need a slice of pizza and a soak in the hot tub.

"I was just being friendly," she says with a smile.

I almost wonder if she knows how she affects me right now.

Maybe all that flirting was for my benefit. But then Riley turns and casually walks back into the house, her towel loosely draped over her shoulders, her wet hair falling down her back in waves, and her swimsuit taunting me all the way to the back porch.

RILEY'S JOURNAL

July 26th

How does each day on the road feel like a week? I bet you'd know the reason, Gladys. I hope you watched me dedicate this trip to you when we painted the cars at Cadillac Ranch today. Did you get a glimpse of what Cam sprayed? A VW Bus.

I still need a name for my VW bus. It will come, but for some reason it feels like I have to name her before we get to LA. It feels superstitious to park her for six weeks in a garage and just to let her sit there, nameless and alone, while we go work on the island.

Today we drove through a lot of open land. A lot. No. More than that. It was wide open spaces for hours on end. But we played games. Besides, we really didn't get on the road until after lunch. We needed a day like that—no hurry, but still progressing west by the time we tucked in for the night.

I kinda like Albuquerque. Not that I've seen much of it, but what I've seen has been sweet. The house we're in has a Native American vibe and the pizza guy was … well, he was hot. Sorry if that embarrasses you. There's just no other word for a man who comes across the way he does. He wasn't forward or cheesy, and some of his moves would have creeped me out coming from someone else, but from him, they just felt fun and flirty.

Of course Madeline and I went on about him for a good half hour after he left. It seemed to drive Ben and Cam nuts. Mostly Cam. He kept showing his irritation with little comments like, "Could we change the subject?" and "So he was cute. What are you going to do about it in the next twelve hours?" and "You'd think you two had never seen a nice looking man before."

Deuce, that was the pizza guy's name … he had this carefree style, sort of in a McRae Williams way. You wouldn't know who that is, I'm sure. McRae is an acrobatic skier, and he's got this sweet, but edgy look to him. That was Deuce. He could charm the pants right off you. Not the actual pants, Gladys! Goodness. But he's what you'd call a charmer. He took my hand and wrote the street address of a double decker donut bus on it. Who does that? It was intimate, but also like something you'd see in a movie. If I were sticking around Albuquerque, I'd definitely see Deuce again.

No. I'm not over Cam. Of course not. Not even close. The world couldn't be that kind to me. I'm afflicted. That's what I am. It's like getting chicken pox, only this itch is more relentless.

Can we just talk about him in a swimsuit, sluicing through the water? I love that word: sluicing. I'm not even sure I used it right, but this is my journal, so it stays. He sluiced like nobody's business. All those muscles. His hair when he emerged from the water … gah. It's not fair for a man to be that effortlessly attractive. And he's not even cocky about it in the least. It's like he barely knows what he's wielding.

And don't get me started on the winks, Gladys. Here and there throughout the day, he'd grin and wink at me. I'm surprised I even have a bone left in my body. I think my skeletal system started melting into putty at the first wink. By the time we arrived in Albuquerque, I should have been a puffy, melty cloud of boneless goo. I'm sorry I'm going on about him to you of all people. But if not you, who?

Anyway, the whole time Deuce was dropping off our pizza and looking like a not-so-bad-boy who would make me forget all my troubles for an hour or two, Cam stood on the porch in full-blown, older-brother protective mode. It was slightly adorable. Cam didn't want me flirting with the pizza guy. Believe me, I wasn't flirting. I was just having a little fun.

Do you know how long it's been, Gladys? Too long. I think I'm going to get brave when we're back at school. I'll take Madeline up on her offer to set me up with someone. How else am I supposed to rid myself of this constant obsession with the one man I can't have?

I'm yawning now. But I still can't sleep. Maybe I'll go out on the patio and watch the night sky for a while. I'm sure I'll get sleepy eventually. Just like I'll get over Cam one day. I will because I have to.

Your name was on a Cadillac today, Gladys. Well, your initials, but it was all you. You had your fifteen minutes of fame.

22

CAMERON

People don't take trips, trips take people.
~ John Steinbeck

I'm in a bed by myself for the first night of this trip. Well, not if you count that bunk bed ... which I don't. Ben was snoring overhead. And when I say snoring, it doesn't really encompass the sound my best friend made. It was definitely far from a quiet night's sleep in a bed of my own.

His snorting and sucking and vibrating sounds would escalate to a crescendo, drop off, and then surge again. All. Night. Long.

I've slept in the same room, tent, or cabin with Ben more times than I can count. He doesn't always snore. But when he does, it's epic. I'm surprised I fell asleep that night.

The house here is tranquil.

After that guy in the beanie left, the four of us ate pizza, swam, and then got in the hot tub where my sister and the woman who seems to have snuck up on me out of nowhere discussed the pizza guy like he was the latest Hollywood heartthrob.

Did you see his beanie?

Oh my gosh, yes. What is it with a beanie?

I don't know. I never thought I'd think they were cute, but he made me a convert.

Right? The way his hair poked out around the edges. Yummy.

And on it went …

He grabbed your hand?

Yeah. And that should have been creepy, right?

It was. It WAS. Creepy is *exactly* what it was.

But, it so wasn't. He was so sweet, and it was like something out of a movie.

A horror movie. A thriller called *Pizza Boy* where the delivery guy charms the tourist and comes back to murder her in her sleep.

My sister sighed at this ridiculous comment, and went on about how romantic having a guy write on your hand was, and it's too bad they weren't staying in Albuquerque so Riley could see Deuce again. Since when is ink poisoning romantic?

Ben, the unusual voice of reason, chimed in with my exact thoughts, *Who names their kid Deuce? Is he a twin?*

Madeline, gotta give her this one, said, *It's probably because he makes the women do a double take.*

I tried my best to put a brake pedal to all talk of the hot pizza guy—ironically, my comments were made following lukewarm pizza. But the girls ignored me and went on swooning. Eventually, they lost interest and we talked a bit about our plans for tomorrow.

While my mind is scrolling through the conversation in the hot tub, alternating with images of Riley in a swimsuit, I think I hear the sliding glass door to the back patio open. I thought I had checked all the locks before I came to bed.

What if the pizza guy is coming back, and he's after Riley in her sleep? I'm ninety-nine percent sure he's not. As much as he rubbed me the wrong way, I'm aware enough to realize that was jealousy, plain and simple—an emotion I'm not used to experiencing at all.

But, on the off chance Deuce is a nefarious pizza boy, and he's back to slice Riley in her sleep, I'm going to check things out.

I hop up, not bothering to put on a T-shirt. I'm in thin summer pajama bottoms and nothing else because, despite the ceiling fan and the way the desert cools at night, there's still a lingering heat in the air from the high temps we experienced all day.

I tiptoe down the hall and out into the sunken living room. Then I walk through the dining room toward the sliding glass doors leading to the deck. A figure is on the porch, leaning on the railing. I can't make the person out in the dark, so I pick up the first thing I see. It's a statue of a cowboy on a horse with a lasso overhead. Man, this thing is heavy.

I step onto the porch, the cowboy statue raised overhead and say, "Halt! Who goes there?"

Whatever. I was in a Shakespeare play in high school. That's the first line that crossed my mind.

The figure whips around from the banister and my brain takes a moment to transfer the awareness of who it is. I swing the cowboy out in front of me and then realize my mistake a second too late.

Riley jumps back. "Sheesh, Cameron. Are you trying to kill me?"

Her voice is high and tight and squeaky.

"No! Oh. Sorry. No. Riley. It's you. I thought you were ..."

She pops a hand onto her hip. "Who did you think I was?"

"An intruder. Maybe."

"And you were going to take me down with that?"

"It's late. I'm tired. It was the first thing I saw."

She softly chuckles. I turn and place the cowboy back inside the doorway where he originally had been standing—or riding.

Stepping back outside, I slide the door shut behind me. Riley's turned back toward the yard, leaning on the railing that frames the deck. Her head's tilted back so she can look up at the insane number of stars overhead. This house is on the outskirts of Albuquerque, so there's not much light pollution here.

"Isn't it beautiful?" she asks in a nearly reverent tone.

"Definitely," I say, not bothering to look up.

She glances over as I step beside her. We're dangerously close considering she's in a summer pajama set and I'm in my pj bottoms. Not only that, my heart is hammering—over Riley. I can barely reconcile the girl I grew up with to the woman standing next to me.

We linger there in silence for a few minutes. It's not awkward or weird. It actually feels peaceful—a familiar comfort settles between us. Riley's easy to be with—like she fits me somehow.

She finally speaks. "I couldn't sleep."

"Yeah. Me neither. It doesn't make sense. I've finally got a bed to myself, and I'm tired enough from driving. But my head was stir-crazy. I couldn't shut it down."

"Mine too."

"What's got you stir crazy?"

She looks at me like she'd tell me, but she'd have to kill me.

"Okay. You don't have to tell me," I say in a joking tone.

"What about you?" she asks.

Yeah. I'm not telling her she's the primary source of my mental disruption.

"Just a lot on my mind, I guess."

"Same."

We're quiet again. A soft breeze kicks up, blowing a few strands of her hair across my chest. I push them back without thinking. Riley looks up at me. I gaze down at her. It would be so easy to bend down and kiss her lips.

I clear my throat and glance up at the sky. She takes a miniscule step away from me, but it feels like a chasm. What did I expect? More than that, what did I want? I know this can't lead anywhere. But I wish, just for a night, I could shut off this voice of reason in my head and do something irrational for once. I wish I weren't the guy who always counted the potential fallout of his choices.

All of a sudden, from out of nowhere an owl swoops down over the yard toward the roof, and then we're bombarded. The sounds of multiple flapping wings and a repeated "ch, ch, ch, ch, ch" noise ring through the air.

Riley's swatting out in front of herself and overhead with rapid flailing motions. Her feet are doing a crazy dance and she's screaming. Really screaming.

I'm ducking and swinging my arms around too, only not as wildly as Riley.

Bats! They're everywhere.

They seem to be disoriented or focused on something around us, but it feels like the scene from the historic thriller *Birds* where a whole flock of crows swarms this guy. A bat bumps into Riley's face while it's flying under the roof of the deck, and she lets out a scream that probably alerts dogs the next county over.

Riley turns and grabs onto me. Her hands grip my shoulders. My free hand lands behind her back and I hold her to me while I swat at the few bats still left flying here and there on the porch. They must have sensed our lack of welcome because they cleared out as quickly as they came. They might be blind, but they aren't deaf. Though, after Riley's screaming they just might be.

Riley's still in my arms. One of her palms rests flat on my chest, and my hand on her back is holding her in place. Her rapid heartbeat thrums against me through her pajama top. She looks up at me, and then her body softens and collapses into me while she cracks up.

"Oh my gosh! Of all the nights. Madeline just faked us out saying she was afraid of bats! We were ambushed!"

Riley gasps for breath between her bursts of laughter.

I can feel the smile splitting my face. I feel so much more than that. Riley hasn't made a move to disentangle herself from me, and I haven't let her go.

"Bats!" she says more seriously. "I bet they were afraid of the owl. Or the owl disturbed some bugs and the bats went in hot pursuit of the insects."

I look down into Riley's eyes. She's looking up at me. We're rooted in place, not separating, just staring at one another. Then the sliding door opens and Ben walks out. His eyes go wide, and a wicked grin takes over his face. Riley jumps back, and I step away just as quickly, making it look like we were about to do something we obviously weren't going to do.

"I'll just ..." Ben says, turning to go back inside. "I heard a bunch of screaming, so ..."

His face contorts as if to say, *Why would Riley be screaming if you are about to kiss her?*

I shake my head vehemently. "Nope. No. Just bats. It was bats. There were bats."

Ben looks around. Of course, there's not a sign of a bat anywhere in sight.

"Baaaaats. Yeah. Okay. Right," he says.

"It was bats. Like a hundred of them. They were swarming us and bombarding us. One hit me in the forehead!" Riley tells him.

"Okay. Sure. Bats. I get it."

Riley and I look at one another.

"I think I'll turn in," I say.

"Yeah. Me too. After washing my face," Riley says.

"Don't let me keep you two from hanging out *bat watching*." Ben emphasizes bat watching like it's code for something else.

"We're not. You're not. It's fine," Riley says. She looks at me and says, "Goodnight, Cam."

"Night, Riley."

When she passes by Ben on her way into the house she says, "It really was bats."

"Mm hmm. I know. Bats."

I don't stick around to hear Ben's take on what he thinks he walked up on. I follow Riley into the house. The feel of Riley in my arms is a tangible memory. If I close my eyes, I can still smell her, a combination of chlorine and that chocolatey warm scent of hers. My skin hums with the memory of holding her.

Eventually, I must drift off, because I wake to sunlight streaming through the curtains and the sound of conversation in the main room. A glance at the clock tells me it's seven thirty. We have to get a move on today if we want to make the sunset over the Grand Canyon this evening. In the hot tub, when the girls weren't raving about that hooligan in a beanie, we all managed to agree it was a goal to make it to the national park before dark.

Everyone quickly showers and dresses so Ben and I can load the bags on top of the van. Then we take off to the address that had been written on Riley's palm for donuts on a double decker bus. She took a photo of her hand before she went swimming so she could preserve the address for this morning.

The top of the donut bus has rows of wooden benches facing one another with slightly rickety tables between each pair of seats. We pull out our donuts and Ben reads us the weather forecast while we eat.

"It says to expect precipitation tomorrow or the next day. At the end of July?"

"Yeah," I tell him. "It's a desert, but this part of the country can get these rogue storms throughout the summer. There's sometimes a lot of wind, even tornadoes come through. And then there are thunderstorms strong enough to cause flash flooding. I'm sure we'll be fine, but I read up on conditions we could expect before we left Ohio."

Riley and I keep glancing at one another. We haven't spoken directly to each other since we were together on the deck before finally going to bed. I don't know what she told my sister about last night—if anything. She's got a shy smile on her face right now, along with a little smudge of whipped cream filling I want to lean over and kiss off her chin.

"I bet the bats take shelter during the storm. It's almost like they never existed," Ben says with a smirk on his presumptuous face.

"What are you talking about?" Madeline asks. "I told you I'm not afraid of bats."

"I know you're not. Riley. Are you? Afraid of bats? Or do you love bats? Are they your favorite?"

"Ben," I say with a warning note in my voice.

Madeline looks around at all three of us. "What is going on with you three?"

Ben can dish it out, but I still trust him not to spill his assumption to my sister. Even if Riley and I kissed and Ben found out, he wouldn't say a thing to anyone. He's got my back.

"Nothing. I'm just being weird about bats," Ben says.

"You are absolutely the weirdest," Madeline says.

"You love my weirdness. It's hot, admit it."

"Right. So hot," she says, laughing at Ben, and then flicking a bit of donut at him.

Ben apparently takes Madeline's reaction as some sort of challenge. He plucks a small bit off his donut and flicks it at her. Before I have a chance to stop them, the two of them are dismantling their donuts. Pieces of pastry are pinging off faces, chests, and arms.

They devolve into a fit of laughter while continuing to assail one another with pea-sized crumbles of what was supposed to be breakfast.

"You guys are picking this mess up," I say.

I regret the words as soon as they're out of my mouth, because the two of them turn and join forces to aim their assault at me. They flick me with tiny morsels of baked goods in rapid fire succession. I open my mouth and try to catch whatever's lobbed at me, but I miss half the pellets. A chunk smacks my forehead and falls to my lap. I look up to see Riley beaming with pride.

"Oh, payback is going to be so severe, Sunshine. You will regret that cheap shot."

"Worth it," she says, popping the last bite of her donut in her mouth and licking her lips while looking straight at me.

I busy myself cleaning up crumbs off the table, reeling from thoughts of Riley and how I'd like to kiss her, hold her, listen to her laugh. Okay. I'm not reeling from my thoughts as much as they are reeling me like a fish on the end of a hook.

We clean up the mess, and then end up getting another batch of donuts for the road when we come downstairs.

Once we're outside Albuquerque, we make good time. Madeline insists we pull off into a small town called Grants to drive through an arched neon sign that says Route 66, so we veer off the highway, drive through while Riley snaps pictures, and get right back on the road.

Aside from that stop, we drive along without interruption for a while, resuming our game of Hot Seat to pass the time. The landscape outside takes on subtle, almost imperceptible shifts as we travel further west. More plateaus appear in the distance. The plants are denser and slightly greener. It's still mostly scrub and desert, but if you observe closely, there's a gradual shift.

I'd really love to keep my eyes and mind on all that's outside the van, but Ben made Riley the tribute as the first passenger in the hot seat.

He asks her, "Who was your first celebrity crush?"

It's almost a cruel question since we both know, and we relentlessly teased her about it for several years whenever we were bored or felt like getting a rise out of her.

"Clark, and you know I'm not lying."

"Claaaark," Ben says in a girly voice.

I shoot him a little look from my spot in the driver's seat. Riley can't see me, unless she catches me in the rearview.

Madeline looks over at Riley, sympathy written all over her face. But Riley surprises us all by flipping the tables and joining in.

"Oh, Clark! You are my seventh grade dream," she coos. "Those gangly legs and barely-there muscles. The way you drew out the studio audience's canned laughter. Whatever will I do without you?"

She laughs at her own joke. Then she looks at me.

I ask her my hot seat question. "What's the biggest mistake you've ever made?"

Considering her comfort with talking about embarrassing moments, I figure this question won't unnerve her much. I'm basically throwing her a bone in my own way. Hopefully no one catches onto the fact that I'm purposely going easy on Riley.

"Telling the guy I like that I've got feelings for him."

She stares me straight in the eyes. I have to look back at the road, since I'm driving, but it's like she was trying to tell me something. Riley likes another guy? And she told him? But telling him was a mistake. Does that mean he didn't feel the same way for her? How do I get answers without being obvious?

Why did I ask that question?

Madeline says, "Hmmmm. Who did you tell you liked them? This I have to think about."

Then she asks, "What's the biggest secret you've ever kept from your best friend?"

Riley swallows hard. I can actually hear the gulping sound from the front seat.

Then she says, "Not telling her who I like."

Riley murmurs, "Sorry, Mads."

"It's okay, girly," Madeline says quietly. "I still love you. And you know me. I'm a bloodhound. I will find out one way or another. You must have your reasons."

"Well, I guess we know your lie," Ben says. "You never told the guy you like that you like him."

Riley nods.

"So, we each get a point from that one except you, Rye Rye," Ben says.

"That's fine, you earned them."

She's not sad ... but she's subdued.

Who's the guy she likes? She hasn't told him. And what am I going to do about it?

"Who's next?" Ben asks. "You or me?"

"Rock, Paper, Scissors?" I ask.

The girls giggle a little from the back seat.

"Nah. I'll just go."

"What's your biggest fantasy?" Madeline asks Ben.

"You seriously just asked him that?" Riley says to Mads.

"Keep it PG," Madeline tacks on.

"It just so happens my biggest fantasy is PG. Thank you very much," Ben says. "Unless you count my dream of marrying Camila Cabello."

"Seriously?" I ask.

"Dude. She's my dream girl. And I'm her dream guy. She just doesn't know it yet."

"Isn't she like twenty-six or seven?"

"She's mature."

"Your perfect match, then," Madeline says, rolling her eyes.

"Tell her for me, would you?"

"Answer the question, would you?" I say.

"Okay. Okay. My biggest fantasy is traveling the world. Like having a year off to go to all these exotic places. I'd visit Fiji, and the Great Wall of China, and tour all around Europe, and Greenland, and Iceland ... New Zealand and Australia. And, if it's really my fantasy we're talking about here, I would have the love of my life alongside me to experience it all together before we settled down to raise our family."

"Camila?" I ask, with a half-smile.

"Obviously, not really. Someone I meet and fall in love with. I haven't met her yet."

"How do you know that?" Riley asks.

"I just know. When I meet the one, I won't be able to get her off my mind. She'll consume me."

"Sounds more like a deadly virus," Madeline teases.

"Love can be like that," Ben says in all seriousness. "You're almost sick with it at first. I haven't ever experienced it. But I've witnessed it a few times—enough to know I want it, and that it's worth the wait."

"Okay, Romeo, have you ever broken the law?" Riley asks. "And if so, what was your crime?"

"I have. We stole the White's tractor and rode it around town in the middle of the night."

"Does that really count?" I ask.

"It does, you felon."

"Even if they'd never press charges, and I'm pretty sure they knew we did it?"

"Even if. We still took someone else's property valued at over five K and did so without their permission."

"Dang. I'm a hardened criminal."

"You are the Sundance to my Cassidy," Ben says. "And now we're on the lam."

I chuckle.

Off to the side of us the horizon begins to grow murky.

"Hey. Do you see that?" I ask Ben.

"Yeah. It looks like a herd of horses or buffalo. Do they even have buffalo out here?"

"Yeah, it's like a massive herd's kicking up dust. Only it's getting taller. What is it really?"

The wind picks up, pulling at the van in inconsistent tugs. I tighten my grip on the wheel. We all watch as this wall of dust grows on the horizon to the left of us, getting taller and taller by the second. Rain starts to fall gently and then hail follows almost immediately.

Riley and Madeline have their phones out. "It's a haboob!" Madeline shouts.

"Tell me you're not serious," Ben says. "What kind of name is that?" Then he starts repeating the word "Haboob. Haboob. Haboob. Oh yeah. That's definitely my new favorite weather term."

"You had an old favorite weather term?" Riley asks.

"It sounds like boob, that's why," Madeline stage whispers to Riley.

They giggle, but then grow serious when they see what I've been watching. This wall of dust looks like some CGI image in an apocalyptic movie.

"It's a wind and dust storm. Looks like it's mixing with a hailstorm. You're supposed to pull over and wait it out," Riley says.

I do just that. We pull off the highway onto the shoulder.

"Turn your lights off," Madeline says.

I do. "Why?"

"Cars behind you won't see you're not moving, and they may try to follow you if they see your lights. It can cause an accident. Just stay off the road, and we'll wait this out."

The hail pelts the car. Thankfully there's a tarp over the luggage up top. As long as it holds, our things should stay dry.

The wall of dust is taller than a mountain, moving our way, but it seems to be shrinking now that it's meeting the point where hail is falling heavily. We sit in silence in the van. The engine's off and I engaged the emergency brake. We don't even have the music Riley had queued up as a distraction anymore.

Ben and I climb out of the front seat and join the girls in the back while the storm rages outside the van. Other cars and semis had been driving ahead of us, but I can't see them through the storm anymore.

23

RILEY

You keep me safe, I'll keep you wild.
~ Unknown

We try to play Hot Seat, but it's a half-hearted effort at distraction with the storm raging around the van. Visibility is gone. The van rattles and rocks in response to the force of the wind. We have no other choice than to wait it out. We're Midwesterners. We know how to do storms. Still, being in a vintage tin can through this kind of an onslaught would shake the nerves of even the most seasoned farmers back home.

Madeline keeps checking her phone. "These types of storms are fast and furious, so it says."

"I'm getting the furious part, loud and clear," Ben says.

The guys folded out the two chairs Duke stowed in this overhead slot. We pulled up the flap table that's hinged to the wall. I'm sitting across from Cameron and his foot keeps bumping or nudging mine. I know there's not a ton of space back here, but it almost seems intentional, especially now that he's stopped wiggling it around and it's resting against mine. I'm not complaining—just confused.

The past twenty-four hours feel increasingly confusing where Cameron's concerned. I don't want to project my smitten hopes all over him and our interactions, but some of it seems awfully close to flirting, or possessive jealousy. Whatever passed between us on the deck last night felt a lot like a kiss about to happen. And from Ben's reaction, I wasn't the only one with that impression. Was Cam really going to kiss me? I look at Cam, that question probably etched across my face. He's in the hot seat.

Ben asks, "What's the biggest misconception about you?"

Cam doesn't even pause. "That I can't loosen up and let go. People see me as some sort of stick in the mud, killjoy, party-pooper, you name it."

"Well, we know that's your lie," Madeline jokes.

Cam doesn't laugh. "I'm fun, Mads. You might not see it. Just because a guy is responsible, doesn't mean he can't let go and have fun."

There's a note of irritation in Cam's voice before he says, "I mean, I stole a tractor, didn't I?"

"Darn straight you did," Ben chimes in.

"Why did your last relationship break up?" Madeline asks, glancing out the window and then back at her brother.

"Low blow," Ben says with a long whistle.

"It's fine," Cam says.

He looks Madeline in the eyes. "I wasn't fun enough, according to her."

I wince. I really do want to take that Stephanie down. What did Cam ever see in her?

My mouth runs ahead of my brain. Maybe it's the storm. It

could be the fact that Cam's ankle is leaning on mine like a private anchor, a tether between us that no one else can see or feel.

"If you had to kiss anyone in this van, who would it be?"

Cam gets this deliciously sexy look on his face. He runs his tongue lightly over his lower lip. He takes his time looking at each of us and stroking his stubble—something he let grow in overnight—as if this is a tough decision and he has to weigh his options. Then Cam combs his hand through his hair and his eyes latch onto mine. I couldn't look away if I wanted to.

"Ben, obviously," he says. And then he lunges for Ben. "Come 'mere. Gimme a smooch, Benny."

Ben literally squeals as he lurches backward, and then he cracks up. "I always knew you had the hots for me, bro. I'm flattered! I'm waiting for Camila, though. Don't go breaking her heart."

"I need you, Benny," Cam carries on. "Get over here."

Cam's arms are outstretched toward Ben and he's wagging his eyebrows and then giving this smolder that definitely makes me wish I were in Ben's chair right now.

All of a sudden, Ben leans toward Cam, grips his cheeks, and places the loudest, sloppiest kiss on Cam's forehead, followed by a raspberry. It's messy, noisy, gross, and completely hilarious.

"That's all the action you're getting from me," Ben says. He pauses and then he looks up through his lashes at Cam. "You haven't even taken me to dinner."

We're rolling. The whole vanful of us. I'm clutching my abdomen, Madeline leans into me and we laugh so hard tears are streaming down our cheeks. I can barely catch my breath.

When the laughter dies down, Madeline turns to me and asks, "What made you ask that?"

"Who knows?" I say in as cavalier of a tone as I can muster. "I just wanted to shake things up, I guess."

I can't even look at Cameron.

Then he says, "Okay. Guess my lie!"

Madeline and I both say, "You don't want to kiss Ben," as if we rehearsed saying it synchronized.

Ben throws a hand to his chest. "What? Rejected so soon? You only wanted me for the moment. I feel so cheap!"

We tally the points. Ben wins. He'll be the one to choose the stops tomorrow—that is, if the weather doesn't choose them for us.

The hail starts to dissipate. The wind dies down almost as dramatically as it started. We're left with a mild rainstorm in the wake of what felt potentially devastating. Our view down the road ahead is restored, even though the rain still falls steadily.

Cam looks around outside and says, "I think it's safe to drive again. I just need to take a look at the roof to make sure everything's still secure up there."

"In the rain?"

"Not much choice in that. We need to get back on the road, and sitting here until this storm completely passes may sacrifice another hour."

He shucks the hoodie he's wearing so that he's only in a thin white undershirt.

"I'll go out with you," Ben offers.

"No use in two of us getting soaked," Cam says. "If I need you, I'll knock on the window. Why don't you help the girls stash the table and chairs?"

Cam steps over the cabinets and into the front seat and then he opens the driver-side door and steps out into the rain. I watch through the window as his shirt goes from dry to wet, clinging to his pecs and abs like a second skin. His hair drips with water. His body disappears up the ladder and we hear his motion overhead.

In no time, Cam's back down and in the driver's seat. I grabbed a towel while Madeline collapsed the table and Ben stashed the chairs. I hand the towel up to Cam and he does this sexy ruffling of his wet hair with it, and then shakes the excess off like he's in some sort of car-abandoned-on-the-highway commercial. Triple A would explode their membership if they made an ad campaign of Cam drying off right now. And then he does it. He pulls off his wet T-shirt, letting it sail over the front seats so it lands in a heap on the floor of the van about three feet in front of me. He grabs his hoodie from the passenger seat and pops it over his head.

I attempt to still my thoughts. Oh, who am I kidding? I'll be seeing images of Cam pulling his wet T-shirt over his rain-soaked head for years to come. If I'm being honest, I'm not trying to resist him like I was. Not when I think of what his eyes seem to be saying every time I look at him. Not when I remember how it felt to be held by him last night.

I'm not afraid of bats, as you'd expect after a traumatic encounter like that one. Nope. I pretty much want to set up a shrine to bats—the unexpected matchmakers of the animal kingdom.

"I'm pretty hungry," Cam says to Madeline. "What's near here that would give us an early lunch stop—or at least get me some protein?"

"You've got hummus and carrots in the mini-fridge," Ben teases.

"Yeah. I'm thinking something more substantial."

Madeline says, "I was just thinking the same thing. There's the historic El Rancho Hotel in Gallup. It's only about forty-five minutes from here. They have a restaurant on site. Listen to this. The Silver Screen Cafe is our original ranch-style dining room with high ceilings, exposed wood beam trusses and rustic cowboy décor. They even have a dish called Duke's Loaded Nachos."

"Awww, man. Duke will love this!" Ben says. "I'm definitely getting some of those."

"Pretty sure they're talking about John Wayne," Cam says.

"Whatever. Duke will still love it."

"I need to call him anyway," Cam says.

He glances at me. "I want to make sure there's nothing special we have to do to your baby here after she survived that dust storm."

"Tina," I say.

"Tina?"

"Yeah. I'm naming her after Tina Turner. She's a legend. She's a survivor. And she always made people take notice of her wherever she went. This van is named Tina."

"It's perfect," Madeline says.

"I love it," Cam says. "Well, I'll be calling Duke about Tina. And then we can eat."

It's still only eleven in the morning when we pull into Gallup. Having ridden out the storm makes it feel much later for some reason. We grab lunch in the hotel restaurant. Everything on the menu's named after someone who was famous in the movies back in the early days of film, like Katherine Hepburn, Humphrey Bogart, and Roy Rogers.

We place our order. Cam puts in a call to Duke, then he joins us at the table when the food is served.

"Duke says check the undercarriage to make sure nothing blew under there and got stuck during the storm. I already checked the front and rear bumpers when I got out in the rain."

I'm pretty sure I blush thinking of Cam in the rain.

Smooth. Really smooth.

"I hate to disappoint," Madeline announces. "But, we're

twenty five minutes from the border between New Mexico and Arizona here. And I have to insist we keep the tradition going."

"Of course you do," Cam says, smiling over at me.

"We're all in on the border photos now," Ben agrees.

I smile around at my friends. So many of my bucket list items had to be sacrificed on this drive, but when I think back over the trip so far, what we've done has been practically perfect in its own way.

The drive to the border goes quickly. The landscape includes more rocky cliffs along the roadside and in the distance. The Welcome to Arizona sign is in a rest area, at the far edge that faces the highway. We pull in, hop out of the van and take photos. My favorite is where Cam and I both make the letter A with our arms overhead and Mads and Ben make a Z with their arms going in separate directions. It's goofy and perfect.

"Next stop, Winslow, Arizona!" Madeline shouts when we're back in Tina, ready to roll. "It's an hour and a half from here."

"I was hoping for the Petrified Forest, but I think we need to skip it," she tells me privately once we're driving. "I don't want to miss getting to the Grand Canyon before sunset."

I make a call to my parents on this leg of the drive.

"Hey, Mom."

"Oh, sweetie. We've been on pins and needles waiting to hear from you."

"I called you last night after we got out of the hot tub."

"I know. And I know I have to let you go away and grow up. Just bear with me while I adjust to it."

"You've had three years to practice," I remind her.

"I know. But this is the first cross-country road trip you've taken. How's it going? What did you do for fun today? Anything interesting?"

"We hit a little storm midmorning."

Ben turns around and his eyes go wide.

I shrug.

He smiles and shakes his head.

Madeline nudges me. Then she says, "It was really little," in a voice intended for my mom to hear.

"Oh, hi, Madeline, sweetie." Mom says, as if Mads can hear her.

"You're not on speaker mom. I'll tell her you say, hi."

"Hi, Mrs. Stewart," Ben shouts from up front.

I put my mom on speaker. "Okay. Everyone, say hi!"

We all shout, "Hi!" and my mom answers.

Then I take her off speaker. "We had donuts on this double decker bus in Albuquerque. They were super yummy. I think you'd have loved that."

"Ooh, that sounds fun."

"And now we're heading into Winslow."

"To stand on a corner!" Mom nearly squeals.

"Yes. As cliché as it is, we will."

Mom starts singing the Eagles' song. I endure a few bars.

"Welp. I'd better go, Mom. I just wanted to check in since we'll be in the Grand Canyon tonight. I don't know how the reception will be."

"Be safe, love bug."

"I will. Give Dad a hug for me."

"I will, sweetheart. Make memories, m'kay?"

"We are, Mom. We really are."

I hang up with my mom after telling her I love her. This prompts everyone to call home. At least we know we've touched base before we get to our campground where we may or may not be able to reach them tonight.

Winslow, Arizona is darling. Of course, I queued up the song on my playlist as we approached town. The four of us belted out the words as we drove through the flat desert outskirts, and then into the center of the historic streets lined with well-maintained brick buildings. There's a bronze statue of Jackson Browne on one corner. In the middle of the street is a giant Route 66 sign painted onto the road.

Legend has it that Jackson Browne's car broke down when he was traveling Route 66 to Sedona. He had to stand on a corner to wait for roadside assistance, and this famous song was born of that hardship.

We shop at the Standin' on a Corner gift shop. More Route 66 souvenirs are collected by each of us. It reminds me, I still have that arrowhead to give to Cam.

An hour away from Winslow is Flagstaff. I'd really like to spend more time here, but we're focused on getting groceries for our overnight camping trip at the Grand Canyon. It's nearly four o'clock, and our campground is an hour and forty minutes north of here. Flagstaff is officially considered the gateway to the Grand Canyon. The town has a population of seventy-six thousand people, but there's a lot to do around here like hiking, water sports, and spending time in the historic downtown.

I will say, grocery shopping with Ben is something everyone should experience once in their lives, at least. Cam's pushing the cart, and true to form, he's on mission. Ben, on the other hand, is acting like a preschooler in a candy shop.

"Ooooh. Pop Tarts!"

"No," Cam says. "Put those back."

"I'll buy them with my own money," Ben pleads.

"We're splitting the cost of groceries four ways."

"I need my own cart," Ben says. "Wanna ride in a cart, Mads? I'll push you."

Madeline smiles until she catches sight of Cam's frown.

"Ben, seriously. You're going to get us kicked out of this grocery store," Cam says. "Focus. We need food for our night at the campsite, and for breakfast in the morning."

Ben salutes Cam. Then he proceeds to pull a box of Cinnamon Toast Crunch off the shelf and plop it into the basket.

"Bro, cinnamon is good for your digestion," Ben says with a wink.

"I just can't with him," Cam says, pinching the bridge of his nose.

Ben walks down the aisle and disappears out of sight.

"I'll drive into the Grand Canyon," I offer. "You've driven a lot today. And you had to deal with the haboob."

Ben pops his head into our aisle seemingly from out of nowhere. "He doesn't mind a little haboob, do ya Cam?"

Cam shakes his head, but he's stifling a grin.

That's why he and Ben work so well together. Despite their history, there's this balance they each bring to their relationship. Like two children on a teeter-totter: one pushes up, the other goes down, then that one pushes the opposite way again. It's a cooperative effort and it works.

"Pause here," Cam says to me and Madeline.

He stops the cart in front of the meat case.

Ben walks over from where he was surveying an end cap full of cookies and baked goods.

"Should we get hot dogs or hamburger meat? Or do you want to roast sausages? I could grill up some onions and peppers and we could put those with the sausages on kaiser rolls."

"Ohhhh yeah. That. And franks and beans," Ben says.

"Nope. No. Nope. No beans for you," Cam says.

"What? We'll be outdoors."

"You'll be officially outdoors. Very outdoors. As in, you and the bears and whatever else is out there. I'm not sharing my tent with you after franks and beans."

"Gross. And TMI," Madeline says. "The sausages sound

good. Let's get mustard too."

We divide and conquer. I grab oatmeal and some oranges. Cam smiles when I plop my choices into the cart and I feel like I'm the winner on the game show *Supermarket Sweep*, only so much more than that. Just a smile from him has me feeling all warm and tingly.

We load our groceries into the back of Tina, and I take over the driving. Cam says he'll take shotgun.

Madeline gripes. "She's my bestie, not yours, Cam."

"You sat with her all day," he answers calmly. "I need to be up here to help with navigation."

"Because I couldn't?" Mads asks, defensively.

"You probably could."

Cameron says that, but he doesn't move.

Am I an awful friend for being happy Cam's fighting to sit next to me?

Maybe. And he probably is only insisting on sitting here so he can help navigate.

But, I'm still a little giddy over him wanting to be near me, whatever the reason.

24

CAMERON

People are just as wonderful as sunsets
if you let them be.
... I don't try to control a sunset.
I watch with awe as it unfolds.
~ Carl Rogers

Flagstaff feels so different from the desert landscape we've been traveling through for days. Everywhere we look we're surrounded by pine trees. Jagged mountain ranges flank the edges of our view. And, even though Albuquerque is about seven times more populated than Flagstaff, we didn't venture into the city while we were there, so it didn't feel as big. Flagstaff feels like the first place where we're not in a small town that's still reminiscent of life seventy-five years ago.

Riley's at the wheel and I'm next to her. Yes. I wanted to help navigate our way to the campground. But I also wanted to be near her. I'm trying not to give in to the urge to figure out what's going on or what I'm going to do about it. Whatever's happening between us feels nearly inevitable if I'm reading Riley's signals right.

I hope I am.

Then again, I hope I'm not.

Thoughts of Stephanie's words to me creep into my mind. Riley's one of the most fun-loving people I know. Would Riley really want something more than friendship with me? I don't know my own mind. When I look at her, laughing with my sister, or even now, watching her focus on the road as we drive closer to the Grand Canyon, I want nothing more than time alone with her and an opportunity to see what might happen between us.

But, if I allow myself to look past the moment, all the reasons this could be the worst idea I've ever had bombard me: our families, my sister, my shortcomings, the difference in the trajectory of our lives right now.

The pine trees line the road on either side of us for a while, and then they spread out until we're driving through more low shrubbery and wide open spaces, only the feel is different than the desert we left behind. This is high desert, I guess. We come to more dense spots of trees, and then the forest thins again so we're riding along wide open spaces. The road merges with another, and then we're in a little shopping area where all the buildings look like mountain tourist spots.

"They've got McDonald's!" Madeline shouts.

"And an IMAX Theater," Ben says.

A short while after passing through that village, we're at the south entrance station to the park. We inch forward behind a line of cars, trailers, and RVs, eventually pay our entrance fee, and head up to Mather campground. Once we find the site we reserved, we pull the van into the curved driveway.

It's around six-thirty. We have an hour until sunset.

Ben and I make quick work of the tent. The girls will sleep on the bed in the van, and Ben and I will be in the tent on the ground, only about ten feet away from them. While Ben and I are setting up camp, Mads and Riley pull together what we'll need for dinner, chopping vegetables and getting out everything we'll need to cook. We leave all that in the van so we can go to the Visitor Center Bus Terminal to catch the orange shuttle to Yaki Point. It's supposedly one of the best spots to watch the sunset over the canyon. No one can come to this point in their own vehicle, so the crowds are thinner than at some of the other viewing spots.

I'm nearly buzzing with excitement. After days on the road, and so many nights in hotels and strange beds, a night sleeping out in nature is just what the doctor ordered. And, though I won't say anything to Riley, Mads, or Ben, seeing the sun dip away over the rim of the Grand Canyon is definitely a bucket list item for me—and not just for this trip, but for my life.

The shuttle is nearly full with over thirty passengers.

Ben leans close to me and says, "I guess we're not the only people wanting to see this sunset."

"Yeah. For some reason, I pictured being this lone traveler out on the point with just the four of us silently watching the sun drop over the opposing rim."

"Well, it will be more of a collective experience," Ben says with a chuckle. "Don't let it dim the excitement you're feeling. I can tell this means a lot to you. And think about it. We're only a day away from here once we're settled on Marbella Island. An hour boat ride and a seven hour drive and we could be here anytime. We can do this again."

"Yeah." I nod. "We can."

The actual viewing spot has a metal railing embedded into the rock. People gather there to watch the sunset. It's seven now, so we're getting close to the drop. There's another flat rock with no protection around it. Not a soul is in that spot.

"Do you guys feel okay watching from there?" I ask.

"I might hang back from the edge a little," Mads says.

"I definitely want to watch from there," Riley says.

We walk out onto the point. I drop down and fold my legs. Ben sits on one side of me and Riley on the other. Madeline sits behind us. I don't blame her. The drop down from here is steep and relentless. Some trees and bushes dot the sides of the cliffs, but one wrong step and your life would be over or radically impaired forever.

We sit quietly, taking in the indescribable beauty of the cavern beneath and across from us. Striations of lavender, peach, tans and creams etch the sides of the canyon walls. Various rock formations seem to rise out of nowhere, pointing heavenward in shapes that defy reason. Michelangelo in all his talent never carved or painted something so breathtaking.

As the sun drops, a hush seems to fall over the four of us, maybe over the whole canyon. What was muted pastel on the rock sediment layers now seems to become more saturated in deeper shades of orange, purple, and even turquoise. The sky darkens incrementally, a charcoal gray meeting the vibrant sunset colors. With each dimming stage of the sun's retreat, the canyon becomes increasingly mystical and enchanting, until the last burst of light seems to flare on the horizon.

The night consumes everything. The moon rises behind us. Movement draws my attention to our left. A few elk are grazing under trees on the other side of the path. I wordlessly point toward them so my friends can see them too. They seem accustomed to human visitors in the park, unaffected by our nearness.

No one speaks or makes a move to stand. It's as if we're all transfixed, trying to absorb everything we just experienced and commit it to memory. I've never been so acutely aware of how small I am as I am at this moment. I look to my right and Riley's soft smile is the first thing I see. I want to draw her hand into mine—to interlace our fingers, to feel her skin on mine, to sit together sharing what we've just experienced in a way that's just for us. But, I can't.

I refuse to allow myself any frustration. This moment is too perfect to wish it away with thoughts of what I'd rather have. She's here. We did enjoy this together. We'll always have the memory of a shared sunset over this canyon.

The shuttle leaves within thirty minutes of sunset, so we eventually break the spell and stand to rejoin the group of travelers taking the tram back to the bus stop.

Once we're back at camp, I start a fire and Ben lights the camp stove. Riley grills the sliced onions and peppers in a frying pan on the stove while I skewer the sausages and brown them in the flames. We gather around the fire with our dinner and eat.

"I am going to sleep like a log," Ben says after he finishes his sausage.

"I think we all are," Madeline adds.

"I'm getting up to see the sunrise," I remind everyone. "It's at five thirty, so I'll be waking an hour before that. And it will be brisk out. Maybe fifty degrees, if that. I won't wake you unless you tell me to."

"Don't wake me," Ben says. "I'd love to see the sunrise, but I'm not pushing it."

"Same," Madeline says.

"If I'm up, I'll go," Riley says.

The firelight dances across her features and I watch her from my seat across the firepit.

"I'll probably wake when you do," Ben adds.

"Good. Welp. Whoever's up. We'll go."

We sit around the fire a little longer, Riley pulls out her guitar and softly sings some songs. Her voice could catch the attention of a record executive, but she seems unaware of her own talent—and especially clueless as to her effect on me.

Everyone starts yawning before nine, so we douse the flames and get ready for bed.

Right before the girls head into Tina for the night, Riley turns toward Ben and me and says, "We're three hours north of the world's largest pistachio. It's thirty feet tall. And I want it to go on record that I'm not even asking to go see this marvel."

I chuckle. "Duly noted. Goodnight, Sunshine."

"Night, Cam. Night, Ben."

"Nighty night, Sunnnnshiiiine," Ben says, exaggerating the nickname for my benefit.

Once the girls are in the van, Ben asks me, "So, are you going to do something about that?"

"About what?"

"Your feelings for her?"

"My feelings?"

"Dude. It's too late, and I'm too tired. Are you going to cross the line with Riley?"

"You make it sound so romantic."

"I'm sure you've got the romance covered. I'm just trying to see where you stand. What are your intentions with our little sunshine?"

"First of all, she's not our sunshine. Secondly, I don't know."

I'm quiet, staring at the embers glowing in the firepit as they flicker from orange to white to nothing. There's something about being out around a fire in the dark with your best friend. It feels like I can safely let all the thoughts in my head out for him to examine.

"To be honest, I'm still messed up about Stephanie."

"Messed up, like you still have feelings for her?"

The sour note in his voice isn't even disguised. There's no love lost between the two of them. And Ben watched me go through a world of grief after our breakup. He's not a fan of Stephanie's at all. I don't talk about her much anymore. What would be the use?

"No. Definitely no feelings for her. Not even anger. I'm just left wondering what I lack."

"You're kidding, right?"

I look over at him, even though I doubt he can make out my face.

"I'm not kidding. She hit pretty close to the mark in her assessment. I was serious, goal-oriented, focused. Maybe I'm not that fun."

Ben's quiet. I give him time to answer. He'll tell me the truth. That's one thing we've always done for one another.

"I'm going to say something, and I hope you really listen."

"I'm all ears."

I poke at a few chunks of burnt wood that still have a little glow to them, moving them apart so they'll die out.

"You don't need to ask me if you're fun. Whatever I think won't make a difference. I have fun with you. But we both know I'm the fun one around here. No one matches me when it comes to the fun factor. If you ask me, you're asking the wrong questions."

"What do you mean?"

"Trying to be what she said you weren't. Since when does she get to be the one who says what you need to be? You're not a match for Stephanie. And, if you ask me, that's a good thing. I would have suffered through for your sake, but I always hoped you'd move on from her. She wasn't a match for you either. She was never satisfied with you. That's a bad omen in a relationship. Don't you want a woman who already thinks you're enough? There are plenty of women who want a strong, responsible, thoughtful man who knows how to let loose at times and knows when to reel it in. That's you. What you need to ask yourself is if you're ready for that woman when she comes around."

"And you think that's Riley?"

"I don't know if it is. But I've been watching you two this trip. Something's different. She's looking at you when you aren't watching, and I'd say she's not disappointed. She's definitely not making a list of things she wishes she could change about you. She looks like she's admiring you half the time, and longing for you the other half."

"What if you're wrong?"

"What if I am? So, you make a move and get shot down. This is Riley we're talking about. You two will move past it. You'll have a laugh down the road—*remember that time I came on to you and you were shocked and straightened me out?*" He pauses long enough for me to seriously cringe at that possibility. "But if I'm right? Well, that's a risk I think you'd want to take. She's a catch. And ... if I may say so, as the man you wish you could kiss ... so are you."

I chuckle. But I'm considering all Ben's words. It's a lot to digest.

He cuts through my thoughts. "I was sure something already happened between you two last night. Bats? Seriously? You two could have said something more believable than bats."

"It was bats!" I say with more volume than I anticipated.

"Whatever you say, loverboy. I'm just saying, make the move. If that sunset told you anything, it's that our days will come and go too quickly. We need to focus on what really matters in life. Don't waste one more sunset wishing away your life. Take action."

"The sunset said all that to you?"

"I'm a poet at heart, my friend. Me and Taylor Swift."

"Okay, Tay Tay. Let's brush our teeth and get some sleep."

IT'S chilly when I wake, and dark. I check the time on my phone. It's four ten. My alarm is set to go off in twenty minutes. I unzip my sleeping bag as quietly as I can and stand, hitting my head on the roof of the tent when I do. The movement wakes Ben.

"Hey," he says, rolling over and looking up at me.

"Hey. I'm getting up to see the sunrise. You coming?"

"Nah. I'll catch it another time. I'm too beat."

"Okay. Suit yourself," I say, pulling on my hoodie, shucking my pajama bottoms and putting on some jeans I had tucked in the corner. The tent fabric is wet with dew and it drips down on me while I'm dressing.

I unzip the tent, then turn and secure it. Then I make a quick pit stop at the restroom. When I'm walking out, I look up and nearly run into Riley.

"Oh!" she says.

"Hey. Good morning. I didn't expect you to be awake."

"I set an alarm on my phone. I realized something after we went to bed."

"What's that?"

"You'll need to drive to the shuttle pick up."

"Oh. Yeah. That's a major unexpected glitch in my plan."

I rub my hand through my hair and catch Riley watching the movement.

"So," she says. "I thought I'd drive us over there. Mads already woke up. I told her we needed to drive to the shuttle. She said, *Keep the bed down and you can do whatever you want.*"

I chuckle. "She never was much of a morning person."

"Truer words were never spoken."

"So ..."

"So, let's go watch the sunrise."

I follow Riley back to camp. Neither of us says much. I'd expect to be anxious or wound up, but she has the opposite effect on me. I'm never more at ease than when I'm with her or Ben. Why haven't I ever noticed how she calms my nerves? Or is this new?

"I'll drive," Riley offers.

I'm glad to let her. We hop into the front seats, and she starts the engine. Madeline rolls over in the bed in the back of the van and makes a noise that's somewhere between a grunt and a groan. Then she's out like a light again.

We park the van, locking it with Madeline inside, sleeping soundly. If she wakes, she has food and water, and there's a restroom right here if she needs it.

Riley and I get on the four-thirty shuttle. They run every half hour until six, and then every fifteen minutes after that. If we hadn't made this one, we'd be on the five o'clock. That was my original plan, but this gives us an even better lead time. We get off the shuttle at a different spot than last night: Yavapai Point. It's touted as being less crowded than the more popular and more accessible, Mather Point.

We find a spot away from the rock half-wall where a few other tourists are standing around in the dusky early-morning darkness. The canyon looks mostly black, like an endless cavern, but we can make out a faint line of the rim across the way.

I put my hand on Riley's back and lead her to a flat rock with no guard rail around it. We're the only two at this spot for now. She doesn't flinch at my touch. Neither of us says a word as we sit down side by side. I put my arms behind me, bracing myself on my flattened palms. Riley mimics my stance and her pinky brushes mine. She looks up at me. Time seems to freeze.

The sun hasn't risen, but there's a pre-dawn light that makes it easier to see her face.

I move my pinky just the slightest bit so it's resting on top of hers.

She gasps, and then she smiles up at me. Her ring finger moves so it's on top of my pinky finger. We aren't watching the sunrise. It's not happening yet. I'm not sure I'll end up turning to see it when it does. I lift my hand, and in the greatest risk of my life, I scoot closer to Riley so we're touching side to side. I pull her arm from behind her, lace our fingers together, and set our clasped hands on my thigh.

Her eyes go wide when she looks at me, but she's still smiling.

I lean in so my mouth is just a breath away from the shell of her ear, and I whisper, "Happy Birthday, Sunshine."

"You remembered?"

"Of course, I remembered."

I give Riley's hand a squeeze. She turns and looks down at our fingers, joined together, then she looks back up at me, a question across her face.

Her features start to become clearer as the light from the sunrise becomes the slightest bit brighter. I look away, toward the rim to our right. A thin line of sun is cresting over the edge. Clouds dot the sky, and the light plays off them in hues of peach, pink, lavender, and the faintest yellow. Sometimes an ethereal ray of light filters through a cluster of clouds, casting its straight rays out across the sky. Riley and I sit together in silence, watching the sun make its way over the rim until it's so bright we can't stare directly at it anymore. The canyon goes from black to charcoal to revealing the natural earthy pastel lines in the rock over a matter of minutes. It almost looks like someone is shining a spotlight across the scene in front of us now. We can easily see to the bottom of the canyon, stretching so far down it almost takes my breath away.

I turn to Riley. She hasn't released my hand.

"Cam?"

"Yeah?"

Her tongue darts out and wets her lower lip. She stares up at me, eyes wide with anticipation. Her brows lift in an invitation, and I know this is the moment everything changes for us. Either I accept her unspoken offer, or I decline and shut her down. All the reasons I should stop attempt to grab my attention like a teen sister impatiently waiting outside the bathroom door, banging and demanding entrance.

I close my eyes for the briefest moment, trying to regain my bearings and still my rambling thoughts—to muster the courage to do what I know we are both waiting for me to do.

Riley's free hand gently cups my cheek.

When I open my eyes, Riley's staring up at me.

There is no way I'm not kissing her.

I bend in and softly brush our lips together.

She hums in response.

"Happy Birthday, Riley," I whisper as I pull back.

She grasps the nape of my neck and pulls me in for another kiss, as if I weren't coming back for more. I lift my hand and cup the back of her neck, and our lips find one another again. She releases my other hand and places her palm on my chest, steadying herself. I feel my heartbeat against her palm, beating for her.

This moment is surreal, and yet it feels like nothing I've ever felt when kissing any other woman.

Riley's hand moves from my chest to my shoulder, and then she grips my arm, clinging to me like she never wants this moment between us to end. Our mouths dance together in the sunrise. My whole body feels alive. I cup her face, softly rubbing my thumb on her cheek.

I need her to know this is so much more than a kiss.

When we pull apart, she rests her forehead on my chin. Then she starts giggling.

It starts soft and light, but soon she's really laughing, fisting the front of my shirt with one of her hands and rocking her forehead on my chin while peals of laughter escape her.

"What's so funny?"

She takes a big breath and finally meets my eyes.

"Did you really just kiss me?"

"Yeah," I say with a chuckle.

Her laughter feels contagious.

"You kissed me. Cameron Reeves kissed me."

"You kissed me too."

I'm not defensive, but I know that wasn't all me. She can't think I made a move on her without her giving me a green light. I would never. Besides, the way she kissed me told me I wasn't the only one.

"Oh, I know I kissed you. I was always going to kiss you. But you kissed me. Cameron. You. Kissed. Me." She giggles some more. Then she looks at me seriously and says, "And you're a way better kisser than I even imagined."

"Thanks?"

I'm so confused. I've never sent a woman into hysterics from a kiss. At least she thinks I'm a good kisser. And what does she mean she was always going to kiss me?

"You were always going to kiss me?"

"Well, I wasn't, of course, because you're Madeline's brother, and you're you, you know. But I was going to kiss you if you kissed me. And you did. You totally did."

She runs her fingers over her lips like she can barely believe we kissed.

"I did. I'll do it again if you need proof," I offer.

"Yeah. That might be a really good idea."

She looks at me and the mood shifts from playful and hesitant to heated in a heartbeat. Her eyes rove mine with a look I can only describe as wonder. Tell me about it. I never in a million years thought I'd be here—on the rim of the Grand Canyon, kissing my sister's best friend while the sun came up over the horizon. But now that I'm here, I can't imagine being anywhere else with anyone else doing anything else.

I lean in and take Riley's mouth like I mean it, wanting her to know this isn't a fluke. I'm not under the influence of the sunrise. It's her—all her. She makes little noises, hums and light moans. I wonder if she even knows she's making them. They are my new favorite sounds.

I run my hand down her hair. It's wild from sleep, untamed and beautiful like her. Something moves me to risk even more. I take my lips away from hers, placing one more kiss on them before I kiss along her jawline, to her neck and right up to the spot where her T-shirt meets her shoulder. She tips her head to allow me easy access to her throat. I kiss my way back up, making a trail to her lips, and then I place a soft, tender kiss on her mouth, lingering to savor her.

When I pull back, Riley's not laughing. She's got a pensive, sated look on her face.

"What are you thinking?" I ask.

"So many things." She sighs this contented sigh. "But mostly, I'm just deliriously happy."

"Me too," I tell her. "Me too."

Riley leans into me, and I wrap my arm around her shoulder. We sit like that, looking out over the canyon together. Then, because we unfortunately can't stay here forever, we stand and prepare to face Madeline and Ben.

25

RILEY

That dip in the road
that sends your belly to your throat ...
that is how it feels when you kiss me.
~ Kellie Elmore

We walk back toward the shuttle together, holding hands.

Me. I'm holding hands with Cameron.

And, he's holding my hand. Willingly. He actually initiated this whole fingers entwined moment between us. We stood from the spot where we watched the sunrise, and he extended his hand. It's not only palm to palm, which is a great way to hold hands too, and I'd be a huge fan of holding Cam's hand that way too. Face it. We could link pinky fingers and I'd be thrilled. But, no. Cam laced our fingers. It feels ... more. And I can barely handle less, let alone the way holding Cameron's hand is making me feel like I could take off and soar over the canyon right now.

Every so often, he rubs his thumb over my knuckles. And when I look up at him, he's smiling down at me with this *no regrets* smile. It's full, and comfortable, and easy.

If you would have told me I'd be sitting on the rim of the Grand Canyon the morning I turned twenty-one, kissing Cameron Freaking Reeves ... well, we all know how likely I thought that was.

My very unhelpful brain keeps trying to bombard me with reality, like the fact that we're on a road trip with my best friend who happens to be Cam's sister. And how supremely unhappy she'd be if she knew about that particular highlight of my birthday. And then there's the small detail that he's about to start his adult life, really adulting in an assistant manager job at a resort, while I'm still the unstable, unfocused college student working a part-time summer job. And, as if that's not enough, I start to think of our parents and what they'll say. Oh, they'd probably be thrilled. Maybe they wouldn't be thrilled. Maybe they'd think this was a horrible idea. This. What even is this?

I'm telling my brain to shush.

Shush, shush, shush, brain.

Enjoy this. Enjoy Cameron. Enjoy the feel of his hand, and the way he's looking at you like he wanted that kiss as much as you did.

"Wow," Cam says as we climb the steps onto the shuttle.

"Wow, the sunrise, or wow, the kiss?"

Oh, my mouth. Why? It would be so very nice to be able to control what comes out of my mouth.

Cameron chuckles, seeming totally unfazed by our kissing or me asking about how awesome it was. And let's pause right here to note the awesomeness of that kiss. It was—whew. I might just have to fan myself thinking of it. Which would be awkward since it's barely fifty-five degrees out.

Cameron's cool as a cucumber right now. Maybe he kisses girls all the time. No big deal. Just another kiss at one of the Seven Wonders of the World. Tra-la-la. Just chillin' with the homies, kissin' on a death-defying ledge as a sunrise that evades words to describe it crests over the rim beyond us.

But I get the feeling Cameron doesn't make a habit of casually kissing girls. And I definitely don't think he'd randomly kiss me. There's too much complication. And Cameron's cautious almost to a fault. If either of the two of us were going to casually kiss someone on a rock ledge, it would be me. And there was nothing casual about that kiss—at least for me there wasn't. I mean, the man kissed my shoulder. Goosebumps rise at the thought of those sweet kisses along my face and neck.

"No. Well, yes," Cam says. "Wow to both those things. But I meant, wow, there's nearly smoke coming out of your ears from all the thoughts obviously whirling around in there."

He taps my temple lightly.

I know I blush. I can feel the heat rise up my neck and onto my cheeks.

"I overthink everything too, don't worry," he says.

But he doesn't seem to be overthinking our kiss.

We grab a seat toward the middle of the shuttle. A couple in their fifties or sixties sits in the seat across from us.

"First time seeing the sunrise over the canyon?" the wife asks me.

Cam still has our fingers interlaced. Our clasped hands rest on his thigh.

"It was," I answer.

"It's something you'll never forget." She looks between me and Cam. "You'll tell your children about it one day. Maybe you'll even bring them here to experience it too. This was our tenth time. Hopefully, not the last."

"Not the last," the husband says.

I start to say "Oh, we're not ..."

And Cam finishes the sentence, "We're not having children anytime soon. Still just starting out."

He obviously gave her the impression we're married or dating seriously, because she says, "Well, there's no rush. Enjoy this time together. Once the kids come it's a kind of busy you've never imagined before ... and you can't just do things like this as easily for a while. Some folks do. But it takes a lot of intention to be a couple who takes their kids all over like that. I wish we had done it more."

Her husband pats her knee and smiles.

Cam leans in toward me so his mouth is near my ear. "I thought we'd have time on the shuttle to talk about how we want this to go once we're back at the van and, you know, around Mads and Ben."

I smile up at him and say, "Me too."

His warm breath caresses my ear and I want to ask him to stay there. He could recite the alphabet, or the Preamble to the Constitution. I don't care, just so long as he talks into my ear in that voice with his head right there. I nearly hum at the way it tickles in the best of ways.

"We've got to get on the road soon, or I'd say we should stay on the shuttle and talk."

I turn my head so I can look at him. "I know. We've got a day of travel ahead."

He nods. Then he leans in with twenty strangers as our witness and places the softest kiss on my lips. I want to stay on the shuttle until I'm twenty-two. Just sitting here with Cam in this unperturbed bubble. Of course, we'd need sustenance and bathroom breaks ... but man, what a year that would be!

Instead, the shuttle's going to stop and we're going to have to get off. Madeline is in the van—either asleep, or awake by now. Cam and I won't be holding hands and kissing in front of her, obviously. What are we going to do?

"Relax," Cam says in a calm voice that could put a saber-tooth on its back, paws skyward while you rubbed its massive belly.

His mouth is so near to my ear that I feel a chill run down me when his words come out. I think I even shiver a little which makes him smile. I don't know how he can be so calm right now.

I lean toward his ear and he bends so my mouth can be closer to him. But when it comes time to speak, I don't know what to say. If I ask him, *What about Madeline?*, he'll think I'm assuming we have something that is going to last past our kiss this morning. Which, obviously, is what I want. But is it what he wants? He is still holding my hand, which would be a universal sign for keeping things going. But I can't assume anything. My dreamy heart will have us taking our kids to the Grand Canyon in no time. I have to keep both feet planted in this situation. No running off into what if, and what could be. If I say, *What did that kiss mean?,* he might think I'm pushing for something. And I would push for everything with Cameron, but I don't want to seem desperate.

So, here we sit; Cam bent toward me; me with my mouth an inch from his ear, like a statue entitled, *Girl trying to think of what to say and coming up blank*. Yes. It's a long title for a statue.

Cam saves me from my frozen state of indecision.

He turns to me and privately says, "I wish we had more time to talk. Here's what I'm thinking. We need to keep things how they have been for now in front of Madeline and Ben. At least until you and I have had time to really talk. Okay?"

It makes sense. Of course, we can't just come back from a

sunrise kiss and be all, "Hey guys, good morning! So ... we kissed!" I know that. And yet, I feel my stomach flip over when Cam says we need to keep things quiet. Am I his dirty little secret?

He leans in again, "I don't regret that kiss. And, yes. It meant something. I wouldn't just kiss you, Riley. Not even for your birthday. We really need time to talk—time we unfortunately don't have this morning. Until we talk about what happened and what we want to do about it, let's not get everyone involved."

"I agree," I finally say. And, I do. I take a deep breath, look Cam in the eyes and say, "It meant something to me too."

Cameron smiles down at me. It's a warm, comforting smile. I relax into him, allowing my head to rest on his shoulder the last minutes of the ride to the shuttle stop.

I realize I'm smiling so hard it hurts my cheeks. Cameron doesn't regret our kiss. It meant something to him. That means I mean something to him.

It's too bad we're here in this shuttle with all these witnesses because I'd pretty much like to break into a crazy celebration dance.

And that's when I remember it. I have his arrowhead in my pocket. I took it with me, hoping to give it to him as soon as the sun came up. Only, he preoccupied me with far more interesting activities, so I forgot.

I dig the arrowhead out of my pocket, string and all. And then I take our clasped hands and turn them so Cam's palm is up, but we're still holding onto one another. I carefully slide the arrowhead into his hand.

"I got this for you."

He looks at it, slipping his hand from mine so he can hold the necklace up to really examine it.

"You got this for me?"

"Yeah."

"But it's your birthday. I should have gotten you something."

"You did." I smile.

The shuttle pulls up to the stop. Cameron slips the necklace over his head and tucks the arrowhead into his shirt. He looks me in the eye with an expression that could be the death of me if we hadn't just shared the best kiss of my life. Then he leans in and softly brushes my temple with his lips. He waits for the other passengers to exit, and then he walks ahead of me to exit the tram. We make our way to the spot where the van is parked. Cam unlocks my door and holds it open, giving me a quick wink before shutting it and running around to the driver's side.

Madeline stirs when my door shuts.

"How was the sunrise?" she asks in a drowsy voice.

"Amazing. Best sunrise ever, really," I say.

"Mkay. I'm going back to sleep."

"Sweet dreams."

A wave of guilt washes over me. Usually, I'd tell Madeline if I had feelings for a guy. I'd definitely always tell her when I kissed someone—especially someone I had been crushing hard on. These past years as my infatuation with Cameron grew, I haven't been such an open book, for good reason. I miss sharing everything with her. If I'm honest, it's put a small wedge between us. Secrets do that in friendships.

Cam is in a different league than any other guy. Hiding our kiss from Madeline feels deceptive and wrong, even though I believe it's the best thing to do for the time being. Cam said it himself. We haven't even had time to figure out what this means and what we'll do going forward. It's not time to bring other people into what's going on between us—especially not my life-long best friend who happens to be his baby sister.

We drive in silence, Cam looking over at me occasionally, always smiling like the cat that ate the canary. Which is gross, when you think of it—a cat with carnage written all over his face. Cam looks more like the cat who kissed the bejeebers out of this canary. He's happy. And that makes me happy.

It's seven when we get back to the campground. Ben's up with the tent packed up and ready to go.

"Hey, you two," he says when we approach the picnic table. "Good sunrise?"

"Yeah," I say, afraid to say more.

I feel like the whole story is a mere breath away from falling out of me.

I can keep a secret. If a friend of mine confides in me, I'll take that story to my grave. But this feels so monumental—bigger than the canyon itself. It's hard to contain something this huge.

"Mmmmm," Ben hums in this cryptic way, looking between the two of us.

When I look up at Cam, he's got that same smile on his face —the one he had after we kissed.

"So glad the trip to the rim went well. Oh, and Happy Birthday, Rye Rye! My gift to you? You call the shots for stops today. I'm giving you my turn."

"What? You don't have to do that."

"I know. It's just the kind of awesome guy I am."

"Awesome and humble," Cam murmurs.

Cam passes behind me and it's everything I can do not to lean back into him. This is worse than being on *Survivor*. Can Riley survive being in Cameron's presence after a kiss of that magnitude? Will she cave? Will the tribe vote her off? Ben might not, but Madeline—yeah. She will. Maybe she'd come around. But I know she's going to be upset about me not telling her about my feelings for her brother. I don't know how I possibly could have told her. It would have gone over like dentures in the ambrosia salad. Trust me. I've been through that one at a church picnic. It's not pretty.

I know I was right to keep my feelings a secret when nothing was going on. But now, everything's different. What's the protocol? Cam's right. We need to talk first.

"Earth to Riley," Ben says.

"Hmm?"

"You're out there, girl—off in space somewhere. Was it hard waking so early?"

"No. Not really. It was worth it."

I glance at Cam. I can't help myself. He's standing behind Ben's line of vision, taking food out of the grocery bags he just brought out from the van. He wags his eyebrows and winks at me. Then he mouths, "So worth it."

Not fair. But I'm here for it anyway. Cam boldly flirting with me? Yes, please.

Ben turns to follow my line of sight to where I'm staring at Cameron. Cam immediately busies himself digging a spoon out of the silverware box on the table. Ben smiles back at me.

"Granola and yogurt?" Cam asks.

I take the bowl he's handing me, and resist the urge to let my eyes linger on his for too long.

"We need to fold the bed so we can hit the road in about a half hour," Cam says in his usual focused and efficient tone. "That is, if we're still stopping in Williams."

"You're kidding, right?" I ask. "They have a zip line that goes over one of their main streets. We are definitely stopping there."

I step toward the van to wake Madeline.

When I look back over my shoulder, I overhear Ben asking Cam, "So?"

Cam nods his head to Ben, and smiles a smile brighter than the sunrise we just shared.

Ben lets out a low whoop.

My eyes go wide, but I can't help but giggle as Cam shushes Ben.

Welp. That solves the easier part of this situation. I had a hunch Ben might be in favor of something happening between me and Cam. Madeline will be another story.

I pull the door to the van open with my free hand.

"Hey, Mads. Time to wake. We're going to fold the bed. Cam's got a quick breakfast ready for you. You can eat while we drive if you want. Why don't you go use the restroom? We're trying to pull out in about thirty minutes."

"M'kay. But we could leave the bed down. I'll sleep while we drive."

"I'm sure we could, but it's probably not the safest choice."

"Yeah."

She stretches her arms overhead and throws off the covers. She's still in pjs, but she has a hoodie on over everything. It was a little chilly overnight. The van kept us warmer than a tent would have, but we still felt the cooler air.

While Mads gets ready, Ben announces he's driving. Cam calls shotgun. The two of us fold up the bed while Ben loads up the breakfast items and everything else around the campsite.

"You doing okay?" Cam asks quietly.

"Never better. You?"

"Same." He smiles over at me. "I just wish we had some time alone."

"Me too. We will. Maybe tonight after we're in LA."

"I'll try to make that happen."

He reaches over and puts his hand over mine. I want to leap across the van and throw myself at him, but I just gaze into his eyes and smile like a big lovesick dufus. He must not mind because he smiles back at me.

Madeline's voice breaks through our moment. She's at the picnic table.

"Hey! There's barely any coffee left!"

"We'll get some at a drive through at the village on the way down. Let's hit the road," Cam says.

His eyes remain locked on mine in a secret exchange, and he hasn't lifted his hand. It feels like we're walking a tightrope. My heart is in my throat. If he keeps his hand here one more second, I'm liable to shout over to Madeline, "I kissed your brother!"

He must sense something, because he steps back.

Once we're loaded up, we drive out the same way we came in, only at the fork in the road outside the park, we take the option heading to Williams instead of Flagstaff. It's an hour drive down the mountain.

Madeline's wide awake by the time we drive into the historic town of Williams. The metal archway over the street says *Gateway to the Grand Canyon - 1881*.

"Oh, man," I say to Madeline as we're huddled together looking at my phone. "We're going to miss the shootout at sundown."

"That's so fun! I can't believe they still do a reenactment."

Ben looks back from his spot in the driver's seat. "Lots of action at sunrise and sundown around these parts." He gets a mischievous grin.

Stinker.

"What happens at sunrise?" Madeline asks.

Not that she'd want to be up to see whatever it is.

"Nothing in particular as far as tourism goes," Ben says. "I just heard it's a romantic time of day."

"You're a weirdo, Ben."

"We've established that, Mads. And still, the women flock to me."

"There's no accounting for taste."

He chuckles and then gives me a pointed look.

Cam and I exchange a glance. I can barely look at him. I feel like my face tells the whole story of our morning.

We find parking and make our way to the zip line which goes thirty miles an hour over the town. It's a less than twenty minute experience total, zipping out backwards, and then shooting back to the landing platform. We pair up: me with Madeline, and Cam with Ben. The ride is tame, going over a parking lot and then crossing the Grand Canyon—Boulevard. We stay seated and ride twice. The view includes the whole town and surrounding mountains.

On the way back down the second ride, Madeline pauses, grabs my arm and shouts, "Oh my gosh! Happy Birthday, Riley! You're twenty-one! I love you, bestie!"

I smile and shout back, "I love you, too."

"Til death do us part!" Madeline shouts.

I repeat it back to her.

I don't know when we started saying that to one another. It's been long enough I can't remember. I know we attended plenty of local weddings when we were children. We somehow latched onto that line. In fourth or fifth grade, we started adding the phrase anytime we said we loved one another. It's a promise that started out silly and came to mean the world to me. No matter what, Madeline will be my friend for life—and I'll be hers.

26

CAMERON

Some of the best moments in life
are the ones you can't tell anyone about.
~ Anonymous

"Bro," Ben says quietly from the driver's seat.

He wags his eyebrows and smiles this overly excited smile I've seen so many times in my life, I probably imagine it in my sleep.

I give him my *chill out* look. So far, Madeline's not acting suspicious, but if Ben keeps this up, she's bound to get curious as to why he's acting like a kid on Mother's Day when his dad told him not to leak the big surprise to Mom.

Ben mouths, "I can't believe this. I'm living in an alternate reality where two of my favorite people end up together."

"Shhhh," I mouth back to him. Then I add, "Or you might end up trying to survive out here in the desert—after I drop you off on the side of the road."

He laughs this amused chuckle.

I raise my eyebrows.

My sister asks, "What's so funny up there?"

"Ben's being a goof," I say.

"What else is new?"

"Right?"

Riley says, "Hey, Ben. We're going to turn off I-40 to take old Route 66. It's going to add about a half hour to the drive, but we'll make two fun stops that we'd miss if we stayed on the main highway."

"Will that put us into LA a lot later?" I ask.

"No, Captain Punctuality. We'll get in around seven-thirty," Riley answers me.

There's a note of extra playfulness in her voice. I'm hoping I'm the only one who hears it.

"Okay," Ben says. "Your wish is my command, birthday girl."

We follow Riley's directions and end up about an hour and a half from Williams in the middle of nowhere. I'm not making it up. This is literally nowhere. If you look up Nowhere on a map, a red X will show on this spot. Two vintage gas pumps sit in front of Hackberry's General Store under the overhang. It looks just as you'd imagine—a run down wooden building with benches and a soda fridge. Dilapidated, rusting cars which will never see another trip on the road are scattered here and there on the property.

We park and get out to look around, each of us going in our own direction at first.

"Hey," Riley says, sidling up to me while I'm looking around the old mechanic's garage off to the side of the store.

"Hey."

Our eyes lock.

That one word uttered by each of us feels heavy and sweet with meaning.

"That's a little freaky," she says, looking around the deserted service bay turned exhibit.

"That mannequin?" I ask, looking down at her.

There's this "mechanic" standing in coveralls next to a vintage car in disrepair. I'll agree he's seen better days. And there's another mannequin—a woman—slumped over on a stool off to the side. Maybe she's the customer?

Riley looks over at the mannequins and back at me.

I stuff my hands in my pockets to ensure I don't accidentally reach out and touch her. I've never felt anything like this longing. I've been attracted to women, obviously. And I had a few serious relationships. But none that felt like I was missing something when that person wasn't near me. I never itched to touch them like I'm craving Riley right now. She's only an arm's length away from me and still, not touching her feels like a loss.

Her warm smile and the way she's staring at me with that playful look in her chocolate eyes feels like a slight compensation for now.

"Yes, those mannequins! They're creepy. Like I'm going to have nightmares about mannequins in service garages for months."

I laugh and Riley laughs with me. Our eyes connect again, the memory of our kiss a palpable secret between us. She blushes just the slightest bit. My tongue darts out to moisten my lips before I even think about what I'm doing. All these things I want to say to Riley cluster in my mind, begging to be spoken. I can't say anything. Not right now.

Ben walks up behind us. "You guys should see inside this place. There's a ton of Route 66 souvenirs, it's pretty cool. And there's this funky mannequin girl sitting on a barstool in the old soda shop next to a working jukebox ... Oh! Like those." He points at the mechanic and the customer. "Freaked me out when I first looked over at her."

Riley looks up at me. "Told you. Nightmares."

"You were the one who wanted to stop here," I tease.

"I still do. This is the place known as the mother lode of the Mother Road. They've got an epic amount of Route 66 memorabilia, and the walls alone are worth the stop."

My smile takes over my face instantaneously at her enthusiasm.

Riley could want to pull over to stare at a tumbleweed right now and I'd be game. Madeline walks out of the store and waves us over, signaling for us to join her.

Riley skips over to my sister. Yes. She skips. I watch her. Ben laughs.

"Dude, you kissed her for the first time ever this morning, and that's all she wrote."

"Pretty much." I don't even try to deny it.

If she were anyone else, I'd think I'd gone mad. But I've known Riley my whole life. Then again, I feel like we've only just met on this trip. Maybe I'll always feel like that. She's the type of person who constantly reveals new facets of herself. I could spend a lifetime discovering her.

"You know you're going to have to name your first boy Ben. And, if it's a girl ... Ben."

The girls disappear into the store. I turn to Ben.

"What are you talking about? We kissed this morning. We haven't even decided what happens from here."

"Dude. It's a done deal. I can see it in your eyes. You have never been like this over anyone. She's it. ... Hence, the name Ben."

"For a girl?"

Why am I even entertaining this conversation?

"They name girls guy names all the time now. Michael, Jerry, Spencer, Carson, Hudson ... Ben."

"When I meet another girl named Ben, we can revisit this

insanity."

"Don't you want to be a trendsetter?"

I shake my head. "There's no baby to name. Reality check. Plus, have I ever wanted to be a trendsetter—ever?"

"No. That's a fact. But there's a first for everything. After all, you took a risk at sunrise. Maybe this is Cameron two-point-O. And as far as babies, that's a not yet," Ben says. "Not yet. But just wait. I predict by this time next year you're engaged."

"Slow your roll, Cupid. She and I haven't even had a chance to really talk since the kiss."

He nods. We walk into the store and shop with Riley and Madeline. Each of them gets a few more kitschy things to add to their growing collection of knick-knacks from this trip. I tell Ben to go ahead. The three of them walk to the van while I secretly buy a vintage T-shirt for Riley that says *I Got My Kicks on Route 66*. It's cream and the Route 66 logo is shaped like the old-school highway signs.

When I get into the van, I toss the bag back to her.

"Happy Birthday, Sunshine."

"Awww. You got me a gift?"

She opens the bag and pulls out the shirt. "I love it! Thanks, Cam."

Her voice feels like a promise. The way she says my name makes my heart swell.

"I got you something too," Madeline says to Riley.

She hands Riley a small box. Inside is a turquoise and silver bracelet.

"It's beautiful," Riley says, clasping it onto her wrist.

The girls hug while Ben starts the engine.

"Where to, Rye Rye?"

"Five minutes down the road. We're going to Giganticus Headicus."

"Whaticus?" Ben asks.

"You'll see-i-cus," Riley answers.

And that starts the next five minutes of all of us adding "icus" to everything we say.

When we reach the shop with a green statue that's a sort of totem style head out front, Riley actually squeals.

"This makes skipping the giant pistachio totally worth it!"

We hop out of the van and take pictures. My favorite is where we all pretend to be picking the statue's giant nose. The shop behind the head statue has souvenirs, but we just browse since we've already purchased memorabilia five minutes ago. We check out the other unique statues around the property, but we don't spend long at this stop.

I decide to drive for a while to give Ben a break.

"Shotgun!" Riley calls out.

"Awww, don't you want to ride in back with me?" Madeline asks with a pouty tone to her voice.

"Um. Yeah. Sure. What was I thinking?" Riley says.

"I'll take shotgun," Ben says, winking at Riley.

Subtlety isn't his strong suit.

The drive from Giganticus Headicus to our next stop takes a little over an hour. I'm glad to be making time on the road again. Tonight we have an AirBnB reservation in West Los Angeles. Then we'll park Tina at Riley's TA's house near UCLA since cars aren't allowed onto the island. I'm eager to be finished with this road trip, even though ending our drive means transitioning into the next phase of life—my job at the resort. More importantly, it means deciding what's next with Riley, and once we figure that out, disclosing our relationship to my sister if there's anything to disclose. From the way Riley's looking at me today, and the smiles she keeps sending me, I'm thinking we'll have something to tell.

Thinking about Madeline's potential reaction ... well, maybe I shouldn't be in such a rush after all.

"Next stop, Oatman!" Riley shouts as we near the town she's decided will be our pit stop for lunch.

Steep hills lead into Oatman which is a mix of ghost town and tourist attraction. As we get closer, the main street comes into view, reminding me of a Wild West stage set. We find parking in the dirt lot on one end of town. It's already one o'clock, so my stomach is staging a protest. I need food.

The first thing I notice as we make our way into town are the wild burros wandering the streets—they are literally everywhere.

"We can get alfalfa at most of the stores in town to feed them," Riley informs me. "And, yes. This is on my bucket list. Feed a burro in Oatman. Check!"

She walks ahead of me and Ben, linking her arm with Madeline's, extending her phone overhead and snapping a selfie with all four of us in the frame and the historic surroundings as our backdrop. We purchase alfalfa, and the burros come over to eat, obviously accustomed to tourists and what we'll offer. The main street of Oatman is fun to walk down, with shops like Outlaw Willie's that boasts "Shotgun Weddings," and an art gallery inside.

Ben waggles his eyebrows and points to the sign as we pass, while Riley and Madeline walk ahead of us. I shake my head at him and mouth, "Not happening." He pretends to pout. I can picture that phone call home now. "Hey, Mom and Dad. Guess what we did while we were touring this great country of ours. Welp. Riley and I had a shotgun wedding."

Yeah. Nope.

Even if we end up dating and our families somehow adjust to this new reality, not one of our parents would be okay with that situation.

It's getting close to one thirty. The streets take on a different tone. We still haven't eaten, and I'm about to suggest we grab lunch. That burro's alfalfa is starting to look pretty appetizing.

I'm thinking about the decibel level of the growling noises coming from my stomach when men dressed in cowboy attire start reenacting a wild-west shootout. It's a scene that may have actually happened in the mining days when this town was founded in the mid-1800s. The cowboys insult one another, someone steals something, and eventually there's a standoff which results in one of the gunslingers falling to his mock death.

After that excitement, Riley leads us to the Oatman Hotel, an older adobe building which no longer rents rooms, but does —thankfully—have a restaurant. All the food has gold-mining themed names. We order our lunch, and then Ben points out the Dollar Bill Bar within the hotel. One saloon wall is covered, floor to ceiling, in dollar bills. The waitress explains to us that miners used to sign a dollar and hang it on the wall to use later if they ran short of cash. Tourists have been pinning money up on that same wall for years.

I take a few dollar bills out of my wallet and Ben takes one from his. I hand one to Madeline and one to Riley. We all sign our dollars and pin them to the wall. I drop back before I rejoin the group at our table, adding + *Riley* to the spot where I had written *Cam*. I take a photo of the dollar on my phone to show Riley later.

We leave Oatman at around two-thirty. We're only a half hour away from crossing into California. Every mile we travel closer to Los Angeles feels like a curtain dropping on my life as a college student. I drive in intentional silence for the next half hour, pondering my future and trying to determine how Riley might fit into it.

I'm assuming she wants to fit somehow. Maybe she won't. I'm not a fun-loving, easy-going guy like Ben. I'm intense, a thinker, constantly getting stuck up in my head instead of enjoying the moment. I set goals and work for them. I take people and situations seriously. Riley might want someone more carefree. But if she's interested in me ... if she feels half of what I'm feeling right now, I want to figure out a way to make something work between us—to give us a shot.

A relationship with Riley is the last thing I'd imagine myself considering. A week ago, we were life-long friends from a small town in Ohio. We'd grown up like siblings or cousins. I never in a million years imagined I'd have romantic feelings for Riley, let alone the types of thoughts and desires I'm experiencing now that we've kissed. And, if she were any other woman, I'd be taking things much more slowly—or not at all. I'm about to start a new job, live in a new place. The timing's not ideal for starting a new relationship.

But I can't imagine not pursuing Riley now that we've crossed the invisible line which had separated us for years. Now that I've tasted her, held her, known what it's like to be the source of her smile and laughter, to be the one who can comfort her when she's feeling uncertain, I can't go back to whatever we were before.

We cross the Colorado River and hop out at Needles for our last state welcome sign. We all put on sunglasses and make hang-ten hands, posing like we're riding surfboards while we stand on the palm-tree-lined street under the Welcome to California sign. Needles doesn't scream what most people imagine when they think of California. From what I can tell, it's a nondescript, dusty, desert town with low mountain ranges in the distance. Still, we captured the moment and made it ours.

The mood has shifted now that we're on the home stretch. Riley and Madeline end up napping in the back seat, slumped together like the best friends they are—leaning on one another as they always have for as long as I can remember. Looking at them now, I question my decision to kiss Riley. It's the first wave of serious doubts I've had since our time together this morning. What will something romantic between me and Riley do to my sister? Will their relationship survive us deciding to pursue something more—if we do?

My eyes focus on Riley. She's resting peacefully, her beautiful face soft and carefree, even in sleep.

I don't think I ever had a choice. She's so much more than I imagined. And like Ben said this morning, *That's all she wrote.*

Ben's quietly reading something on his iPad in the front passenger seat. My eyes are on the road, but I'm deep in thought. Our traveling adventures are basically over. Next stop, Barstow. Trust me, from what I've seen of that town, Barstow's not a place you stop in to get some *Wish You Were Here* postcards.

We drive two hours from the California-Arizona border to Barstow and pull in at five-thirty. It's hotter than Satan's back porch, but we find a clean Jack-In-the-Box and use the restroom. Riley and Madeline have that sleep-saturated grogginess written all over them. Their hair is rumpled, and they walk like they're half-drunk when they first exit the van. We grab some fries, cheap tacos, egg rolls, and sodas and we're on our way, headed to Los Angeles, which is a little over two hours away.

"Two more hours left of the road trip of a lifetime," Riley says once we're back on the road.

Her voice lacks its usual enthusiasm.

She smiles a moment later, and says, "But we're an hour away from the world's tallest thermometer. It still works." She pauses for dramatic effect. "Do I need to see it? No. I don't. No. Really. I'm good. I'll pass. No more landmarks for this traveler."

I chuckle. "I'm not driving an hour in this heat to see a thermometer that tells me it's hot enough to fry an egg on the highway."

"New bucket list item! Fry an egg on the highway!" Riley shouts, glancing at me in the rear view mirror with an expression that makes me want to pull over somewhere so I can have time alone with her right now.

We drive along I-15. Shades of tan and cream fill the landscape as far as the eye can see. Dried vegetation extends toward low beige and peach hills in the distance that almost look like a mirage at times. The only thing breaking up the monotony of tan is the gray freeway stretching endlessly in front of us. At times a car or semi rushes past us. It's six fifteen when the van starts to run funny. I check the gauges and pull over. We're running hot.

"Guys, I'm going to kill the engine and call Duke," I say.

"I'll call Triple A," Ben says.

I dial Duke's cell.

"Hey, Cam. What's up?"

"Not much, Duke. The van's been running great. We did hit that haboob in Arizona."

"A what? You hit a ... did you say you hit a boob?"

"Um. No. We definitely did not hit ..." I clear my throat and lower my voice. "A boob."

Ben hears me, even though he's on the phone with Triple A. He starts cracking up like the twelve-year-old he can be at times like this.

"A haboob," I repeat. "It was that dust storm. Like I told you, there was hail. I only mention it now because the dust or debris might have done some unseen damage. I checked everything after the storm, but you never know."

"Man, I'm glad it was that thing and not what I thought you said. And, yeah. A storm can do unseen damage. What has you calling?"

"The engine was running hot, so I pulled over. I wanted to check with you as to what we should do."

I look over my shoulder into the back seat. Riley's pulling a box out of the cabinet. She's setting things out on the counter. What even is all that?

"You probably want to check your fluid levels. Especially the coolant. If you've been running the A/C through the desert, it may simply need to be topped off. Do you know how to do that?"

"I do. I'll check everything and call you back."

Duke tells me he'll be waiting for my call. Ben says Triple A is on their way. I step out of the front seat into what can only be described as a wall of heat. If you've ever sat in a sauna, you know this feeling. It's dry, but it's hot enough to make me feel a little bogged down and almost drowsy.

I pop the back of the van and check the coolant and oil levels. Both are low. I pull the coolant jug out from where Duke stored it and top off the tank. We sit and wait. The engine needs time to cool off after it ran hot.

Riley's been busy while I checked out the fluids. By the time I take my seat behind the wheel again, everyone's got a custom iced coffee drink. Mine even has oat milk and stevia. Just how I like it.

"When life gets tough, call your barista," she says with a wink. "Coffee makes everything better."

I don't know about coffee, but I do know Riley makes everything better—infinitely better.

27

RILEY

If we wait until we are ready,
we will be waiting for the rest of our lives!
~ Lemony Snicket

By the time we make it to the rental in Los Angeles, it's after nine thirty.

We made it. We drove all the way from Ohio to the West Coast. I feel different. Not only because Cam kissed me, though that definitely changed everything.

The rental is a darling two bedroom home tucked into the Hollywood Hills. It's less than a half hour from UCLA, which is where we'll be dropping Tina for the coming six weeks with my TA, Janessa. She's got a house she inherited from her grandma with garage space and only one car.

"We'll take the queen bed," Cam volunteers as soon as we walk in the door.

"Um. What?" Ben asks. "They are half our size. I don't want you all snuggled up on me for the night."

"I'm not going to be all snuggled up on you," Cam says.

His voice isn't irritated, but his exhaustion from today's trip, especially that fiasco of a breakdown in the middle of nowhere, is showing now. He's still more pleasant than most people would be under the circumstances. It's one of the things I adore about him. He can be borderline grumpy, and definitely straightforward, but he's never downright edgy or mean. I guess that's because he keeps so much inside—always mulling things over in that gorgeous head of his.

"We can take the queen," I offer, looking at Madeline for her agreement.

"Yeah. We can."

We order Chinese delivery even though we're all exhausted. If there's such a thing as eating in your sleep while you take a shower, that's what I want to do right now.

It's only shortly after we've gotten the suitcases into our rooms that the delivery person rings the doorbell.

"I'll get it," Cam says.

Ben chuckles. "That way, no one will be writing on Riley tonight."

Madeline smiles over at me like we share a secret admiration for Deuce. He was cute, but that night feels like years ago. Now, I'm so focused on her brother, I couldn't even joke about how adorable another guy is.

I open the large double french doors and step onto the terrace patio. The view is incredible. We can see across the Hollywood Hills and over the Los Angeles valley from here.

Cam brings the bag of food out and we all plop into chairs around the firepit, not bothering to light the flames since we're all going to bed as soon as we eat. My eyes find Cam's several times when no one is looking. He seems to be trying to tell me something, but I can't figure out what.

We eat our fill of broccoli beef, kung pao chicken, and sweet and sour shrimp straight out of the containers, using chopsticks and passing each box around to the next person for them to eat their share. We're too tired to bother with plates. As soon as she's finished eating, Madeline announces that she's going to shower and get in bed.

"I'll be in shortly," I tell her. "I just want to sit out here and relax. Go ahead and get in bed. I'll meet you there. I'll be quiet if you're already asleep."

"Oh, I'll be asleep, trust me. You won't even need to be quiet."

Once Madeline's inside, Ben turns to me and Cameron. "I think I'll turn in too. I'm sure you're in good hands out here, Riley."

I smirk at him. It's honestly good to have him in on our temporary secret, but in another way, every time he says something like that, my heart breaks a little for Madeline. She deserves to know. And she will. I just don't know how she'll take it—whatever *it* is. We still have to determine what we're doing here.

The moment the door snicks shut, Cam looks over his shoulder to make sure the coast is clear, and then he moves to sit next to me on the love seat. His hand lands on my thigh just above my knee, and he gives me a gentle squeeze. Despite how exhausted I was when we got here, Cam's touch awakens everything in me. His nearness is exhilarating.

"Hey," he says, turning toward me.

His voice is soft with an edge of grit. This is the voice he uses with women when he's attracted to them, not the voice he always used with me in the past. I got the same treatment as

Madeline and Ben for years. Now I get to see this side of Cameron—the side reserved for romance.

"Hey," I answer, surprised at the quaver in my voice.

"Are you nervous?" he asks.

His hand makes a light brushing movement on my leg.

"No. Not nervous. I mean, if Madeline walks out, we'll be in a beyond awkward position."

I giggle apprehensively and then I feel like the teen version of me—crushing on him when he seemed larger than life.

He simply smiles down at me, draping his other arm behind my back.

"It would be less than ideal for her to come out here. But I already thought of that."

"And?"

"And," he raises his phone. "I have Ben on standby. He'll signal if Madeline does anything besides shower and hit the sack."

"Tricky."

"I prefer, resourceful. Or, thoughtful. Or, ingenious. Or, *Wow, Cam, you thought of everything*."

I laugh lightly, barely able to believe I'm here, tucked into his side, his hand now rubbing lazy circles on my knee, the view of Los Angeles spreading across the valley beyond this terrace.

"May I kiss you?" Cam asks. "We should talk, and we will. But I've spent all day wanting to kiss you again, and ..."

His voice trails off when my hand reaches up to cup his jaw, running my fingers down the stubble that's grown in today as we made our way across Arizona and California. I tilt my head up and my eyes flutter shut. I don't see Cam lean in, but I feel his breath as he moves nearer and then brushes a kiss across my lips. I flatten my palm on his cheek, nearly gripping his face to hold him to me. His arm that is behind me tugs me near and holds my shoulder.

Obviously, we're on the same page—*get close to me and stay here while I show you what you've been missing.* Cam's lips dance across mine in sweet caresses, then he deepens the kiss, making a low growling sound when I meet his intensity with my own longing.

I loved this day, but he's right. I can't begin to count the times I wanted to grab hold of his hand, or have him put his arm around me—or do this, kiss like our lives depended on it.

Cam's hand on my knee shifts from comforting brushes of his fingertips, to a firm grip as his fingers span my knee. It's as though he needs to anchor himself, or plant his hand somewhere to keep himself in check. I run my hand down his chest, then loop it behind his neck, gripping onto his hair and raking my fingertips through the wavy strands on top and then running my palm across the shorter hair closer to the back of his neck. He growls, or hums, or purrs—some sound that lights me up from my toes to the tip of my head.

Cam slowly ends our kiss, like a driver carefully bringing a race car to a graceful stop. He pulls back and meets my eyes, his at half mast, but a crinkle in the corners from the sated smile on his face. Then he bends in and kisses the tip of my nose, and then places another soft kiss on my lips.

He rests his forehead on mine, running his hand down my hair.

"I won't stop," he says, almost as if he's warning me.

His eyes search mine. "Where have you been hiding, Sunshine? And why did it take me so long to find you?"

"I've been right here."

My answer feels lame—so much less romantic than his question.

"Waiting?"

It's a question, but not really.

"Mm hmm. Waiting for you."

I admit it, even though I feel completely exposed to him.

"How did I get so lucky?"

"You're lucky?"

The tone of my voice feels vulnerable and raw.

"To have you? To know you feel this way? Yeah. I'm beyond lucky. You're ..."

He doesn't finish. A selfish part of me cries out, wanting to ask him what I am, but I stifle the question. He'll tell me someday. If not tonight, at some point he will. And the way he's looking at me, the way he kissed me, that tells me all I need to know. This isn't one-sided, not by a longshot.

A wide smile breaks across my face.

"Your smile is beautiful," Cam says. Then he chuckles. "That's so cheesy."

"I'm here for all the cheesy lines. Keep 'em coming, Reeves."

He's pulled back slightly now, but he's still near enough that I can barely make out the flecks of gold around his iris in the dim glow of the twinkle lights overhead. He's looking in my eyes like he can see straight into my soul.

"I love when you call me Reeves. Am I capping out on the cheesiness yet?"

"Not even close. I love when you call me Sunshine."

"It fits you."

He smiles at me, brushing his thumb across my cheek.

"Man, I want to kiss you again."

"Do it," I egg him on.

"We need to talk. Talk first. Then more kissing. Definitely more kissing."

He pushes back and I move with him. I'm not going to make this easy. I've waited years—years—for the unbelievable impossibility of Cameron Reeves wanting to kiss me, or even to have him think of me as anything beyond a second little sister. I'm not about to let him go all business-first on me right now.

I lift his hand off my leg and then I move so I'm sitting sideways across his lap, looping my arms around his neck.

"What was it you wanted to talk about?"

I tilt my head up toward him, daring to brush a kiss along his chin. His bristly scruff there makes my lips hum, so I kiss him again.

"Riley," he nearly groans. "Oh man, you're dangerous."

"Am I?"

My voice is innocent, and this is way too fun.

He makes a noise that sounds like he's being tortured, and then he grips the back of my head and his mouth crashes down on mine with a relentless passion I didn't know he had in him. I got what I wanted—whewee—and then some. This is not tame and thoughtful Cam. It's not five-year-plan Cam. This is a side of Cam I unleashed. I have a feeling he's never let loose like this with anyone else, and I soar with the feeling that I'm the one making him crazy.

Cameron's hands grip my shoulders, but then he's roving over my back, even lightly gripping my hair and tilting my head to give him better access while he kisses my neck and around to my ear where he nips lightly, causing me to squirm from the chills coursing through me. He kisses his way back to my mouth, carefully, but with a hunger I didn't know he was capable of expressing.

I feel the moment his resolve surges. Cam's hands brace my shoulders, he pulls his head back, looks me in the eyes, and shakes his head. His smile is wide and full.

"Talk. We need to talk. Do I have to take one of those chairs over there, or are you going to behave yourself?"

His words are definite, but his eyes are playful.

I move off him. He's right. We do need to talk.

"I'll behave," I promise.

He gives me this half-scolding look as if he doesn't believe me. I raise my hands to prove my innocence.

"Can you blame me?"

"No." He smiles. "Not at all. It's all a little surreal. But amazing. And if I didn't have my eye on what tomorrow has in store for us, I'd keep you out here for hours until you fell asleep in my arms. Though, that would definitely get Madeline's attention."

"She was pretty wiped out."

"Not so wiped out she wouldn't notice you not coming to bed at some point."

I nod. Madeline. She's so important to me. I chose UCLA because of her. I even picked my major to match hers just to ensure that we'd remain close over the past three years and this coming one. The idea of possibly hurting her guts me. Cam and I do need to talk. So much is on the line—and everything will become more complicated tomorrow when we land on Marbella Island.

"So," Cam says, taking my hand in his and lacing our fingers so that our palms match up and face one another.

He holds our hands up between us, studying the way we fit together with a soft smile on his face.

We allow our hands to drop to the sofa cushion between us, rearranging them, but keeping them clasped together.

"I wouldn't usually have this kind of conversation with a woman before I've even taken her to dinner."

"You've taken me to dinner. And lunch. And breakfast."

"On this trip, yes. Just the two of us? No. I haven't even taken you on a date, Riley."

His voice sounds slightly pained—like he broke a personal code of ethics.

"This morning was quite a date," I say, trying to assuage his unnecessary guilt.

"A date over the Grand Canyon."

"Yes. Best date of my life. No one will ever top that."

He smiles. I rub my thumb over the back of his hand.

"The point is, in an ideal world, I'd take you out. We might kiss. We might not. I'd ask you out again. Then, I'd definitely kiss you."

"Oh, you would, would you?"

"I would."

He smiles over at me with a look that's full of longing and promise, and then his tongue darts out to wet his bottom lip—it's sexy, and alluring, and extremely distracting.

"You can't do that and expect me to focus."

"Do what?"

I mimic his action, letting my tongue peek out and run across my lip.

Cameron stands and walks over to the chair across the fire pit from me.

"What are you doing?" I ask in a higher pitched tone than I expected.

"Making sure we talk." He takes a breath and lets it out, plopping onto one of the chairs. "As I was saying, I would date you. Then we would kiss, if I were serious. And we would take things step by step. But you're not like the other women I've dated."

"All the women of Cameron Reeves. Should this be a television special, like *The Bachelor*?"

"Women I've dated, I could count on both hands. Women I've gone out with long term, two."

"Oh."

"Yeah. I'm not exactly into casual—anything."

He's right. Cameron is serious. When he takes something on, he's committed, whether it's a sport, a hobby, a service project, or driving across the country. Why would I think he'd be any different when it came to being romantically involved with someone?"

"So, if you weren't you, and I was in this stage of my life ..." His voice trails off. "I wouldn't even pursue a second date. Maybe I wouldn't have even had a first date. I'm about to start a new job—the first job of what I hope becomes a life-long career. I've never lived on this island. I need to focus, to make a good impression. It's not ideal timing for a relationship."

"I get it." I try to keep my voice level, masking the disappointment coursing through my veins, straight to my heart.

"No. I don't think you do."

Cameron stands again and walks over to me. He grasps both my hands in his as he takes a seat on the couch next to me.

"You aren't another woman. You're you—Riley. This is different. For one thing, I've known you forever. We have a history. For another thing, I couldn't stop whatever this is between us if I wanted to—and I definitely don't want to. I just don't know how to make this work. You'll only be on Marbella for the next six weeks. Then you'll go back to UCLA. I'm going to have to put most of my energy into my job. I won't be free to just hang out and give us the attention we deserve."

He looks nearly stricken. My heart feels like someone pumped it full of helium. I'm glad he's holding my hands, or I'd be liable to float away on the sheer happiness of hearing his words.

"Cam," I say softly, making sure he's looking straight in my eyes. "We'll make it work."

I don't know how. But knowing Cam wants this—seems to want it nearly as much as I do—makes me sure we'll figure it out. We have to.

"Are you sure?" he asks. "I feel like this isn't fair to you. I'm asking a lot of you. You'll have to share me with my career for now. And then we'll have to figure out how to stay connected when we're separated by an hour's boat ride and almost two hours' drive."

"I'm very sure. I've been sharing you for a long time now. I finally get to claim a piece of you for myself. I'm more ready than you know."

He smiles down at me, obviously not aware of the depth of my feelings or how much I've wanted this and for how long. I'll tell him someday. Not now. It's too soon.

"Should we tell Madeline? Like tomorrow?" I ask. "She needs to know."

My voice reveals the wariness in my heart. As much as I want to tell Madeline—to come clean, and to hope that she'll be as happy for me as I would be for her, I know that may not be a realistic outcome. She might be angry and feel betrayed. More than likely she'll be worried about how this change will impact our friendship.

"I agree one hundred percent," Cam says. "She deserves to know. And I don't want to keep you or my feelings for you a secret any longer than I already have. We can tell her first thing in the morning—once we're all up and packed."

"Good. And if she doesn't take it so well ..."

Cam's quiet, obviously pondering my words. "She'll come around."

"Are you sure?"

"No. I'm not sure. I'm just counting on the fact that she loves both of us enough to get past her initial knee-jerk reaction if it's less than ecstatic. Ultimately, she'll want us to be happy. And she'll be happy for us eventually—after she sees that she's not losing anything by sharing you with me."

We both know Madeline is possessive of me. She's as deeply connected to me as I am to her. She might view this development between me and Cam as a sort of betrayal at first. But Cam's right. She will probably come around once she has time to adjust to the idea.

"I won't give her any reason to feel jealous of me," Cam says. "I respect your friendship."

"And I'll make sure to put an effort into spending enough time with her so she doesn't have any reason to think you've taken me over."

"When she sees you are still making room in your life for her, she's bound to feel more open to us dating. And if you decide you want to try to make something work with me long term, she'll have to adjust."

"I already know what I want, Cam."

He smiles. "Yeah? Me too."

He leans in and kisses me softly. It's the sweetest kiss of my life. It's not like I've been running around kissing a whole bunch of people. I haven't. But I know a special kiss when I feel one, and this kiss feels like a soft summer breeze, or the way it felt to be held when I scraped my knee as a child. It's tender, comforting, intimate, and full of emotion. I kiss Cam back, pouring everything I feel for him into my kiss. I gently cup his face in my hands. He runs his fingers through my hair like a comb, smoothing the strands with each stroke. I lean into him. When I pull back, he tugs me toward him so my head rests on his chest. He places one more soft kiss on my forehead. I snuggle in, loving the feel of his heartbeat under my cheek.

"So, we'll tell Madeline tomorrow," Cam says.

"Yep. Tomorrow."

"Thank you for giving me a chance, Sunshine."

"I've been waiting to give you a chance," I remind him.

"Happy Birthday, Riley," he nearly whispers into my hair.

All I can think is, *best birthday ever*!

RILEY'S JOURNAL

July. 28th

BEST BIRTHDAY EVER!

Gladys! Oh, how do I tell you everything? There's no way.
My eyes are about to drift shut from exhaustion. We made it to our place in LA—not the place I share with Madeline through the school year, but this rental we got for the night. Anyway, we made it here late after overheating on the freeway and having to call Triple A. That all worked out, don't worry.

Even though we were wiped out, we were also starving. So, we ordered take-out to eat on the patio.

But who cares about all that?

The BIG NEWS is this:

Cameron kissed me!!!!!!!!!!!

He kissed me. And yes, I kissed him back. Of course. Well, actually, I did everything in my power to let him know he should kiss me. And then he did. Boy, did he. Our first kiss was over the Grand Canyon. Not literally over it, like we weren't dangling there or anything. We were sitting on a rock outcropping. The sun wasn't even up when he bent in and took my mouth in a kiss to end all kisses. It could have been a scene right out of a movie.

I'm writing this now, and I can still barely believe it. Gladys, it might be weird for you to hear about the details, so I'll keep it vague. Just trust me when I say I lit up like the annual Christmas tree. You know the one they always light in the town square next to the fountain? I felt that kiss from my toes to the roots of my hair and everywhere in between. The man can kiss.

Fast forward to tonight ... There's a lot to tell between kisses, but I have to get this out or I'll bust wide open. And I need sleep—I feel like I could sleep like a baby sloth. But not before I write about this day.

Today was delicious torture. Everywhere we went after sharing that kiss, I'd catch Cam's eye, or notice him watching me. And we couldn't do anything about it because we haven't told Madeline yet. We did tell Ben—or he guessed. I don't know. All I know is he's in on the fact. And he's acting like such a typical Ben about it, teasing, nearly blowing the details out in front of Madeline. It's not that I don't want her to know. I want her to know more than anyone else. I'm just scared. What if she's mad? Or jealous? What if her reaction messes up what Cam and I have just started pursuing with one another?

Tonight, after we were sure Madeline was asleep, Cam and I sat out on this beautiful patio and talked. And kissed. And talked. And kissed.

First, we talked about us—what we want, what we're up against, and what we're going to do about it. I'm so grateful Cam shared his thoughts and feelings with me. He didn't say everything, but he said enough for me to know this isn't one-sided. And we know the timing is less than ideal. But here we are.

So, we're going to make it work. You know more than anyone how much I have wanted Cam. If there are obstacles, so be it. I've never met a man like Cameron. I've never felt for anyone the way I feel for him. You know I fought my feelings for years. I'm not going to walk away over a little bit of challenge—like the distance between us once I go back to UCLA, or the fact that his life is definitely going to be lived on Marbella Island, at least for the foreseeable future. I don't have a clue where my future will take me. So much is up in the air.

But what's not up in the air is how I feel about Cameron. And that has to count for something. I get the sense that his feelings are pretty strong for me too. Can you believe it, Gladys? I know you're rooting for us. At least, I believe you are.

After we figured all that out, we had to talk about when to tell Madeline. I've already been hiding my feelings for Cam from her for so long. I figured nothing would come of them. So, why complicate things between me and my best friend by confessing how I felt about her brother?

But then we kissed. Not me and Madeline, of course. Me and Cam.

Now my secrecy about my feelings for Cam is going to blow up because we crossed a line we can't ever uncross. Not that I'd want to go back. I don't. I just don't know what to do about the fact that I've withheld so much from my best friend. She deserves my honesty.

And when you top all that off with the fact that I haven't shared my confusion over my future with her, I'm in a pickle—one I fermented myself.

I still don't even know if I want to be a teacher. Well, I'm pretty sure I DON'T want to be one. I feel like a lousy friend having kept all this to myself. I just never wanted to disappoint her. And so much of this hasn't felt clear until this trip. It's like it took this road trip to make me see myself and what I really want in life.

So, we're going to tell Madeline first thing tomorrow. I want her to know, even if it means her getting mad at me and Cam for a bit. Our friendship will survive. At least I hope it will. It just has to.

Maybe she'll surprise me and be really overjoyed. Either way, Cam thinks in time she'll be happy for us. After all, if things go well, down the road we could be actual sisters. Can you imagine? But, one thing at a time. First, we have to get through breaking the news to her tomorrow.

I have to go to sleep, Gladys. I just wanted you to know. I turned twenty-one today and it was definitely the best birthday ever (if you don't count breaking down in the middle of an oven-level hot desert … but we won't count that. We'll just count the good stuff … like Cam's kisses … and the way he looks at me … and the fact that he wants to pursue a relationship with me … I think I might just float off my bed when I think of it all—of him.)

28

CAMERON

A tourist is a fellow who drives thousands of miles
so he can be photographed
standing in front of his car.
~ Emile Genest

My cell vibrates on the bedside table at the same time as my sister comes running into the bedroom where Ben and I are tucked into a king bed. It's the last night we'll be sharing a mattress, and I couldn't be happier. It turns out, Ben's a foot warmer. And I don't mean he's warming my feet. Nope. He puts his icy dogs on my calves in the middle of the night. He denies it of course, but let's think about it. Would I make this up? No. I would not. I spent half last night in a sort of cat-and-mouse chase game under the covers, trying to keep my legs a safe distance from Ben's feet.

On the island, we've already arranged to share the rental of a small two-bedroom, upstairs apartment. Two-bedroom is the operative phrase in that configuration. Ben's feet in his room, me and my toasty calves in mine.

Madeline would usually knock. She just bombarded her way in here, looking frantic and waving her phone around over her head.

"Answer the call, Cam!" she shouts.

How does she know I've got a call?

"It's Mom!"

"Okay. Calm down."

The first call goes to voicemail, and then my phone starts vibrating and ringing all over again.

Ben rolls over. "Make it stop." He lifts his head and looks at my sister. "Man, Mads, you look awful in the morning."

She crosses her arms over her chest and glares at Ben.

I pick up my phone and say, "Hello," while Ben says, "What's she doing in our room?"

"Cameron?" My mom's voice sounds panicky.

"Yeah, Mom. Are you okay?"

"We're fine. I'm fine. It's fine."

"Three fines usually doesn't mean you're fine. Did something happen?"

"Your dad fell off the ladder. He was up there cleaning the gutters. I told him to call Chris St. James, but he said, *The day I don't clean my own gutters is the day I ought to retire and start improving my golf score.*"

I rub my eyes. Riley and I were up late, and I feel the residual impact of not getting enough sleep.

Riley.

I want to smile at the thought of her, but I'm too consumed with concern for my parents.

"He turned wrong and fell from about four steps up. He hit his head on the pavers I have on the side of the house. They think he may have broken a bone in his arm. We're in the ER at

Soin Medical Center in Beavercreek. They're doing a scan—an MRI—and then they'll x-ray his arm."

Mom's words come out quickly, and then she sobs a little.

"I wish I were there, Mom."

"It's okay. We've got support. You know that. I just want you and Madeline to know. We'll keep you posted."

"If I need to come home to pitch in, you tell me, okay?"

"You're about to start your new job. It's not like college, Cameron. You can't just leave and take schoolwork with you to turn in later. They won't want to let you go now that you're there."

"We don't officially start our jobs for nearly a week. We'll be in orientation. I'm sure they could spare me if there's a family emergency. Just let me know."

"I will. I'll keep you posted."

"I love you, Mom."

"Love you too, sweetheart."

"I'm sure Dad will be okay."

"I don't know what I'll do if he isn't."

"Don't go there. He's going to be fine. Was he talking?"

"Yes. He kept talking about how stupid he was, and then saying how this still doesn't mean he's ready to retire."

I chuckle. That's Dad. "He'll be fine."

"Yeah. He probably will." She's quiet for a moment. I hear a long sigh. Then she says, "When did the tables turn, baby boy? How is it you're comforting me when I used to rock you to sleep?"

"I'm too big to rock these days. You'd throw your back out trying."

"I'm proud of you, sweet boy."

"Thanks, Mom. Call us. We're here for you."

"I will."

We hang up and I look over at Madeline. Riley appears in

the doorway behind her, she's still in pajamas, and her face looks like she just woke up. She rubs her eyes with the back of her hand.

"What's going on? Is everything okay?"

"My dad fell off a ladder."

"Oh, no! Is he okay?"

"He hit his head. May have broken a bone in his arm. He's talking, so that's good news. I'm sure he'll be okay."

Madeline looks shell-shocked. Riley steps up next to Madeline and wraps her arm around her shoulder, tugging her into a hug.

Riley's eyes connect with mine. We share a wordless conversation. It's obviously not time to tell Madeline about our relationship—not with this tragedy hanging in the air. She needs our support, not to have to process one more thing today.

"Are you okay?" I ask Mads.

"I'll be okay. It's just so hard. It makes me think of Mom and Dad as mortals. I guess I like picturing them being here forever."

I nod. "He'll be okay."

I'm not sure of it, but it seems like he will, and Madeline needs assurance right now.

"I think he will too, but I wish we were there."

Madeline leans into Riley, hooking her arm behind Riley's back and allowing Riley to comfort her. I watch the two of them, so grateful they have one another. As goofy as Ben can be, he's the guy I lean on like that too. When times are serious, he sets aside his playful nature and shows up in ways that no one else does for me. And then he busts out a joke or two just to keep everyone smiling. I need that—both his sincerity and his levity.

"Anything I can do?" Ben asks.

"I don't think so."

"How about I go on the breakfast run?"

"Sounds perfect."

I look at the clock for the first time this morning. It's already a little after ten. I don't know the last time I slept til ten.

"It could almost be a lunch run. Look at what time it is!"

"Yeah. We needed it. All that travel took it out of us. Especially the van breaking down yesterday. We owed it to ourselves to take a day to sleep in without any scheduled wake-up."

Our bus to Ventura Harbor doesn't leave until two thirty, so we've got time to relax here at this rental until after lunch.

I had hoped we'd tell Madeline over breakfast. She's still slumped into Riley's comforting embrace. It's obvious she's on overload until we hear more about Dad. Telling her will have to wait. Which also means I'm going to have to keep my distance from Riley. I'm too likely to reach out and touch her if we get too close to one another.

It's funny how I never had that urge before, and then something awakened in me, and now I can barely be in the same room with her without feeling this undeniable need to be closer and to have some part of me touching some part of her.

Ben gets out of bed. He's wearing Spider-Man pajama bottoms. They say *I'm A Marvel* between the images of Spider-Man slinging webs and standing in that squatted stance he's famous for.

Madeline's brows raise as she looks at Ben. He's not wearing a shirt, but that's not what's got her attention. It's his ridiculous pants.

"Nice PJs, Ben," she says, still clinging to Riley like a life preserver.

"You know it. It's like they made them just for me." Ben twirls like he's on the catwalk. "I'm a Marvel, ladies. Get back. Unh-huh. Oh yeah."

He's flexing now. Turning so his back is to Riley and Madeline and winking over his shoulder at them. Then he walks forward and blows them an exaggerated kiss. He leaves the room after this display has all three of us cracking up.

From the hallway he shouts, "I'm going to get breakfast. Text me your orders. I'm not only a marvel, I'm marvelous. Say it. Let me hear you!"

Not one of us says it.

From the bathroom I hear him, "Aren't you hungry? I'm charging for breakfast in compliments."

Riley's wiping a tear from her eye. Then she says, "Oh, Ben! You are marvelous. And I want a breakfast burrito with salsa and bacon."

"Coming your way," Ben says as he walks back into the bedroom, pops open his suitcase and grabs out a few things to change into.

He looks between me and Madeline. "Reeves children, get with the program or starve."

"You're the best," I say in a deadpan voice. "I'll take a burrito too. Same as Riley."

Ben can't help himself. He says, "Ohhh, matchy matchy. So cute."

Riley's eyes go wide. She looks over at me. I try to feign neutrality, letting Ben's comment slip away without a reaction.

I get out of bed so I can shower and change before Ben's back with breakfast. Riley watches me and I watch her watching me. The feeling of her eyes roving across my muscles is nearly tangible. She looks away, clearing her throat, and I grab my things and pass between her and Mads on my way to the bathroom. I'm torturing both of us, getting this near to her. Here's hoping I can relieve the tension with a kiss and some quality time alone together sometime later today.

We hang out all morning at the rental. Ben reads a book on his Kindle out on one of the loungers. The girls sit on the same loveseat where Riley and I kissed and shared our hearts last night. They seem deep in conversation. I spend time on my laptop, going through the emails the employment office at the resort sent me this week and then looking at every page on the resort website—again. I already familiarized myself earlier this summer, but now that my job is starting in six days, I want to refresh myself to the point of being able to recite every detail.

I glance over the rim of my computer at Riley. Madeline's staring across the property at the incredible view beyond the terrace railing. I wink at Riley and lightly wag my eyebrows. She smiles a shy smile and then gives me a warning expression. I smile back. I'm not going to jeopardize my sister's feelings. I'm careful. It's also slightly excruciating having to hold back from being near Riley, so a little harmless flirtation is an indulgence I'll give us both.

I'm not thrilled about keeping us a secret from my sister any longer than we have to, but there's something to say about this side of temporarily sneaking around. It's fun to flirt behind Ben and Madeline's backs—exchanging a private moment shared only between Riley and me. Still, I'll feel much better when we let the cat out of the bag.

We eat a light lunch of snacks we had left in the van. Riley makes us all iced coffees. Then we pack our bags and hoist them up on top of Tina for the last time.

Mom calls when I'm securing the luggage with the tie-downs. I pull my cell out of my shorts pocket and answer quickly.

"Hey, Mom. Any news?"

I push the speaker button so Madeline can hear Mom too.

"Yes. His head is mostly fine. No concussion, only a minor contusion—which means a bruise to the brain in one spot. They want him to stay here so they can monitor his symptoms and make sure he'll rest. You know your father. He's not going to stay put unless someone straps him down or locks him up."

"I do. I'm glad he's getting good care."

"He also broke his arm. Fractured the ulna. He'll be in a cast for six weeks. Thankfully, it was his right arm."

Dad's left-handed.

"I'm staying here with him. Mrs. Stewart went back to Bordeaux to get me some things. There's a hotel just across the road from the medical center. I'll get a room."

"I'm glad you have her," I say, realizing Madeline's not the only person Riley and I are going to have to spring our news to —eventually.

We're going to have to tell our parents.

"Is Madeline there?" Mom asks.

"She's right here. I have you on speaker. We're loading up the van to take it to Riley's friend's and then we're heading to the shuttle boat that will take us to the island."

"So fun. Enjoy every minute of it. Love you, Cameron. Love you, my sweet Maddy girl."

"Love you, Mom!" we both shout.

I hang up with Mom and look down at Madeline.

"I feel much better," she says. "I'm still going to be stressed until Dad's released from the hospital, but it could have been a lot worse."

"It sounds hopeful," I agree. "Ready to load up?"

Everyone takes one last tour through the rental to make sure we haven't forgotten anything, and then we climb into the van. Riley asked me to drive since LA traffic can be a hairball. She's sitting in the back with Madeline, and Ben's in the shotgun seat for our last ride of the trip.

"Do you guys mind if we go to Santa Monica to take a photo at the beach with Tina—the four of us standing in front of her with the ocean at our backs?"

"I'm game," I say.

Yes. It's true. I'd say yes to almost anything for Riley. Besides, I'm missing the beach after a few months in Ohio and the past few days of nothing but desert as my view.

"Take me to the beeeeeeeach!" Ben howls.

Madeline laughs. "Let's do it."

After a little over a half-hour drive, we pull into the huge parking lot north of the Santa Monica Pier. This place is always packed. But we're on a mission to park Tina so we can take a picture in front of her. Santa Monica is the official end of Route 66, so it's fitting we get our last shot of the trip here.

I pull toward the end of the lot, right where it meets the sand, and park. We're not in a space, but the van is parallel to the shore, so we can stand along her side and take this last photo. Riley sets up her little tripod. We all line up next to the van, Madeline nearest to the driver's door, Riley next to her, me next to Riley, and Ben closest to the back of the van. Madeline loops her arm around Riley's shoulder and this sets off a chain reaction of us all linking our arms around one another. It's the first time I've touched Riley since our time together on the terrace last night. Her hair brushes my arm and she glances up at me with a slight flush to her cheeks.

It's like a switch was flipped once I realized I had feelings for her. Now every glance, every touch, every thought makes my body and mind hypersensitive and focused on her alone.

Riley counts to three and we all smile at the camera on her cell. Then she shouts "Goofy faces!" and we all pose with crazy expressions—tongues out, crossed eyes, the works. For the last pic, we all separate and on Riley's count, we jump. She snaps the shot and catches us midair in front of the van I'll always remember. This trip means more than I expected it to. It's the trip where I first kissed Riley, a woman I never expected to steal my heart.

After taking Tina to Riley's friend's house and parking her in the garage, we catch a one-hour bus to Ventura harbor where we'll meet the shuttle to Marbella Island. Charter boats leave the harbor three times a day. We're going out on the late-afternoon cruise.

It pulls into the dock at two thirty for boarding. We walk down the gangplank, each of us tugging our suitcases behind us. I'm buzzing with anticipation and nerves, and the awareness that we still have to figure out how and when to break our news to Madeline. Maybe tomorrow, when we're all settled in. Now that we know Dad is as good as cleared, she's probably in a better headspace.

The boat is a double decker with the capacity to hold one hundred fifty passengers per ride.

We're greeted by one of the crew wearing a royal blue Island Charters polo shirt.

"Hi, I'm Kaci," she says, as we step from the dock onto the boat. "You can sit anywhere. Stow your luggage inside the lower cabin at the back. Welcome aboard the Sea Sprite."

We find seats upstairs on the open top deck where viewing is uninhibited by windows. The air is cooler once we're out on the water for the one-hour ride over to Marbella. About a half-hour after we board, the captain comes over the speaker system announcing that we're entering a dolphin feeding ground.

"Between one and two thousand dolphins swim in this channel daily for this two-mile stretch right around this time of day. They swim until they locate a food source and then they surround their meal and work together to catch fish."

We look over the edge of the boat and dolphins are literally everywhere, as far as the eye can see on both sides of the boat, jumping, swimming at a pace that surpasses our speed, and playing in the wake of the boat as they go.

A few minutes later, the outline of Marbella becomes more clear. Terracotta clay tile rooftops and white stucco buildings stand out among the green vegetation. As we draw nearer, the red of the beach umbrellas fills the shoreline. Finally, we're able to make out the pier which stretches into the ocean alongside a harbor filled with moored sailboats and motorboats that look like they're in mint condition and cost as much as my childhood home.

"We're here," Kaci tells us. "Grab your bags and follow me. I'll introduce you to Summer. She's the resort employee who will show you around and help you get settled."

We retrieve our luggage from the lower deck and follow Kaci to the front edge of the boat. A blond woman wearing a white polo, tan pressed cotton shorts, and white boat shoes is standing ready to greet us.

"Hey guys, I'm Summer. Kaci probably already told you that. I'll be your welcome hostess and island guide." She looks me in the eyes and says, "You must be Cam."

"Hi, Summer. Nice to meet you. You got it right. I'm Cam. How did you know?"

"Employee file. They gave me each of your photos so I'd recognize you."

Ben cuts in before Summer can call him by name and officially introduce herself. He's putting on his schmoozy face. Here we go.

"Hi, Summer. I'm Ben. I always loved summer. It's my favorite season." He pauses to wag his eyebrows. It sounds cheesy, but he's got this down. I've seen it hundreds of times. He finishes by saying, "And now I have even more reason to love that season."

Summer looks at Ben, and I expect the usual swoony response from her.

She crosses her arms over her chest, and says, "Well, hi,

Ben. You were pretty cute ... until you opened your mouth." She gives him a smirk that says he needs to watch himself.

I chuckle. Ben stands still, obviously at a loss for words for one of the first times in his life. I don't think I've ever witnessed a woman not completely taken under by his charms. Grandmas, little girls, all women our age—even if they are only going to be friends with Ben, still find him charming. I just gained a whole lot of respect for Summer, even though Ben looks shell shocked. Maybe especially because he does.

"Whoa," I say to him under my breath. "Never saw that coming."

He shakes his head as if trying to come out of a trance.

Then he says, "I think I'm in love."

29

RILEY

Everyone knew that all islands
were worlds unto themselves,
that to come to an island
was to come to another world.
~ Guy Gavriel Kay

Marbella island is glorious.

You'd barely know you were in California anymore except for the tell-tale chaparral on what appears to be the undeveloped side of the island. We can just barely catch a glimpse of the distant hills over the tops of the trees, beyond the developed hillsides filled with scattered homes and winding roads this side of the island facing the pier. The scene spreading out in front of us takes my breath away. I actually gasped when I stepped onto the wooden pier with its thick wood pylons spaced every six feet or so down the bending path it makes toward shore.

I applied online for the barista position at the resort coffee shop, C-Side Coffee Co. My official interviews took place over two Zoom calls. The cafe manager, Clarissa, talked to the owners of Bean There Done That to check my references, and I guess to ascertain if I could actually make a good cup of coffee, which we all know I can. Before I knew it, I had secured a temporary job serving caffeinated goodness to guests of Alicante resort for all of August and half of September. It's the last six weeks of summer, and I guess Marbella attracts more tourists this time of year, so they are in the position to need seasonal help.

All that to say, I've never stepped foot on Marbella Island before this moment. I saw photos on the website, but they didn't come close to doing the exotic beauty justice. Everything here feels curated, planned out so that residents and guests to the island experience refined island living and an escape from every other reality on earth.

The pier ends on a soft sand beach with evenly spaced palm trees lining the back edge. Behind that is what would appear to be a street, only there aren't cars on Marbella. The only vehicles people drive here are golf carts, mopeds, scooters, and bicycles. A micro-truck drives by, probably delivering something to one of the quaint shops on the other side of the street.

North of the pier is a harbor full of private boats moored in tidy rows. In front of those ships sits a smaller pier, much shorter than this one, about a football field's length away, and a boat launch. South of the pier, the sand stretching along a beachfront is dotted with red beach umbrellas and loungers. When my eyes lift, I see the terracotta roof and white stucco of the resort. The main building is set back about a block from where we're standing, but there are smaller villas and what seem like condos tucked away between trees.

"This is so beautiful," I say to Summer.

"It really is. I just started working here in June. My agent got me the gig."

"Your agent?"

"I'm an aspiring actress. There's a show that's going to be starting on the island next month. I auditioned for the part of the mermaid."

When I don't say anything, Summer continues. "It's not like I dream of playing mermaid roles in island theater productions, but we take what we can get in the hopes that each role gives me increased exposure so I can go for the next big thing. Someday, I'll get my break. It just takes that one role to get noticed and then a career can skyrocket."

"I'd love to see the show," Ben says. "I did a little theater in my high school days."

Summer completely ignores Ben.

I've never seen a woman react to Ben with anything but kindness and interest. Usually, women our age throw themselves at Ben like fans at a Harry Styles concert. He's admittedly gorgeous, and he's got charm to spare. He's funny, but also knows when to be serious. And he's got a heart of gold—loyal almost to a fault.

Summer's not impressed with Ben at all. If he weren't pouting like a kicked puppy, it would be hilarious.

"Peter Pan," Ben continues as if Summer didn't hear him. "John Napoleon Darling. That was my role. I had seventeen lines."

He's babbling now, which usually is my job. I'm the blurting girl who can't reel in her thoughts when she's nervous. It's never Ben. He's goofy, but he's always on his A-game, especially when it comes to charming women. If I were meeting him for the first time like Summer is, I'd be running for the hills right now.

She does glance over at him after he recites his very short acting resume to her. Again, she doesn't say anything. Cam catches my eye. He's obviously entertained by Ben's floundering. I smile over at Cam, hoping it looks like a friendly smile and not an *I want to be alone with you to kiss and talk and kiss again—and soon*—smile.

"Let's ditch your luggage," Summer says to Madeline and me. "Then we can take these two to their apartment." She looks at Cameron. "The landlord gave me your key."

"You already have the key to my apartment?" Ben asks. "Feel free to use it anytime."

He wags his eyebrows and it makes him look almost smarmy. I want to take him aside and pour ice water over his head, or whatever would snap him out of this spiral of weirdness.

Madeline looks at Ben with raised eyebrows. "Did you get seasick on the boat ride over? Or catch some ocean-borne virus that messed with your head? What has gotten into you?"

Then Madeline looks at Summer. "He's definitely a huge goofball at times, but he's never like this. I don't know what's gotten into him. Trust me. He's really a nice, mostly-normal guy. Women usually throw themselves at him."

I giggle. I don't know why. Watching Madeline defend Ben's honor to this near-stranger strikes me as funny for some reason.

"Mostly normal?" Ben asks. "I'm totally normal. I'm so normal, they put my photo under the word *normal* in the dictionary."

"So normal," Cam mutters. "There's your proof."

Madeline shrugs and shakes her head. She tried. What can we say? It's not Ben's day to woo the local island women—or at least not this one.

Summer takes us to a golf cart parked next to other golf

carts. On the side of each cart there's an emblem that looks like an island and the words *Alicante Resort and Spa.*

"These all belong to the resort," she explains. "Employees get to use them for carting guests around or running resort-related errands. Guests can check them out too. They just have to see the front desk in the main building or the concierge. So, hop in!"

"Wait," Ben asks. "You're a resort employee?"

"Yes," Summer says in an exasperated voice.

"But I thought you came here to be a mermaid ... in the play."

"I came to take the role of a mermaid, but that job hasn't started yet, even though we're already scheduling rehearsals. And it pays in clams."

"Seriously?" Ben asks.

Summer spears him with a look. "No. But it may as well. So, I needed another gig. Working part-time with guest services allows me to rent a room in the employee dorms at a discount and I make a little money. I'm your typical starving artist."

These are the first words she's said directly to Ben since she made that comment about him being pretty before he opened his mouth back on the dock.

"Resourceful," Ben says.

"I guess," Summer answers, never making eye contact with him.

We're all in the golf cart, so Summer takes off, navigating down narrow roads that run between buildings then wind back behind the resort and up a hill until we're at a three-story building that looks like a modest apartment complex. The exterior is simple, but clean.

"Here we are. Employee dorms. I'll show you two to your room."

We hop out and Summer leads us through the double glass

doors at the front of the building, and then we take an elevator to the third floor. My first impression was accurate—the rooms are very much like the dorms Madeline and I lived in our freshman year at UCLA. Two twin beds line opposing walls, a bank of closets and dressers is across the wall on either side of the door we entered. The view out the window, though, is stunning. The bay can be seen off in the distance beyond treetops. And looking inland from the shoreline, we have a clear view of the whole resort with its pools, lazy river, and various cabanas and patios.

Summer goes through her spiel about the dorm setup. "There's a lounge on each floor with couches and chairs, a microwave and coffee pot. If you want to do any fancier cooking you can use the kitchen on the first floor. And there's a barbecue out back. Also, you have community showers and toilets down the hall. And there's a game room and TV lounge on the first floor. Women are up here. Men on floor two. Couples live in the few apartments on the first floor."

"Couples? Like they're married and they both work here?" I ask.

"Yep. If they don't already live on the island, or they don't want to shuttle in from the mainland, they have the option of accepting an apartment on the first floor."

We leave our bags in the room and accept our keys from Summer. Then we get back in the golf cart and she drives us over to Ben and Cam's apartment. Their place is much nicer than the dorms. Not that those are awful, they are just a bit spartan and utilitarian. Ben and Cam have one of two upper apartments in a four-plex. The building is a deep mustard yellow with a terracotta roof like the ones on top of most of the buildings around here.

We ascend the steps to their entry and Summer hands the key to Cam. He opens the door and we all walk into a nice living room with an adjoining kitchen. There's a balcony off the side of the living room with barely enough space for the two chairs and a little table between them. The guys walk down the hall and check out their bedrooms.

"I call dibs on this room!" Ben shouts out in his typical style.

"King bed?" Madeline guesses to me.

"I bet."

"You can have it," Cam says from somewhere down the hall. "This room has a sweet view."

The guys ditch their suitcases in their rooms, and we all head back downstairs with Summer. She tours us around the front side of the island, telling us about different parts of the island, like the fishing village further north of the resort area. Then Summer explains that the backside is owned by a wealthy family who leaves it open for public use, but they are strict about not developing that side of the island. A small portion of Marbella is also owned by the Nature Conservancy. Summer mentions that Marbella Island is twenty-five miles long and nine miles wide. That's bigger than I expected.

Outdoor enthusiasts come to hike, camp, and kayak on what the locals call "the backside." I'm thanking the heavens that Ben doesn't make a joke about backsides. Seeing his track record with Summer today, I'm shocked he's able to contain himself.

Summer explains that over the years, Hollywood producers have rented the island for filming major motion pictures. She lists off a bunch of movies we've heard of. Then she says, "That will explain the wild emus, chimpanzees, kangaroos, and a variety of other animals roaming the island. They have no natural predators here, so they just multiply and live freely back there. Sometimes they wander into town. It's always a commotion when they do, but it adds to the charm of this place, if you ask me."

"Wait," I ask. "You mean they brought animals here for filming and just left them here?"

"Yes. The Davis Foundation—the family who owns the backside—allowed it. They wanted to protect the animals and give them a sanctuary."

At this point, Ben leans in toward Cam and quietly says, "It's a wild backside."

I saw it coming. Glad it wasn't worse. I'm pretty sure Summer didn't hear Ben. Then again, if she and Ben become friends, she'll hear plenty more where that came from.

After driving us around to see various neighborhoods and shops, Summer parks the cart in a designated area at the resort and gives us a tour of the buildings, telling us about various amenities the resort offers as we go. As employees, we get discounts on massages, and there's a free pilates class once a week, and yoga on a different day in the dorm lounge with the resort yoga-pilates instructor, Aria.

It's nearly dinnertime by the time we're finished touring.

Since none of us have groceries yet, we decide to eat in one of the restaurants on the resort property. There are lots of dining options around the main town on Marbella, which is called Descanso. The name means *rest* in Spanish. And Marbella means *beautiful sea*. Summer told us that. She knows a lot for only having been here a month. I guess they taught her all she needed to know to do her job well.

Ben invites Summer to join us. "Do you want to eat dinner with us? We'd love to thank you for your time and the tour. It's the least we can do."

There he is. Our Ben. At least he's showing her the not-so-dorky side of himself now.

"No thanks," she says. "I've got dinner plans."

If only you could see Ben's face. I'm not sure what it is about Summer, or if it's just the fact that she rejected him and Ben's a typical man in hot pursuit of whatever he can't have. Is it the allure of the chase or something more? I've never seen him so instantly set on a woman.

Dinner's casual, since we're now on our own dimes. Our parents treated us for the expenses on the trip, but we all agreed once we landed on the island we weren't going to take further advantage of their generosity. We never could have had the experiences we did if they didn't help pitch in for the road trip. But, we're all adults, we need to be self-sufficient now.

Cam calls his mom once the meal arrives so he and Madeline can check in on their dad. Mr. Reeves is doing well. Stable. Madeline seems relieved, but still weighed down, naturally.

Madeline excuses herself to use the restroom after our meal. The three of us remain at the table, chatting and finishing the last of two slices of cheesecake we ordered for dessert.

"Can you slip out tonight?" Cam asks me.

"I thought you'd never ask," Ben answers in a falsetto.

Cam sends him a look. "Bro, you are not in red hot form today."

"I know," Ben says, shaking his head. "I literally struck out."

"Is that the first time a woman has denied you?" I ask.

Ben nods, this look of confusion on his face.

I chuckle. I can't help it. "Welcome to the human race."

"I want my mojo back." He pouts.

Cam looks at me, obviously wanting an answer to his question.

"I could try. Maybe I'll tell Madeline I want to spend some time alone on the beach to think about the trip. I hate lying to her."

"I think we can tell her tomorrow. She seems to be doing much better. I just want to wait until this day has passed since we got such heavy news this morning. We can tell her at breakfast."

"That's a plan," Ben agrees. "I don't like knowing something she doesn't. It feels slimy."

I nod. It does feel slimy, even though we delayed telling her for her own good.

"Text me if you are able to get away," Cam says, brushing his fingertips across my knuckles.

My body tingles everywhere simply from that innocent touch.

Madeline and I decide to walk the mile from the resort to our dorm. The weather is cooler, but not cold, an evening breeze flowing in from the ocean. At one point she links her arm through mine and we walk together like that—arm in arm.

"Are you doing okay?" I ask. "With your dad and everything?"

"I'm better. Still pretty shaken. It's a good distraction being here. I'll check in with my new boss tomorrow after lunch. Do you want to know something funny?"

"Always." I give her arm a light squeeze.

"When I applied for the job, Public Area Attendant, I thought I'd be standing around or something. I didn't realize that was a fancy name for housekeeping."

I chuckle. "Didn't you read the job description?"

"Honestly?"

"Yeah."

"I just wanted to be here with you. I didn't care what I did. There was only one barista job and I wanted you to have it. Face it, you were born to serve coffee." She looks over with a shy grin. "That sounded worse than I meant it. I mean, you have a gift for hospitality and for crafting beverages. It's always extra-special when you make it. So, I wanted you to get that job. I just took the next thing that I saw."

"At least it's public areas. You won't be cleaning toilets."

"Yeah. I read up on it this afternoon on the boat ride over. It's sweeping and picking up trash, and keeping the public areas looking immaculate. My mom will have a heyday when she hears this is my new job."

"She will. I'm pretty sure if they saw your room, you wouldn't have made the cut."

"What is my life? If I were exposed I wouldn't even be hired for seasonal housekeeping!" She giggles. "But admit it. I'm not as bad as I used to be."

"True. But still. I'd have to say housekeeping was never a position I saw you applying for or even qualifying for."

She laughs. "Welp. Here I am, a housekeeper at a resort. I know it's for six weeks, so I'll be fine. Then I'll finish preparing for my true calling—our true calling."

She winks at me and gives a light squeeze to our enjoined arms. I feel like a tool. It's on the tip of my tongue to tell her I don't know my calling yet. But considering Cam and I have a more pressing bomb to drop tomorrow morning, I let it slide. We can have the *I don't know what I'm going to be when I grow up* talk after she absorbs the *I'm madly in love with your brother* talk.

Love.

Am I in love?

I might not be, but I'm careening toward it at mach speed.

30

RILEY

I want to go on a road trip. Just you and me.
The highway, the radio, the blue sky, the back roads,
and windows down.
We'll talk about everything and nothing.
We'll sing our hearts out,
and we'll make memories we'll never forget.
Just you and me.
~ Unknown

"I just feel like taking a walk along the beach—alone." The lie tastes bitter on my tongue.

I do feel like a walk along the shoreline. Being at the beach soothes me in ways nothing else does—the rhythmic lapping of the waves, the infinite water stretching out to the horizon, obliterating everything else from view. Life gains perspective when I'm at the beach.

But I'm not walking alone tonight. I'm meeting Madeline's

brother for our clandestine arrangement. Yes, we're protecting her. But are we really? When she finds out, every minute Cameron and I pursued one another without telling her is another grain of salt in the wound. I feel like spilling it all right here, right now.

"I'm so tired," Madeline says. "It's been an inordinately long day. All the worry over my dad made it doubly long."

There's my answer. She's not in the headspace to swallow one more big chunk of information, let alone one so emotionally charged as me being with Cam.

"I'm so sorry about your dad. I know he'll be getting better. He's too much of a fighter to let this take him down long term."

"Yeah. I know. I just ache knowing he got hurt, and thinking how bad it could have been."

"Of course, you do. Get some rest. You'll feel better in the morning."

Until we drop a bomb on you, that is.

Ugh. I'm the worst friend right now. I don't know what else to do, but this—well, it just feels wrong.

I grab my backpack, rifle through it for my lipgloss, and toss the bag back on my bed. Things go flying out, but I'll get to them later, after I meet Cam. As badly as I feel about covering things up with Madeline, the thought of seeing Cameron makes flutters erupt in my belly, spreading through my chest and legs. I've got it bad for him—it's even more intense now that he has shown me how he feels about me.

A mirror hangs on the back of the door to our room. I step over to it and apply the gloss.

"Why go to the trouble of glossing your lips for a walk on the beach? Are you planning to pick up some local lifeguard? I think you do that in daylight, not the pitch of night."

"Yeah. I'm not trying to pick up a lifeguard," I deflect.

"Okay. Well, be safe. Take your cell."

"I will. If Summer hadn't told us about the low crime rate here, I wouldn't feel so open to wandering around at night. I've gotten used to being on guard on campus. But then being home got me more relaxed again. I'm glad we can be less concerned here. I love a walk at night."

"Me too," Madeline says on a yawn.

"I'll be quiet when I come back."

"No need. You know me. A marching band could come home with you, and I'd be sawing logs while they belted out their song, tubas and bass drums and all."

"Yeah. Love you, sweet Mads."

"Love you too, girlfriend. 'Til death do us part."

"'Til death do us part."

I pop the door open, carefully shutting it behind me, and walk to the elevator with a knot in my stomach. Tomorrow. She'll know tomorrow. For better or worse—speaking of vows.

I text Cam once I'm out of the apartment. He's waiting a block down the road, standing in front of someone's house with his hands in his shorts pockets. I see his smile through the darkness when I'm only a few feet from him. All uneasiness sloughs away as soon as we're close enough to touch one another.

My hand instinctively reaches for his. He clasps it and then draws me in for a hug.

"This day has been great, but so much torture," he murmurs into my hair. "I've wanted to hold you all day."

"Yeah?" I look up at him.

"Oh yeah." He places a kiss on my forehead and my smile takes over my face.

"It's been a day rife with temptation," I agree.

"Oh?" he asks.

The teasing note in his voice does things to me.

"Definitely."

"And what were you tempted to do, Sunshine?"

"Touch you. Kiss you. Hold hands. Like this."

I lean my head up and he meets me, kissing me with a kiss that relieves all the tension of the day, fulfills the anticipation, and yet stokes a fire that feels like it's only going to burn higher and hotter with every movement of his lips on mine.

We hold onto one another, savoring the kiss, reconnecting after a day of forced separation. His free hand runs across my back. He never unclasps our enjoined hands. He cups my face and pulls away enough to look into my eyes.

"I'm still in awe. And I feel so dumb. I can't believe you've been right here all along. You're amazing. Do you know that?"

"I'm ... okay."

I'm not feigning humility. I just don't know what he sees. I'm a decent person. I'm not ugly, but I wouldn't ever make the cover of a magazine. I'm kind. I have a fairly good sense of humor. But the way Cameron's looking at me, you'd think I was so much more than I am.

"Okay? You're kidding, right? You're beautiful in such a natural way—when you wake up and your hair is all disheveled, when you're climbing into a hot tub. Well, then you're beyond beautiful. You're captivating when the sunrise reflects off the highlights in your hair. When you laugh. When you pull out that notebook you write in and focus so fully that you seem lost to the world around you. And you're funny, adventurous, full of life. Not to mention the way you make me feel."

"Wow."

It's all I can say. For years, I've dreamed of being with Cameron. Rightly so. He's a man, not a boy now. He's responsible, thoughtful, and beyond gorgeous. He's funny, but also deep. There are things about him that draw me to him, and I can't even find words for what they are or why they matter. I just know I want him more than anything else I've ever wanted. To hear him say all that about me? It's beyond what I ever could have asked for.

Cameron tugs me toward himself. He holds me in his arms and I melt into his embrace.

Then he says, "Let's go walk on the beach."

"That's what I told Madeline I'd be doing."

"Madeline."

"Yep. Madeline."

We walk, holding hands, toward the shoreline. Guests from the resort are on loungers or walking along the south side of the pier. Cameron turns so we're headed north toward a less populated section near the water's edge. We pass the moored yachts and sailboats. Then the coastline becomes less developed. A tall craggy cliff rises up on the island, but there's a wide beach between it and the shore pound. Rocks, washed-up seaweed, and shells dot the ground around us.

When we've walked a while in silence, Cam turns me toward him and kisses me again.

It's possible I'll never get used to kissing Cameron. As soon as our mouths connect, an exhilarating, yet comforting chill runs through me. He shifts from hungry and intense to tender and sweet. I'm here for all of it. I match his movements, running my fingers through his hair, cataloging his muscles with my palms, lacing my fingers in his belt loops to anchor myself when I feel like I'm going to come undone from the sheer bliss of being taken over by him.

We kiss for a while, no rush, nothing else pressing in on this moment we're sharing. When we pull apart, his mouth lifts in a coy smile.

"And you can kiss," he adds. "Dangerously good kisses."

"Should I come with a warning label?" I tease.

"You definitely should." He pauses, running the back of his hand down my cheek. "Not that it would stop me. It wouldn't."

"I never pictured you as a reckless man."

"I'm not. But with you, apparently I am."

Cameron lightly tugs on my hand. "Let's sit."

I follow him to a large rock on shore, set back from the incoming tide. He sits and then he pulls me down between his legs so my back rests against his chest. He nestles his head next to mine, his chin on my shoulders. Then he wraps his arms around me from behind.

We sit like that, quietly watching the white foam crest and fall, ebbing onto the sand and retreating. Then Cam says, "I've been thinking about what you said that day about not knowing your future."

"Yeah. Me too. Not so much about that day, but I'm constantly thinking about what I'm going to do."

I pause, realizing this is all about me. He's the one starting a new job.

"Are you nervous about your new position?"

"Not really. I probably should be. But I've studied and prepared. I've gotten so acquainted with Alicante and Marbella I could give a better tour than Summer. I'm ready. I feel excited to get started and dive into everything. I'm sure I'll have a learning curve. Mostly, I can't believe I landed this job right out of college."

"They're lucky to have you."

"Thanks. I'm lucky to have you."

"You need to stop."

"Nope. I'm making up for lost time. Get used to it, Sunshine. I'm going to spoil you, and flatter you, and kiss you, and share life with you—especially during any free time I get while we're here together. The next six weeks are going to fly by."

"That's what I wanted to talk about."

"About this summer?"

"About my plans."

"I'm all ears. I want to hear your thoughts."

"Welp. I had a lot of time on the road to do some thinking. Sometimes I would be driving and there was nothing but the road ahead, mountains off in the distance, and the desert surrounding us. It gave my mind the space to work through things."

"Yeah?"

"And I didn't come to anything solid. I still don't have a clue what I want to do long term. But I know what I don't want. I know that with a clarity I didn't feel before we took our trip."

"And what's that?"

"I don't want my bachelors in education. I'm spending my parent's hard-earned money to get a degree I don't want. It feels wrong. I do want to finish my bachelors, but not in education."

"What would you do it in?"

"Business, I think."

"Okay."

"Okay? Just like that?"

"We're young. It may feel like we're past some expiration date, but we've got years ahead of us to correct any missteps and to take risks. We can choose a direction and change our minds later. Did you know there was a guy in my degree program in his fifties? He decided he wanted to get into hospitality, so he went to SDSU to get his degree along with all of us in our twenties. I admired him. And seeing him taught me a lesson. It's never too late to pursue your dreams. Well, I mean it's too late at some point. But it's usually not too late when people think it is. You just turned twenty-one. You've got time to figure out your goals and your path."

"So, I was thinking, what if I dropped out of UCLA and did a business degree from an online school that costs way less? I'd save my parents money. I'd be doing my thing instead of following Madeline while she does hers. I don't want to hurt her. It will gut me if she gets hurt over this, but I also have to live my own life. I think part of why I've been so confused is because I kept making decisions based on what I thought she wanted. She never asked that of me, but I didn't trust the strength of our friendship to endure me picking something that would separate us."

"And now you do?"

"I can't say I do. I'm pretty sure she's going to be mad at me either way. And I can't blame her. Tomorrow morning, when we tell her about us, she's not going to be happy that we started something and hid it. But I think she'll get past that. At least, I hope she will. I just know I can't live in her shadow. I have to figure out what I want, and then trust that our friendship can go the distance."

"I wonder if Ben is doing what you were doing with Mads."

"Maybe. You mean following you so you two don't break up?"

"We could use a different term. We shared a bed, but he's not my boo."

I laugh and Cam's laughter rumbles across my back. He squeezes me closer and I lean into him. This place, nestled into him, is my new favorite spot on earth.

"I feel a lot of feelings for you, Riley. You sort of ambushed me."

"If I recall, you were the one who leaned in and kissed me on my birthday."

"You're darn straight I did. And that opened up the lid on a box I guess I'd capped shut. I'm just overwhelmed by you."

His candor takes me by surprise. I want to reward it with equal honesty and vulnerability.

"If you ever read that notebook—my journal—you'd get an eyeful of how much I thought and felt for you—for years."

"Years?"

"Yep. I think I told you that already. But yes. Years. I've been pretty smitten with you, Reeves."

"Well, the feeling's mutual, Stewart."

"Oh, is it now?"

"Definitely. I'm obsessed. I can't stop thinking about you. Even when Ben and I were in our apartment after dinner, he kept teasing me. I wasn't really present. I was thinking about you, waiting for you to text, confirming you could come out and meet me."

I'm silent, soaking in the reality of what Cam's telling me.

He turns my head with his pointer finger and thumb gently gripping my chin. Then he places a kiss on my lips. Our mouths meet and fireworks erupt across my skin, traveling through me, setting me alight with longing for him.

I hum into his mouth and he answers me with a growl or a groan. It's so masculine and completely different from the Cam who needs to be on time and follow all the rules. I love discovering this side of him—a side that seems to be only for me.

He pulls away, kissing my neck and then my cheek. I've never had a man kiss anything but my lips. Cam's kisses fall all over my ear, my throat, my face. I love the way he seems lost in our connection.

We rest back into one another, silently holding this newness between us.

"Are you sure you don't want to finish at UCLA?" he asks.

"I'm sure. I don't know if I'll stay at the apartment with Madeline. I don't want to abandon her. Then again, she may not want me there after we break our news."

"I don't think she'll be that upset. Maybe at first, but not enough to want you out of her life or the apartment."

"I hope not." I pause. "After seeing this island today, I could imagine staying here. Finishing my degree online."

"Wow."

"Wow, good? Or wow, I'm crazier than you thought I was."

"Maybe a dash of both. I'd love to have you stay here. There's a lot to consider, though. You just got here. You may hate it in a week. What would you do for work? Where would you stay?"

"I know. It's just a thought for now. I wanted to tell you what I was thinking. We'll see."

"Yeah. We'll see."

Cam's quiet for a little while, running soothing strokes up and down my arm with his hand.

"I wouldn't want you to choose anything just for me—just for us to be together. You're not like other women, Riley. I told you I don't do casual. No matter where you are, I want to give this the best shot we can. I'm committed to that. As new as this feels, it's also very old and established. It's not like we just met. I know you—even though in some ways I'm just getting to discover other parts of you I never knew, or was too dense to notice. I know I want to make this work, and I'm willing to have a long-distance relationship while you finish up school if that's what it takes."

"Thank you."

My voice is soft and careful. I can barely believe the words I'm hearing. I want to wrap them up in tissue paper and collect them.

Cam turns my head so we're gazing at one another, only the dim light of the stars and moon and the reflected light from the ocean defining his features. "Thank you, Sunshine—for giving me this chance, for waiting for me. I promise you won't regret it."

31

RILEY

The worst pain in the world
goes beyond the physical.
Even further beyond
any other emotional pain one can feel.
It is the betrayal of a friend.
~ Heather Brewer

I quietly open the door to our room, careful not to wake Madeline, even though she's right. A herd of elephants could barge through and she'd sleep soundly through the commotion.

When the door swings open, the light on her bedside table clicks on.

Not good. Something in my heart knows I'm about to experience one of the greatest pains of my life. The foreboding penetrates my gut with a throbbing and knotting sensation I can't shake.

"Hey," Madeline says.

Her voice is flat. Too flat. She sounds crushed.

I know Madeline as well or better than I know myself. Something is seriously wrong.

"Is it your dad?"

"Nope."

"What is it?" I ask, walking in and shutting the door behind me.

I sit on the edge of my bed, and that's when I see it.

My journal, splayed open, laying on the bedside table like evidence in a crime scene.

"You read my journal?"

It's not an accusation, even though it sounds like one. I'm in no position to stand on high moral ground right now. If she read my journal, she violated my privacy. But I violated her trust, so we're nowhere near even.

"I wasn't going to. After you left for your walk—if that's even what you did—I got up to use the restroom. When I came back into our room, I noticed some of your things had fallen out of your bag onto the bed, and then I saw a few were scattered on the floor. I bent over to pick them up for you, and when I lifted your journal off the bed, it fell open. I saw Cam's name ..."

"So you read what I wrote about him."

"I shouldn't have."

"That's not ... I mean, yeah. You shouldn't have. But ... I should have talked to you."

"Ya think?"

She's mad. I knew she was from the way her tone lacked emotion.

"I had reasons."

"What reasons, Riley? What possibly could have motivated you to keep such a huge secret from me? Oh. And not just one secret. Do I even know you? I thought we were best friends."

I'm quiet. She's right. I kept secrets.

I didn't tell her I was wrestling with my thoughts about the future. I withheld my feelings for Cameron from her. And when Cam and I got together, we intentionally kept our relationship hidden.

"You don't even have anything to say for yourself? You kissed my brother. You kept your feelings for him a secret for years. Years, Riley! You purposely hid these things from me. And you don't want to be a teacher? Why wouldn't you tell me that? What do you think I am? Some fragile piece of glass? I tell you everything. And from what I can see, you tell me nothing—nothing important."

I feel the wetness on my cheeks and realize I'm crying. I've messed everything up. What can I say? There's no defense for my choices. Yes. I had reasons. But in the end, she's right. I should have come to her.

"Are you just going to sit there and look at me without giving me the dignity of a response? I'm hurting over here, Riley. I feel so betrayed—by the two people who matter most to me in life. No, make that three. Ben knows too. Oh my gosh! Riley. Ben knows and I don't. Do you know how that makes me feel? Give me something to hang onto here. You can't just sit there letting me yell at you and not say anything."

She starts to cry. That makes my tears fall more furiously.

"I'm sorry," I say so softly I wonder if she can even hear me.

My head is spinning like I just got off a high-speed carousel. I feel like I'm going to puke.

I start to sob. Not because I feel sorry for myself, but because I betrayed my best friend and hurt her in ways I can't imagine. I feel her anguish and it's breaking me. I'm the cause of her pain.

"I ..." I start to speak, but the words get caught in my throat.

I gather my thoughts and look over at Madeline. "I don't want to hurt you. I never wanted to hurt you."

"Then talk to me now, Riley. I don't know what we can do about this, but you owe me that much. Tell me what you were thinking. Help me understand why you would shut me out of the two most important parts of your life."

A sob breaks free when I absorb her words. I knew what I was doing, but on another level I had no idea. Hearing her lay it out like this feels like knives running along sensitive skin.

"Okay," I say. "I'll start with Cam."

My mind thinks of him holding me tonight. How right it feels to be in his arms—how us finally finding something together feels like the very thing I've waited for. I can envision a future with him. I've been imagining one for years, but now that he's feeling the same way for me as I do for him, and the fact that he's telling me he's willing to work for our relationship, I know this isn't just me fantasizing.

And a future with Cam means Madeline and I will be connected whether she forgives me or not.

I grab my pillow and hold it to my front like a shield, sitting back and crossing my legs on my bed. Madeline stays where she is, tucked under her covers, her head on her pillow. I sniffle and take a deep breath, trying to stave off my tears long enough to give Madeline the answers she deserves.

"I don't even know when I started having a crush on Cam. It was years ago. At first it was probably innocent—like a kid who looks up to someone and thinks they're cute."

I blush. Admitting all this to her feels so vulnerable, and a little weird. He's still her brother.

"At some point, those feelings grew deeper. I guess the older I got, the more I saw the qualities Cam had that other guys lacked."

"And that's why you never dated other guys?"

"Pretty much. I tried. I fought the feelings I had for Cameron."

"So I read."

"You read it all?"

"Not all, but enough. I stopped because it hurt. And because at some point my conscience kicked in and said even though you wronged me, two wrongs don't make a right. That's your journal. Your thoughts. Your feelings. It's not mine to read and search through. You had a reason it was all in there and not out here between us."

"At first I didn't tell you about Cam because I thought it would make things awkward. And I thought the feelings would pass. I never imagined he would ever notice me, let alone think of me as anything other than his second baby sister. So, I determined to fight my feelings and keep you out of it so things didn't get weird between us."

"We can have things get weird, Rye. We'll get through that. Deception is far worse than weird, wouldn't you say?"

Madeline sits up, the intensity of her emotions obviously too much for her to remain lying down.

"Agreed. Obviously."

"Go ahead. I'm still listening."

"I was even fighting the emotions I felt for him on this trip. And then we spent time together, driving and talking. He and I had some serious talks while you and Ben crashed in the back seat. I still thought he was just being Cam. I saw him. I always saw him. But he never saw me.

"But then he started calling me Sunshine, and sometimes even winking at me. I still didn't know. If I thought something was going to happen between us, I would have told you. Up until the morning of my birthday, I never imagined ..."

"And then he kissed you at sunrise over the Grand Canyon."

"Yes." I can't help the dreamy tone to my voice.

My mind drifts to the memory—how Cam shocked me with that kiss, but then I'd never felt so right as I did in that moment. It wasn't merely because I'd wanted him for so long. It was him. It was us.

"I've gotta hand it to him," Madeline says. "That's a pretty romantic move. Unexpected."

"I don't think he planned it. How could he have? He asked you and Ben to come watch the sunrise too."

"So, you two kissed. Why didn't you tell me then?"

"We were so surprised, and caught up in the moment. And the four of us were on a schedule that morning. We had to get on the road, so Cam and I didn't have time to process what happened and talk things over with one another. We wanted to discuss everything with one another before we talked to you or Ben. I know that makes no sense—even as I'm saying it, it seems so simple. We should have just told you. But at that point I wasn't even sure where Cam's head was at. We were going to tell you first thing this morning, since we talked last night, but everything happened with your dad."

"I get that. It does make sense in a way. What were you supposed to do, march into camp and announce, '*Hey, Mads, we kissed!*'?"

"But I could have pulled you aside at some point yesterday. I should have."

"Probably. Yeah. Definitely. Waiting ... it just made me feel left out and unimportant."

"You're not. You are one of the most important people in my life. I chose UCLA for you."

"We'll get to that."

"Yeah."

"But first, I have to ask. Gladys?"

"Mm hmm." Tears break free hearing Gladys' name from Madeline's mouth.

"She's our grandma. Why are you writing to her? If that's the Gladys you are writing to."

"It's her. You know how many times I went to her house after school. And pretty soon she felt like she was my grandma too. When she passed I missed her so much it hurt. I didn't expect to miss her like I did. So, one day I wrote her a letter. Pretty soon I found myself writing to her anytime I had a fear or something to work through that I didn't want to face alone, or a special moment I wanted to cherish."

"Or a secret to keep."

"Yeah. Or a secret to keep."

"I had no idea you missed her so much."

"The journal helps. I feel like I'm still connected to her when I write my letters to her."

"Does Cam know?"

"About Gladys?"

"Yeah."

"No. You're the first."

"Well thank God for that, at least."

I'm quiet, reminded acutely of her pain and how I'm the cause.

"So, you don't want to be a teacher?"

"I thought I did. I love kids. But the further we went along in our program, the more I realized I don't want to teach. I have no idea what I want to do."

"Why did you stay with that major?"

"You."

"Me?"

"Yeah. I wanted to be near you. We've always shared everything. When we started applying for colleges, I was so afraid we'd drift. So I applied where you did, picked your major. I just wanted to be sure we'd stay together. It sounds so misguided right now."

"Actually, it sounds sweet. But it also shows me you don't trust me. If you did, you would have come to me. You would have shared that fear and told me what you were thinking. Instead, you held everything in and kept me at arm's length. I thought you trusted me more than that."

What can I say? She's right.

"What else?" Madeline asks.

"What do you mean?"

"What other secrets are you keeping from me?"

"Nothing." I pause, and then I realize there's something. "Except, I didn't walk alone tonight."

"You met Cam."

"I did. We really were going to tell you in the morning. We just knew you'd been through so much over your dad today."

"Again, not trusting me. I'm a big girl, Riley. I can handle crisis and sadness—and difficult truths. I'd far rather hear the truth and have to grapple with it than find out the three people I love most in the world colluded to keep me in the dark. How would you like being the odd man out?"

"I'd hate it. So much."

"Exactly."

I want to ask her if we're good, but I know that's selfish. She needs time. It's the least I can give her after what I put her through. I think I need time too. I need to figure things out—like why I kept such massive secrets from my best friend instead of trusting her.

"I love you," I say before I even think better of it.

"I still love you too." Madeline's voice is sullen and careful, like loving me is a hardship instead of the gift she's always treated it like in the past.

"I need sleep," she says.

"I'll do whatever it takes to make this right."

"I know you will. I just don't know what that is yet."

We don't say anything else. I brush my teeth, change into pjs, and climb into bed.

"Rye?" Madeline says when the lights are out and we're both under our covers.

"Yeah?"

"I'm not mad anymore. I'm just hurting big time. You really hurt me. You all did, but you most of all. And I'm sorry I read your journal. It wasn't meant for me."

"I'm not sorry you read it. I wish you had found out another way—a less hurtful way—but I want you to know it all. I always did want you to know."

"M'kay. Goodnight, Rye."

"Goodnight, Mads. I love you."

She doesn't answer me, and she doesn't say *'Til death do us part*. I don't expect her to, but I miss those words in a way that feels like a hole going straight through me.

What if we don't come back from this?

What if I did so much damage that we're never the same?

Is a romantic relationship with Cam worth losing my best friend?

My tears fall quietly, soaking my pillow. I eventually fall asleep with regrets and an ache in my soul that feels like it will never go away.

32

CAMERON

You will know if a person truly loves you
if he is willing to wait for you no matter how long.
~ Unknown

Ben and I fix breakfast while I send a group text to the girls inviting them to join us. Ben woke early and went out to pick up some groceries so we could finally start eating at home after a week of having nearly every meal at a restaurant.

Riley and I are going to tell Madeline about us this morning, so I figured eating in was a good call. That way, Madeline is free to let us have it if she's upset.

My cell pings with a message notification. I pick it up off the kitchen counter.

Riley: *She knows.*

Just those two words. They tell me so much. If this were good news, Riley might call, or she'd add something about how Mads knows, but she's good with it, and they are on their way.

I wait for something more. Nothing comes.

"Madeline knows," I tell Ben.

"Oh boy. How'd that go?"

"I don't know. Riley didn't say yet."

Ben lets out a low whistle.

I check my phone again.

Nothing.

"Should I call her?"

"Madeline or Riley?"

"I don't know."

"Welp. If you don't know, it's best to wait."

"Seriously. That's awful advice."

"It's solid and you know it. Come on. Let's eat. We'll feed the girls if they show up later."

"I don't know if I can eat."

"I'll make you an egg white scramble. You'll eat."

Ben turns to the stove and starts fixing one of my favorite breakfasts.

We're halfway through breakfast when my phone pings with a text. I have it face up, next to me on the table. I tap Riley's message.

> **Riley:** *She read my journal last night while you and I were on the beach. We talked when I got home. We really messed this up, Cam. I messed up more than you did. She doesn't want anything to do with me this morning. She wants space to process. I can't come over when she's like this. She already feels like it's the three of us leaving her out of things.*

"Son of a monkey!"

I pick up my phone, take my plate to the kitchen, and grab my apartment key.

"Where are you going?" Ben asks.

"I need to talk to my sister."

"Whoa. Whoa. Whoa. Slow your roll." Ben holds his hand up like a policeman stopping traffic. "And did you just say, son of a monkey?"

I glare at Ben. He chuckles like the impervious man he is. "Son of a monkey. I'm using that for sure. Dude. You just qualified for AARP with that one."

My hand is on the door handle.

"Give me your phone."

I don't know why, but I relinquish my phone to Ben.

Ben reads the text, whistles low again, and then says, "Okay. What's the move?"

"The move?"

"What's your plan, hot shot? You can't just go in there like a blazing ball of testosterone."

"I don't have an actual plan, per se. I just have to get through to Mads. We weren't trying to hurt her. Things rolled out in a sequence. It wasn't subversive. We wanted her to know. We were protecting her."

"And she asked for space. And she knows where you live."

"Your point?"

My hand is still gripping the door knob.

"She needs space. Giving her what she needs will help her come around. Send her a text if you want. But don't go over there. And let me read it before you hit send. You need a second line of defense in the state you're in."

I nod, dropping my hand and sticking it out so Ben can hand my cell over.

"Thanks."

"You'd do the same for me. Heck. You have done the same for me. That's what we do for one another."

"Should I text Riley?"

"Text her back, yeah. But I might give her some space too. Otherwise, Madeline's going to feel like she's being disregarded and excluded again. Until things are straight with Mads, you two need to be patient."

"I'm usually a very patient man."

"You are. And that's how I know Rye's the one."

"You know that?"

"Definitely. You're like a different version of you since that kiss, maybe a few days before the kiss when you coined that nickname. That's when your icy heart started to thaw and you saw the light. You're this unhinged, spacey, slightly obsessed version of yourself." Ben makes a dreamy face. "It's a beautiful thing." He chuckles, and then his tone is serious again. "That's love, man."

"Love."

I don't say it like a question. More like I'm trying on the thought for size. I don't know if I love Riley. On one hand, I've always loved her—like family. She's definitely out of the family-zone now. I think of her kisses, and even with this much distance between us, my body responds immediately to the memories of her in my arms. But am I falling in love? I don't know.

Who am I kidding? I'm falling. I might not be there, but I'm careening toward love without any power to stop myself—not that I'd want to. The idea of falling in love with Riley brings a smile to my face.

Of course, Ben notices.

"Love. Told you, man. You've got it big."

I shake my head lightly. I'm not fighting it.

I plop on the couch and start typing a text to Madeline first.

Ben's right. For now, she needs to come first. That's the only way we'll make this right. But if Madeline's being unreasonable, there will be an expiration on this grace period. I'm not giving Riley up. Madeline will have to get over herself if she doesn't come around. I only hope Riley feels the same way I do.

Cameron: *Hey, Mads. I know you heard about me and Riley. I'm not going into things on a text. She told me you want space. Just know I love you. I don't want to hurt you. You matter. We were trying to pace ourselves and make sense of what happened and where things were going before we talked to you or Ben, but Ben guessed. He reads me like a book.*

Riley and I want you to know about us. It was poor thinking on our part not to tell you right away. Just know you're not an afterthought.

I love you, Goob. I'm here if you want to talk.
Ben put me on house arrest when I tried to rush over to talk this morning. You can thank him for me honoring your request for space. Let's talk when you're ready. Or I'll just sit still and listen while you yell at me. I'd say you could throw things at me, but I've got orientation starting this afternoon and I can't start a new job with random bruises.

Sorry you're hurting. Really, I am.

I hand my phone over to Ben. He reads the text, nods, and hands my cell back to me so I can hit send.

"You pulled out the Goob."

"I did."

I called Madeline Goober when we were really little. I don't remember how it started. I heard the word somewhere and it stuck. She went through a phase where she threatened to do horrible things to me and my property if I used the nickname. But since we've been away from one another, I've noticed she smiles affectionately when I pull it out, since I only use it sparingly, and never in public. I'm not using it to butter her up. She has every right to be upset. I just want her to know she's still my Goob.

Once I hit send on Madeline's text, I type a response to Riley.

Cameron: *Hey. I can only imagine how brokenhearted you are over Mads. Give her time. She'll come around. You're her person. You guys will get through this. And I'm here. But Ben, in his unexpected wisdom, said we ought to stay away from one another while Madeline processes everything. For the record, I hate that idea. But I think he's right. At least for a little while. Madeline felt left out. Us seeing one another will only reinforce that feeling. We need to help her get past the hurt. What do you think? I already miss you. Just popping that here in case you start thinking this is easy on me. And, I texted Mads. I told her she could yell at me or talk. I'll listen. We'll get through this, Sunshine. I'm not a quitter—and you're worth waiting for.*

Madeline's text comes through the second I hit send on my message to Riley.

Madeline: *Thanks. I am hurting. I just need space. It's more than you two kissing and starting something behind my back, and keeping me in the dark on purpose. As if that's not enough. It's also a lot with Riley. More than you may know. Then again, you may know, considering everyone knows* *everything but me. Anyway, thanks for letting me have space. I'll let you know when I'm ready to throw rotten veggies at you. I definitely am taking you up on that. And you're paying for the veggies.*

I set the phone down, feeling a little relief. If she's joking about veggies, there's hope. Then again, she might not be joking. But there's still hope. The cell buzzes on the coffee table.

Riley: *Thanks for all that. You're right. Or Ben's right. I already was going to suggest we take some space while Madeline sorts out her thoughts and feelings. I miss you too, but I'm used to wanting you and not having you. I can wait. I've waited this long.*

Cameron: *I don't want you to get used to waiting for me. Not anymore. I'm here now. Not going anywhere. This is a blip. We'll wait it out, at least for a little while. If it drags on, I'll take action. I want time with you while we're both here on Marbella.*

Riley: 😘

I stare at that emoji for a while.

Ben asks, "What's going on?"

"Riley sent me an emoji."

"Which one?"

"That's the thing. I don't know what it means."

"Hand me your phone, grandpa."

I ignore the dig and hand over my cell.

"It's the kissy face. It's like she's sending you a kiss."

I can't help it. I groan.

Ben cracks up. "Man, this is entertaining. I love it."

"So glad to be your entertainment while I suffer."

"Yeah, well, you can laugh at me when I'm half-gone for a woman."

"Like yesterday with Summer?"

"Dude. Leave her out of this."

"Exactly," I say with a smirk.

Ben and I tidy up the kitchen and then I start feeling squirrely, so we explore the village around our apartment a little before we have to each show up at our respective jobs for orientation.

Ben is going to be on staff with water sports. He'll help with boat rentals, boat tours, SUP lessons, surf lessons, kayaking, snorkel tours and whatever else falls under that part of what the resort offers. It's a job that pays less than the position I landed, but it's not the equivalent of a summer job any high-school kid could cover. He had to have a background in hospitality and certification in lifeguarding and pass the proficiency tests for other water sports.

I show up in the lobby of the main building of the resort to meet Shaw, who is the head of guest services and my direct boss. After introducing me to key staff members, Shaw shows me the computer system we use for tracking amenities and special requests. We run down the calendar for upcoming events. Shaw and I review the status of a few upcoming on-site weddings, a celebrity impersonator conference, and a pirate shindig. At the beginning of September there's a big three-day meet the author event they host annually here on the island. I've got tasks to complete already to help arrange details for the authors who will be coming in for that weekend.

I'm grateful to have work to distract me. Even with the whirlwind of orientation, my mind constantly drifts to thoughts of Madeline, and even more so to Riley.

33

RILEY

Travel isn't always pretty.
It isn't always comfortable.
Sometimes it hurts, it even breaks your heart.
But that's okay. The journey changes you.
It should change you.
~ Anthony Bourdain

I show up at C-Side Coffee Co. at noon. The coffee bar has a fully open back wall which leads right out to a patio that faces the beach. On the other side of the patio railing is sand leading right up to the ocean. Boats are moored nearby. There's a very "island" feel to the interior, with wooden rafters and a teakwood front to the bar at the center of the room. Stools face the counter where baristas craft drinks, and thoughtfully spaced bistro tables fill the dining area. Tables with umbrellas shade the patio, and twinkle lights are strung overhead in the outdoor space.

The owner of C-Side, Clarissa, has tanned skin, brown hair with blond highlights, and a personality that immediately makes me feel like I've known her forever. She steps around the counter when I walk in and pulls me into a much-needed hug. I nearly cry after all I've been through in the past twenty-four hours with Madeline and the way things are still so up in the air between us.

"I've been so looking forward to meeting you, Riley. Your bosses at Bean There Done That couldn't say enough about you. Apparently, you're a natural when it comes to serving customers and preparing drinks."

"I love being a barista," I say honestly.

Then I hear the words I just said as if they are a revelation. *I love being a barista*. I know it's not an elementary school teacher, or an assistant manager, or a rocket scientist, but it's what I love. You wouldn't even have to pay me. Of course, I'm not telling Clarissa that. I'll take a paycheck, thank you very much. But, wow. This is what I love. Why did it take a two thousand two hundred seventy mile trip for me to see what was right in front of me all along?

"So," Clarissa says, completely oblivious to the fact that I'm having a life-epiphany right now. "Let me show you around. Bianca will be in at one, and she'll work the bar. You can either watch or help. It's totally up to you. In the meantime, why don't you make me a drink."

"What do you like?"

"Make it something that says *vacation*, or *island coffee*. Surprise me."

She's so laid back. I love her already.

I step behind the bar, feeling a comfortable ease with my surroundings instantly. While I familiarize myself with the set up, I make conversation.

"Of course, I could make you a coffee lemonade, or a coffee

and orange juice. Those are both becoming popular lately. There's a fun twist to an iced latte I saw the other day. It's an iced strawberry latte. You can use fresh strawberry syrup and crushed strawberries as a base for a traditional latte. Or, there's the classic affogato. Just coffee over ice cream. Simple, delicious, and nothing says summer like ice cream. But that doesn't scream *Island*, or *Vacation*."

Clarissa is smiling at me.

"What?"

"I already love you and you haven't even made me a drink."

I blush. "I felt the same way when you pulled me into a hug. It's been a long day—well, yesterday was—and I felt right at home with you."

"Long day?" Clarissa asks.

I'm pulling out ingredients, and talking as I do. My head's under the counter when I answer her.

"Yeah. Long day. I had a misunderstanding with my best friend. Totally my fault. Anyway, it's not quite resolved. So, I'm still a little preoccupied. But when I got here and you welcomed me, a bit of that heaviness lifted."

"That's always hard. Is your friend here on Marbella?

"She is. She's doing temp work too. And her brother and another friend of ours are working here full-time as of this week."

Clarissa hums.

"Your drink is going to take a few minutes. It's my special version of a specialty."

"Ooooh. I'm intrigued."

"Have you followed the Dalgona craze?"

"Do I own a coffee shop?"

"Okay, fair enough. I saw this drink where you make Dalgona and put it over coconut milk."

"You've got my attention, Riley."

"Only, I make my Dalgona with real coffee. As long as the sugar to coffee ratio is right, you still get a whip that stands up pretty well."

Clarissa smiles while I get busy pulling out the coconut milk I saw in the fridge, sugar, and the cold carafe of coffee from another fridge. I place a bowl on the counter and pour in milk, coffee and sugar, and then I start the whipping process that takes around four minutes. Clarissa silently watches me with a soft smile on her face.

A couple who had been at a bistro table along the back wall steps up to watch me.

"What are you making?" the middle-aged man asks.

I explain the drink as I pour coconut milk over ice in the glass, and then top it with the foam topping I just whipped up.

I place the drink in front of Clarissa, grabbing a paper umbrella at the last minute to pop into the top of the foam. I lightly dust the top of the drink with some vanilla cookie crumbs.

"Enjoy," I say.

Clarissa takes a spoon from the setup on the bar and scoops some of the foam first, then she sips the coconut milk through the straw. The couple smiles at us, leaves a tip in the jar, and walks out toward the patio.

"Divine!" Clarissa says, licking her lips. "Oh my goodness! Why do you have to be seasonal? You are just the barista I've been looking for."

"Really?"

"Yes. Between the way you feel like a kindred, and the ease with which you move in drink prep, to the way you handled those customers. Your previous bosses were right. You were born to do this."

"That's funny. Those are the exact words my bestie said to me the other day."

"Well, she's right. Why don't you make her one of these—or whatever she likes—and bring it to her as a peace offering. It might not solve your problem, but in my experience, free coffee always helps."

I stay on at C-Side working alongside Bianca and Clarissa until dinnertime. The day flies by and I barely realize I've been there over five hours when Clarissa tells me I should go home and rest. I'm off tomorrow, but I start full-time in two days, working from six in the morning until two in the afternoon since those are their prime hours.

Clarissa nearly has to push me out the door. It's not like I have much waiting for me. With Madeline taking space and Cam agreeing to keep his distance to give her the time she needs, the only person I could hang out with tonight is Ben. Clarissa stops me and says, "Don't forget the drink for your bestie."

"Oh, yeah!"

I pull out the ingredients and make Mads a chocolate, chocolate chip frappe with decaf coffee as the base, since it's late. Summer's sitting outside the cafe in the drivers' seat of a golf cart when I walk out through the patio area carrying my peace offering for Madeline.

"Hey, Riley."

"Hey, Summer."

"Need a ride home? I just dropped a VIP guest off here for a dinner date at Toscano's."

Toscano's is a fancy Italian restaurant on the resort property that faces the ocean on the other side of C-Side.

"I'd totally love a ride. Thanks."

"I'm heading to the dorms anyway. Assuming that's where you're going."

"Yep. I'm bringing Madeline a coffee drink."

"Oh, to be friends with the barista." She smiles and winks over at me before throwing the cart into reverse.

I approach my apartment with a dry tickle in my throat and a shaky feeling all over. I keep telling myself it's just Madeline. She's still my best friend. We'll make this right over time.

"Knock, knock," I say as I walk in.

"Hey," she says, looking up from the book she's reading.

"I ... uh ... I brought you this. It's a chocolate, chocolate chip frappe, which was always your favorite. I didn't know if you ate, or if you'd want it. It's decaf since it's after five." I look at the clock. "Well, nearly six now. Summer was outside the cafe when I got off work, so she drove me. Which is probably for the best since it would not have been as fresh if I had to walk all the way up here. It would separate. You know how that goes. The icy part rises up and the liquid sinks. Which is weird. You'd think the icy part would be heavier. I never thought about that before. Why wouldn't the ice sink?"

"Rye?"

"Yeah?"

I'm still standing with the door open, just inside the threshold, and it only now dawns on me that I haven't even shut our door.

"You're rambling."

"Sorry. Yeah. I guess I am."

"You never ramble with me."

"I know."

I walk over and extend the drink toward her, waiting to see if she'll take it.

"Thanks."

"You're welcome. I hope you like it."

"I already like it. Because you made it."

I smile a shy smile at her. And then a tear slips down my cheek. I don't want to cry. I try to subtly wipe at it by doing this cough thing while I move my hand up to my cheek. It probably looks like I just lost control of all motor function.

Madeline takes a sip of her drink and hums. "This is really good. If you plan to buy my friendship back with coffee drinks, I might be down for that."

"If that's what it takes."

"Hey," she says, sobering her tone.

"What?" I walk toward my bed, slipping off my shoes. It's technically dinnertime, but I'm not the least bit hungry. My mood has dropped like a thermometer when a cold front blows in.

"I should have seen it," Madeline says. "The way you always got all babbly and blurty around Cam. It's a telltale sign with you. I spent a lot of time thinking over the past ten hours. I overlooked all the signs that you were crushing hard on him. And I get why you wouldn't tell me at first, and how the kiss snuck up on you. I understand needing to figure things out with him before you talked with anyone else. If we hadn't been on the trip I probably would have understood more. But we were all together. And you hid it from me. Once Ben knew, I wish you had told me."

"I wish that too."

"So, you really like him?" She takes another sip of her drink.

"I do. A lot."

"It's so weird. I mean, I know he's cute, objectively speaking. But he's so serious and you're so fun. He's so on-track, and you're so in-the-moment."

"You know what they say."

"Love is blind?"

"No." I chuckle. "Opposites attract."

"Well, you two are living proof."

I want to ask her where we stand, but I don't want to upset the fragile balance of whatever's going on here between us.

"I did do a lot of thinking today."

I nod.

"And you're still my best friend."

I smile over at her.

"And I can't trade Cam in."

"Nope."

"So, I guess all I'm saying is we need to rebuild what was broken. And you need to figure out why you wouldn't trust me with the types of things people usually tell their best friends."

"It was just fear—fear of losing you, fear of this stage of our lives, fear of you not wanting me to be with Cam. It wasn't so much not trusting you as it was fear."

"Which still boils down to trust, Rye." She takes another sip of her drink and sets it on the side table. "If you trusted me, you wouldn't have been so afraid. So the real question is, can you trust me now? Because trust means not trying to control the outcomes. It means risking that the things you fear might actually happen. It means taking a leap knowing the person you trust has your back."

Instead of answering Madeline, I decide to show her that I want to trust her. Words are cheap. Action is what matters.

"I had a good day at C-Side."

Madeline's brows draw in at the shift in topic.

"Stick with me, this is going somewhere good. It has to do with trust."

"Okaaaay."

"Anyway, it feels like I've known the owner forever. I came in during a lull and she asked me to make her a drink. I did. She loved it."

"Of course," Madeline smiles this proud smile, and I feel another tear threaten to fall.

"Customers started pouring in. This other barista, Bianca,

and I handled the orders and conversation. It was so much busier than Bean There Done That."

"Was that hard?"

"It was ... exhilarating."

"Made for it," Madeline says, picking her drink up off the side table and tipping it toward me to emphasize her words before taking another sip.

"That's the thing."

I take a deep breath.

Here goes.

"My parents are paying for UCLA. It's not cheap. Clarissa, the owner of C-Side, said she wishes I could be full-time. I'm toying with the idea ... thinking about ... just considering, it's not a decision. I'm just in the thinking-it-over stage. It's not even in my journal yet."

"What are you thinking?" Madeline's face is soft and careful.

"What if I quit UCLA, finished my degree online somewhere much cheaper. What if I stayed here and made coffee drinks for resort guests?"

"After one day, you're thinking of all this?"

"I thought about quitting UCLA while we were traveling. I did mention it to Cam briefly. After today, a whole plan seemed to form itself in my mind. Am I crazy?"

"Maybe a little."

"What do you think I should do?"

"I'm trying not to be selfish here."

"I've never lived away from you. I've been less than a few blocks from you my whole life."

"I know. Maybe it's time."

"To live apart?"

"To trust our friendship to go the distance."

34

CAMERON

True love is usually the most inconvenient kind.
~ Kiera Cass

Madeline: *Meet me at the pools in back of the main building after you get off work. I'm ready to talk.*

Cameron: *I'll be there. Thanks, Goob.*

We've spent three days on the island. Two of those, my sister has been on radio silence. That means I haven't seen or heard from Riley either. I'm aching to spend time with Riley. We haven't even been texting since the whole point of this separation is to give Madeline time to sort things out without making her feel excluded.

Dad's out of the hospital and at home mending. It's a strong, tangible reminder that broken things heal given time and proper care. Hopefully our relationship—mine with my sister—will recover too.

I walk to the main building, the same one I left less than an hour ago when I finished orientation at Guest Services. After getting Madeline's text, I wrapped up work and hurried home to clean up and put on a fresh polo shirt over a swimsuit that doubles as a pair of shorts. I don't know if she wants to swim or just talk, but since we're meeting at the pools, I'm coming prepared. And I can't help but hope she's bringing Riley, even though I know she isn't. She wants to talk to me. That's a good sign. At least, I think it is.

Regardless of how things go, I'm going to tell Madeline we've given her enough time to think for now. She can have more time to dwell on her feelings and thoughts, of course. She can think about everything that happened until she's old and gray. But I'm done putting space between me and Riley as a way of doing penance. Riley and I possibly could have made some better choices. Maybe we couldn't have. But we never meant to hurt Madeline, and the two of us don't need to stay apart forever to prove we care for my sister. We've made our point.

When I walk past the back terrace and out toward the pools, I see Madeline right away. Her eyes meet mine and she stands from the lounger where she had been waiting for me. She's wearing a suit, but she's got a coverup dress over it.

I walk over and join her.

"Hey, Goob."

"Hey, Cam. I'm glad you came."

"Of course, I'd come."

I make a show of looking all around Mads, on the ground, and behind me.

"What are you doing?" she asks, her voice slightly amused.

"Looking for vegetables."

She smiles and lets out a huff of a laugh. Then she raises

her hands in innocence.

"No vegetables will be harmed tonight."

"I'm sure the produce workers union will be relieved to hear it."

I extend my arms for a hug. Madeline steps into my arms and gives me a squeeze.

When she pulls back, her eyes meet mine and her face looks somber. "Sit down, Cam. We do need to talk."

I take a seat. "Man. I feel badly for those parents of your future students. You've got that stern teacher thing down pat. Parent-Teacher conferences are going to be scary times. Do they have a special course in that? Intimidating Parents 101?"

She giggles a little. Then she says, "Cam. Be serious. Since when did you turn into such a goofball?"

"Since I started falling for your best friend."

It's like I'm watching a cartoon the way Madeline's mouth pops open.

"You love her?"

I pause. Do I? Something like a movie montage flashes across my mind—Riley and me as kids, all the time our families spent together, Riley laughing, her crying when she fell off her bike ... Riley looking up at me like I'm her hero. Riley jumping off the boat to swim with me in the Res. Ben and me running away from her when we stole her diary. Riley at my ball games. Riley serving me at the coffee shop in Bordeaux.

And then the trip. Our talks, her smiles, those big, chocolate, doe eyes of hers. The way she insisted on seeing the most ridiculous landmarks and stopping at every state welcome sign. The night she quizzed me about Stephanie. Our games of Hot Seat, and Road Trip Bingo. Her in her sleepy, early-morning beauty when she'd just woken up. The way she responded to my kiss the morning of her birthday. Our talk on the beach the night we arrived in Marbella.

Mostly, I'm acutely aware of how it felt to finally let Riley into my heart.

"If this isn't love, I'm getting awfully close."

"Okay."

"Okay?"

"I mean, it's weird. You're my brother. She's my best friend. It feels wrong—or at least super-awkward—but on the other hand, when I really think about it, nothing ever seemed so right."

"So, you're okay with it?"

"I'm still hurting about the trip and how you two didn't trust me to handle the fact that you had feelings for one another."

"I'm really sorry, Mads. I am. I'd do anything to handle that whole thing differently—if there were a better way."

"That's the thing. I don't know if there was. I've had time to consider what my reaction would have been. I'd like to think I wouldn't have gone all Black Widow on you. But maybe I would have still felt betrayed. We can't change any of what happened. It's done. You and Riley are sorry. I know you are. We have to move forward and call it water under the bridge."

"Well, thank you for that."

"You're dying to see her, aren't you?"

"Pretty much."

"I appreciate you staying away while I sorted through what you two did. It meant a lot that you two did that for me."

"You matter, Mads—to both of us. You're not outside the circle. I'm pretty sure Riley would ditch me for you in a hot minute."

"Well, let's hope it never comes to that. And I wouldn't be so sure. It wasn't my name filling those journal pages. It was yours. Cam this. Cam that."

I can't help smiling at the thought of Riley spilling thoughts and feelings about me in her journal.

"Jealous?" I tease.

"I was." Madeline sighs and smiles over at me. "But then I had one thought that changed everything."

"What was it?"

"I can't imagine either of you ending up with a better match. And I wouldn't want to see you with anyone else."

I smile. I feel the same way. Over the past two days, Madeline isn't the only one who's been doing a lot of thinking. I've thought about my future—and Riley.

"Don't keep secrets, Cam. Not ones I should know about. I need to know you're not going to do something like this again."

"Okay. You have my word. I never meant to hurt you."

Madeline picks up her phone and types something. I sit still, watching her.

She sets her cell aside, looks over at me, and says, "Don't break her heart, or I will come after you."

I laugh. It's a laugh filled with relief and amusement.

"She's here," Madeline says.

I feel it. I don't know how, but I sensed a change in the air and my only thought was, *Riley.*

And then I see her—Riley—coming through the double doors onto the terrace and down toward the pools where Madeline and I are sitting. Our eyes lock and everything else melts away.

I stand, watching her as she makes her way down the stone steps and across the pavement, past arranged seating areas with strategically-placed potted plants and thick wicker lawn furniture until she's finally standing right in front of me.

Riley smiles up at me and I pull her into my arms. We hold one another as if we haven't seen each other in months, not days.

"Welp. I'll just be ..." Madeline says from behind me. "Yeah. I'll just ... I'll see you two later."

Riley tilts her head so she's looking around me at Madeline and mouths, "Thank you."

I don't bother looking. My eyes are fixed on Riley. She might vanish like a mirage if I don't keep her in my sight and grasp onto her like the rare treasure she is.

"Bye, Mads," I say, still staring into the depths of Riley's soft brown eyes.

Then I turn my attention fully to my girl.

"Hey," I say to Riley. "You look gorgeous."

"I do? I spent the morning serving coffee, the afternoon at the pool, and then took a nap. I'm pretty sure I look a mess."

"A beautiful mess." I lean in, inhaling her scent. She's caramel and cocoa and warmth. "My beautiful mess," I murmur into the top of her head.

"Yours?"

"If that's what you want."

"It's what I've always wanted, Cam."

I look down at her, taking her chin between my thumb and pointer finger and I brush the softest kiss to her lips.

It's too soon to feel this much, isn't it? Still, I feel the words on the tip of my tongue. *I love you.* I don't want to scare her off. It feels so fast, but on the other hand, I'm late to the party. All these years she wanted me. I've known her better than I know most other people in my life. Why wouldn't I love her?

Instead of staying up in my head, debating how to tell her the overwhelming thoughts running through my mind, I determine to show her.

I loop my hand behind Riley's head. I'm about to kiss her when she opens her mouth to speak.

"Cam?"

"Hmmm?"

Our faces are inches from one another. She fills my senses, taking up the space that's been rightfully hers all these years.

I was too oblivious to see what was right in front of me all along.

"I have a lot of big feelings for you," she pauses and searches my face with her eyes. "Is that going to freak you out?"

"Not in the least. Because it just so happens, I have a lot of big feelings for you too."

I brush a piece of her hair back, trailing my fingers along the skin of her cheek and down her neck.

"Kiss me, then," she says.

I chuckle.

Then the air between us shifts, a seriousness and longing replacing the playfulness as soon as I look into her eyes and find her invitation written all over her face. I pull Riley to me. Our lips connect, and I'm home. She's so unexpected, and yet as familiar as my own name.

Her lips are soft, pliant and responsive. She kisses me, raking her fingers through my hair, playing with the longer strands on top and then scraping her nails through the shorter cut near my neck and around my ears. My hand caresses down her hair as we deepen the kiss. My fingertips skate along her neck and down her shoulder, stopping when they hit the strap of her suit.

I pull back. "What do we have here?"

"My swimsuit?"

"Did you plan on swimming?"

"If you want."

"Have you eaten?"

"No. But I'm not hungry right now. Are you?"

"Not for food, no."

She giggles and a blush rises up her cheeks.

Before I know what she's doing, Riley's scooping up the skirt of her sundress and pulling it over her head, revealing her swimsuit. She tosses the dress on a lounger, ducks out of reach, and walk-runs toward the deep end of the pool nearest to us. The pools are such a royal blue that they look other-worldly. Underwater luminaries illuminate each clover-shaped pool, and the twinkle lights strung between the palms overhead reflect off the water's surface.

In one fluid movement, Riley's diving into the pool, away from me.

I shuck my polo, kick off my shoes, and follow her.

When I catch up to Riley, she's halfway across the pool. My arms wrap around her waist and she squeals. I tug her into me, keeping us both afloat with small kicks of my feet treading underwater.

"Remember the summer you learned to swim?" I ask her.

She laughs, her head falling back, exposing her neck to me. I want to place my lips on her skin, but tonight is about more than kissing. We've been apart, giving us a rocky start to this newness between us, and I want to rectify every misstep. I long to connect with Riley on every level, to remind both of us what we share and the real depth of our bond. We belong together. It may have taken us years to get here, and we may have nearly wrecked our early days together, but that's not going to be the story we tell in years to come. We're going to tell the story of our love and how she waited for me to wake up from a stupor, and then I made up for my blindness every day we shared going forward.

I don't know her plans for the future. The last we talked, she was considering staying here, but her ideas might have stemmed from a first-day honeymoon kind of impulse. It's very typical Riley—all in with everything she has before she's given things adequate thought. She needs to really weigh out her options. She may have done that by now. If she hasn't, I'm going to help her see the importance of her choices.

I can't expect her to alter her life so dramatically for me. In all probability, she may be going back to the mainland in five weeks, leaving me here. Our connection will be tested far more than it has been over the past few days. I want her left with no uncertainty as to how I feel, or how destined we are to be together.

"I remember that summer," she says, reaching up and pushing a wet lock of hair off my forehead. I feel it flop back down as soon as her hand moves away. "Do you want to know what I remember?"

"Tell me," I say, holding her to me and allowing the pool water to swirl around us, warm and soothing.

"You." She smiles this soft smile at me. "I remember you, in the lake behind the boat. I stood on the casting deck, staring my certain death in the face, and you kept shouting up at me, 'Just jump, Riley. I'm here. You'll be okay. No one's going to let you drown.'"

"I think it took you most of the afternoon to finally take that leap."

"But you were there. I swallowed half the lake, and Dad jumped in after me. I'll never forget the look on your face."

"I felt like I had betrayed you. I told you that you wouldn't drown, and then I thought you might."

"You were right, though. No one was going to let me drown."

"And I never will," I whisper to her like it's a declaration about so much more than watersports.

I lean in and brush a soft kiss to her forehead. Her arms loop more tightly around my neck.

"I've made some decisions, sort of," Riley says.

"What kind of decisions?"

"About my future. I hope you don't mind, but I needed to bounce my thoughts off Madeline first. It's not like she's always going to be the first person I go to about big things, but for a while, I think I need to err on the side of including her. I promise I'll talk to you after I have a better feel for what I'm doing."

"I don't mind. She's your best friend. You should confide in her."

Riley nods, her warm smile hits me like a shot to the heart.

"I don't want you to stay here just for me," I tell her. "Not that you are staying here. You mentioned it on the beach. I don't even know if that's a consideration now that you've had a few days to think things over."

"It is still a consideration. It's kind of all I've been thinking about. And I called my parents. We had a long talk. I'm not making any decisions based solely on my feelings for you. I'd be lying if you being here wasn't a big factor in my decision, but I've learned my lesson. I'm not making my major life decisions centered around one person anymore."

I smile down at her, stroking the back of my hand down her cheek. "Well, I hope you factor me in a little bit."

I hold my fingers up, pinching my pointer and thumb together until they nearly touch.

"I factor you in a lot."

"Oh, yeah?"

"Mm hmm."

I lean in, cupping the back of Riley's head. The water swirls around us. She tugs me near and we kiss. I'm lost in her. Lost ... and found.

I hear the shout before I feel the tsunami of water crash over both of us, interrupting our moment with jarring intensity.

"Cannonbaaaaallll!"

Ben.

I might just kill him in his sleep.

Then again, if it weren't for him nudging me into action, I might have missed Riley entirely.

35

RILEY

The road of life takes us in different directions,
but we always find a way back to one another.
~ Unknown

The last six weeks have flown by like a sweet summer breeze blowing in with the tide.

Each passing day, I know with increasing certainty that I have found my place here on Marbella. Not only my place, but my person.

After Madeline met with Cam and basically gave us her blessing, we knew it was time to share the news of our relationship with our parents. We set up a Zoom call. Yes. I know. But we couldn't decide which set of parents to tell first. And, knowing our families, as soon as one mom knew, the other would find out, and not from us. So we told them we wanted to talk to them all at once now that we were all settled on the island. Even Ben's parents were there. The three sets of parents all gathered at my childhood home for dinner, and then we called them after they finished eating.

Cam started in by telling them that we were grateful for their support and the opportunity we had to travel across the country. Then he said we all spent a lot of time together and the bond between the four of us was so much stronger as a result. I thought that was a creative segue. Ben coughed at this point and mumbled, "Some bonds got strengthened more than others." Cam gave him an elbow to the ribs.

Then Cam said, "And we have some news." Before the next words were even out of his mouth, my mom gasped and said, "Oh! My! Riley and Cam finally got together!" Our dads turned to one another and exchanged a high five while the four of us sat in Cam and Ben's living room in some form of shell shock. Our moms hugged. It was a bit chaotic on their end of the screen. We had thought we needed to break it to them gently. The joke was on us.

I nearly teared up when Mrs. Reeves said, Gladys always predicted this. She said, 'I'll be tarred and feathered if those two don't end up married one day.'" Leave it to Gladys—my adopted gram.

Once that call was out of the way, Cam and I settled into a routine. Madeline has gotten pretty used to us being all lovey-dovey around her. She still complains at times. But it's mostly for show. You can tell she's really happy for us.

Cam and I work staggered shifts. I go in early—leaving the dorms at five thirty to get to the shop before the sun even fully rises over the horizon. I finish up my shift at two. Madeline works the same hours, giving us afternoons together to lounge around the pools or on the beach, where she ogles lifeguards and occasionally even engages in harmless flirting.

I'm no fun anymore, according to her, since I won't look at any of them, or their strong muscles, or whatever feature she's pointing out on a given day. Cam has happily ruined me for other men. He did that a long time ago, but now that he's actually mine, I'm gone. So gone.

Cam ends his workday around five or six most days, unless there's a special event. But the resort is good about comping his time. If he works extra, he gets to take the following morning off, and Clarissa, being a romantic at heart, insists I take the time off with him. We've become known among the resort employees. Rumor has it there's a pool going regarding when Cam will propose. I'm surprisingly in no rush. We just started dating. I want to give us the gift of time to experience each stage of our relationship before we rush into the next.

And, yes. I'm staying. I already applied and was accepted for a transfer to an accredited online college to finish my bachelors. I'm taking a few extra business courses that I missed as prerequisites, and then I'll be enrolled in a degree that fits me better than education ever did.

Madeline's leaving today.

We're in our dorm and she's packing the last of her things.

"I'm going to come back at least one weekend a month," she says.

We've already discussed this multiple times.

"I know. And the three of us will come see you once a month."

"And I'll come back and work next summer, even though I'm pretty sure I hope I never have to empty another trash can again in my life."

"Maybe you can get another position then."

"I don't really care what I do, as long as we're together."

"Me either."

I look over at her and her eyes meet mine.

"We're going to be fine," I assure her. "You're not shaking

me. Don't even think I'm going to drift away or let you disappear either."

"I know. 'Til death do us part. Besides, one of these days that brother of mine is going to officially make you my sister."

"Not one of these days soon, though?"

"We'll seee-eeee." Her voice has a sing-song tone to it.

"Not soon. Mads. Tell me it's not soon."

"It's not soon. He hasn't said a thing. I just see the two of you—especially him. He's so head-over-heels for you. It's going to happen."

I can't help smiling. "We're in no rush."

"I've got my money set on this spring."

"You went in on the bet?"

"Heck yeah, I did." She giggles.

She zips her suitcase shut and tugs it over to the door.

Then she takes one last look around the dorm room and lets out a long sigh.

"Goodbye, dorm."

I will not cry.

I hold the door open so Madeline can tug her suitcase out behind her and then we make our way to the elevator and out the front door where the guys are waiting for us in a golf cart.

We ride in silence to the dock—me and Madeline in back, our arms around one another's shoulders, Ben and Cam up front.

When we get to the waterfront, the shuttle boat is already there.

"Take care of Tina for me," I say to Mads before she grabs her suitcase handle.

"Here. I've got that," Cam offers, taking Madeline's luggage before she can.

Madeline and I link arms and walk out the long dock—the

same pier we stared down for the first time six weeks ago when our lives seemed headed in a totally different direction.

When we get to the end, I hold onto her.

"Don't go," I say without thinking.

"Text me every day. FaceTime. Call. Butt dial. You name it."

"I'm butt dialing you daily, Mads," Ben says from behind me. "With my ..."

"Put a lid on it, Ben," Cam says. "I swear you forget she's a girl half the time."

"I guess I do," Ben says, but he's still smirking, amused at his own humor.

"It's okay, Benny," Madeline says. "I get you. Just tone it down around Summer, would you?"

"I don't know what it is about that woman." He shakes his head. "She brings out the worst in me."

We all laugh. Then the crew member on the boat calls out, "All aboard for the mainland."

I look at Madeline and a tear slips down her cheek. I reach over and brush it.

"If you need me, you call me. Day or night. I'll hop a boat and catch an uber. Whatever it takes. I'll be there."

"Same," she says.

We hug and hold onto one another, crying into each other's hair.

The crew member approaches us and says, "We have to push off. Time to board."

I reluctantly release Madeline. Ben pulls her in and squeezes her tight, and then Cameron gives her a longer hug. As soon as he releases her, he wraps his arm around my shoulder and holds me to himself like an anchor.

The three of us stand there, watching Madeline board the boat. We wait until we can see her on the top deck, waving to us. And then we stand in silence, watching until the boat is so far across the channel it looks like a speck on the water.

I look up at Cam. He smiles down at me.

"Any regrets that you're not on that boat with her?"

"I'll miss her like someone cut off my arm." I sigh and lean into him. "But, regrets? No. Not one. I'm right where I belong."

EPILOGUE

CAMERON - SIX MONTHS AFTER MADELINE LEFT MARBELLA

Wait for someone who won't let life escape you,
who'll challenge you and drive you
towards your dreams.
Someone spontaneous who you can
get lost in the world with.
~ Beau Taplin

"Why won't you tell me where we're going? It's my vacation too," Riley whines into my shoulder.

She's snuggled in toward me on the bottom deck of the shuttle boat. It's too cold this time of year to ride up top. We could if we were feeling it, but we're all about the hot cocoa and another chance to have Riley as close to me as humanly possible. Maybe that's just me. She seems to be into it as much as I am, though.

And, yes, I did not tell her where we're going. It's a surprise, which, by definition means she can't know the details. She agreed to let me plan everything, but now that we're underway, the suspense is eating at her. She'll know soon enough.

We arrive in Ventura harbor at eight thirty in the morning and catch the bus to LAX from the harbor. It's a Monday, so the airport is busy, but not bustling. Travelers dressed for spring break getaways surround us as we make our way through TSA and head to our gate. Then the crowd changes in appearance. More guys in cowboy hats and boots, a few oil-executive types, and other nondescript passengers mingle at our gate.

Riley, being the intelligent woman she is, checks out the sign behind the flight attendants.

"Amarillo? We're going to Amarillo? Is this just so you can have that steak again, Cam?"

"While I do think of that steak more often than is probably healthy or natural, no that is not the only reason we're going to Amarillo. Hang tight, Sunshine. More will be revealed."

"You love this, don't you?"

"Love what? You? Yes. I love you. There aren't words for how I love you."

She smiles up at me and kisses me on the cheek.

"I love you too, even if you drive me nuts by torturing me with surprises that have no clues. Everyone knows you're supposed to give clues."

"They do, do they?" I smile into her eyes, and then I bend in and place a kiss on her temple.

"I don't think I knew what I was doing when I wrote about how much I thought we were meant to be together in my journal. I had no idea you were capable of such cruelty. I think I need to reconsider my life choices."

"Oh, do you now? You might want to wait a hot minute before you go tossing the man who planned this trip for you to the curb. Give me a chance, Sunshine. You won't regret it."

"Hmph." She crosses her arms and fakes a pout. But she's smiling. I know my girl, and she loves surprises. And this one is going to be one she'll never forget.

We board the plane that takes us to Dallas where we have a two-hour layover. Then we take a second plane that lands in Amarillo at three forty-five. I loaded Riley's Kindle with cozy mysteries, her favorite genre of books. I brought all the snacks she loves—Red Vines, Moose Munch, and Funyuns. Those are all stashed alongside my trail mix and rice cakes. I open my backpack to pull out a new snack every so often, and she doesn't disappoint. She's as giddy as I hoped she'd be—as if she's never had junk food and I'm a genie with a magic backpack full of delicious, non-nutritious snacks. We grab our luggage off the carousel and pick up our rental car. I wanted so badly to rent a VW van, but that wasn't an option, so we got a four-seater sedan instead.

We're only eight minutes from the hotel, but we've got a stop I need to make before the sun sets in three and a half hours.

I queue up my road-trip playlist—the one I put together specifically for this trip. It has a few of the songs we listened to on our drive last summer, and some other songs I picked for Riley, like *I Met A Girl* by William Michael Morgan, *Just the Way You Are* by Bruno Mars, *Brown-Eyed Girl* by Van Morrison, *This Kiss* by Faith Hill, and *I'm Yours* by Jason Mraz. And I sing along with each one, glancing over at her regularly to catch her smiling back at me.

"What is this playlist?" she asks just as *Falling In Love At A Coffee Shop* by Landon Pigg starts to play.

"What? This old thing?" I ask with a wink.

"Yes, you." Riley playfully swats at my arm. "This old thing. Did you put this together?"

"I might have thrown a few songs together. Why? Do you like them?"

"I do. Very much. They seem to have a theme."

"Really. What would that be?"

"Love. Falling in love. Finding the one."

"Huh. That's a coincidence if I ever heard of one." I wink again.

"Caaaammm."

"Sweet Sunshine of mine."

She audibly sighs. Over the past nine months, I've gone from calling Riley, Sunshine, to making all sorts of sunshine-related spinoff nicknames. If she didn't smile so big each time I used one, I'd stop. But she loves it, so I'm dead set on becoming a solar-poet. Or something like that. She makes me do ridiculously extravagant things—and I'm not complaining in the least.

This trip is a case-in-point. I spent nearly a month pulling together the details of what we'll do and how everything needs to happen.

Riley looks out the front window and then surveys the landscape surrounding us. "We're not going to the Big Texan. Cam, where are we going?"

I'm fully prepared for this question and I have just the answer—it's enough of an answer to satiate her curiosity, but it's not anywhere near giving away what's going to happen. Not a lie, just a close-to-true diversion tactic.

"Next stop, Twitty, Texas!"

Riley starts laughing lightly and then her laughter grows until she's doubled over.

"Wait! Wait. Twitty? Did you say, Twitty?"

"Yes ma'am," I answer in an East Texas accent. "Twitty, Texas. The very town that inspired the name of the late, great Conway Twitty, otherwise known as Harold Lloyd Jenkins."

"Oh my gosh!" Riley says, still laughing. "Stop it. That accent. And how do you know his actual name?"

Still using my accent, I say, "When one sweeps the love of his life off to Twitty, Texas, one does his research, little lady."

"Love of his life?"

"Yes, ma'am. I reckon."

"Cam. The accent. You're killing me. Stop." She's laughing, and I feel like I just won the lottery.

"In honor of the great Conway Twitty, I picked out this here ditty," I say, barely holding in my laughter.

I cue up *Fallin' for You for Years*. I sing along, making my voice sound all old-school Conway for her. I look over at her as I croon out the lyrics in a full-blown, bad-karaoke style, raising my eyebrows, using one of my hands to gesture, putting it over my heart at one part of the song, then pointing at her when the song sings about falling for her for years.

I have been. It took a while to see it, but once I admitted my feelings, I began to realize how long I had felt something for Riley. I had blocked out all my attraction to her because she's my sister's best friend. But it's always been Riley for me. I know that now.

We drive along for two hours, me distracting Riley with our own version of the Hot Seat game. And, no, I'm not telling you what questions we ask one another or what our answers are. Some things should remain between a man and his woman. Then we play the license plate game, which proves difficult when there aren't too many cars out this way with anything but Texas or Oklahoma plates. It is Route 66, but it's a Monday in the middle of March, not exactly the height of tourist season.

Finally, we're about a mile away from our destination.

"We're almost there," I say.

"We are? Twitty? We're almost to Twitty?"

And that right there, that's why I love her. One of the many reasons.

Go ahead. Look up Twitty. Now, see how you react when you think of five hours of time on planes to get to that little western hamlet. No. Add an hour on a boat, and an hour and a half on a bus before all that. Then get in a car and drive through a whole lotta nothing. Would you be excited, or would you be planning where to bury my body when you killed me for ruining your vacation? Not Riley. She's pumped. Twitty, here we come—sort of.

I drive two miles down the highway, and then I pull off. Then I get right back on the highway going the opposite direction. And I drive one mile until we come to ... the Welcome to Texas sign.

She sees it before I say anything, and she starts bouncing in her seat.

"Cam! Cameron Reeves! Did you? You did!"

Then, something I didn't expect happens. Riley starts crying.

"Cameron. You did this for me. You promised you'd bring me back here one day. And you did."

"I'll always keep my word to you, Riley."

I pull over to the side of the road so we can get out and take a whole slew of pictures.

"Do you remember why we missed this sign the first time through?" I ask her as we're walking back to the rental car, her hand folded into mine.

"Because I was playing junior therapist in the dark of night while I drove and you rode shotgun."

"That's when I knew."

"You knew what?"

"I knew you weren't Riley, the little girl I grew up teasing half the time and protecting the other half. I saw you that night. And the next morning I wanted to kiss you. It scared me half to death."

"Didn't scare you too badly," she says. "You kissed me two days later."

"I couldn't not kiss you."

She turns to me, and I cup her jaw, tilting her head up so my mouth can brush a kiss over her lips. We stand there kissing at the edge of Texas. A semi blows its horn and scares us half to death. Riley jumps so abruptly that our teeth bang together. We pull apart, laughing.

"Well, let's go have some steak and get a good night's rest. I've got a few more things planned for tomorrow."

"I'm not even going to ask. I think I like your surprises."

"I'm glad you do."

We drive back to The Big Texan and when we pull into the parking lot, I shoot off a text. We walk into the restaurant, and the hostess asks us if we want a table for two.

"No thanks," I say. "We're meeting some people here."

Riley gives me a questioning look. I glance around and see them, so I lead Riley to our table.

"Oh my gosh!" she squeals when she catches sight of Ben and Mads at a table. "You had Ben and Madeline join us?"

"We're recreating a section of the trip. For old times sake."

Riley hugs Ben, and then she and my sister hug and cry, and hug some more.

When they separate, Riley looks at me and says, "Cameron Reeves, you are a romantic at heart."

"I guess I am—or maybe you just inspire me."

"I can live with that."

We eat a steak dinner, and check into our room. Ben and I share a bed, and Riley and Mads are in the other. First thing in the morning, Ben and I wake and bring pancakes back to the room. I mull over the memories of the last time we were here. I never dreamed I'd be in a committed relationship with Riley back then.

After breakfast, we check out of the hotel and drive just outside town to Cadillac Ranch. Riley notices where we are just before we pull into the little parking area off the highway. Two other cars are already here this morning.

"Did you bring paint?" she asks me.

"I got you," Ben says, holding up a plastic bag full of cans he picked up for me yesterday.

I pop the car keys in my pocket and pat on top of the bulge there. We walk across the field and when the two couples who beat us here come into view, Riley's hand goes over her mouth.

"Mom? Dad? Mr. and Mrs. Reeves? What are you doing here?"

Riley looks over at me, her brows knitted together.

"We wanted to see you, hunny," Riley's mom says just as I told her to.

"Want to see what we painted?" Riley's dad asks.

He winks at me.

I walk a little bit ahead of Riley, clasping her hand in mine and taking her to the last car. The one where she later told me she sprayed an homage to Gladys: *This one's for you, G.R.*

When we round the last car, she reads the words sprayed across the car. They fill the whole space and they're everything I want to say to her this morning.

Will You Marry Me, Sunshine?

I drop to one knee, in front of my best friend, my sister, our parents, and the woman who so thoroughly stole my heart. And I ask her. "Will you?"

"Oh! Oh, Cam!" She slaps her hand over her mouth and does a little running man dance, minus the hand motions.

"Cam. You! What? Oh my goodness. You're proposing. Here. You're proposing marriage. Here. And you're on one knee. Asking me to be your wife. And you invited my parents here. And your parents. And Ben. And Mads. And you. And me. And you're asking. Right in Gladys' spot. Cam."

"Sunshine?"

I chuckle. No one can blurt and babble like Riley.

"Yeah?"

"Will you marry me?"

"What? Oh! Yes! ... Yes! Yes! Oh my gosh! Yes!"

She falls to her knees in front of me and cups my cheeks in her hands. "I couldn't marry anyone else, Cam. My heart is yours. It always was. It always will be."

"I love you, Sunshine."

I pull the ring out of my pocket—my gram's ring—and place it on Riley's finger. She stares at it and then back at me. Her eyes glisten with tears. We're still kneeling here, looking at one another as if we're the only two people in the world.

"I love you, Cam."

"I love you more, Sunshine."

I lean in and kiss her. And she kisses me back, cupping my face and slanting her mouth over mine while I hold us both steady. I run my hand down her hair and savor the feel of her in my arms.

I'm so lost in our kiss that I barely register Ben saying, "Okay, folks, let's take a tour of these cars, shall we?"

~

The End

~

Here's to all the places we went. And here's to all the places we'll go. And here's to me, whispering again and again and again and again: I love you.

~ John Green

Share the book love ...

Something you can do really quickly:
If you loved ***Are We There Yet?***, you can help other readers find this story by leaving a review on Amazon.

~

If you enjoy Savannah Scott's writing, check out the Getting Shipped Series, you can find all the books on Amazon.

Ben and Summer's story will be out November 15th, 2023 in ***Fish Out of Water***. To get updates on all the Marbella Island stories, sneak peeks at Savannah's writing, and to be included in exclusive giveaways, sign up for Savannah's weekly email.

Sign up at
https://www.subscribepage.com/savannahscottromcom

~

A little backstory ...

I moved to California when I was 20 years old—to come to graduate school. I drove an old Honda that could have given someone tetanus with all its rust. My sweet dog, Bear, rode in the back. And I pulled a U-Haul trailer behind me with all the possessions that meant anything to me packed tightly inside.

This was in the days before cell phones (when dinosaurs roamed ... or at least kids ran wild, playing outdoors until the streetlights came on). So, I had a CB radio tuned to Channel 4 where I could communicate with truckers as I drove from Springfield, Ohio to Burbank, California.

I drove historic Route 66 through two blizzards, a couple other storms, and a holdup due to an escapee from prison who held a couple hostage in their barn.

I didn't have Riley to pick tunes, or Cameron to keep me on schedule. I didn't have Ben to make me laugh, or Madeline to keep me company.

And I didn't stop all the places these four did, but I had my own adventures and made many memories.

And the trip changed me, as trips will.

When I got to California, I settled in, and within a little over a year, I met my future husband—a surfer from LA.

That's my story. I'd love to hear yours. Connect with me at SavannahScottBooks@gmail.com or follow me on Instagram at @SavannahScott_author

All the Thanks ...

A story is birthed in one imagination, but it is raised by many hands and hearts.

I want to thank **Gila Santos,** for walking alongside me through this project, and for believing in me. Your keen eye for story and your passion for my books continues to bless me deeply.

Tricia Anson, thank you for being one of the best proofreaders and personal assistants out there, and for being a dear personal friend. Thanks too, **Kari Cheney**. You two are the keepers of my sanity. Here's to the snort laughs we share, the answered prayers, and all the daily goodness. You two are a gift to me. (What she said!)

Kirsten (Kiki) Oliphant, you helped me find my wings. You believed in me. You taught me. Our friendship is a treasure. I'm so grateful to be doing author life with you.

To my **Awesome Advanced Readers** and the **AMAZING Bookstagram and Bookish Community** on Instagram and Facebook. You people bless my socks off—as evidenced by my nearly-constant bare feet.

Thank you to my oh-so-talented sister, **Mary Hessler Goad** for the cover design. This cover the best yet. You have outdone yourself!

Jessica Gobble, My first and best cheerleader, my ride-or-die, my pie-hoarding secret-keeper, the one I laugh most with and cry with first. You are the sister of my heart, and my soft place to land. You believed in me before I believed in myself. And now we all can thank you. I may have never stepped out to write like this if it weren't for you. I love our road trips! Let's go on another adventure soon!

Jon, my not-book boyfriend, Thank you for believing in me and supporting me. There aren't words for the way you have made it possible for me to pursue my lifelong dream of becoming a full-time author.

And the biggest thanks to God for making me a storyteller and giving me the gifts I've received on this journey.

And to the readers who faithfully read Savannah Scott romcom books — that's **YOU**. Thank you for believing in me and loving the stories I weave.

You are the best!

Made in the USA
Columbia, SC
04 February 2024